MW00389460

PRAISE FOR JEFF EDWARDS BOOKS

"Jeff Edwards has created a superb thriller that grips the reader from beginning to end. Brilliantly executed."

— **CLIVE CUSSLER**, International bestselling author of '*RAISE THE TITANIC*' and '*THE ROMANOV RANSOM*'

"A taut, exciting story by an author who knows his Navy — guaranteed to keep you turning pages well into the night!"

— **GREG BEAR**, New York Times bestselling author of '*KILLING TITAN*' and '*DARWIN'S RADIO*'

"Jeff Edwards spins a stunning and irresistibly-believable tale of savage modern naval combat."

— **JOE BUFF**, Bestselling author of '*SEAS OF CRISIS*' and '*CRUSH DEPTH*'

"Brilliant and spellbinding... Took me back to sea and into the fury of life-or-death combat. I could not put this book down."

— **REAR ADMIRAL JOHN J. WAICKWICZ, USN (Retired)**, Former Commander, Naval Mine and Anti-Submarine Warfare Command

"Edwards wields politics and naval combat tactics with a skill equal to the acknowledged masters of military fiction."

— **THE MILITARY PRESS**

"Smart and involving, with an action through-line that shoots ahead ... fast and lethal. I read it in one sitting."

— **PAUL L. SANDBERG**, Producer of '*THE BOURNE SUPREMACY*' and '*THE BOURNE ULTIMATUM*'

STEEL WIND

Jeff Edwards

Braveship
BOOKS

Aura Libertatis Spirat

STEEL WIND

Copyright © 2018 by Jeff Edwards

Braveship Books

www.braveshipbooks.com

Aura Libertatis Spirat

The tactics described in this book do not represent actual U.S. Navy or NATO tactics past or present. Also, many of the code words and some of the equipment have been altered to prevent unauthorized disclosure of classified material.

This novel has been reviewed by the Defense Office of Prepublication and Security Review, and is cleared for publication (Reference 17-S-1071).

Cover Artwork & Design by Rossitsa Atanassova

Library of Congress Control Number: 2018946485

ISBN-13: 978-1-64062-047-6
Printed in the United States of America

To my little brother, Eric, who is
everything I hope to be when I grow up.

ACKNOWLEDGMENTS

I'd like to thank the following people for their assistance in bringing this book to life:

ENG4 Michael Allen (USGC) for helping me get at least some of the Coast Guard details right; John R. Monteith for tracking down unclassified information about nuclear submarine reactor shielding; STSCM(SS) Ernie Pooler (USN, Retired) for entertaining and helpful sea stories about his experiences as Chief of the Boat aboard USS *Dallas*; Kyung Hyun and James Minchul Kim for help with Korean language translations; Svein Johannesen for providing insight into the Hague Conventions, Thomas A. Mays for guidance in keeping the notional engineering stats of the *Kang Chul Poong* within shouting distance of the laws of physics; FORCM (AW/SW) C.J. Mitchell for relieving *some* of my ignorance on the mechanics of the U.S. Navy Reserve; and Barry Campbell for help with the geography of compartments on *Los Angeles* class SSNs.

Also, I owe a huge thanks to the people at **www.timeanddate.com**, who probably have no idea that I exist. Without their online tools, date calculators, and event timers, it would have been difficult—if not impossible—to keep track of events occurring across multiple time zones.

As always, any errors that have crept into this work were purely of my own making.

I'd also like to thank the merry (and motley) band of advance readers, proofreaders, kibitzers, and literary meddlers who have once again conspired to make me seem more competent than I actually am.

And most of all, my wife, Brenda, for firing frequent, relevant, and fascinating research leads in my direction until I had enough cool ideas to write this book.

Offshore where sea and skyline blend
In rain, the daylight dies;
The sullen, shouldering swells attend
Night and our sacrifice.
Adown the stricken capes no flare —
No mark on spit or bar, —
Girdled and desperate we dare
The blindfold game of war.

— *The Destroyers*, by Rudyard Kipling

Let's pretend it's not the end of the world,
Act like we got a future up ahead.
Diggin' fallout shelters in your mama's basement,
Only ninety miles from bein' dead.

Cold war tango in the Caribbean —
Shit is heatin' up way too damned fast.
Better hope your house ain't on the target grid,
Or you can say goodbye to your own ass.

— *Caribbean Tango*, by Nuclear Death Kitten

PROLOGUE

USCGC SAWFISH (WPB-87357)
CARIBBEAN SEA, SOUTHEAST OF PUERTO RICO
SUNDAY; 22 FEBRUARY
0739 hours (7:39 AM)
TIME ZONE -4 'QUEBEC'

The white hull of the Coast Guard patrol boat *Sawfish* cut cleanly through the morning swells. Driven by a pair of 1,500 horsepower v-8 diesels, the boat's twin screws carved parallel tracks of foam across the rolling wave tops.

The *Sawfish* helmsman knew her job. She kept the patrol boat in precise position, a hundred yards off the starboard beam of the suspect ship.

Standing to the helmsman's left, at the port side bridge windows, Master Chief Ray Whitaker watched through binoculars as his boarding team made their final approach. Even with the binocs, faces were generally indistinguishable at this distance. But he could make out the silhouettes of all five team members, dark blue coveralls, helmets, and flak vests contrasting sharply with the bright orange pontoon hulls of their boat.

Whitaker exhaled slowly through his lower teeth. He didn't like the look of this one. He didn't like it at all.

The suspect ship, the Motor Vessel *Aranella*, was ignoring all radio hails. Pushing forward at a steady eighteen knots, the big freighter showed no signs of stopping to comply with repeated boarding demands from the *Sawfish*. That in itself was cause for concern, but something else was wrong here. Something Whitaker couldn't quite put his finger on.

According to the pre-boarding report, the MV *Aranella* was registered under the flag of Liberia, with ownership held by the Consolidated Maritime Group: a tidbit of knowledge that added to Whitaker's suspicions.

On paper, CMG was an international consortium of chartered dry-bulk carriers, with corporate headquarters in the Liberian capital city. In reality, the entire company infrastructure amounted to a website, a single bank

1

account, and a dead-drop post office box in downtown Monrovia.

It was a shell corporation, designed to hide the identities of the real ship owners. Protect them from litigation and prosecution whenever their nebulously-registered vessels carried prohibited cargoes, or engaged in other illicit activities. Unfortunately, misleading registries and so-called "flags of convenience" were perfectly legal under international maritime law.

Yet another loophole through which the profiteering corporate snakes of the world could slither. But even *that* wasn't the source of Whitaker's unease. It was something else....

Ray Whitaker was a Boatswain's Mate Master Chief, a seasoned sailor, with two and a half decades of service in a no-nonsense profession. He didn't believe in premonitions—at least not the kind of mumbo-jumbo psychic bullshit you saw in movies. He chalked up the uneasy feeling to some unnoticed detail picked up by his subconscious. Some speck of half-processed information niggling at the fringes of his awareness.

His fingers tightened on the binoculars. The rust-streaked hull of the *Aranella* towered like a wall of black steel above the small orange shape of the boarding boat. As always, the visual pairing was absurd: an eighteen foot semi-inflatable motorboat the color of a child's toy, trying to bring a 40,000 ton cargo ship to heel.

Appearances aside, the size disparity between the vessels didn't mean a thing. The success or failure of a boarding operation was dependent on the quality of the team, not the size of their boat. And Whitaker's people were top-notch. Every sailor in that boat was smart, motivated, well-armed, and highly trained. Under the able leadership of Whitaker's second-in-command, BMC Aldo Salazar, the boarding team was ready for anything that a merchant crew could possibly throw at them.

Even so, Whitaker had both of the topside .50-caliber machine guns manned. If his team got into trouble over there, the *Sawfish* would come rushing in with fifty-cals blazing.

He wasn't expecting anything that serious, of course. Non-compliant boardings could get pretty hairy, but they rarely devolved into outright violence.

Whitaker swept his binoculars down the length of the suspect ship's deck again, searching every crane housing, hatch cover, and gunwale for signs of human presence. Nothing. Not a single person visible anywhere. He shifted his visual search to the ship's dingy white superstructure, scanning catwalks, watertight doors, and port holes. Still nothing. Even the freighter's bridge windows were empty of faces and movement.

The crew of the *Aranella* was hiding.

They might be concealed in hidey-holes all over the ship, determined to make the crew roundup part of the boarding as difficult as possible. That had happened before, although Whitaker had never understood what the hell people thought they stood to gain from pissing off a Coast Guard inspection team.

The freighter crew might also be lurking at some ambush point down in the bowels of the ship—ready to attack the boarding team with wrenches, lengths of pipe, and the sorts of improvised weapons that are easily available in a shipboard environment. That had happened before too. Not often, but a few times. Whitaker couldn't understand what people expected to gain from that kind of stupid shit either.

If you were caught smuggling, then you were *caught*. Get over it, put your fucking hands in the air, and accept the consequences. Serious jail sentences were rare, and any monetary fines would be paid by the ship owner. Attack the boarding crew and you were looking at hard prison time. It just wasn't a smart move, but that didn't stop it from happening sometimes.

Whitaker exhaled through his lower teeth again, and shifted his binocs to cover the boarding team. The orange boat was alongside now, the coxswain keeping his craft shoved snug against the hull of the freighter.

As Whitaker watched, one of the team members stood up, braced against the motion of the boat by the hands of his two nearest shipmates. That would be BM3 Connors, who was well practiced in the art of robot tossing.

Connors lifted the small dark shape of the Recon Scout robot on the end of a short nylon lanyard. He spun the little burden in a circle above his head, picking up speed with each revolution, like a cowboy swinging a rope lariat. Then, at some instant timed by his training and his internal clock, Connors let go of the lanyard. The small two-wheeled robot arced high into the air, and came tumbling down onto the deck of the freighter where it bounced three or four times and skittered to a stop. Another perfect throw by the resident *Sawfish* robot tosser.

Manufactured by Recon Robotics of Edina, Minnesota, the Recon Scout XT was a 1.2 pound throwable micro-robot, designed as a mobile surveillance sensor for battlefield use. Less than eight inches wide and only four and a half inches high, the tiny machine was basically an impact resistant video camera on wheels. It could transmit sixty degrees of visual or infrared video back to the handheld Operator Control Unit in real time.

Whitaker's communications headset crackled with the sound of Chief Salazar's voice. "Team Alpha to *Sawfish*—we are in position. Video feed should be coming on line now."

Master Chief Whitaker lowered the binoculars and checked the display monitor zip-tied to the metal framing between two bridge windows. The seventeen-inch screen was several times larger than the handheld display of the robot's Operator Control Unit. Which—with the typical irony of life in the Puddle Pirate Navy—meant that the *Sawfish* bridge crew would have a better view of the *Aranella* than the men who were doing the boarding.

The display pulsed with digital static and then resolved into a grayscale image of an electrical junction box and wiring conduits bolted to the side of the *Aranella's* superstructure. Well, the robot would no doubt be looking at more interesting things in a few seconds.

Whitaker thumbed his mike button. "This is *Sawfish*. Video is coming in five-by-five. Be careful over there, Chief. I don't like the smell of this one."

Salazar's reply came immediately. "Team Alpha to *Sawfish*—roger *that*."

On the video monitor, the robot's point of view swung to the left as BMC Salazar took control of the little scouting machine.

Whitaker caught a close-up glimpse of black high-laced boots topped by bloused pant legs in some mottled multi-shaded pattern. It took him about a quarter of a second to realize that he was staring at camouflage uniform trousers, tucked into the tops of combat boots. The camera pulled back, to reveal several figures crouched behind the raised steel gunwale on the *Aranella's* starboard side.

Then the video screen went dark. That was when the shit hit the fan....

Whitaker yanked his binoculars back up to eye level and was just zeroing in on the boarding team when seven or eight camo-clad forms appeared over the top of the freighter's waist-high gunwale. Every one of them instantly began firing down onto the boarding team, raking men and boat with bursts from short-barreled assault rifles—all set for automatic.

The orange pontoon hulls of the boat deflated visibly as the five Coast Guard sailors jerked and shuddered under the vicious hail of bullets. They were all down in a couple of seconds, but the gunfire didn't let up.

Whitaker could barely make out the screams of his injured and dying men across the distance. The staccato rumbles of the assault rifles were much easier to hear.

"Left full rudder!" he shouted. "Full speed ahead! Fifty-cal mounts, fire at-will!"

The deck heeled under his feet as the bow of the *Sawfish* swung left and leapt toward the *Aranella*.

The helmsman followed her orders flawlessly, but she failed to repeat back the commands she had been given.

Master Chief Whitaker ignored the young sailor's departure from bridge protocol. Somewhere behind him, she was softly chanting, "What the fuck? What the fuck? What the fuck?"

Both of the *Sawfish* fifty cals opened up, peppering the gunwales of the *Aranella* and sending the uniformed attackers diving for cover.

Whitaker grabbed the microphone for the 1MC, and his voice boomed out of every speaker throughout the *Sawfish*. "Attention all hands! Boarding Team Alpha is under heavy fire! We are closing the target vessel to engage. This is *not* a drill!"

He released the button and let the 1MC mike drop, snatching up his binoculars in time to see three watertight doors on the *Aranella's* superstructure fly open. The range between the two vessels was diminishing quickly.

Men in camo uniforms appeared in the three doorways, joined immediately by one more on the freighter's starboard bridge wing. All four of the newcomers pointed long cylindrical objects toward the incoming patrol boat.

Four quick flares erupted and four ribbons of smoke streaked across the remaining stretch of water separating the freighter from the patrol boat.

"Incoming!" Whitaker screamed. "Hard right rudder! *Now!*"

The bow of the *Sawfish* swung sharply to the right, and Whitaker had to grab for a handhold to keep his footing.

Two of the hurtling projectiles shot past the port side bridge windows, to detonate against the wave tops somewhere in the distance. The third rocket slammed into the port side hull below the main deck where it exploded with the force of a grenade, tearing through the 3/16 inch steel plate like so much aluminum foil.

Flames and black smoke boiled out of the ragged hole. The port diesel had been hit. Robbed of half her motive power, the *Sawfish* began to slow.

The last rocket struck the forecastle forward of the superstructure, killing one machine gunner instantly, and leaving the other unconscious on the deck, bleeding from a dozen wounds. The shockwave blew in the forward bridge windows, sending fragments of shattered safety glass flying with the speed of bullets.

Something—glass, a scrap of superstructure, maybe a chunk of the rocket warhead—struck Whitaker high on his right chest, punching through ribs and organs like a gunshot, and sending him sprawling backwards.

He lay on the deck; vision blurred; ears still reverberating with the unbearably loud sound of the explosion; brain not quite processing.

There was pain. More pain than he had ever imagined possible—in many parts of his body. But nothing compared to the pulsing core of agony that had claimed his chest.

He lost track of his surroundings. Momentarily forgot who he was, and how he had come to be here.

Gradually, his senses returned. The smell of burning. The murmurs and cries of injured men and women. Vision throbbed and wavered back into focus, and he found himself staring up at the overhead, the once-pristine paint now riddled with gouges and streaked with soot.

His thoughts stumbled along in the wake of his senses, shock-addled brain sluggishly regaining the ability to reason, and remember.

He needed to do something. Needed to get his boat and his crew—what was left of them—out of danger. Needed to report the attack....

One attempt at getting up was all it took. The already staggering pain in his chest shot up to unimaginable intensities. His vision went gray and he nearly lost consciousness again.

Okay... standing up was no longer on the menu. Maybe he could turn his head.

He did. A couple of yards away, his helmsman was struggling to her feet. One arm dangled limply, and the left side of her young face was smeared with blood.

Whitaker's first attempt at speech turned into a wet cough that sent his vision spiraling back into the gray zone.

He took several slow and cautious breaths before he tried again. His voice came out in a low rasp. "Does she...." He had to stop and swallow before continuing. "Does she... answer the helm?"

The helmsman looked around dazedly before catching sight of her Officer-in-Charge. She shook her head as if to clear it, and blinked several times. "What was that, Master Chief?"

Whitaker swallowed again. "Does she answer the helm?"

The sailor glanced around and located the familiar shape of the control console. "Just a minute.... Let me check...."

A few seconds later, she looked back and nodded. "Helm still answers."

Whitaker closed his eyes. Good. They had rudder control and the starboard engine was on line. However bad the damage was, the *Sawfish* could maneuver.

"I think I'm going to lose consciousness again," he said. "So I'm giving you your orders now."

"Okay," said the helmsman. "I mean aye-aye. What are my orders, Master Chief?"

It was getting harder for Whitaker to talk, and he seemed to have lost the ability to raise his eyelids. "If you would be so kind," he whispered, "please get us the fuck out of here."

The helmsman might have acknowledged the order. If so, BMCM Ray Whitaker was no longer around to hear it.

CHAPTER 1

USS BOWIE (DDG-141)
SOUTHEASTERN GULF OF MEXICO
SUNDAY; 22 FEBRUARY
0754 hours (7:54 AM)
TIME ZONE -6 'SIERRA'

Captain Zachary Heller sat in his raised command chair at the center of CIC. Dimly-lit and low-ceilinged, Combat Information Center was the focal point of the ship's integrated weapons and sensor suites. From their consoles around the perimeter of the compartment, Heller's CIC crew operated the radars, infrared detectors, optical sensors, missiles, guns, lasers, and torpedoes that gave his warship dominion over the fish of the sea, the fowl of the air, and every living thing that moveth upon the earth.

That final part—if Heller had spoken it aloud—would have earned him a lengthy and tedious lecture from his father. The last in a (previously) unbroken line of orthodox cantors, Abba had never really forgiven him for leaving synagogue to attend the U.S. Naval Academy. Even now, more than a decade and a half later, Abba referred to his son's chosen career path as: 'running away to join the Navy.'

If the old man were here right now, the crew might see their vaunted commanding officer catch an earful for perverting the words of the Torah. The thought brought a smile to Heller's lips. Wouldn't that be a sight?

Abba would not be impressed by any of this. Not the supersonic missiles. Not the vast computer processing capacity of the integrated combat systems. Not the radar-gobbling stealth technology that made USS *Bowie* an electromagnetic wraith. Not the autonomous robot drones that extended the ship's detection envelopes. Not even the 200-kilowatt laser that the crew had taken to calling the "death ray."

The highest-ranking officer in Abba's chain of command was a few million paygrades senior to the Chief of Naval Operations. Or so the old man believed.

Heller didn't need supernatural leadership to make his life interesting. Nor supernatural enemies, for that matter. The flesh-and-blood kind were

8

quite enough to occupy his time.

His eyes went to the two horizontal banks of video monitors that covered the forward bulkhead of CIC. The upper row was dedicated to tactical feeds: four 65-inch ultra-high-definition display screens, each one showing a sprinkling of color-coded symbols that marked every aircraft, submarine, and ship within USS *Bowie's* area of responsibility. Blue for friendly, white for neutral, yellow for unknown.

The other available color-code (red for hostile) had not yet appeared on the tactical displays outside of training scenarios. The ship had just completed workups for her first deployment. She had never seen combat or real-world action of any kind. That would undoubtedly change at some point in the future, but—for now—she was un-blooded and unproven.

The lead vessel of the 'Flight Four' *Arleigh Burke* class guided missile destroyers, the *Bowie* was the U.S. Navy's most advanced warship. Her design incorporated every cutting-edge stealth technology known to the American defense industry. As a result, she resembled previous *Arleigh Burke* destroyers in hull-form only. From the main deck up, she was a study in minimal profile trapezoids and oblique angles, her steel structure sheathed in radar-absorbent chromogenic polycarbon.

There had been a lot of hype about the ship in the media, including some flagrant exaggerations of her capabilities. The *Bowie* was stealthy and tough, but she was not invisible and she was not invulnerable. To Heller's mind, using either one of the *I-words* to describe a ship was just begging fate to bite you in the ass. Right up there with calling the *Titanic* "unsinkable." Just a bad idea all the way around.

He shifted his eyes to the lower bank of display monitors. These screens were smaller and there were five of them—each displaying 72 degrees of real-time video from the topside camera arrays. Taken together, the screens provided a full 360-degree view of the world surrounding the ship.

Of all the ship's cool new gadgets, this was one of Heller's favorites. As with most warships, CIC aboard the *Bowie* was located in an internal compartment for maximum protection against hostile fire. On other ships, that would mean isolation from the outside world, leaving the captain to construct a mental picture of the battlespace around him from sensor feeds, status boards, and verbal reports. But Heller had a panoramic window into reality, a high-resolution view of the sea stretching to the horizon in all directions. He didn't have to guess at what was going on out there. He could *see* it.

When the sun went down, he could toggle the cameras to low-light mode or the infrared band and keep right on seeing while the world was in darkness.

The Navy should have done this years ago. Decades ago. For now, Heller was content to have the capability on *his* ship. The rest of the Navy could catch up later.

His self-congratulatory reverie was interrupted by a voice in the earpiece of his headset. "Captain, this is the TAO. Your presence is requested in Sonar Control."

Heller keyed his mike. "Sonar? What's up?"

The Tactical Action Officer paused before answering. "Uh... I'm not sure, sir. Apparently they're tracking... *something*..."

Heller thumbed his mike button again. "If they've got contact, why don't they report it over the 29MC?"

The TAO hesitated again. "I... uh... I don't think they're calling it a contact, sir."

Heller felt himself frown. "What are they calling it, then?"

"They're just saying that they've got something weird, sir."

"Did you say weird?"

"Yes, sir."

Heller snorted. "Well, I guess I'd better shuffle on down there. I certainly don't want to miss out on seeing something *weird*."

⚓ ⚓ ⚓

Chief Michael Scott was leaning over an operator's shoulder at a display screen when Heller entered Sonar Control. At the sound of the opening door, the chief looked up and made the traditional announcement. "The captain's in Sonar."

The ship's Undersea Warfare Officer, Ensign Moore, stood over the Sonar Operator's other shoulder.

Heller crossed the compartment in a few long strides. "What have you got, Todd?"

The ensign rubbed the back of his neck. "Something weird, sir."

"So I've heard," Heller said. "What is it?"

Chief Scott pointed toward the operator's display screen. "We honestly don't know, Captain. But you should take a look at this."

Heller looked. The sonar was in passive mode—transmitting nothing into the water—listening for sounds made by possible submarines. The majority of the display was taken up by a scattering of green pixels in apparently random shades and intensities, representing the ambient acoustic sources of the ocean environment. Biologics, wave action, shipping traffic, seismic activity, oil platforms, and everything else making noise in the water column.

A contact would appear as one or more discrete lines on the mottled green display, running vertically if the source was maintaining a constant bearing, or slanting gradually to the right or left as the bearing of the source changed. And the screen did show several sets of contact lines, no doubt associated with the oil tankers and shrimp boats currently being tracked by the *Bowie's* radar.

But Heller had not been called down to look at anything so prosaic as a routine surface track. The "something weird" stood out on the sonar display like a slash of green so bright that it was nearly white, running from the left edge of the screen toward the right edge at an angle close to horizontal.

The vertical axis of the display represented elapsed time, and levels of brightness were an indication of target strength. To generate that kind of intensity and bearing rate, the weird thing had to be both extraordinarily loud and incredibly fast. Maybe louder and faster than anything in the water could possibly be.

Chief Scott gestured to the Sonar Supervisor. "Put this thing on the speaker, so the captain can hear it."

The Sonar Supervisor, a twenty-something second class petty officer, nodded in acknowledgement and pressed a soft-key on a touch screen control panel. Sound erupted from speakers in the overhead: a rush of high-register white noise, like the hissing rumble of an impossibly-enormous waterfall, or ten-thousand pans of bacon all frying at the same time.

Heller said the first thing that came to mind. "That *is* weird."

Ensign Moore nodded. "Yes, sir. It's definitely that."

"I've been in the sonar game since Noah was a seaman-deuce," Chief Scott mumbled. "I've never seen anything like this."

As if his words had somehow broken a spell, the strange waterfall/bacon roar quickly died away to silence. Within a few seconds, the noise level in Sonar Control dropped back to the whir of electronic cooling fans and the background whisper of the air conditioning vents. On the display screen, the stripe of brilliant green began to fade.

The operator held up a hand. "Sonar Supe, it just dropped away to nothing. Contact has disappeared."

The second class petty officer nodded. "Sonar Supervisor, aye. Log the time and last bearing."

Heller looked at Chief Scott. "Any chance this is some kind of system error? Maybe a hardware problem, or a glitch in the software?"

"We'll certainly check, sir," the chief said. "But frankly, I don't think it's a gear problem. Whatever that was, it was coherent, it was always limited to a discrete bearing, and it showed consistent movement over time. That doesn't sound like a system hiccup. That sounds like target motion."

"How fast was it going?" Heller asked.

"We didn't have time to do target motional analysis," Ensign Moore said. "Without TMA or a bearing cross-fix, we can only guess at the range. Any speed estimate we come up with would be iffy at best."

Heller nodded. "If that's what we've got, that's what we've got. So let's bracket it. Give me your best-case, and your worst-case."

The Sonar Supervisor and the USW Officer both reached for paper and pencil.

Chief Scott did the calculations in his head, and finished first.

"If the contact was close, say within a couple of thousand yards, speed could be as low as a hundred-fifty knots or so. If it was farther away, like maybe ten or fifteen thousand yards, we're looking at three-hundred or four-hundred knots."

Heller was stunned. Even the low end of the chief's guesstimate was insanely fast for an object moving underwater. And the thing *had* to be underwater. If it was on the surface, it would be visible on radar, not to mention the eyes of the topside lookouts and the lenses of the camera arrays. Even with perfect radar stealth and total invisibility—neither of which existed outside of science fiction movies—any surface craft moving that fast would be throwing a rooster tail like a rocket boat, and cutting a wake that should be visible for miles.

The damned thing *had* to be submerged, but *nothing* could travel that fast under the water. The hydrodynamic drag alone would make it impossible.

No... That wasn't quite true. The Russians had that crazy-assed supercavitating torpedo, the *Shkval*. Those things had been clocked at two-hundred knots or better. But Heller had heard audio recordings of a Shkval in action. They sounded like jet engines on steroids, not frying bacon. Besides which, Chief Scott was one of the top acoustic analysts in the fleet. He would recognize a Shkval from its acoustic signature.

Maybe the chief had dropped a decimal place in his mental speed calculations. He *had* come up with his answer pretty quickly.

That theory fell apart as soon as the Sonar Supervisor glanced up from his own figures. "My numbers match yours, Chief."

The USW Officer took a few seconds longer. Then he looked up and nodded. "I've been over my math several times, Captain. I make the top-end more like four-hundred-fifty. Call the median just about three-hundred knots."

Heller shook his head. "Nothing moves that fast under water. *Nothing*."

The chief raised his eyebrows. "With all due respect, Captain, *something* damned well moves that fast. And whatever it is happens to be sharing our stretch of the ocean."

CHAPTER 2

WHITE HOUSE
WASHINGTON, DC
SUNDAY; 22 FEBRUARY
9:11 AM EST

President Charles Bradley brushed past the two Secret Service agents and through the door of the White House Situation Room. His movements were brusque this morning. There was not a hint of his usual folksy demeanor.

Political caricaturists liked to depict his angular face as a rather robotic-looking triangle, softened only by twinkling eyes and the trademark Chaz Bradley grin. He didn't feel much like smiling right now, though. In fact, he felt a nearly overpowering urge to throw things and scream at people.

Such mercurial impulses were rare for him. He never indulged them, and they usually didn't last very long. His friendly manner and nearly perpetual smile were not pretense. He truly was a jovial man by nature, just not so much on this particular morning.

He strode to the head of the long mahogany table and dropped into his chair without a word. This was the sixth time in as many weeks that he'd been called away from a quiet Sunday breakfast with his wife. *Six* times.

Paige was a wonderfully patient woman. She understood the incessant demands of the presidency, but *six times in a row?*

She hadn't said a word when the Sit Room Duty Officer had called Chaz away from the breakfast table. She had lowered her fork, laid her folded napkin beside her plate, and slid back her chair. She had timed the maneuver with care, getting to her feet in synchronization with her husband.

The message was clear.... If Chaz Bradley had become too high and powerful to share a simple meal with his wife, then breakfast was cancelled.

Paige had gotten all of about three bites this time, so she would be in a lovely mood by the time he made it back to the residence.

Chaz settled into his chair and tried not to think about his next

14

conversation with the first lady. He stared down the length of the table where his military advisors and key security staff were standing at attention. He waved for them to sit. "Alright, what is it this time?"

Chairman of the Joint Chiefs of Staff, Air Force General Nicholas Boosalis, took position at the far end of the table.

The barrel-chested officer had earned his wings flying B-52s at the close of the Cold War. In those days, his aircrews had called him 'the Greek with a beak,' a reference to both his heritage and the long aquiline nose that dominated his bulldog face. They had occasionally shortened the nickname to just 'the Greek' or 'the beak.' Such informal appellations had fallen by the wayside when he'd been awarded the silver stars that adorned each epaulet of his dress uniform. At least within his earshot.

The wall-sized flat screen display behind him showed the presidential seal against a background of dark blue. The image was repeated on six slightly smaller screens along the two adjoining walls.

General Boosalis cleared his throat. "Good morning, Mr. President. We apologize for interrupting your breakfast."

Chaz resisted the urge to add the word, "*again*."

On all seven screens, the president's emblem vanished, replaced by a photograph of a nondescript-looking cargo ship.

The general continued. "This is the Motor Vessel *Aranella*, a forty-thousand ton bulk freighter registered to a dummy corporation under the Liberian flag. Approximately two and a half hours ago, the U.S. Coast Guard patrol boat *Sawfish* attempted a routine inspection boarding of this vessel."

On the screens, the freighter was joined by the image of a long hulled white boat with the familiar diagonal Coast Guard "racing stripe" across its bow.

The president glanced at the blue-jacketed briefing folder on the table in front of him, but didn't touch it. He looked back up at the general. "I assume that your use of the word 'attempted' was not accidental, so I'm guessing that something went wrong. *Badly* wrong, if it was serious enough to yank me out of breakfast with the first lady."

General Boosalis nodded. "Yes, sir."

He thumbed a slender remote. The display screens changed to a brief black and white video clip, starting with a close-up view of combat boots and camouflage pants, pulling back to a quick glimpse of crouching uniformed men, going black, and then starting again.

The general allowed the snippet to play through several times before speaking. "This short video recording came from a reconnaissance robot deployed by the Coast Guard boarding team. It was relayed to Sector San

Juan by a second class petty officer in temporary command aboard the *Sawfish*. As far as we can tell, the robot was disabled or destroyed only a few seconds after being activated, presumably by one or more of the unidentified personnel shown in the video. Immediately afterward, approximately seven hostiles opened fire on the boarding boat with automatic weapons. All five friendlies on the boarding team were down in seconds."

At the mention of casualties, Chaz's mind went instantly alert. He felt his posture straighten of its own accord as he made the mental shift from irritated husband mode to president mode.

Like any other man, he was subject to the distractions and irritations of everyday life, but this wasn't some political or diplomatic foul up. American service members were dead. He owed them his full concentration. It was time to get his head in the game.

The video clip was replaced on the screens by another photo of a long hulled white boat, this one visibly damaged in numerous places, and trailing black smoke from a gaping hole near the stern.

General Boosalis nodded toward the screen. "This shot was taken from a Coast Guard helo called in to provide emergency evacuation for wounded personnel aboard the *Sawfish*. Based on a rapid assessment of visible damage, and the initial reports of the surviving crew members, we believe the hostiles launched approximately four over-the-shoulder rockets. Probably some variant of light anti-tank weapons, two of which the *Sawfish* maneuvered to avoid, and two of which did most of the damage you see here."

Secretary of Defense Mary O'Neil-Broerman leafed through her own briefing folder. "Can you give us a breakdown of casualties?"

"The *Sawfish* is a *Marine Protector* class patrol boat," the general said. "Eighty-seven feet long, with a standard crew of ten. During boarding operations, they split into two groups of five. One group forms the boarding team, while the other group remains aboard the patrol boat, standing by with fifty caliber machine guns to provide cover. At this time, it seems likely that all five members of the boarding team were killed within seconds of the onset of hostilities. Two of the personnel aboard the *Sawfish* were killed during the subsequent rocket attack. Of the three survivors, one is in critical condition and another has relatively minor injuries."

"So we're talking nine out of ten," SECDEF said. "Seven dead and two wounded. Basically, we got our butts handed to us."

The general nodded. "I'm afraid so, Madam Secretary. Round one definitely goes to the hostiles."

SECDEF raised an eyebrow. "Meaning that round two will go differently?"

The expression that crossed General Boosalis's face was a bit too feral to qualify as a smile. "Yes, ma'am. That's the idea, anyway."

"We can talk about round two later," Chaz said. "Right now, I want to know more about this mystery ship. Specifically, why is a rust-bucket freighter carrying a contingent of heavily-armed commandos? What sort of cargo requires that much protection?"

"We don't know yet, Mr. President," the general said. "But we're coming up with some interesting leads."

He thumbed the remote again, and the display screens were filled with a wireframe map of the world, with North and South America occupying the central axis. Another touch of the remote and a red dotted line appeared, beginning at the eastern edge of the Korean peninsula, jogging northeast past the Japanese islands, and then swooping southeast across the Pacific to a point below the southern tip of South America. From there, the dotted line swung north through the Atlantic, and then curved northwest into the Caribbean Sea.

General Boosalis lowered the remote. "This is an early reconstruction of the *Aranella's* voyage track, pieced together by the National Maritime Intelligence Center. The ship departed Wonsan, North Korea on the fourteenth of January, with an undetermined cargo. As you can see, it followed a highly circuitous route, avoiding all established shipping lanes, all known operating areas for active naval forces, and the coastal patrol areas for every country along the way."

National Security Advisor Frank Cerney tugged at his striped Princeton necktie. "They also went a hell of a long way to sidestep the Panama Canal."

"That's correct, sir," the general said. "Detouring around the horn of South America added about eleven thousand miles to their voyage. At an average speed of eighteen knots, that works out to twenty-five additional sailing days, give or take a few."

Chaz allowed his eyes to trace the red dotted line on the display. These people—whoever they were—had travelled more than three weeks out of their way to evade inspection by the Panama Canal Authority. Then they had massacred the first Coast Guard team to stumble into their path.

To Chaz, this was the most difficult part of any crisis. The earliest stages, where you *knew* that something of monumental importance was unfolding, but you didn't have enough information to plan intelligent action—or even to understand what the hell you were up against.

He looked back to the general. "We have no idea what that ship is carrying?"

General Boosalis shook his head. "Not at this time, Mr. President. Plenty of speculation, but no actual indications."

Chaz suppressed a sigh. "We've got dead service members and a U.S. vessel on the verge of sinking. For the moment, I'll settle for wild-ass guesses."

The general hesitated for several seconds, as if choosing his words carefully. "The, ah... leading theory would be weapons of mass destruction, sir."

SECDEF flipped her folder shut. "Are we really going to jump straight to WMDs? At what point did that become our default assumption for *everything*?"

"It's not exactly a default assumption," the national security advisor said. "I'd call it an educated guess, based on analysis and extrapolation of what little information we have at this moment."

The secretary of defense opened her mouth to speak, but Chaz gestured for the national security advisor to continue.

"If we assume that the cargo is illegal—which seems probable, given the extreme measures taken to protect it—then we only have so many possibilities. We can probably rule out drugs, because we've intercepted shipments of narcotics from North Korea in the past. When they get caught, they write off the cargo, deny everything, and let their couriers or smuggler crews rot in prison. What they *don't* do is attack U.S. vessels, or murder our boarding teams, because they know we'll be forced to take major action in response. By that same logic, we can rule out human trafficking, illegal currency or counterfeit smuggling, and conventional weapons smuggling. Again, we've got precedent on how the North Koreans react. They lawyer-up, count the cargo as a loss, and throw their people to the wolves."

His fingers returned to fidget with his necktie, a seemingly unconscious habit. "The Panamanians actually caught a North Korean ship smuggling conventional missile hardware through the canal in 2014. The North Korean government paid about three-quarters of a million in fines and got the ship out of hock, while loudly denying everything in the press. No firefights. No secret commando squads. No rocket strikes against the inspection team. They just sat back and waited for the story to die down."

"In other words," Chaz said, "this has to be something in a completely different league. Something they would consider worth the risk of a U.S. military response."

"That's how we see it, sir," said the national security advisor. "But I'd like to let General Boosalis get back to his briefing. He has a bit more bad news to deliver."

Chaz turned back toward the far end of the table. "Okay. Let's have it."

The general lifted his remote and four more dotted course lines appeared on the screens, each one closely paralleling the projected movements of the *Aranella* until the overlapping tracks entered the Caribbean Sea south of Grenada. At that point, the tracks of the five ships diverged, each taking a different route through the Caribbean.

Except for the track of the *Aranella,* which ended at the ship's current position southwest of Puerto Rico, the tracks continued on their individual courses until they reconverged at the southern end of Cuba.

"Does that mean what I think it means?" Chaz asked.

"I'm afraid so, sir," the general said. "The National Maritime Intelligence Center believes that at least four other freighters have followed this same general route over the past several months. Departing Wonsan, North Korea with unknown cargoes and delivering them to the port of Santiago de Cuba. NMIC believes that the variations in routing through the Caribbean were intended to avoid repetitive patterns that might trigger our traffic analysis software."

"Why are we just finding this out *now*?" SECDEF asked. "We should have been on top of this thing six months ago, when it first started."

National Security Advisor Cerney released his necktie. "With all due respect, Madam Secretary, we don't have the resources or the personnel to monitor the movements of every cargo vessel on the planet. We keep a close eye on the ones that approach our waters, but we can't watch them *all*. And these particular ships have gone to a lot of trouble to avoid our usual areas of interest. If the last leg of their track didn't pass through the Sector San Juan Security Zone, we would have never noticed the *Aranella*. As it is, we were lucky to catch one ship out of five."

"We *haven't* caught it," Chaz said. "Not yet. I assume that's what we're here to discuss."

"Affirmative, sir," General Boosalis said. "We've put together several mission packages for your consideration. Option number one is code-named *Brilliant Thunder*...."

CHAPTER 3

MOTOR VESSEL ARANELLA
CARIBBEAN SEA, NORTHWEST OF NAVASSA ISLAND
TUESDAY; 24 FEBRUARY
0417 hours (4:17 AM)
TIME ZONE -5 'ROMEO'

Major Pak Myong-sun stood at the sink of the cramped washroom compartment and thought about vomiting again. He hated the idea almost as much as he hated actually having to do it. He knew he'd feel better afterwards, but the notion of (yet again) huddling on his knees in front of the metal toilet was humiliating—as an officer, as a soldier, and as a citizen of the Democratic People's Republic of Korea.

Pak prided himself on never revealing such weakness in front of his men. Even so, he must have lost nearly ten kilos since the beginning of the voyage. His face, which had been lean to begin with, was becoming almost skeletal. As members of the Maritime Special Operations Force, his men were trained to be observant. They couldn't have failed to notice their leader's sickly complexion, or the fact that his carefully-tailored uniforms now hung loosely about his frame.

His squad had been on this *byung-shin* ship for nearly forty-one days, and Pak's stomach had refused to acclimate itself to the ceaseless lurches and rolls of life at sea. They had all trained for seaborne missions, of course. But MSOF soldiers did most of their work from *Sang-O* class submarines, and the older subs that westerners called the *Romeo* class. Maybe an hour or two on the surface every now and then, pitching and rolling with the waves, but the majority of time spent running deep, free from all the queasy motions of the ocean's mixing layer.

As far as he could tell, his men had conquered their own stomachs within a few days. And here was Pak Myong-sun, still waiting for his gut to accept the transition; still fighting his body's desire to blow rice and kimchi all over the deck. He'd always assumed that he would eventually acclimate, given enough prolonged exposure to shipboard motion. But that didn't seem to be happening.

20

He should probably get it over with. Bow to the inevitable, and surrender his latest meal to the rusty steel bowl of the toilet.

He settled for washing his face in the sink again. It was time to recheck his men. The *Aranella* was only about seven hours from port, which meant that the American retaliation would happen within the next two or three hours.

They would try to seize control of the ship; he was sure of that. If they wanted to destroy the *Aranella*, they would have done it already. Sent in jet fighters to pulverize the old freighter with anti-ship missiles.

Same thing for a torpedo attack from an American sub; if it was going to happen, it would have happened already. That meant they were going to try for another boarding, probably backed up by helicopters and a surface ship or two. Things would get ugly, but Pak's men had some nasty tricks lined up. And if the American attacks could not be repelled, there was a plan for that too.

Swallowing a belch flavored like stomach acid, he reviewed the timeline in his head. Starting the clock at the first attempted boarding, it would have taken the American government two or three hours to decide on a plan of action. Then, roughly eight to twelve hours to prepare a response force. Add another thirty hours at twenty-plus knots to move their surface assets into position. That should put their earliest attack window somewhere around two hours from now.

Not that Pak was foolish enough to rely on his own mental estimates. The Americans would attack when they were ready, with no regard for any calculations or predictions he might make. His squad needed to be prepared for immediate action.

He swallowed another nasty belch and backed out of the washroom. His rifle, a stubby close-quarters version of the Norinco CQ, lay on his bunk next to the handheld radio and the gray plastic shape of the initiator unit.

He was slinging the rifle strap over his shoulder when the radio crackled with an incoming signal. "*Sojwa! Sojwa!*" ("Major! Major!")

It was the voice of Lieutenant Gyo. Pak listened, waiting for the man to continue his report. Nothing else came. The only sound from the radio was the quiet sizzle of background static.

Pak picked up the radio and squeezed the transmit key. "*Chungwi, bogoseoleul jegonghabnida.*" ("Lieutenant, make your report.")

No reply.

He squeezed the transmit key again. "*Modeun jig-won-eun jigeum bogo!*" ("All personnel, report now!")

More dead air.

Years of training asserted themselves automatically. Senses sharpening of their own accord, he felt his body begin to prepare itself for combat. His pulse rate accelerated and adrenaline flooded his bloodstream, driving all memories of seasickness from his mind.

He tossed the radio onto his bunk and drew the Type 66 Makarov from the holster on his hip. His left palm wrapped around the slide of the pistol, muffling the mechanical sounds as he racked a 9mm round into the chamber.

Moving as quietly as his boots would allow, he cat-footed across the small cabin and pressed his ear against the door for several seconds. He heard three or four distant thumps, spaced fairly close together, like someone using a hammer. Suppressed gunfire? Or just one of the engineers banging on a clogged fuel purifier? The *Aranella* was a noisy old pig, so he couldn't really tell which.

Possibly he was overreacting. Possibly there was nothing more going on here than a simple radio failure. Possibly....

Makarov at the ready, he opened the door a couple of centimeters and peered out through the crack. The poorly-lit passageway was empty.

He slipped out through the door without consciously deciding to move. Padding quickly and quietly down the dim corridor, ears straining to pick out any sounds not natural to the heartbeat of the ship.

There was another cluster of muted thumps somewhere off in the distance, still not clearly identifiable as gunshots.

Pak reached the stairwell at the end of the passageway. The battered aluminum stairs led to the decks above and below. He began climbing, moving toward high ground with the Makarov pointing the way. His goal was one of the catwalks that ran along the exterior of the freighter's superstructure.

He wanted to get topside, to check for signs of swift boats, or helicopters, or any other indications that the ship had been boarded. He also wanted to check on the lookouts he had stationed on deck, and get a peek through the bridge windows, to make sure that control of the ship was still in friendly hands.

Another cluster of muffled bangs, definitely from above him this time. There was no longer any doubt; they were gunshots.

He reached the deck above and was about to start up the next set of stairs when something large came tumbling down the steps toward him. Even as Pak was leaping backward out of the line of fall, he realized what the something had to be.

Sergeant Mok's body struck the landing and lay unmoving on the faded deck tiles, blood trailing from a tight grouping of bullet holes in his chest.

The veteran soldier's sightless eyes were wide with shock.

Pak's own shock was nearly as intense. *Shi-bal!* How had the Americans gotten on the ship so quickly? Why hadn't the sentries raised the alarm?

It took a half-second to reign in his runaway thoughts. No. Those questions didn't matter anymore. What mattered was the mission: destroying the invaders and protecting the cargo.

He took a two-handed grip on the Makarov and prepared to climb the steps. The imperialist intruders might be able to kill a few unsuspecting sentries, but Pak was alert and ready for combat. He would show the Americans how a true Korean soldier fights. And when it was over, *their* blood would be staining the deck tiles. *Their* lifeless eyes would be staring into eternity.

His own death might be seconds away, but he didn't care. His veins throbbed with the fire of coming battle. This was what he had trained for. What he had been born for.

He was stepping over Mok's body—ready to sprint up the stairs and slaughter his enemies—when he heard something that turned the fire in his veins to ice. The ceaseless pulse of the engine was slowing. Even as he listened, the last rumbles of the monster diesel faded away to silence.

The ship was stopping!

The realization struck Pak like a fist in the sternum. The ship could not stop—*must* not stop! Throughout all of the briefings and the training for this mission, there had been two inviolate orders which took precedence over everything else. Two rules which were never to be broken, no matter the provocation or circumstance. The cargo *must* be protected. And the ship must *not* stop until it reached the ordered destination.

But now the ship *was* stopping.

Pak knew instantly what that meant. The Americans had seized the bridge, or possibly the engine room. Either way, they already had control of the ship. There would be more of them coming aboard now, from swift boats, or swimmer delivery vehicles, or that helicopter fast rope maneuver that their Navy SEALs were so famous for.

He stood with one foot on the bottom stair, torn between his orders and years of trained-in compulsion to engage with the enemy. Evading battle wasn't just abhorrent to him; it was stomach turning. Worse than the wrenching nausea of the seasickness he had never managed to conquer.

But he had been given orders for this situation, and they were unmistakably clear. His only job now was to destroy the cargo. It could not be allowed to fall into the hands of the imperialist aggressors.

With supreme reluctance, he turned away from the stairs, away from the call of battle, and began to move downward into the depths of the ship.

⚓ ⚓ ⚓

It took him five minutes to reach the cargo holds. Twice he had to scramble for hiding places as enemy patrols swept past. He'd gotten a peek at the second group. American Navy SEALs, he was certain.

Some of them would be searching the ship for Pak's men, and members of the crew. Some would be looking for the cargo holds, but the *Aranella's* passageways were an unfamiliar labyrinth to the intruders, and Pak knew his way around.

At last he made it into the amidships cargo bay, sealing the watertight door behind himself. He shackled the dogging lever in the down position with a length of chain and padlock kept there for that very purpose.

Getting through the heavy steel door would take the Americans several minutes. They'd need a cutting torch, or a bundle of correctly placed breaching charges. Either method would give Pak the time he needed.

He surveyed the cargo hold. Illuminated by overhead sodium vapor lights, six transporter erector launchers were chained to cloverleaves on the deck; each one looking like a cross between a battle tank and a brutishly massive ten-wheeled truck. Cradled on the back of every mobile launcher was a Rodong-2 intermediate-range ballistic missile.

Pak knew that the missiles had all been modified. He hadn't received any training or briefings on the weapons themselves, beyond the need to protect them, and the steps of the procedure he was about to carry out. But he'd seen enough unmodified Rodong-2 missiles to know that these were different.

The warhead section of a conventional Rodong-2 was relatively slender, perhaps a third the diameter of the main missile body. These missiles had broader warhead sections, almost bulbous when seen in profile.

He had silenced all speculation from his men about the reconfigured missiles. It was not their place to know what sorts of weapons the ship was carrying. Their job was to deliver the cargo or destroy it. Nothing else.

After the first boarding attempt, Pak had ordered his demolitions man to set the explosives in place: eight high-yield satchel charges at key points around the cargo hold. The electrical detonators were already rigged. The red and black twisted pair wires had been strung and routed to a common collection point, where they formed a pencil-width bundle held together by friction tape.

All that remained was for Pak to connect the wires to the electrical initiator unit, and set the timer. The resulting explosion would obliterate the cargo and crack the *Aranella* in half; probably sinking both halves—not that the fate of the ship would matter by then.

He reached into his hip pocket for the initiator. His fingers felt only fabric.

Moving faster now, he used both hands to pat down all of his pockets. They encountered nothing that felt like the familiar shape of the initiator. Then his fingers frantically plumbed the depths of every pouch and recess in his uniform. It wasn't there.... The initiator wasn't there!

He wanted to scream. Where *was* it? Where could the *byung-shin* thing have gone?

It came to him then—an image of the device, lying on the bunk in his sleeping compartment, next to the discarded radio unit.

Jen-jang! Si-bal! Jen-jang! (Shit! Fuck! Shit!)

Could he make it up to his compartment without getting caught? Even if he somehow managed that, he'd never get down here again before the Americans found this place.

In confirmation of this thought, the dogging lever of the watertight door began to rattle. The intruders had arrived.

There was no choice. He would have to resort to the final emergency measure.

Even the idea cranked Pak's already-high adrenaline level up another notch. The sound of his own pulse was loud in his ears.

He rushed to the second launcher truck on the port side. He had practiced the procedure at least fifty times, as part of his mission training. He'd never expected to actually *use* it.

Standing at the midsection of the launcher, he twisted four snap-latches a half turn to clockwise, and swung open a maintenance access panel. Inside, his fingers located a rectangular metal box and freed it from a pair of holding clamps. He flipped up the lid, exposing a key hole with bezel, a small LED readout window, and an open jack for a multi-pin cable connection. The box was a special feature of this one launcher vehicle, put here for this very purpose.

He plunged his arm shoulder-deep into the maintenance opening and groped until he found the main circuit bus. His fingers identified the third cable from the left, rechecked its position, and then unscrewed the outer locking collar that held the cable in place.

New sounds were coming from the direction of the entrance door. He could hear the low roar of equipment at work. The air began to smell of heating metal. Probably an exothermic cutting torch. It didn't matter. This wouldn't take long.

He pulled his arm out of the access hole, bringing the end of the cable with it. Careful not to crimp the array of pins, he aligned the index slot on the cable head with the corresponding tab on the metal box's connector jack.

A few quick turns of the locking collar to seat the cable properly, and the emergency trigger device was ready to go.

The key hung from a steel chain around his neck. Warmed to body temperature from weeks of continual contact with his skin, it felt nearly alive to his touch.

He slid the key into the trigger device's lock bezel. Only then did he pause to consider what was about to happen.

This was not a practice run. The box in his hand was not a dummy, and the warhead of this missile was not an inert mockup.

When he turned this key, *everything* would be over. His mission. His career. His life.

In training, they'd assured him that turning the key would start a fifteen-minute timer. The countdown would appear in the LED readout window of the trigger device, telling Pak how long he and any remaining men of his squad would have to reach the life boats. When the timer hit zero, the missile's fuel tanks would detonate, destroying all of the weapons in the cargo hold, along with the ship itself.

Pak hadn't believed that part of his training. He was morally certain that the trigger device was set to detonate the warhead, not the fuel tanks. He was equally convinced that the so-called timer was a sham, designed to create the false impression that Pak might have a chance of surviving the emergency destruction procedure.

He resented the deception, along with its implied insult to his integrity as a warrior and a Korean citizen.

He didn't need to be tricked into doing his job. He knew his duty, and he understood the consequences.

The air carried an increasingly heavy stench of burning metal. There was a loud clang from the direction of the entrance door. The Americans would be coming in now.

It was time....

He turned the key.

The force that had once annihilated Hiroshima ripped through his bones and flesh at the speed of light, vaporizing every atom of his body, along with the ship, several thousand tons of water, and every living creature within the bomb's sphere of destruction.

Pak Myong-sun never saw the double-flash of the detonation, nor the toroidal fireball that followed the initial blast of radiant energy.

A few billion particles of his carbonized residue rode into the sky on the column of superheated smoke and debris that formed the stem of the growing mushroom cloud.

CHAPTER 4

FOXY ROXY
CARIBBEAN SEA, NORTH OF NAVASSA ISLAND
TUESDAY; 24 FEBRUARY
4:31 AM
TIME ZONE -5 'ROMEO'

Jonathan Clark was looking the other way when it happened. Later, when he had time to think back, he'd realize that was probably what saved his eyes.

For him, the whole thing came out of nowhere. He was enjoying the quiet night and the calm sea. The trade winds were providing a friendly eight-knot push out of the northeast, and the air temp was somewhere in the mid-seventies, making his cargo shorts and sleeveless USMC tee-shirt perfect for a bit of easy sailing under the stars.

A quarter moon was creeping toward the top of the mast—still an hour or so from meridian. Under its silvery glow, the hull of the *Foxy Roxy* cast a faint white oval against black waves, her mainsail a curving triangle of shadow against the Milky Way.

Below decks, Cassy was asleep in the forepeak, sharing the narrow berth with forty pounds of American Staffordshire Terrier. Roxy (the mutt in-question, and the namesake of the boat) was a good dog. Smart and obedient. But no amount of training could dissuade her from her self-appointed mission as a canine heating pad. It was no use trying to explain that humans don't always *need* a furry furnace draped across their legs—*especially* in warm weather. Regardless of the temperature, Roxy was convinced that sleeping humans would wither and perish without her snuggly-drooly protection.

Roxy had come into Jon's life as a therapy dog—a gift from the VA to help him cope with PTSD after the raging clusterfuck of Afghanistan. That had been a smart move on the part of some VA headshrinker. The dog was good therapy. The *best*.

No.... Cassy was the best therapy. She knew how to make the nightmares go away. She could ride out his sudden bursts of anger and

28

terror, then patiently guide him back toward reason and calm. She had an almost flawless instinct for when to let him rage, and when to reel him back in.

She also understood the importance of this ramshackle old boat. The soothing influence of waves and unbroken sky. The solitude of open horizons. The chance to let his defenses down.

None of this reached the level of conscious thought for Jon. Quite the contrary, he was busily engaged in *not* thinking. His forebrain was operating on autopilot while his hindbrain subliminally tracked the tension of the inhaul line, the ghostly digits of the compass, the boat's angle of heel, the positions of the stars, the chuckle of swells against the hull, and countless other cues about his vessel and the sea around him.

Jonathan Paul Clark—former U.S. Marine Corps staff sergeant, late of the 1st Reconnaissance Battalion, Bronze Star recipient, Purple Heart winner and certified Post Traumatic Stress Disorder basket case—was at peace with himself. Or as close to peace as he'd managed to get in a very long time.

So naturally, this was the moment when war reentered his life.

His head was turned to the right, his face tilted into the warm northeasterly breeze. Without warning and without sound, the blackness of the night was stripped away by a flash many times brighter than the sun. Everything within sight was instantly illuminated by a searing actinic light, like the firing of a flashbulb the size of a football stadium.

The light was gone in some tiny fragment of a second; the world plunged back into darkness even before Jon's eyelids could reflexively snap shut.

His body obeyed other automatic responses as combat reflexes kicked in. He found himself on the deck of the boat's cockpit, crouching behind the dubious cover of the formed fiberglass benches and transom.

His tightly closed eyes did nothing to blot out the large triangles of pinkish-purple that hovered in the left quadrant of his vision. Some analytical module of his brain recognized that the purple blobs had the same general shape as his mainsail. The nylon sail must have acted as a half-assed mirror, reflecting some of the brilliance of the flash back into his face.

If he'd been looking the other way, his retinas would be toast. At the very least, he'd be flash-blind. Maybe for a few hours. Maybe forever.

Through the open companionway he heard a yelp from Roxy, and the sound of someone stumbling around. Then Cassy's voice, sleepy and confused. "Was that a lightning strike? What *was* that?"

"Get down!" Jon shouted. "Lay on the deck!"

He could hear more stumbling.

"Did you shine a flashlight in my face or something?" Cassy asked. "That wasn't funny."

"*Down!*" Jon yelled. "On the deck! I need a minute to recon."

More movement from the forward cabin, the scrabbling of paws and several thumps. Then Cassy's voice again, muffled this time. "Okay. We're down. We're safe. Do whatever you need to do."

Jon got to his hands and knees, staying low and scooting his body around until he was facing toward the southwest—the direction from which the flash had come. He raised his head slowly, barely peeking over the top edge of the gunwale.

His left peripheral vision was still pretty much screwed, but he could see straight ahead and to the right. Way out on the dark horizon, a colossal doughnut-shaped fireball was climbing into the sky. Then came a sound, like the rumble of distant freight trains.

Cassy called again. "Honey? What *is* that?"

Jon felt his sphincters threatening to loosen. "Oh God...."

The growing fear was audible in Cassy's voice. "Jonnie? What's going on? Talk to me!"

"It's a nuke," Jon said, not really believing his own words.

"A *what?*"

"A nuke," he said again. "A nuclear fucking explosion."

"It *can't* be," Cassy said. "That's not *possible.*"

Jon watched as the billowing column of smoke and flame formed themselves into the mushroom cloud of Cold War nightmares.

Just then, another analytical module of his brain activated itself. "Fallout...."

He was on his feet in a second, reaching for the pilot's wheel and the inhaul line. "Stay down and hang on! We're turning into the wind."

"What?"

Jon didn't stop to answer. He threw the wheel over and ducked as the long aluminum boom swung sharply above his head.

The boat heeled to port as he brought the bow around to starboard. The glowing numbers of the compass scrolled and the stars shifted unseen in the heavens.

"Into the wind," Jon mumbled to himself. "Into the wind.... Into the wind...."

When he had his craft on a northeast heading, as close to the wind as he could manage, he started to think about the next step. Should he hoist the headsail for extra speed? Or fire up the diesel?

It would have to be the diesel; Cassy could handle that without coming topside. He wanted to keep her below deck.

He heard more fumbling. "I'm coming up," Cassy called.

Jon's hands tightened on the pilot's wheel. "Stay below!"

"That's not happening," Cassy said.

Her head appeared in the open companionway, blonde hair tousled, eyes puffy with sleep. "I don't have to take your orders," she said. "I'm in the Navy Reserve and you're a civilian now, Mr. Ex-Jarhead. Only one of us has rank these days, and it isn't you."

She was going to say something else, but she looked past Jon, and caught sight of the glowing cloud formation in the distance. "Is that a nuke? I mean, that *can't* be an actual nuclear detonation, can it?"

"I didn't ask for identification," Jon said. "But it sure as hell looks like one to me."

CHAPTER 5

SWIFT, SILENT, AND LETHAL:
A DEVELOPMENTAL HISTORY OF THE ATTACK SUBMARINE

(Excerpted from working notes presented to the National Institute for Strategic Analysis. Reprinted by permission of the author, David M. Hardy, Ph.D.)

Imagine you are a soldier, armed, highly-trained, and alert. You're as combat-ready as your leaders can make you. Your mission is to descend into a darkened cellar, locate an adversary, and kill him before he can kill you.

Here's the catch.... Your enemy is as least as well armed and prepared as you are. He knows the cellar better than you do, because he lives there. His vision in the dark is about seventy percent more acute than yours. And—just to make things truly challenging—he's significantly quieter than you are. He'll almost certainly find you before you find him.

You're equipped with a flashlight, but the cellar is large; your circle of light can only illuminate a small area at any one time. And the instant you flick the power button, your enemy will know precisely where you are.

That's the scenario. You've got your orders. It's time to go down into that cellar and do battle.

I can almost hear your objections....

This is not a fair fight. The odds are stacked against you and even the environment favors your opponent. Only by extraordinary luck could you expect to come out of this alive.

What I've just described may seem like a hypothetical no-win situation, but it's not. In fact, it's a fair analogy for the conditions faced by a surface warship engaged in combat with an attack submarine.

Over the past four decades, the U.S. Navy has conducted more than three-hundred antisubmarine warfare (ASW) exercises involving submarines, surface ships, aircraft, satellites, and autonomous vehicles, equipped with a broad range of acoustic and non-acoustic sensor packages. The resulting operator logs, sensor recordings, and metadata have

32

consistently reinforced the difficulty of detecting an evasive submarine in a complex ocean environment.

In approximately 90.1% of recorded events, the submarine(s) gained sonar contact on the surface vessel(s) before being counter-detected by any surface unit.

In approximately 78.3% of those engagements, the submarines were able to conduct accurate (simulated) torpedo and/or missile attacks against their assigned surface targets before counter-detection occurred.

In the majority of cases, the submarines gained contact first, held contact longest, and were often able to complete all tactical objectives without being detected by surface units. Conversely, surface ships were able to detect, localize, and kill the submarines in only 12.6% of recorded exercise engagements.

The numbers were less one-sided if ships were assisted by friendly aircraft, but tactical parity was achieved only when friendly submarines were assigned to support the surface units. As the latter scenarios tend to reflect sub-vs.-sub engagements rather than ship-vs.-sub, they shouldn't be considered indicators of surface ship antisubmarine capabilities.

Even when supported by dedicated ASW aircraft, a surface warship will be defeated by an attack submarine nearly four times out of five.

This brings us back to the thought experiment with which we began. A surface warship is not unlike our fictional soldier in that imaginary cellar. To complete its mission—and sometimes simply to survive—a ship must detect an adversary which has superior stealth capabilities, higher sensor acuity, and the ability to hide among the thermal and acoustic features of the ocean.

The tactical significance of this imbalance is obvious, but the global strategic implications are less intuitive.

Since the middle of the twentieth century, the general public has learned to think of jet aircraft as the primary means of transportation between continents. People have begun to factor the oceans out of their mental equations. Most people rarely—if ever—journey by ship, so it's natural for them to assume that nothing of importance travels by sea. This assumption is false.

At maximum capacity, the airfreight industry can handle a small fraction of the cargo needs of our global economy. Per the U.S. Department of Transportation Maritime Administration, about ninety-five percent of the world's trade goods are transported by ship. In other words, the vast majority of food, textiles, raw materials, medical supplies, fuel, and building materials in the world are vulnerable to submarine attack at some point during the shipping process.

Ocean transport is vital to the economies of nearly every country on Earth and it is absolutely fundamental to the survival of countless millions of people. If the sea lanes are interrupted for a sufficient period, our technology-dependent civilization will grind to a halt.

Under the right conditions (or rather, the *wrong* conditions) a relatively small number of submarines could threaten not only global trade and economics, but the futures of nations.

How did these deadly machines evolve? Where did they come from, and *why*?

Some historians mark the beginning of submarine warfare with a submersible attack craft called the *Turtle*, built during the American Revolution. Others trace the origins to the fourth century BC and Alexander III of Macedon: a man known to history as Alexander the Great.

CHAPTER 6

The hand shook him again. "Mr. President, I need you awake. I need you awake *now*!"

Chaz Bradley opened his eyes and blinked two or three times. Three Secret Service agents stood over his bed.

The nearest agent spoke. "Mr. President, we have a confirmed Wildfire Event. We have orders to escort you down to the bunker."

In the bed next to Chaz, Paige turned over and lifted her head. "What's going on?"

"You too, ma'am," the agent said. "We need to get you both down to the bunker immediately."

Chaz searched his memory for the code word *Wildfire*. He'd heard it before. Seen it in briefings, probably. But it was one of the obscure terms that he hadn't bothered to memorize. Something esoteric that he was never going to need.

He glanced up in time to see a look pass between the Secret Service agents. Chaz might not remember the significance of code word, but he knew what that look meant. If he and the first lady didn't get moving pretty quickly, the agents would sacrifice decorum for expedience and physically bundle them both off to the bunker, willing or not.

Out of respect for his office, the agents would avoid using force if they could possibly avoid it. But their priorities were set by law, and reinforced by rigorous indoctrination and training. The president's personal safety was a matter of national security. His personal dignity was not.

Chaz sat up and rubbed his eyes. "Refresh my memory," he said. "What's a Wildfire Event?"

"Nuclear detonation," the nearest agent said. "On or in close proximity to U.S. soil."

Paige and Chaz were both out of bed and reaching for robes before the

35

man finished his sentence.

"Is this a drill?" Chaz asked. "Tell me this is a drill."

The agent gave one shake of his head. "I'm afraid not, sir. National Command Authority is reporting a confirmed Wildfire Event."

Chaz wanted to grab the man and shake him. "Where? Are we under attack? How many detonations?"

"I'm sorry, Mr. President," the agent said. "CP didn't brief us on specifics. I don't have any answers for you, sir. And we really *do* have to get moving."

He and Paige started toward the door, belting their robes as they went. The three agents took up a triangular formation around them.

What followed was somewhere between a rapid shuffle and a SWAT maneuver, the agents maintaining a three-sided human barrier around their protectees, taking the fasted route to the emergency elevator.

The bulletproof steel doors opened on-cue, no doubt triggered by some watchful Secret Service agent in the Command Post.

The protection detail hustled Chaz and Paige inside, not relaxing formation when the doors closed and the car began to descend.

Chaz stifled the impulse to fire off a dozen more questions. It wouldn't do any good. The agents had been told only enough to communicate the urgency of the situation.

So the brief elevator trip was made in silence.

⚓ ⚓ ⚓

The PEOC (short for *Presidential Emergency Operations Center*) was a hardened citadel three levels below the East Wing. Nicknamed the *bunker* during the Reagan administration, the cylindrical shelter was protected by a layered forty-foot blast shield of steel plating, Kevlar, and high-tensile ferroconcrete. The facility housed self-contained life support modules, office spaces, living quarters, computer networks, a communications complex, and an operations room that mirrored the capabilities of the West Wing Situation Room.

When they were through the armored blast doors, Chaz turned and gave his wife a quick hug. "You gonna be okay?"

Paige nodded. From the look in her eye, she was every bit as curious and worried as Chaz was, but she understood the rules of the game. She was an active first lady, deeply engaged in a wide range of high-profile social issues, from health care, to education reform, to immigration, to women's rights. But her sphere of access and influence did not include national security.

As a human being and marriage partner, she was the equal of her husband. But only one of them had been elected to the highest office in the land.

They couldn't stay together for this next part. She would be politely escorted to the living quarters, and he would move on to the operations room.

She gave him a wistful smile and returned his hug. "I'm alright. You go ride the pony, Cowboy."

And she let the Secret Service agents lead her away.

CHAPTER 7

CUBAN REVOLUTIONARY ARMED FORCES HEADQUARTERS
HAVANA, CUBA
TUESDAY; 24 FEBRUARY
0527 hours (5:27 AM)
TIME ZONE -5 'ROMEO'

General Rafael Garriga turned up the volume of the phonograph and lowered the needle onto the spinning record. When the hissing crackle of the old shellac disc was joined by a swell of fifties-era bolero music, he walked quietly across his office and locked the door.

The precautions were not strictly necessary. Between the heavily paneled walls, the plush carpeting, and the tight-fitting oak door, his office was effectively soundproofed. Besides which, no one who valued his life or freedom would dare to open the general's door without knocking. To get even that close, any potential visitor would first have to make it past Garriga's secretary, Allita, stationed at the end of the hall.

Together, the music, the soundproofing, the locked door, and the secretarial barrier provided as close to a guarantee of privacy as any man could expect in Cuba. And Garriga would not have risen to General of the Army without taking every protective measure available to him.

He settled into his leather chair and unlocked the lower left drawer of his desk. Inside was a mahogany humidor bearing the engraved emblem of *Hoyo de Monterrey*, along with a bottle of *Havana Club Seleccion de Maestros*. The cigars and the rum were for important visitors. Garriga never touched either one, except when social circumstances demanded.

In truth, he rarely sampled any of the pleasures that were supposed to be coveted by powerful men in his country. He kept a beautiful young secretary, because such things were expected. On two or three occasions, he had allowed subordinate officers to catch sight of him groping Allita's backside or breasts in passing. These displays—infrequent as they were— had the intended effect: spreading the idea that the general's secretary was also his mistress.

Garriga sometimes considered taking the woman to bed, to lend

38

substance to the rumors, if for no other reason. Allita would almost certainly not refuse, given his influence over her career and even her life. But such thoughts were no more than idle notions. He felt no desire for her.

Allita might be a virgin for all he knew, although that seemed rather unlikely. Her presence, accompanied by a perfunctory sexual gesture now and again, was enough to convey the intended impression. Outside of her competence as a secretary, that was all he needed her for.

Garriga didn't lust after any of the usual trappings of success. Sex; money; fine clothes; alcohol; elegant houses; automobiles; gourmet food; he acquired all of these things because they were necessary symbols of power. He didn't care about any of them.

The list of things he *did* care about was short. Very short. Most of the items on that list would have frightened the living Jesus out of anyone who ever discovered the truth.

The list—brief as it was—did contain a few articles of an unthreatening nature. One of those was the ancient phonograph. Another was the recording of Mendo Balzan now playing on the old machine.

Both items were several decades past their expected lifespans. They were old now, and worn to the point of near failure. The machine and the recording had been almost new when they'd come into his possession.

Garriga had been a boy then, not yet seven years old. He could still see his father, the young lieutenant standing tall and proud in the drab olive uniform of Fuerzas Armadas Revolucionarias, rifle over his shoulder, eyes shielded from the April sun by the stiff brim of a flat-topped "Castro" cap.

Even as a child, Rafael Garriga had recognized his obligation to be brave. He had not run forward to clutch at his father's leg. As badly as he had wanted to, he had not pleaded for his father to stay, and ignore the call to duty.

Unshed tears blurring his vision, he had watched his father climb into the back of the truck with the other soldiers. Stood waving silently as the truck drove away, toward that place called *Bahía de Cochinos*, the Bay of Pigs.

Garriga had listened to this record a thousand times in the half century since his father left to fend off the invasion. Maybe two thousand times. The voice of Mendo Balzan and his accompanying orchestra were nearly lost beneath the sizzle and static of the worn grooves.

There were other memories of Garriga's father. Memories of the aftermath. The formerly strong lieutenant wasting away in the back bedroom of their tiny house in San Cristóbal after the doctors had done what little they could. Shuddering with fever, drenched in sweat and despair, surrendering his life one painful centimeter at a time.

Garriga would never know who threw the grenade that cut his father down. Maybe one of the ex-Cuban stooges. Maybe one of the CIA operatives fighting alongside the traitors. Either way, the Americans had been behind it. The funding, the weapons, the training, *all* of it had come from the Americans.

For his birthday in May of 1961, Raphael Garriga had received three gifts which he carried to this day—his father's phonograph machine, his father's favorite record, and the purpose that would dominate his existence.

He had waited decades for his chance to repay the injuries done to his country and his family. And now, instead of exacting a well-deserved revenge, the weaklings who mismanaged his government could not wait to ingratiate themselves with the Americans.

The strength of Cuba, the *spirit* of Cuba, had died with Fidel. Garriga was sickened by the ease (and even eagerness) with which his beloved country had surrendered its honor.

He pulled out the humidor and bottle, and laid them on top of his desk. At the back of the drawer he found the metal lock box and pulled that out as well. The box was heavy, so he set it down carefully next to the rum bottle. He twisted the combination dial through all the proper turns until the lid opened.

Inside were two 9mm pistols, six magazines of ammunition, and an Iridium model 9788 satellite phone.

He pulled out the phone and pressed the power button. It took a few seconds for the device to cycle itself online, locate the proper satellite signal, and synchronize with the company's commercial encryption stream.

When all was ready, he punched in the number from memory, beginning with the international access code, 00, and then the country code, 850. The device was specifically programmed not to remember phone numbers. Another precaution that was probably unnecessary.

Eight or nine annoyingly-electronic rings later, the Korean answered. "This is not our agreed-upon time," he snapped.

"I don't *care* what we agreed upon," Garriga said. "You didn't tell me that your warheads are unstable."

The Korean's voice was hard. "Our warheads are perfectly stable. Our weapons technology is—"

Garriga cut him off. "I don't remember anything in the plan about nuclear explosions a hundred and fifty kilometers off my coast. If that wasn't an unstable warhead, then what the hell happened? Are you blowing up random parts of the Caribbean? Or does Jamaica suddenly have nuclear weapons?"

The Korean grumbled something in his own language, and then shifted back to Spanish. "It was *our* weapon, but it was not an accident. It was a contingency measure."

"What does that mean?"

"Our delivery vessel was intercepted by hostile forces. Possibly U.S. Navy SEALs. Our senior man aboard apparently found it necessary to detonate one of the warheads, to prevent compromise of the cargo."

"Apparently?"

"The man died in the explosion," the Korean said. "We can hardly question him."

Garriga forced himself to breathe slowly. The Americans again. Always it was the damned Americans.

"Our final shipment is in transit," the Korean said. "After delivery, we can move forward with the next phase of the operation."

Garriga was surprised. "Another shipment? The Americans are alerted now. They'll intercept it."

The Korean spoke with cold amusement. "We planned for this possibility. We have something unusual prepared. If the Americans go after our shipment, I believe they will very much regret it."

Garriga opened his mouth to ask a question, but the satellite phone emitted the low-pitched squeal of a terminated connection.

He returned the phone to the lock box and spun the combination dial. Across the room, the record had reached its end, and the phonograph needle was bumping rhythmically in the final groove.

CHAPTER 8

NATIONAL MARITIME INTELLIGENCE CENTER (NMIC)
SUITLAND, MARYLAND
TUESDAY; 24 FEBRUARY
1014 hours (10:14 AM)
TIME ZONE -5 'ROMEO'

Lieutenant (junior grade) Sheila Marek was busily engaged in not thinking about peanut butter crackers. The rumbling in her stomach was growing louder and more frequent now, and the vending machine was only about fifteen steps away—just outside the door of the analysis center.

One package of crackers couldn't hurt anything, right? One tiny little package. That would be what? Two hundred calories? Two-ten? An extra half-hour on the stationary bike would knock that out.

But the Navy Physical Readiness Test was rushing toward her like a freight train. If she was going to pass the weigh-in, she needed to drop seven pounds over the next three weeks.

She'd worked out a detailed plan to reach her goal. X number of calories per day.... X minutes of cardio.... X number of sit-ups.... She had all the variables factored, and there was no room on her fitness spreadsheet for visits to the vending machine.

At the back of the refrigerator were three zip-locks full of celery, each bearing her name in neat black Sharpie. She knew she should grab one of those. She also knew that she wouldn't. The celery thing always seemed like a great idea, until the time came to actually eat it.

Why couldn't some Brainiac in the snack industry figure out how to make celery taste like peanut butter crackers? She'd be all over that in a heartbeat.

She tapped the left-hand display of her operating station and called up the next page of the alert queue. Every ship in the queue fell into one of three categories. Either it was a potential security threat; or it was suspected of criminal activity; or it had departed from its expected navigational routing.

She selected the top ship on the list and windows opened automatically on her other two screens. The center display populated with data about the ship's displacement, crew roster, cargo manifest, history of inspections, previous ports of call, scheduled ports, and numerous other details—any of which might (or might not) be significant. The right-hand screen showed a map of the ship's geographic location, with the planned voyage track depicted in white, and an unexplained course change highlighted in red.

The explanation for the vessel's deviation was captured in the amplifying information. An engineering casualty: some kind of damage to one of the line shaft bearings. The ship was diverting to the nearest port for emergency repairs.

As Marek cleared the ship from the alert queue, a pronounced growling noise issued from her midsection. She ignored the biological distress call and summoned up the next ship in the queue. The Motor Vessel *Lecticula* was a 38,000 ton general cargo carrier registered under the Liberian flag.

What kind of name was *Lecticula*? It sounded like a sultry vegan vampire from bad teenage fan fiction. (Although Marek would have been hard pressed to name an example of *good* teenage fan fiction, come to think of it.)

Her eyes slid down the screen to the ship's owner of record. Consolidated Maritime Group. That made sense. Since the explosion of that other CMG ship, the MV *Amaretto* or whatever, the alert algorithm was tagging every vessel in the Consolidated Maritime fleet.

One glance at the ship's movement history and she sat up straight in her chair. Holy shit! It was the same route.

The white line of the voyage track started in North Korea, swung northeast of the Japanese island chain, and then hooked down around the southern tip of South America before looping up to cross into the Caribbean south of Grenada. Except for the variation on the final leg, the MV *Lecticula* was following the exact same route that the other CMG ship had taken. The MV something-or-other that started with 'A'. The one that had nuked itself close to Cuba.

Same shifty-ass corporate owners. Same dead-end registry. Same snaky routing—the long way around South America to avoid the Panama Canal. Even the same general class of expendable rust-bucket freighter.

The *Lecticula* was north of Aruba now, and moving northwest toward Cuba. They were doing it again. The bastards (whoever they were, and whatever they were up to) were doing it again.

Marek tabbed the messenger icon on her op screen and started a chat session with Commander Caramicio. When the chat window was open, she typed, "Got a sec?"

The commander's reply popped up almost immediately. "Sure. What's up?"

Marek thought about typing out an explanation, but that would take too long. She typed, "Can you drop by my console? I've got something you need to see."

His reply was three words. "On my way."

Marek leaned back in her seat to wait for the commander. It wouldn't take long. His office was only a few doors down the hall from the analysis center. And then things would ramp up quickly.

When the excitement was over and the short-fuse reports had gone up the chain of command, Marek would reward herself with some peanut butter crackers.

She was already mentally revising her fitness spreadsheet; factoring in another half-hour on the stationary bike.

CHAPTER 9

Sitting behind the historic *Resolute* desk, President Bradley gazed into the cluster of television cameras with the air of a stern-but-loving father. There were still twenty seconds or so before the cameras went live, but his face was already composed for his coming address to the nation. He was all business tonight: the famous Chaz Bradley grin nowhere in evidence.

Camera positions had been selected by lot. CNN held the coveted center spot, flanked on the left by the Fox News camera, and on the right by C-SPAN. The whitehouse.gov camera—which would stream live video directly to the White House website—was far off to the side, yielding floor space to networks who had drawn less advantageous real estate.

The cameras were being operated from remote, crews controlling pan, tilt, and focus from a string of news vans lined up along the curb of West Executive Avenue.

At exactly 7:30pm, the warning light above every camera flipped from red to green, and the president began to speak.

"Good evening, my fellow citizens. On October twenty-second of nineteen-sixty-two, President John F. Kennedy sat at this very desk and announced the presence of Soviet nuclear missiles on the island nation of Cuba. That reckless act on the part of the Soviet Union would come to be known as the Cuban Missile Crisis. It brought our planet to the verge of a nuclear conflict which might have marked the extinction of life on Earth.

"Tonight, more than a half-century after our closest brush with Armageddon, we find ourselves again facing the same situation. It is my unpleasant duty to inform you that the government of North Korea is now following in the ill-conceived footsteps of the USSR."

He paused to let this pronouncement sink in. His next words were taken nearly verbatim from JFK's 1962 broadcast, partly as an homage to the

45

long-dead president, and partly to underscore the extreme gravity of the
current threat.

"Within the past week, unmistakable evidence has established the fact
that a series of offensive missile sites is now in preparation on that island.
The purpose of these bases can be none other than to provide a nuclear
strike capability against the United States."

The president hesitated, feeling both the weight of repeating history and
the foreknowledge that future generations of scholars and pundits would
endlessly deconstruct every syllable now issuing from his lips. He resisted
an impulse to clear his throat before continuing.

"I have conferred with President Diaz-Canel, and he emphatically
denies any knowledge of North Korean missiles on Cuban soil. His
assurances will understandably be met by a degree of skepticism within
certain quarters of our own government, but I remind my colleagues in all
branches of leadership that our neighbor to the south is not the tiny island
that many of us imagine it to be. The Republic of Cuba has more open land
and wilderness than our own state of Kentucky, with a national population
of only eleven million. It is not beyond possibility—or even credibility—
that a number of truck-based launcher systems could be smuggled into the
country without the consent or awareness of top Cuban officials. I am
therefore disposed to take President Diaz-Canel at his word in this matter,
until and unless we receive evidence of collusion on the part of his
administration.

"We do not currently enjoy diplomatic relations with the Democratic
People's Republic of Korea. We have no ambassador to North Korea, and
our attempts to establish a dialogue with their government are not being
acknowledged."

President Bradley's expression hardened by some infinitesimal fraction
that was somehow visible to the cameras.

"Like President Kennedy before me, I would prefer to find a peaceful
diplomatic solution to this situation. Offered the choice, I would rather
extend the olive branch than take up the sword. But—also like President
Kennedy before me—I will not stand by and allow the United States to be
threatened with nuclear weapons.

"A few minutes ago, I ordered a full naval blockade of the waters
surrounding Cuba. Until this crisis has been resolved, U.S. warships will
intercept, board, and inspect every vessel that attempts to enter the
blockade area—regardless of registry or nation of origin. If any of our
inspection teams encounter armed resistance, they will engage and
neutralize the antagonists with overwhelming military force.

"We are prepared to take any measures necessary to prevent the introduction of additional North Korean weapons onto Cuban soil, but such reactive efforts are clearly not sufficient to deal with the threat that already exists.

"There are an unknown number of nuclear missiles stationed less than a hundred miles from our coastline. Their presence constitutes a direct threat to our national security. I am therefore ordering U.S. strategic nuclear assets to DEFCON 3, and taking all U.S. military forces to yellow alert.

"I speak now to Supreme Leader Kim Yong-nam. You have put your nation and your people in dire peril. I place you on notice, sir. Any misstep on your part could lead to the gravest possible consequences.

"I urge you to move with the utmost caution, and make your diplomatic representatives available for immediate discussions. Do not provoke us. If you seek anything other than a peaceful conclusion to this situation, I give you my solemn promise that you will *not* like the outcome."

CHAPTER 10

HOBGOBLIN 7
CUBAN AIRSPACE
WEDNESDAY; 25 FEBRUARY
0027 hours (12:27 AM)
TIME ZONE -5 'ROMEO'

Officially, the Hobgoblin Unmanned Aerial Vehicle loitering 51,000 feet above Matanzas province did not exist. In fact, the Hobgoblin program itself had no official existence whatsoever.

The U.S. Government Accounting Office carried no budgetary allotments for a persistent wide-area surveillance drone program operated by the CIA. The Department of Defense, the National Geospatial-Intelligence Agency, and the National Reconnaissance Office had no records of any such program. The funding stream for the drones was nearly as covert as the drones themselves—buried in an unintelligible federal appropriations bill for the rehabilitation of toxic landfills.

But the UAV cruising through the stratosphere over Cuba was quite real, and so was the ARGUS imaging pod attached to its belly.

Short for *Autonomous Real-Time Ground Ubiquitous Surveillance*, ARGUS had been developed by BAE Systems under contract with the Defense Advanced Research Projects Agency. The core components of the system were two video processors, four image-stabilized telescopic lenses, and 368 cell phone cameras—each with a scan density of 5 megapixels—for an aggregated image resolution of 1.8 gigapixels.

A single ARGUS pod could surveil fifteen square miles of territory in real time, providing continuous high-detail scrutiny of an area roughly three times the size of downtown Los Angeles. It recorded everything within range of its camera array, internally storing a million terabytes of video a day, and simultaneously streaming the compressed and encrypted camera feed to orbiting communications satellites for relay back to a waiting ground station.

For the Hobgoblin ARGUS pod, the ground station happened to be a CIA safe house in a Boca Raton business park. The pod's video stream

48

was woven into the Ku band uplink signal for a second-tier commercial satellite television provider by a multiplexing software bot implanted in the satellite company's server architecture. The bot, like the Hobgoblin program itself, was as inconspicuous as the CIA knew how to make it.

With sunrise six hours away and the moon only a quarter full, much of the terrain lay in shadow. The ARGUS pod was operating in infrared mode; cameras tracking heat blooms from oil wells, refineries, the Matanzas Bay supertanker facility, and the sugar mills that processed the harvest from the province's numerous cane fields.

There were hundreds of industrial buildings, garages, and warehouses, any one of which might contain a North Korean mobile missile launcher— or a dozen. That didn't include the thousands of work sheds, cane cribs, and shanties scatted across the countryside. And Cuba had fourteen other provinces besides Matanzas, every one of which held uncounted opportunities for concealment.

For all of its extraordinary surveillance abilities, Hobgoblin 7 was seeking an unknown number of hiding places for an unknown number of missiles. By comparison, the proverbial search for a needle in a haystack would have been an order of magnitude less challenging.

But Hobgoblin's tiny engine sipped liquid hydrogen slowly, burning only enough fuel to generate the meager voltages needed to power the drone's high-efficiency electric motors. The LH2 in the drone's tanks was sufficient to cruise the skies of Cuba for another five days—long enough to scan many *many* haystacks.

CHAPTER 11

USS BOWIE (DDG-141)
CARIBBEAN SEA, NORTHWEST OF GRAND CAYMAN ISLAND
WEDNESDAY; 25 FEBRUARY
0104 hours (1:04 AM)
TIME ZONE -6 'SIERRA'

Zack Heller was dreaming when the call came. An odd rambling dream in which he could slide through walls like a ghost, but small items kept disappearing right when he needed them. His wallet. His cell phone. His wristwatch.

Every time an article vanished, a bell would ring somewhere, as if an unseen entity was keeping score. The absent possessions were mounting toward some inexplicable critical mass of 'missingness.' A vaguely-perceived threshold of loss, below which Heller would forfeit the ability to accomplish an important task.

The exact nature of the goal wasn't clear, but—in the twisted logic of the sleeping brain—that didn't make the task any less vital.

Just as he was realizing that his car keys had gone missing, he heard a different ringing sound. Not the scorekeeper's bell, but something else....

He was double-checking his pockets when the new and different ring repeated itself.

His dream folded in on itself and retreated toward infinity, a shrinking origami trick composed of whimsy and random thought.

Hovering for a second in the liminal zone between sleep and waking, his mind tried to weave the noise into the fabric of receding fantasy.

The ringing sound came a third time, and his brain finally recognized it for what it was. His eyes fluttered open in the semidarkness of his at-sea cabin. He rolled onto his side and fumbled for the phone on the bedside table, pulling the handset loose from its retaining bracket.

He yawned as he lifted the phone to his ear. "Captain speaking."

The voice on the other end belonged to Heller's executive officer, Diane Dubois. "Sorry to wake you, sir. We have classified Flash message traffic. Immediate execute orders."

Heller yawned again, tugged the sheets aside and sat up on his bunk. "Thanks. I'll meet you in the wardroom in about five minutes."

"See you there, sir," the XO said.

Heller hung up the phone and reached for his coveralls.

Immediate execute? Maybe the brass had finally decided to do something about that mystery contact: the unidentified acoustic source that had torn across the sonar screens like a bullet on Sunday morning.

Or maybe it was the president's blockade. Orders to join the naval surface force that would cut off all sea traffic to Cuba.

He yawned one last time for good measure. Better go find out...

⚓ ⚓ ⚓

Four and a half minutes later, Heller was seated at the wardroom table with a cup of black coffee in one hand, and a hardcopy radio message in the other.

```
//SSSSSSSSSS//
//SECRET//
//FLASH//FLASH//FLASH//
//250651Z FEB//
FM   USSOUTHCOM//

TO   COMFOURTHFLEET//
USS PHILIPPINE SEA//
USS GETTYSBURG//
USS HUE CITY//
USS BOWIE//
USS LASSEN//
USS ROOSEVELT//
USS WALTER W WINTERBURN//
USS FARRAGUT//
USS LITTLE ROCK//
USS SIOUX CITY//
USS WICHITA//
USS MAHAN//
USS INDIANAPOLIS//
INFOCARSTRKGRU EIGHT//

SUBJ/SURFACE BLOCKADE TASKING/IMMEDIATE EXECUTE//
```

```
REF/A/RMG/ONI/241522Z FEB//

REF/B/RMG/USSOUTHCOM/241019Z FEB//

NARR/REF A IS OFFICE OF NAVAL INTELLIGENCE
ASSESSMENT OF PROBABLE DPRK MISSILE DEPLOYMENTS ON
THE ISLAND OF CUBA.//

NARR/REF B IS PINNACLE OPREP 3 NUCFLASH ISSUED BY
U.S. SOUTHERN COMMAND FOLLOWING 240935Z NUCLEAR
DETONATION IN CARIBBEAN SEA.//

1. (CONF) AS OUTLINED IN REF A, ONI IS EVALUATING
THE PROBABILITY OF NORTH KOREAN MISSILES ON CUBAN
SOIL. THE NUMBER AND TYPE OF WEAPONS ARE UNKNOWN
AT THIS TIME, BUT COULD INCLUDE VARIANTS OF THE
RODONG-2 AND/OR TAEPODONG-1 SHORT- TO
INTERMEDIATE-RANGE BALLISTIC MISSILES, MOUNTED ON
SELF-PROPELLED TRANSPORTER ERECTOR LAUNCHERS. BOTH
OF THESE WEAPON DESIGNS ARE CAPABLE OF CARRYING
NUCLEAR PAYLOADS.

2. (SECR) THE NUCLEAR DETONATION DESCRIBED IN REF
B OCCURRED DURING A FAST ROPE BOARDING OF THE MV
ARANELLA, A NONCOMPLIANT MERCHANT VESSEL EN ROUTE
FROM WONSAN NORTH KOREA TO SANTIAGO DE CUBA. TEN
(10) MEMBERS OF SEAL TEAM TWO WERE ABOARD MV
ARANELLA AT THE TIME, ENGAGED IN CLOSE-QUARTERS
COMBAT WITH AN UNIDENTIFIED MILITARY CONTINGENT,
TENTATIVELY IDENTIFIED AS NORTH KOREAN SPEC-OPS.
ALL TEN U.S. NAVY SEALS HAVE BEEN MISSING SINCE
THE EXPLOSION, AND ARE PRESUMED DEAD. IT IS
POSSIBLE/LIKELY THAT THE DETONATION WAS
INTENTIONALLY TRIGGERED BY THE DPRK CONTINGENT, TO
PREVENT SEIZURE OF THE VESSEL.

3. (SECR) NATIONAL MARITIME INTELLIGENCE CENTER
ANALYSIS OF MV ARANELLA VOYAGE TRACK INDICATES
THAT THE SHIP AVOIDED PANAMA CANAL TRANSIT TO
PREVENT INSPECTION OF CARGO. EXAMINATION OF
ARCHIVED VOYAGE TRACK DATA SHOWS THAT AT LEAST
FOUR (4) OTHER CARGO VESSELS HAVE FOLLOWED THE
SAME ROUTE OVER THE PAST SIX (6) MONTHS, DETOURING
```

AROUND THE HORN OF SOUTH AMERICA TO BYPASS THE
PANAMA CANAL.

4. (SECR) NATIONAL MARITIME INTELLIGENCE CENTER
HAS DETERMINED THAT MV LECTICULA IS CURRENTLY EN
ROUTE FROM NORTH KOREA TO CUBA FOLLOWING THE SAME
VOYAGE TRACK.

5. (SECR) USS PHILIPPINE SEA, USS GETTYSBURG, USS
HUE CITY, USS BOWIE, USS LASSEN, USS ROOSEVELT,
USS WALTER W WINTERBURN, USS FARRAGUT, USS LITTLE
ROCK, USS SIOUX CITY, USS WICHITA, USS MAHAN, AND
USS INDIANAPOLIS ARE DIRECTED TO DETACH FROM
CURRENT DUTIES AND DEPART THEIR RESPECTIVE
OPERATING AREAS UPON RECEIPT OF THIS MESSAGE.
PROCEED AT BEST AVAILABLE SPEED TO INTERNATIONAL
WATERS IN VICINITY OF CUBA FOR NAVAL BLOCKADE AND
SURFACE INTERDICTION OPERATIONS.

6. (UNCL) BY PRESIDENTIAL ORDER, ALL U.S. MILITARY
FORCES ARE NOW AT DEFCON 3.

7. (CONF) NO VESSELS, REGARDLESS OF FLAG OF
REGISTRATION OR NATION OF ORIGIN, WILL BE
PERMITTED TO CROSS THE CORDON LINE WITHOUT
SPECIFIC CLEARANCE FROM US SOUTHERN COMMAND.

8. (SECR) COMFOURTHFLEET WILL ISSUE RULES OF
ENGAGEMENT, STATION ASSIGNMENTS, ADDITIONAL
ORDERS, AND AMPLIFYING INTELLIGENCE.

9. (SECR) THE USS HARRY S. TRUMAN CARRIER STRIKE
GROUP WILL RECEIVE SURGE ORDERS VIA SEPARATE
CORRESPONDENCE.

10. (UNCL) STAY SAFE, STAY SHARP, AND BE READY FOR
ANYTHING. ADMIRAL COOK SENDS.

//250651Z FEB//
//FLASH//FLASH//FLASH//
//SECRET//
//SSSSSSSSSS//

Heller skimmed the message quickly, and then re-read it more slowly
to ensure that he hadn't missed anything on the first pass. When he was

done, he handed the printout back to his executive officer, Lieutenant Commander Diane Dubois. "What's your take on the situation, Di? Is this going to turn into the second Cuban Missile Crisis?"

The XO laid the message on the table top and reached for her coffee cup. "If I had to guess, Captain, I'd say that's what our buddies in North Korea are hoping for."

Heller took a swallow of coffee. "Go on...."

"The Soviet Union was a no-shit nuclear juggernaut, with enough warheads to jump-start the apocalypse. They were the real deal. The North Koreans have got a few nukes in their pocket, but—next to the Soviets—they barely qualify as street corner punks."

She paused. Heller motioned for her to continue.

"Only we're not treating them like street corner punks," Dubois said. "We're reacting to them exactly the same way we reacted to the Soviet Union back in the bad old days. The president is ramping up our DEFCON level and calling out a full naval blockade, just like President Kennedy in 1962. Hell, he even compared them to the Soviets in a national address."

"You think that was a mistake?"

"I think it's a PR wet dream for the North Koreans," she said. "They're a third world cesspool and we just elevated them to the level of a global superpower."

"What *should* we be doing? Better yet, what would you be doing if *you* were the president?"

The XO shrugged. "No idea, sir. Could be this really is our best option. I certainly can't think of anything better. All I'm saying is that we're giving Kim Yong-nam and his cronies a free ticket to the Armageddon Club."

"They've got nuclear missiles ninety miles off our coast," Heller said. "Maybe they *belong* in the Armageddon Club."

He took another pull from his coffee. "Remember when they launched the first Hwasong-14? Thing came out of nowhere. We were busy laughing at their repeated failures to deploy a long-range missile, and then they popped out an ICBM while we weren't looking. *Nobody* was expecting that."

"True," said the XO, "but the Hwasong hasn't got the legs to reach most of the U.S. mainland, even if it doesn't blow up in flight like most of their long-range missiles do."

"It hasn't got the legs *yet*," said Heller. "But they'll get it figured out. Have you ever watched video clips of *our* early ICBM tests? Check out some of the compilations on YouTube. Spectacular Redstone and Atlas explosions, speeded up and set to Looney Tunes music. Pretty funny stuff.

Like Elmer Fudd and Daffy Duck were in charge of our ballistic missile programs. But you know *what*? We climbed the learning curve, eventually. We got the hang of the ICBM thing. And so will the North Koreans."

The XO said nothing.

After about thirty seconds of silence, Heller set down his coffee cup. "Better wake up the navigator and have him lay in a course for Cuba."

CHAPTER 12

FOXY ROXY
WINDWARD PASSAGE, SOUTH OF GREAT INAGUA
WEDNESDAY; 25 FEBRUARY
6:11 AM
TIME ZONE -5 'ROMEO'

Roxy's ears twitched a couple of times; then she raised her head from the deck. She hesitated there, with her muzzle turned instinctively into the early morning breeze, nose gently snuffling.

The dog had been sleeping on Jon Clark's feet—carrying out her self-imposed duty as warmer of human appendages—so Jon felt the shift in her weight when she moved.

He lifted a hand from the pilot's wheel and reached down to pat Roxy's neck. "What are you after, girl? Mermaids? Another seagull?"

Roxy lumbered to her feet and padded over to the port side gunwale, blunt claws clicking softly on the nonskid fiberglass of the cockpit decking. She stared out past the railing into the gloom.

Jon tried to follow her gaze, straining to pick out whatever the dog was searching for in the tenuous pre-dawn light. The bomb had gone off more than a day ago, but his retinas didn't seem to be recovering from the reflected brilliance of the blast. The left quadrant of his vision was blurry and partially occluded by purplish triangular afterimages: a fact that he had (so far) managed to keep to himself.

His eyes would probably return to normal over time if he left them alone to heal at their own pace. Until then, he was learning to compensate by relying more on his forward and right peripheral vision.

He turned his head a bit to the left until he found an angle that made better use of the undamaged areas of his retinas. Then he spotted them: two shadowy forms a few thousand yards away, nearly invisible against the dark ocean. Ships, both churning up trails of spray in their wakes. They were hauling ass. Way too fast to be freighters or cruise ships. Probably warships.

He wondered how Roxy had picked up on them from this distance.

56

Could she hear the whine of their turbine engines? Maybe some frequency up in the spectrum of dog whistles, too high for human ears to detect? Or was the wind carrying stray whiffs of exhaust gases?

Jon heard nothing but the murmur of water against the hull of his boat and the quiet creak of the rigging. He smelled nothing but salt air and the light musty aroma of a recently-bathed canine crew member. Whatever the dog had cued on, it was too subtle for basic human senses.

Jon shifted his grip on the helm and leaned forward to rap his knuckles against the teakwood coaming of the open companionway. "Cass? Can you come up here for a minute?"

There was no sound from below decks.

Jon gave it thirty seconds and then rapped harder. "Hey, Doc. Get your butt up here. I need you to do some of that Navy shit."

A minute or so later, Cassy lurched unsteadily through the companionway, rubbing one eye and sagging against the aft bulkhead of the cabin for support. "If you woke me up to make coffee, you're a dead man."

"I've already got coffee," Jon said.

Cassy changed hands and began rubbing her other eye. "Right. And who are you again?"

Jon smiled. "I'm your husband. Or at least that's what Roxy tells me."

Cassy waved a dismissive hand. "You can't trust a word Roxy says. She's a dog. She'll say anything if you promise her bacon."

"I don't have any bacon," Jon said.

"Then why the hell did you wake me up? I'm not the kind of girl who gets out of bed for strange men with no bacon."

Jon gestured to the west, the same direction toward which Roxy's snuffling nose was still pointed. "What are *those*?"

Cassy stared blearily into the distance, rubbed her eyes some more, and then tried again. Eventually she managed to focus on the objects of Jon's question. "I'm pretty sure those are ships."

"I can see that," Jon said. "What kind of ships *are* they?"

His wife shrugged. "I don't know. *Fast* ships?"

Jon sighed. "I was hoping that the Navy taught you something besides how to hand out Motrin."

"I'm a part time Hospital Corpsman," Cassy said. "I can pop an 18 gauge IV needle into a vein or apply a pressure bandage in my sleep. I can name all 206 bones in the human body. I can read medical charts, update medical charts, and occasionally even *find* medical charts. But identifying ship silhouettes is about four-thousand miles outside of my training pipeline."

"Sounds about right," Jon said. "In the Jarheads, every Marine is a rifleman. I just figured that you squids might have something similar. You know... like maybe... every sailor is a *sailor*?"

Cassy rubbed the bridge of her nose with an extended middle finger: the old fashioned (but still understood) covert method of flipping the bird. "I'm the *other* kind of sailor."

"What kind is *that*?"

"I'm the kind who patches up dumbass grunts who step in front of bullets."

And beneath Jon and Cassy's long-standing cross-service banter, that part happened to be true.

They had met at the Multinational Medical Unit in Kandahar. Cassy had been attached to the MMU's trauma team when Jon came in on a CASEVAC helo with shrapnel in his neck and a 7.62mm round in his left thigh. She had taken over stabilizing the wounded Marine until the triage doctors had worked their way around to him.

It might be an overstatement to say that Cassy had saved the life of the man who later became her husband, but Jon didn't think so.

He could still remember seeing her face for the first time, being comforted by the evident concern and competence in her expression as she went about the business of keeping his damaged body alive.

Jon's physical injuries had healed long ago, but Cassy continued working her slow and patient magic on the wounds that didn't show. The ones that tended to yank him out of sleep, to leave his heart thundering in his ribcage and his muscles trembling with unneeded adrenaline.

So he accepted her little taunt with a nod. "Fair enough, Doc. I'll take a Motrin pusher over the other kind of sailor any day of the week."

"And twice on Sunday," Cassy said.

"And twice on Sunday," Jon echoed.

The sun was beginning to peek over the horizon now, and visibility was improving by the minute. Jon looked out toward the distant ships, tearing across the waves under the growing light. "I only know amphibs, aircraft carriers, and submarines," he said. "If we rule out those, what does that leave?"

Cassy looked at the ships again. "Too big to be tugboats, and too fast to be minesweepers. I don't know.... Cruisers? Destroyers? Maybe Littoral Combat Ships?"

Jon nodded. "If the wind stays with us, we can make Key West in about four days. Then maybe we can find out what in the hell is going on down here."

He didn't mention the other reason for wanting to get to Key West....

Fallout. Thankfully, the nuke had gone off downwind, and Jon had turned the boat into the wind almost immediately after the blast. Theoretically, that should have been enough to keep the *Foxy Roxy* outside of the bomb's fallout footprint.

Jon and Cassy had also done two saltwater scrub downs of the boat's topside surfaces, followed by showers for themselves and the dog, cutting heavily into the freshwater reserve tank. For all of that, Jon wouldn't stop worrying until he, and Cassy, and Roxy had all been tested for radiation exposure.

He looked south toward the shadow of Cuba's landmass on the horizon. It wasn't too late to double back to the U.S. Marine Corps base at Guantanamo Bay. Gitmo was a lot closer than Key West, and the base would have medical facilities and (probably) decontamination equipment.

But Cuba was *too* close. Too close to the site of the nuclear explosion. Too close to whatever the fuck was coming unraveled down in this part of the world.

Cassy was oblivious to the doubts and questions bouncing around inside of Jon's head. The specifics, at any rate. She nearly always seemed to know the general line of his thoughts.

If she knew this time, she was keeping it to herself. For the moment, her eyes were glued to the speeding warships. "I don't know what you guys are doing," she said softly, "but good luck and keep safe."

CHAPTER 13

USS ALBANY (SSN-753)
CARIBBEAN SEA, NORTH OF GRAND CAYMAN ISLAND
WEDNESDAY; 25 FEBRUARY
0823 hours (8:23 AM)
TIME ZONE -5 'ROMEO'

Roughly 420 nautical miles southwest of the *Foxy Roxy* (and 300 feet down), the *Los Angeles* class fast attack submarine USS *Albany* was gliding quietly through the water column.

The submarine was not technically silent. The *Seawolf* class boats were quieter, and the *Virginia* class subs were quieter still. There were acoustic emanations; the laws of physics and the limitations of noise-reduction technology saw to that. Even so—under most circumstances—the acoustic source levels of a *Los Angeles* class sub were low enough to be largely masked by the ambient noises of the ocean environment, or dissipated by the mechanics of absorption and volume spreading.

So the *Albany* was quiet. *Damned* quiet. And she was on the hunt.

In the sonar room, Chief of the Boat Ernie Pooler leaned over STS3 Rivera's shoulder to have a look at contact *Sierra Two-Three*. Between merchant ships, fishing boats, pleasure craft, and all of the U.S. warships rushing in to join the blockade, the BQQ-10 broadband display was a tangled mess of surface contacts. Enough easy targets to warm the heart of any bubblehead.

But the main target of interest was isolated on a narrowband display for the *Albany's* towed array.

Sierra Two-Three appeared on the green waterfall style display as a series of parallel lines, with lower frequencies toward the left side of the screen and higher frequencies toward the right. The relative brightness of each frequency was an indication of signal strength. Some of the contact's frequency lines were clearly visible, while others were so faint and intermittent as to be barely detectable.

Currently, *Sierra Two-Three* was classified as *POSS-SUB high*, indicating that the contact was probably (but not definitely) a submarine.

As the sonar team continued to collect and analyze acoustic clues, the contact's classification might be downgraded to NON-SUB or upgraded to PROB-SUB.

To hedge against the second of those two possibilities, the *Albany* had Mark-48 ADCAP torpedoes loaded and prepped in tubes one and four. The attack center was manned, and the targeting team was busily refining its fire control solution on the off-chance that the encounter devolved into a shootout.

U.S. submarines did this as a matter of routine, treating unknown (and sometimes known) sonar contacts as potential enemies—going through the full sequence of steps and procedures leading up to a torpedo or missile launch—stopping just short of hitting the button. This hair-trigger level of readiness kept the crews in continual training for combat, and gave U.S. subs the ability to react within seconds to changes in the threat situation.

If *Sierra Two-Three* turned out to be a non-submarine, the Mark-48s would remain in their tubes and the contact would be relegated to low-priority status: tracked for purposes of situational awareness, but otherwise ignored. If—on the other hand—*Sierra Two-Three* proved to be a submarine, the *Albany* was already prepared for action.

The thing was, there shouldn't *be* any other submarines here. Master Chief Pooler had read the threat board, the OPTASK ASW SUPP, and the most recent update from Blue Force Tracker. There weren't any friendly subs in the area, and there was no intel whatsoever about non-U.S. submarines anywhere near the Caribbean.

On top of that, the power plant noise from this contact had some frequency patterns in common with the old Chinese *Han* class fast attack boats. The *Hans* has been the first (and rather crude) generation of nuclear submarines to come out of Asia. Tactically limited and noisy as hell, most of them had been pulled out of service more than ten years ago.

Sierra Two-Three probably wasn't a *Han* class sub, but it appeared to have some similar engineering characteristics. That was strange. Almost as strange as the fact that the damned thing was here at all.

Master Chief Pooler straightened up and massaged his lower back. He'd wander out to the attack center and see how the target motion analysis was coming along.

He was just turning to leave when STS3 Rivera sat bolt upright. "What the fuck? Did the processors just crash or something? Narrowband just went snake-shit!"

Pooler and the Sonar Supervisor both stepped forward to look at the narrowband display. The top of the screen, where new information appeared, was suddenly bright with broad and fuzzy tonal lines, clustered

mostly in the higher frequency range. A blast of sound so intense that it
almost resembled acoustic jamming.

The disturbance was visible on the broadband display too, a swath of
green that cut across the screen at an improbably shallow angle, so brilliant
that it eclipsed the cavitation signatures of the noisy surface contacts.

The bearing of *Sierra Two-Three* had suddenly begun changing at a
ridiculous rate. The contact was moving fast. *Impossibly* fast.

After a minute or so, Master Chief Pooler left the sonar team to their
own devices and went out to stand next to the CO in the attack center. As
he'd expected, the fire control team was scrambling to stay on top of the
contact's ludicrously fast motion.

The bizarre run of *Sierra Two-Three* lasted just under four minutes.
Then the contact vanished from broadband and narrowband, leaving no
trace of its massively loud signal, or even the weaker acoustic signature
that resembled a *Han* class reactor plant. When the contact (whatever it
was) throttled back to a quieter mode of operation, it was evidently out of
detection range.

Based on TMA, the contact's estimated range at the start of the run had
been in the neighborhood of 16,000 yards. If the estimate was even close
to accurate, *Sierra Two-Three* had moved something like twenty nautical
miles in less than four minutes. The contact's speed through the water had
to be up around three-hundred knots.

That was crazy. It was impossible. But it had happened.

CHAPTER 14

All but five of the 2,000 seats were empty. With the lights out, the windowless main meeting hall of the North Korean government was a 4,300 square meter cavern of echoing darkness. A lone ceiling lamp cast a circle of illumination on the platform at the front of the room.

This was not an official meeting of the Supreme People's Assembly, or even the much smaller National Defense Commission. A gathering of either group would have been pointless. Most members of the fatherland's governing party were figureheads, whose only purpose was to rubber-stamp the proclamations of the Supreme Leader.

The five men seated within the cone of light were not part of that mock administration. They were not puppet delegates or token legislators. Between them, the five composed the entire body of the *haengdong wiwonhoe*, a term which could be translated loosely as *action committee*.

They sat at the head table, with Supreme Leader Kim Yong-nam in his usual chair at the center position of honor. To his right were General Pan Sok-ju (Minister of State Security), and Cho Song-taek (Director of the Propaganda and Agitation Department of the Workers' Party of Korea). On the Supreme Leader's left were Sun Jin-sung (Chairman of Central Committee Bureau 121, the cyber warfare branch of the North Korean government), and Gyo Pyong-il (Chairman of the infamous Central Committee Bureau 39, which managed state-sanctioned illicit activities, including the counterfeiting of foreign currencies, illegal arms dealing, drug production and distribution, and trafficking in humans).

Collectively, these men controlled the military, the economy, the media and communications infrastructure, and even the criminal underworld of their country. Four of them deferred only to Kim Yong-nam, while Kim himself deferred to no one at all.

With more than twenty smaller conference chambers to choose from, the Mansudae Assembly Hall had plenty of rooms more suited in size and layout to the action committee, but—at Kim Yong-nam's insistence—the committee always met in the main hall.

Although he never spoke of it, the proportions of the room and the darkness were a sort of physical metaphor to Kim. The ranks upon ranks of empty chairs symbolized the common people of North Korea: voiceless and impotent in their numbers, and utterly in the dark. By contrast, Kim and his handful of trusted advisors basked in the light of knowledge, power, and privilege. Which was as it should be.

He motioned toward General Pan Sok-ju. "Tell me about the ship."

The general's head dipped in a gesture that might have been either a nod or a bow. "Sir, the *Lecticula* is passing west of Jamaica, and proceeding at normal speed. We expect the American blockade vessels to attempt intercept sometime in the next four to six hours."

Kim nodded. "Is everything in place for our counter stroke?"

"I can only speak for the military preparations, sir," the general said. "We have confirmation that the *Kang Chul Poong* is ready for combat. I assure you that the blockade will not prevent the *Lecticula* from reaching Santiago de Cuba."

Cho Song-taek raised a tentative finger. "If one may ask, what happens after that? The Cubans have been warned about our ship, and they know the nature of its cargo. Even supposing that they are foolish enough to allow the ship to dock, there will be no chance of smuggling the missile launchers ashore. America's surveillance drones and reconnaissance satellites are watching now."

"The ship will not attempt to dock," said Kim. "It now has orders to anchor in the harbor without offloading cargo."

Cho Song-taek started to respond; then the set of his features changed as he began to recognize the propaganda potential in this new situation. "A message for our comrades in Havana?" he mused. "Armed nuclear warheads at the doorstep of Cuba's second largest city?"

Kim Yong-nam didn't answer. His headache—a continual and unwelcome companion for months now—was beginning to gain strength again. The pain was a distant throb, easily ignored for the moment, but it was definitely getting stronger. He would have to take the pills soon, before it gained momentum toward its full and crippling potential.

He looked toward the man who was essentially the Minister of Cyber Warfare. "What is the status of our diversion? Is that ready as well?"

"Of course, sir," said Sun Jin-sung. "We await only your order."

Kim consulted his watch: a Bulgari Magsonic Sonnerie Tourbillon that cost slightly more than a high-end Ferrari. "Initiate the diversion three hours from now. We will give the American Imperialists something to think about when the steel wind begins to blow."

CHAPTER 15

IDYLWOOD POWER SUBSTATION
IDYLWOOD, VA
WEDNESDAY; 25 FEBRUARY
9:12 PM EST

In a strictly technical sense, the malware designated as *Kumiho* was not a virus. Nor was it a worm, a zero-day vector, or even a Trojan horse, although it shared certain properties of all those types of malicious code. Kumiho was a cyber weapon, custom-tailored for the SCADA protocol used by the power grid of the Eastern United States.

Developed and deployed by military hackers from Central Committee Bureau 121, the weapon was (ironically) woven into an authorized security update for the IEC 61131 industrial programming language. Folded safely into the script structure for Programmable Logic Controllers, the weaponized code was now recognized as an approved feature of the software, which made it impervious to virus scans and intrusion detection routines.

In Korean folklore, kumihos were malevolent nine-tailed fox creatures with magical powers. In the old stories, a kumiho could assume the guise of a beautiful woman to deceive young boys and devour their livers.

This Kumiho had no mystical abilities, but its powers of deception had enabled it to remain undetected since its insertion the previous September. And—while the weapon knew nothing of young boys or livers—it was no less dangerous than the mythical creature for which it was named.

After lying dormant for nearly half a year, Kumiho received its activation signal at 9:12 p.m. and eleven seconds. The malicious software went immediately to work. Following a predetermined sequence, it transmitted an electrical overload alert, a high temperature warning, and a major component malfunction report to the first transformer on the substation bus: a 230 kilovolt step-down unit that was roughly the size of a compact car. Any one of these fault conditions would have been enough to trigger the automatic load shedding routines built into the transformer's programmable logic controller. Taken together, they constituted a serious

66

enough threat to demand more drastic action.

The PLC had no way of determining that the fault signals were counterfeit. The unit did exactly what it was designed to do: it slammed the gigantic oil-cooled circuit breakers open to isolate the "damaged" transformer from the electrical bus, and forced an emergency shutdown.

But Kumiho wasn't finished yet. Before transformer one could complete power down procedures, its PLC received an emergency restart signal, cancelling all previous alerts. The mammoth breakers slammed shut, bringing the still-charged transformer back into circuit without performing any of the usual safe-start procedures.

The instant the breakers closed, the cycle began again. A new set of counterfeit fault signals forced the giant transformer into isolation and shutdown mode.

Within seconds, the cyber weapon had instigated the repeating emergency cycle on every transformer in the substation. All along the power bus, breakers snapped open and closed with juttering metallic bangs.

The substation's load balancers tried (and failed) to stabilize the wildly oscillating power output of the station. The quiet hum of normal operation was replaced by what sounded like an army of drunken carpenters blindly pounding on anything within reach of their hammers.

If properly trained human operators had been on hand, they could have manually switched the transformers out of circuit and shut down the PLCs at the first signs of failure. Most—if not all—of the ensuing hardware damage might have been prevented. But very few local power substations are manned, and this site was not one of the lucky exceptions.

The first physical destruction occurred in less than a minute. One of the abused breakers fused itself in the closed position and an attendant junction box arced with overvoltage and exploded into flames. This was quickly followed by a series of cascading equipment failures.

In a surprisingly short time, the Idylwood Substation was no longer a functional part of the eastern regional power grid. It had become a smoking chaos of berserk machine assemblies, rapidly tearing themselves to pieces.

⚓ ⚓ ⚓

Approximately thirty-four miles to the northeast and twenty-five miles to the southeast, variations of the attack were playing out at the Elkridge Substation in Baltimore, Maryland, and the Whittington Road Substation in White Plains.

By 9:16 p.m., all three substations were out of commission due to catastrophic equipment failure. The Idylwood and Elkridge sites were both shaping up into major fires.

The three affected substations formed a scalene triangle covering just under 421 square miles of territory. Within the boundaries of that triangle lay the cities of Washington, DC; Arlington, Virginia; and some forty-odd smaller cities, towns, and communities.

The North Korean cyber assault team had planned well. The average temperature in the Washington Metropolitan Area was 34 degrees Fahrenheit and falling when the capitol city of the United States lost all electrical power.

CHAPTER 16

WHITE HOUSE
OVAL OFFICE
WASHINGTON, DC
WEDNESDAY; 25 FEBRUARY
9:16 PM EST

Chaz Bradley smiled when he heard Paige's voice on the other end of the line. He'd had a lot of calls over the last several days, and very few of them had been anything to smile about.

It was nice to spend a few minutes chatting with his wife about something... *anything* ...that didn't involve a national emergency.

Paige was calling from the Secret Service limo on her way back from Annapolis. She'd been asked to deliver the keynote address at a fundraising dinner for the Maryland Women's Caucus. Chaz was sorry to have missed it.

She was a gifted orator. Witty, engaging, and far more naturally eloquent than her husband. Chaz hoped that someone had recorded the evening. It was bound to be worth watching.

"How did your speech go?" he asked. "Did you knock 'em dead?"

Paige chuckled softly. "I doubt they even remember me."

"What?"

"*Nobody* remembers my speech. I guarantee it."

"Why is that?"

"I got upstaged by Emmaline Halloway. She did her ad lib rendition of Cirque du Soleil, and totally stole the show."

Chaz tried to reconcile Paige's words with what he knew of Ms. Halloway. The woman was large, intimidating, and—quite possibly—the most stoic human being on Earth. She had once referred to the infamous 9/11 attacks as, "*that disturbance in New York.*"

"Okay," Chaz said. "This I've got to hear."

"It was a shoe malfunction," Paige said. "Sergio Rossi, I think, but they might have been knock-offs. Gray leather pumps, pointy toes, and that ultrathin stiletto heel Rossi is famous for."

Chaz gave a mock sigh. "You're determined to drag this out all night, aren't you?"

"Well," Paige said, "it turns out that those thin stilettos have a weight limit. Emmaline broke a heel, and that's when everything went to pieces. She lost her balance and tumbled onto her well-padded rump. There was quite a bit of thrashing on the way down, and she kicked over the lectern in the process. It toppled off the stage and crashed into the front row of tables. People were knocking over chairs trying to get out of the way. And our dear Emmaline was bellowing like a wounded cow the whole time."

"You're making this up," Chaz said.

Paige chuckled again. "Actually, I'm not. If there's not already a cell phone video of it on YouTube, there will be soon."

Chaz Bradley laughed. For the first time in days, his body gave itself over to something other than tension.

He was still laughing when Paige spoke again. "Just a second! Are you seeing this?"

Chaz made an effort to chop his laughter off short. "Seeing what?"

"Looks like a blackout," Paige said. "We're a mile or so past the Anacostia on the 50, and everything just went dark."

"Everything?"

"As far as I can tell," Paige said. "Nothing shining but car headlights. Everything else is pitch black."

The laughter was gone as quickly as it had started. "Maybe it's localized," Chaz said.

"Maybe."

"Hang on," Chaz said. "I'm going to set the phone down for a second."

He stepped over to the bank of windows behind his desk and pulled back the sheer drapery. Through the triple-paned bulletproof glass, he could see the lights of the White House grounds, but nothing beyond. Except for vehicle lights on Constitution Avenue, everything outside of the fence was dark.

He was reaching for the phone when Agent Hugh Parrish, head of the Presidential Security Detail, walked into the Oval Office without knocking.

Parrish crossed the rug toward his protectee at just short of a trot. "Mr. President, we've got a problem. I'm going to need you to step away from the windows."

CHAPTER 17

SWIFT, SILENT, AND LETHAL:
A DEVELOPMENTAL HISTORY OF THE ATTACK SUBMARINE

(Excerpted from working notes presented to the National Institute for Strategic Analysis. Reprinted by permission of the author, David M. Hardy, Ph.D.)

The writings of Aristotle credit his student, Alexander III, with employing divers and "underwater devices" to destroy submerged defenses during the siege of Tyre in 332 BC. Descriptions of the battle don't specify the nature of the underwater devices and the texts don't contain any terms which could reasonably be translated as "submersible" or "submarine."

Nevertheless, a growing number of historians associate the birth of submarine technology with Alexander's tactical experiments, a notion that may have been reinforced by a series of Renaissance paintings which depict the Greek warrior exploring the sea bottom from a transparent diving bell.

Apart from similar diving bell experiments over the next few centuries and China's legendary (but probably apocryphal) Han Dynasty submersible, the next attempt to conquer the ocean depths occurred around 1502 AD.

While serving as military engineer for an Italian nobleman, master artist and inventor Leonardo Da Vinci created plans for a submersible craft which he referred to as "a ship to sink another ship." His notes were deliberately vague, making it difficult to determine whether the craft would operate under water or only partially submerged.

He was secretive about the design because he considered it the most dangerous weapon ever conceived, predicting that submersible warships would bring new levels of horror to a planet that was already too proficient at making war.

Where Da Vinci's descriptions of submarine construction were frustratingly nonspecific, William Bourne's later writings on the subject were far more detailed.

16th century painting of Alexander the Great lowered in a glass diving bell

Bourne—a mathematician and former gunner in the British Royal Navy—wrote navigational manuals for sailing vessels. His book, *Inventions or Devises*, published in 1578, described an enclosed craft capable of mechanically decreasing the volume of its hull to submerge beneath the water.

The vessel consisted of a wooden frame covered in waterproofed leather, propelled by oars that penetrated the hull through watertight ports.

Although Bourne's apparatus for submerging would be made obsolete by floodable ballast tanks, his descriptions showed that the problem of depth control was solvable.

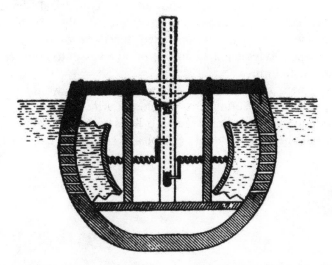

Conceptual drawing of submarine mechanism (attributed to Bourne)

In 1623 a Dutchman named Cornelius Drebbel, employed by King James I of England, built what may have been the first working submarine. Drebbel didn't use Bourne's depth control mechanism, but he adopted the method of propulsion recommended by *Inventions or Devises*.

Written accounts of Drebbel's craft described a decked-over rowboat propelled by twelve oarsmen. According to these reports, the *Drebbel I* made a journey down the Thames River submerged to a depth of fifteen feet.

James I may have witnessed a demonstration, but reports that the king took an underwater ride are dismissed as exaggeration.

The crude submersible was limited to low speeds, shallow depths, and dives of short duration. It's also worth noting that reports only describe movement in a downriver direction, suggesting insufficient power to maneuver against the current. Nevertheless, Cornelius Drebbel had proven that a manmade vessel could travel under the water.

Thirteen years later, French theologian Marin Mersenne applied mathematical reasoning to the problems of hull construction. Aware that water pressure increases by about one half pound per square inch (PSI) for every foot of depth, Mersenne realized that hulls constructed from wood and leather risked being crushed even during relatively shallow dives. Balancing material weight against ability to withstand pressure, he determined that copper plating would be more suitable for the hull of a submarine.

Mersenne's calculations also showed that cylindrical shapes could better withstand the water pressure at greater depths. As his research progressed, the mathematician concluded that the ends of a submarine's hull should taper, to reduce drag and permit the vessel to reverse direction without having to turn.

Over the next few decades, Mersenne's findings would do little to influence naval engineering. In the long term, however, all of his recommendations—from metal pressure hulls to tapered cylindrical hull shapes—would become standard principles of submarine construction.

CHAPTER 18

USS BOWIE (DDG-141)
CARIBBEAN SEA, NORTHWEST OF JAMAICA
WEDNESDAY; 25 FEBRUARY
2308 hours (11:08 PM)
TIME ZONE -5 'ROMEO'

From his command chair at the focal point of Combat Information Center, Captain Zachary Heller swiveled to take in the video feeds from the topside camera arrays. Between the quarter moon and a sky full of stars there was plenty of ambient illumination for the cameras to operate in low-light mode.

If necessary, the cameras could shift to the infrared band, allowing them to "see" heat signatures even under conditions of total darkness. But staying in the optical band kept the image resolution much higher, and made the video displays more naturally intuitive.

Evolution had spent half a billion years creating and refining the sensory organs that led to stereoscopic vision in modern primates. Human beings were genetically wired to interpret images based on visual wavelengths of light. By contrast, the ability to understand infrared imagery was a strictly learned behavior, receiving no assistance from human instinct or biology.

Heller's abba might disbelieve (or *want* to disbelieve) the teachings of Darwin, but Heller himself had no doubts about the realities of evolution. Natural selection had endowed the human animal with certain physical abilities and limitations. Like any military leader worth his rank insignia, he tried to factor human physiology into training scenarios and operational planning as much as possible.

In training situations, his standing order required the crew to work with the topside cameras in infrared mode at least eighty percent of the time, because reading the IR video displays took a lot of practice. During real-world operations, he preferred to keep the cameras in the optical band, where interpretation was instinctive.

It was a lesson he'd learned during his junior ensign tour aboard the old

USS *Gettysburg*—train the hard way; do it the easy way. So far, that theory seemed to be paying off. The *Bowie's* CIC team was nearly as proficient in IR mode as they were in optical mode, despite the limitations of human visual processing.

The Motor Vessel *Lecticula* was well outside of the shipping lanes, and running without lights. Probably the ship's master didn't hold any real hope of slipping past the blockade in the dark. He was a sailor; he knew that radar didn't give a damn about darkness. More likely, it had been a purely reflexive decision. (If you're trying to do something sneaky at night, you turn your lights off.)

Whatever the motivation might have been, the lights-out trick wasn't working. The cargo ship was easily visible on radar, and she stood out just as clearly on display screen #3. In low-light mode, the cameras were limited to grayscale, but the clarity was exceptional.

On the video display, the MV *Lecticula* looked like exactly what she was: a poorly-maintained bulk cargo carrier, nearing the end of her operational life. And that end might be only minutes away if the ship continued to crowd the blockade line.

The Rules of Engagement were explicit. Ships approaching the blockade area were to be warned three times over bridge-to-bridge radio channel 16, which international law requires major vessels to monitor at all times. Any ship that failed to heed the radio calls would receive a single warning shot across the bow. If the would-be blockade runner continued to approach, it was to be engaged with naval artillery and either disabled or sunk.

Standing by for this task was the guided missile destroyer, USS *Mahan*, currently bearing 253 degrees from *Bowie*. The *Mahan* was interposed between the MV *Lecticula* and the do-not-cross line of the blockade area—positioned far enough back to stay out of the immediate blast zone in case the aging freighter suddenly went up in a nuclear fireball. Nobody wanted to be rubbing elbows with a nuke if the *Lecticula* self-destructed like her sister ship, the MV *Aranella*.

USS *Bowie* was in the backup position, lurking three and a half nautical miles behind the *Mahan*. If the old cargo ship miraculously evaded her more-nimble pursuer, the *Bowie's* mission was to engage the target and finish the job.

A voice broke over bridge-to-bridge channel 16. It was the radio talker from USS *Mahan*, with the first warning call. "Motor Vessel *Lecticula*, this is United States warship Seven-Two. You are approaching an area under naval blockade. If you continue on your current course, you will be fired upon. If you approach within fifty nautical miles of the Cuban coast, you will be fired upon. You are directed to alter course immediately and depart the area."

After fifteen or twenty seconds of empty static on the channel, another voice came over the radio, an interpreter aboard the *Mahan* repeating the warning in Korean.

There was no response. The *Lecticula* continued toward Cuba at eighteen knots.

The warning came again after a minute or so—first in English, then in Korean. Still no response. The freighter didn't slow or turn.

"They're showing us their game face," Heller said. "My money says they'll blow off the third warning too. They won't turn until the *Mahan* drops a five-inch round across their bow."

A few seconds later, a voice came out of a speaker in the overhead. Not the measured tones of the *Mahan's* radio talker. A younger female voice, speaking over the *Bowie's* 29MC antisubmarine warfare announcing circuit. "All Stations—Sonar has passive broadband contact off the starboard beam! Bearing two-nine-one with extremely rapid left bearing drift. Initial classification: POSS-SUB, confidence level low!"

Heller's eyes flitted to the tactical displays. The new sonar contact appeared as a red line from the symbol representing USS *Bowie* to the edge of the display screen. The line was angled at 291 degrees: the current bearing of the possible submarine from *Bowie*.

Without echo ranging from active sonar, or a cross-fix from another sensor, there was no way to know the contact's range. The possible sub could be anywhere along that line of bearing, from fifty yards to fifty-thousand.

Heller keyed his headset's microphone. "Sonar, this is the captain. Is this our high-speed mystery contact? The one we were tracking on Sunday?"

"Captain—Sonar. Looks like it, sir. The broadband swath is so bright it's nearly burning up our scopes. Extremely high bearing rate, and the audio sounds like a giant pan of frying bacon."

On the tactical display, the red line of bearing was sweeping rapidly to the left. The contact was hauling ass. It was the same guy alright, moving like an underwater missile.

Heller saw a new line of bearing appear: sonar tracking data from USS *Mahan*. The two red lines intersected to the northwest of the *Mahan*.

The cross-fix would give both ships vital range information about the strange submerged contact, allowing them to calculate course and speed to build firing solutions if the POSS-SUB turned out to be hostile. Unfortunately, the destroyers had been expecting surface action, not antisubmarine warfare. Neither ship had manned up a full ASW team, and it would take at least a couple of minutes to get the proper watch stations covered. Given the speed of the contact, they might not *have* a couple of minutes.

The appearance of this new threat was not a coincidence. It couldn't be; the timing was too precise. Somebody had planned this.

Bridge-to-bridge channel 16 came to life again as USS *Mahan* issued the third warning to the MV *Lecticula*.

Heller ignored the call. The freighter wasn't the problem here. If the unidentified sonar contact turned out to be a hostile submarine, the tactical situation could turn into a shit sandwich in about two nanoseconds.

He keyed his mike and began issuing orders without waiting for acknowledgements. "Bridge—Captain. Stand by to crack the whip on my command. Break. TAO—Captain. Call away Condition One-AS. Prepare for immediate ASW action. Break. Sonar—Captain. Is Chief Scott in Sonar Control?"

"Captain—Sonar. Affirmative, sir. He's standing right beside me."

Heller nodded to himself. "Captain, aye."

As soon as Heller was finished speaking, the Tactical Action Officer punched the button to jumper his own headset into the 1MC General Announcing Circuit. When he keyed the mike, his voice came out of speakers all over the ship.

"This is the TAO. Now set Condition One-AS. Man all antisubmarine warfare stations, and prepare for immediate ASW action! Now set Condition One-AS."

Hot on the heels of this announcement came the Sonar Supervisor's next report over the 29MC. "All Stations—Sonar has hydrophone effects off the starboard bow! Bearing two-seven-six, correlated to the current bearing of POSS-SUB contact. Initial classification: submerged missile launch!"

Heller's eyes automatically scanned the tactical display screens for hostile missile symbols. There were none.

The Tactical Action Officer keyed his mike and spoke into the net. "Air—TAO. Can you confirm missile emergence?"

The Air Supervisor's report was three or four seconds in coming. "TAO—Air. That's a negative. SPY shows no air contacts within ninety degrees of bearing two-seven-six. We have no tracks consistent with missile trajectories."

The "SPY" he referred to was the AN/SPY-1D(V)4 phased-array radar: the nucleus of the Aegis integrated sensor and weapons suite. With a peak power output of nearly six million watts and a high data-rate computer control system, SPY was the ship's all-seeing eye, capable of detecting and tracking more than two hundred simultaneous air and surface contacts. But for all of that power and capacity, the radar wasn't seeing any signs of the (supposed) missile launch detected by sonar.

The door to CIC clanged open and the Undersea Warfare Officer, Ensign Moore, hustled in, followed by an enlisted Sonar Technician. The sailor dogged the watertight door behind himself and both men practically ran to their respective consoles.

Ensign Moore—whose watch station at Condition One-AS was Undersea Warfare Evaluator—made a bee-line for the Computerized Dead-Reckoning Tracer, jacking his headset into the communications panel and configuring the unit for operation.

The Sonar Technician moved just as quickly to the Underwater Battery Fire Control System and began prepping his station for a combat engagement.

Even as they were readying their equipment, another update broke over the 29MC. "All Stations—Sonar. Hydrophone effects now reclassified as supercavitating torpedo. Possible Shkval class. Be advised, torpedo is *not* incoming. I say again, hostile torpedo is *not* incoming. Broadband shows extremely rapid left bearing drift. Torpedo appears to be locked on the *Mahan*!"

Heller checked the tactical displays again. A red hostile-torpedo symbol had appeared, and it was gobbling up the distance separating it from USS *Mahan*.

The *Mahan* was increasing speed and changing course. Following doctrine, her captain was executing the *crack-the-whip* maneuver: a rapid sequence of tight turns, designed to confuse enemy torpedoes by creating multiple propeller wakes at close intervals.

But the flashing red symbol wasn't moving at fifty knots, or even sixty. If it really was a Shkval, its speed would be upwards of two-hundred knots. *Crazy* fast. Like the crazy-assed submarine contact that had launched it.

Heller keyed into the tactical net. "USWE—Captain. Unidentified sonar contact is now designated as *Gremlin Zero-One*. You have batteries released. Engage and kill as soon as you have a valid fire control solution!"

Ensign Moore's fingers darted over the soft-keys of the CDRT's touch control window. "USWE, aye. Break. UB—USWE. I've got good bearing cross-fixes from *Mahan*. Stand by for range updates directly from the CDRT."

"UB, aye."

This was a reversal of the usual information flow. For passive broadband contacts, range was normally calculated by the Underwater Battery Fire Control System, and then forwarded to the CDRT for display and tactical decision-making. But in this case, the USW Evaluator already had the range information on his screen, from the bearing cross-fixes. There was no need to wait for the UB computer to work through its target motion analysis algorithms.

The fire control operator examined the incoming data and keyed his mike. "USWE—UB. Contact is well outside the range envelope for over-the-side torpedoes."

"USWE, aye. Target *Gremlin Zero-One* with Anvil, and inform me as soon as you have a firing solution."

"UB, aye."

Heller's gaze was locked on the tactical displays. The crack-the-whip maneuver had never been intended to evade supercavitating torpedoes, and it wasn't working now. On the screen, the red hostile-torpedo symbol was closing inexorably on the blue friendly-ship symbol that represented the *Mahan*. The speed differential was simply too drastic to overcome. It was like watching a butterfly try to outrun a bullet.

Suddenly, a circular blue icon appeared on the screen close to the latest cross-fix for *Gremlin Zero-One*. It was a water entry point symbol. *Mahan* had launched an Anvil. Getting in a last-second shot at the enemy submarine.

But the hostile sub was also moving at supercav speed. By the time the *Mahan's* weapon acquired contact, it was chasing a target with a speed advantage of more than a hundred-fifty knots. Falling farther behind with every second, it had no chance at all of catching the unknown submarine.

Sadly, the enemy's weapon was on the opposite side of the speed advantage problem.

Heller was watching when USS *Mahan* lost her race against the supercavitating torpedo.

Seen from the tactical displays, it was nothing more than the silent merging of two colored icons. The story captured by the topside cameras was altogether different.

It played out on video screen #4 in flawless high-resolution monochrome. The unlit form of the warship—a shadow against dark waves—was suddenly caught in a flare of brilliant illumination. A monstrous geyser of spray erupted amidships as the seawater under the destroyer's keel was instantly flashed to steam.

For some brief part of a second, the thermal pulse of the explosion heated structural supports and hull plating into the ductility range of steel, robbing the hardened metal of its tensile strength. Simultaneously, all support beneath the hull was taken away by the expanding bubble of vaporized water. The overpressure of the shock wave finished the job.

The destroyer was ripped in half, with both of the mangled sections pummeled repeatedly by massive hydrostatic shock reverberations.

There would be fire, and shrapnel, and the screams of dying sailors, but none of those horrors were visible through the curtain of smoke and falling water.

And there was no more time to watch, because it was USS *Bowie's* turn to fight.

⚓ ⚓ ⚓

Anvil (USS *Bowie*):

An armored hatch sprang open on the destroyer's aft missile deck, revealing a weatherproof membrane that capped the top of a vertical missile cell. The membrane disintegrated a millisecond later as the *Bowie's* Vertical Launch Antisubmarine Rocket (ASROC) roared out of its cell and hurtled into the night sky on a silver-orange column of flame and smoke.

Code-named *Anvil*, the ASROC's flight profile was decidedly unlike that of other missiles. Instead of blasting toward an aerial intercept point, or dropping toward the waves for a sea-skimming trajectory, the ASROC tilted over to forty-five degrees and climbed toward the apex of a pre-calculated ballistic arc.

At an altitude of ten thousand feet, it reached the top of the curve, and several things happened in quick succession. A pair of explosive blocks in the airframe detonated, shattering the stainless steel bands that clamped the missile body together.

The fiberglass aeroshell split into two halves, which were torn apart by aerodynamic drag and flung in opposite directions. The ASROC flew to pieces, exactly as it was designed to do. Out of this expanding assortment of discarded components dropped the missile's payload: a flight-configured Mark-54 torpedo.

From an engineering perspective, the ASROC was a hodgepodge of dissimilar technologies, cobbled together in a fashion that would have made Rube Goldberg proud. According to persistent rumors among the ASW community, the weapon's code-name had been inspired by classic Chuck Jones cartoons in which the hapless Wile E. Coyote devised improbable contraptions to drop anvils on the head of his animated nemesis, the Road Runner.

Whether or not the rumor happened to be true, ASROC was a surprisingly effective standoff weapon—capable of throwing a lightweight antisubmarine torpedo many thousands of yards with remarkable accuracy.

Freed from the junkyard of parts that it no longer needed, the Anvil's torpedo fell toward the sea, completing the second half of the ballistic curve.

When the weapon dropped past two thousand feet, a parachute deployed from the tail section, throwing the torpedo into a nose-down attitude and slowing its rate of descent just enough to survive collision with the water.

The weapon hit the ocean hard enough to fracture its nosecone along a set of pre-scored stress lines. The collapse of this last remnant of aerodynamic fuselage absorbed some of the impact shock, and protected the fragile sonar transducer in the head of the torpedo.

As the Mark-54 sank into the ocean, seawater flowed in through tiny vents, activating the saltwater batteries. The torpedo's internal computer cycled itself online and began routing battery power to the sensors, the main electrical bus, and the guidance module.

When the pre-start logics had all been satisfied, the computer spun up the turbine engine. The guidance module performed a quick evaluation of orientation and depth, and then initiated a clockwise search pattern.

The sonar transducer and seeker logic had no trouble locating the noisy target. The torpedo locked on to the submarine's broadband acoustic signature and accelerated to attack speed.

⚓ ⚓ ⚓

USS *Bowie*:

"USWE—Sonar. We have weapon startup. Anvil has acquired the target."

Ordinarily that report would have elicited cheers and whistles among the CIC crew, but the watch standers were stunned by what had just happened to the *Mahan*.

There wasn't much to cheer about anyway. On the CDRT and the tactical displays, USS *Bowie's* Anvil changed from a water entry point symbol to a friendly-torpedo symbol and began to move. It lagged behind the enemy sub from the start, losing ground just as quickly as the *Mahan's* weapon had done.

The cross-fixes were gone now. *Mahan* had lost sonar contact somewhere amid the speed and frantic turns of her crack-the-whip maneuver.

The lone line of bearing from the *Bowie's* sonar continued to drive left, sweeping counterclockwise like the secondhand of a clock running in reverse. *Gremlin Zero-One* was still moving at incredible speed.

Then the strange contact was suddenly absent from the sonar scopes. Just like in the earlier encounter, the powerful broadband signature evaporated without warning, as if someone had pulled a plug, or flipped an 'off' switch.

Heller's eyes went back to the topside camera displays. The forward half of USS *Mahan* had capsized and was foundering. The aft section of the ship was on fire, and going down quickly by the stern.

A few miles to the southwest, the Motor Vessel *Lecticula* had crossed the blockade line and was continuing on course for Cuba at an unwavering eighteen knots.

For a half-moment, Heller thought about trying to chase down the hostile submarine, but that would be futile. He already knew the sub could outrun his ship. Even if the *Bowie* managed to get within ASROC or over-the-side torpedo range, the submarine would activate its supercav drive and leave Heller's weapons in the dust.

Besides, there were two more pressing matters to attend to. Luckily, Heller's crew could handle both of them at one time.

He keyed his mike. "Bridge—Captain. Close to within five-hundred yards of USS *Mahan* and start the search for survivors. Break. TAO—Captain. The Motor Vessel *Lecticula* is now designated as *Hostile Surface Contact Zero One*. You have batteries released. Engage and kill contact with Mount 61! Kill that son of a bitch! Kill it *now*!"

CHAPTER 19

STEEL WIND (KANG CHUL POONG)
CARIBBEAN SEA, NORTHWEST OF JAMAICA
WEDNESDAY; 25 FEBRUARY
2317 hours (11:17 PM)
TIME ZONE -5 'ROMEO'

The *Steel Wind* slowed to normal operating speed. The gimbaled rocket nozzle in the submarine's stern and the capillary vents in her bow fell silent.

Without a continual flow of steam from the vents, the gas envelope shrunk and then collapsed, increasing hydrodynamic drag on the hull by a factor of nine just as the rocket's exhaust was throttling back to zero.

A trio of much slower (and much quieter) electrically-driven impeller pods took over the job of propulsion and steering. Once again, the wild ride was over. Her first combat engagement had been a total success, with the burning wreckage of the American destroyer as proof.

In the taxonomy of warships, the *Steel Wind* was an anomaly. She did not fit into any of the established categories of combatant vessels. Her builders had no intention of replicating the concept in future constructions, so she was not the lead boat of a new class. She was operationally deployed and fully combat-ready, so she could not be considered a test platform or a prototype. She had no hull number, no vessel registry identifier, and no distinguishing markings of any kind. Her only designation was *Kang Chul Poong*, an obscure Korean phrase which translated roughly as *wind of steel*.

The peculiarities of this odd craft did not end with her lack of formal nomenclature. Nearly every facet of her design represented a departure from established principles of submarine architecture.

In place of the elongated tear drop hull forms favored by most navies, the *Steel Wind's* shape was a simple cone: 8 meters across the base and 48 meters in length, for an overall volume of 804.25 cubic meters.

The upper curve of the hull was not interrupted by the raised sail and conning tower found on nearly all modern attack submarines. The normal arrangements of bow and stern planes were also absent, replaced by the less effective impellor pods—chosen because they didn't interrupt the gas envelope while the sub was in supercavitation mode.

Instead of the customary black paint scheme, the hull had an amber-yellow sheen which resembled aging varnish. The unusual color was caused by a superhydrophobic coating of manganese oxide polystyrene nano-composite, which reduced hydrodynamic drag when the gas envelope was not activated.

The reactor that drove the sub was atypical as well. In place of the double-loop pressurized water reactor variants used by other submarines, the *Steel Wind* carried a single-loop boiling water reactor: a configuration more commonly installed in shore-based nuclear power facilities. In normal operating mode, it drew distilled water from a closed circuit of feed tanks and condensers, generating just enough steam to drive a pair of small electric power turbines. In supercavitation mode, saltwater was siphoned directly from the sea, rammed through a stack of osmotic membrane filters to reduce salinity and remove particulates, then injected straight into the reactor vessel to generate steam for the rocket thruster and the capillary bow vents that created the gas envelope.

The propulsion system of the *Steel Wind* would have been impossible to build in most countries, not because other nations lacked the technical capacity, but because the submarine spewed great quantities of radioactive steam into the sea with no regard for the ecological consequences.

The North Korean engineers who designed the sub had been ordered to disregard any damage their creation might cause to the ocean environment. The safety of the *Steel Wind's* crew was a slightly higher priority, but only in the short-term.

If the sailors all came down with leukemia or liver tumors in two or three years, that was an acceptable price. They needed to survive long enough to complete their mission: a few more weeks or a month at most. After that, their cancer-ridden bodies could be buried as Heroes of the Republic, the highest honor accorded to any citizen of North Korea.

The crew hadn't been told that, of course. The officers and men of the *Steel Wind* had been repeatedly assured that the four-ton experimental radiation barrier was more advanced (and far more effective) than the 100+ tons of lead shielding used on submarine reactors of similar size.

That assertion was half-true. The experimental barrier really *was* more advanced, at least in terms of material science. It was a high-tech laminate composed of silicon carbide ceramic, boron carbide ceramic, and aluminum oxide ceramic, alternating with micro-thin layers of lead and tungsten foil.

The part about being more effective was not just an exaggeration; it was an unqualified lie. The lightweight laminate barrier was nowhere near as efficient as a conventional lead shield, but it was the best protection that could be managed within the narrow space and weight constraints of the submarine's design.

The increased exposure would eventually lead to the death of every man serving aboard. The irony of that had not been lost on the engineers who had designed the submarine, nor on the man who had ordered her into battle.

The *Steel Wind* would kill her enemies quickly, but her friends would die slowly.

CHAPTER 20

FOXHALL CRESCENT
WASHINGTON, DC
WEDNESDAY; 25 FEBRUARY
11:51 PM EST

Working by flashlight, Secretary of Defense Mary O'Neil-Broerman shepherded Knut into the back of the waiting Pentagon limousine. The Golden Retriever scrambled onto the seat and immediately began sniffing leather upholstery, carpet, door handles, and everything else within reach of his nose, his tail wagging madly at the prospect of an unexpected car ride. Like most dogs, Knut viewed riding in a vehicle as one of the great pleasures in life, right up there with a good long scratch behind the ears.

Under other circumstances, Mary would have smiled at her dog's puppyish antics, but there was little room in this night for lightheartedness.

Except for the occasional flicker of candlelight or a storm lantern in some of the windows, every house on Calvert Street Northwest was dark. The streetlamps and security lights were out as well, turning the well-tended avenue into a tunnel of deep shadow.

Mary's house was the darkest of them all. Steve was in Chicago on business, and the housekeeping staff had gone to their own homes, to huddle through the blacked out winter night with their families. Now that Mary had come to fetch Knut, her beautiful 1951 split-level was empty of life as well as light. For the first time in her memory, the house seemed like a dead thing.

A few yards away she could hear the quiet movements of Sergeant Monroe, the Army CID agent assigned to her protection detail. The soldier was in plain clothes—black suit blending into the unremitting night as he searched the darkness for possible threats.

Sergeant Monroe had offered to handle this errand without her. He had practically begged Mary to sit safe in her Pentagon office while he sent someone to rescue her pet from the deserted house.

Mary had refused of course. Knut was too good a watchdog to allow strangers in his house without a fight. Someone—the dog, the Army errand runner, or both—might have gotten hurt in the process. Mary wasn't willing to risk that. Nor did she want the furniture damage that would likely result from the attempted capture of an unhappy and overexcited Golden Retriever.

Better to come pick up Mr. Handsome herself and introduce the Army protective agent as a friend, thereby avoiding bites, bruises, and broken antiques.

His preliminary olfactory inspection of the vehicle complete, Knut promptly plunked himself down in Mary's seat.

She nudged him. "Scoot your butt over, silly boy. Mama needs to get in the car."

The dog shuffled sideways, making barely enough room for his human to sit. Mary climbed in after him and the CID agent closed the door behind her.

Satisfied that his protectee was buttoned up behind the relative safety of bulletproof glass and armored body panels, the sergeant took his seat beside the driver and the car began to roll.

Mary had learned to accept the security precautions without comment, but they always struck her as being unnecessary. Unless you counted the conspiracy theories about the death of James Forrestal, which Mary didn't, no one had ever tried to assassinate a secretary of defense. As a member of Cabinet, as well as de facto deputy commander-in-chief of U.S. military forces, the position wielded a great deal of authority, but no assassin in history had ever been tempted enough to have a serious go at killing a SECDEF.

From Mary's perspective, that simple fact made the hard car limousines and the heel-and-toe bodyguards rather ridiculous. Not just overkill, but absurd overkill.

The car reached the end of the driveway and turned west on Calvert. Outside the sweep of the headlights, the world was dark and powerless. Not because of some accident or natural disaster, but because of a deliberate attack against the city's vital infrastructure.

The North Koreans were doing a lot of things that no hostile nation had ever done before, and no one seemed to have a clue what those crazy bastards were going to try next. Now that she thought of it, maybe the guards and the armor weren't such a bad idea after all.

When the limo turned left onto Rock Creek Parkway, Mary reached for the car phone. Her government-issue cell phone was capable of making secure calls, but getting the encryption to sync up usually required a lot of tinkering. With the limo's STE phone, the process was simple: click the Fortezza-Hyper crypto card into the slot, and press the 'Secure' button.

The phone would do the rest.

Mary carried out these two simple steps and then called up the speed dial number for Rear Admiral Cynthia Long, Commander of the Office of Naval Intelligence.

The time was a minute or two before midnight, but the call was picked up after the first ring. "Admiral Long's office, Lieutenant Jessup speaking."

Mary settled back into the upholstery. "Lieutenant, this is the secretary of defense. Go secure on your end, and then please get me Admiral Long."

Following a rapid succession of low-pitched audio tones, the green 'SECURE' light illuminated on Mary's phone.

"Ma'am, the line is now secure," Lieutenant Jessup said, "but the admiral is in a briefing at the moment."

"Then go drag her out of it," Mary said.

There was a pause before the lieutenant spoke again. "Ma'am, the admiral is meeting with senior ONI staff. She left orders not to interrupt her."

Mary bit back the urge to raise her voice. She'd run into this particular wall before. Military personnel, especially the junior ones, sometimes had trouble taking civilian authority seriously. As they saw it, if you weren't wearing a uniform, you couldn't possibly be very important.

No problem. Nothing Mary couldn't fix with a bit of minor calibration.

"I understand," she said. "Could you please take a message for Admiral Long?"

"Of course, Ma'am," said Lieutenant Jessup.

"Good," Mary said. "Kindly tell the admiral to have her letter of resignation on my desk no later than seven a.m. Sorry, that would be oh-seven-hundred hours to you."

There was complete silence on the other end of the line.

Mary spoke again. "Did you get that written down? Can you repeat it back to me?"

The young officer's words came out in a rush as he tried to stammer a response.

Mary cut him off. "If your boss can't find time for my calls, I'll replace her with someone who can. Do I make myself clear, Lieutenant Jessup?"

"Yes, Ma'am! I mean, yes, Madam Secretary! I'll get the admiral on the phone right away!"

Mary reached over and stroked the top of Knut's head. "You do that," she said. "And if I'm not talking to Admiral Long in the next sixty seconds, I'm going to hang up this phone and wait for her resignation to hit my desk."

"Yes, Ma'am! I'll be right back!"

Less than half of the sixty second deadline had elapsed when a female voice came on the line. "Admiral Long speaking. What can I do for you, Madam Secretary?"

Mary was looking through the limousine's windows when she spoke. A pile of what looked to be chairs was burning on the sidewalk, six or eight people crowded around its circle of light and warmth. Farther down the block, a car was in flames.

"One of our most capable warships has been cut to ribbons by some type of North Korean super-submarine that's not supposed to exist," Mary said. "We don't know the body count yet, but it's not going to be pretty. We've got a few dozen nuclear missiles sitting right off the coast of Florida, and the citizens of our nation's capital are burning cars in the street to keep from freezing to death."

Mary checked her wristwatch. "I'm scheduled to brief the president in about forty minutes, and I very much suspect that I'm going to be out of a job before the sun comes up."

"So here's what you can do for me, Admiral. You can tell me how in the name of *God* we let this happen...."

CHAPTER 21

USS ALBANY (SSN-753)
CARIBBEAN SEA, SOUTH OF LITTLE CAYMAN ISLAND
THURSDAY; 26 FEBRUARY
0213 hours (2:13 AM)
TIME ZONE -5 'ROMEO'

The voice was hushed but urgent. "Wake up, COB!"

Master Chief Ernie Pooler grunted, fumbled absently at his gray Navy blanket, and resumed snoring with the abandon of a tranquilized lumberjack.

A hard sleeper by nature, he was down so far into dreamland that he was practically comatose.

The star of his dream was a pigeon. Not just any old pigeon, but the one that had gotten itself into the ventilation sump aboard USS *Dallas*.

It had been a pitiful looking thing, skinny and bedraggled. Instead of surfacing and letting the bird fly away to fend for itself, the CO had decided to keep it aboard for the rest of the deployment. One of the engineers had improvised a cage, and the untidy creature had been adopted as the 128th member of the crew. Every watch section had fed the damned thing, and after three and a half months of overindulging on bread crumbs, crackers, and potato chips, the pigeon had become too fat to fly.

When the *Dallas* hit homeport at the end of the cruise, the CO had walked down the brow with that overweight feather ball riding on his shoulder like a parrot out of some old black and white swashbuckler flick.

The actual experience had been surreal enough, but the dream version of the bird was even more outlandish. It was dressed in a sequined tuxedo jacket, complete with black cane and rhinestone top hat. Unlike the real pigeon, whose vocalizations had been limited to the usual repertoire of twitters and coos, the dream bird could belt out show tunes like Mitzi Gaynor. It was singing now, nonsensical lyrics about dancing waffles and a lovesick toaster jilted by a pair of salad tongs.

Just as the musical avian was ramping up to the refrain, someone laid a hand on Pooler's upper arm and shook it. "COB, wake up!"

Master Chief Pooler came alert with a promptness rarely found in deep sleepers. He rolled over and pulled back his privacy curtains to face the Messenger of the Watch.

The young sailor was dimly illuminated by the glow of a red-lensed flashlight. "Sorry to wake you, COB. But the Skipper wants to see you in the Control Room."

Pooler yawned. "Tell him I'm on my way."

The messenger nodded. "Aye-aye, COB." He turned and disappeared down the darkened aisle of the berthing compartment.

As soon as the sailor was out of the way, the master chief climbed out of his rack and dressed by touch. With a career's worth of practice at late night awakenings, he moved quickly, quietly, and confidently in the dark.

Chief Petty Officer berthing—known by long-standing Navy tradition as the "Goat Locker"—was one deck below the Control Room, and about seventy feet forward.

Pooler covered the distance in well under a minute, and walked straight to the commanding officer. "Morning, Skipper. You wanted to see me, sir?"

Captain Townsend held out a metal clipboard with a hardcopy message attached. "Morning, COB. Have a look at this."

The master chief accepted the clipboard and began to read.

```
//TTTTTTTTTT//
//TOP SECRET//
//FLASH//FLASH//FLASH//
//260653Z FEB//

FM    COMSUBLANT//
TO    COMSUBRON SIX//
USS ALBANY//

SUBJ/ASW TASKING/IMMEDIATE EXECUTE//

REF/A/RMG/CNO/260547Z FEB//

NARR/REF A IS CHIEF OF NAVAL OPERATIONS TACTICAL
SUMMARY OF LIVE-FIRE HOSTILITIES IN VICINITY OF
CUBAN NAVAL BLOCKADE.//

1. (SECR) AS OUTLINED IN REF A, U.S. NAVY SURFACE
UNITS IN THE CARIBBEAN SEA WERE ATTACKED BY AN
UNIDENTIFIED HIGH-SPEED SUBMARINE AT APPROXIMATELY
0411Z. GUIDED MISSILE DESTROYER USS MAHAN WAS SUNK
```

BY SUBMERGED WEAPON CURRENTLY ASSESSED AS POSSIBLE
SUPERCAVITATING TORPEDO. PERSONNEL CASUALTIES
HIGH.

2. (SECR) ACCOMPANYING GUIDED MISSILE DESTROYER,
USS BOWIE, WAS NOT TARGETED BY HOSTILE SUBMARINE
FOR REASONS UNKNOWN AT THIS TIME. BOTH DESTROYERS
ENGAGED CONTACT WITH VERTICAL LAUNCH ANVILS.
WEAPONS ACQUIRED TARGET BUT FAILED TO INTERCEPT
DUE TO EXTREME SPEED DISADVANTAGE.

3. (SECR) BASED ON IN-SITU TARGET MOTION ANALYSIS,
SUBMARINE CONTACT MAY HAVE REACHED SPEEDS
EXCEEDING THREE-HUNDRED (300) KNOTS. ACOUSTIC DATA
COLLECTED BY USS BOWIE SUPPORTS THE POSSIBILITY OF
NEW/UNKNOWN SUPERCAVITATING PROPULSION SYSTEM.

4. (SECR) HOSTILE SUBMARINE IS ASSUMED TO BE NORTH
KOREAN IN ORIGIN, BUT THIS CANNOT CURRENTLY BE
VERIFIED.

5. (TS) SUBOPAUTH CONFIRMS NO FRIENDLY SUBMARINES
WITHIN TWO-HUNDRED (200) NAUTICAL MILES OF CUBAN
BLOCKADE ZONE.

6. (SECR) LAST KNOWN POSITION OF HOSTILE SUBMARINE
WAS LATITUDE 18.55N/LONGITUDE 79.06W, TIME 0413Z.
LAST ESTIMATED COURSE WAS 218 DEGREES.

7. (TS) USS ALBANY IS DIRECTED TO RELOCATE,
ENGAGE, AND DESTROY ALL UNKNOWN SUBMARINE CONTACTS
IN THIS AREA.

8. (UNCL) GOOD LUCK AND GOOD HUNTING! ADMIRAL
POTTER SENDS.

//260653Z FEB//
//FLASH//FLASH//FLASH//
//TOP SECRET//
//TTTTTTTTTT//

Pooler lowered the clipboard. "Skipper, this has got to be our anomalous contact from yesterday morning. The one that started out looking like an old *Han* class boat, and then kicked into hyper drive."

"*Sierra Two-Three*," the captain said. "I guess we can shit-can our theory about a software glitch in the BQQ-10."

Pooler shook his head. "There's no such thing as a supercavitating submarine. And if there *was* such a thing, it wouldn't be built by the North Koreans. Those boneheads can barely handle indoor plumbing."

"Maybe we've become a little too accustomed to underestimating them," the captain said. "Those '*boneheads*' have managed to build nuclear reactors and nuclear warheads, in spite of our best efforts to stop them. And they just blew away a U.S. Navy destroyer. They evidently have more on the ball than we give them credit for."

"I can't argue with you there, sir," Master Chief Pooler said. "But a supercavitating drive system for a submarine would take a quantum leap in propulsion technology. I just can't believe North Korea is capable of that."

Captain Townsend reached for the message clipboard. "Where the thing came from is irrelevant, COB. The North Koreans could have picked it up at *Superweapons-R-Us*; I honestly don't give a damn. All we need to know is that it's real; it's out there, and it's sinking our ships."

CHAPTER 22

USS BOWIE (DDG-141)
CARIBBEAN SEA, NORTHWEST OF JAMAICA
THURSDAY; 26 FEBRUARY
0658 hours (6:58 AM)
TIME ZONE -5 'ROMEO'

The helo pilot's voice came over the Navy Red speaker in Combat Information Center. *"Bowie,* this is *Sky Wolf Four-Three.* Mark my position, we've got another one. Over."

Captain Heller lifted the Navy Red handset to his ear and keyed the transmit button. He waited a half-second for the *crypto burst,* a rapid string of warbling tones that the UHF transceiver used to synchronize its encrypted signal with the secure communications satellite. "Roger, *Sky Wolf.* Is this one alive? Over."

There was another warble of synchronizing crypto. "This is *Sky Wolf Four-Three,* that's a negative. Floating face down with no indications of movement. Over."

Heller keyed the circuit again. "Understood, *Sky Wolf.* Your position is marked. Resume search. Out."

He lowered the handset. Another body. That brought the tally to nine so far, plus three survivors. Only twelve crew members located, out of the *Mahan's* complement of 281, and three-quarters of those scant few were dead.

Of the three survivors, one was fighting for her life in the *Bowie's* sickbay; another was nearly as critical; and the third had escaped with minor burns, contusions, and a ruptured eardrum.

The search would be easier now that the sun was up, assuming that there was anyone else to find. Anyone who had not been vaporized by the explosion, or trapped inside either half of the sunken wreck.

There was no point in sending for rescue divers. Whatever was left of the *Mahan* was lying at the bottom of the Cayman Trench, under about 3,000 fathoms of water. The pressure at that depth was more than 8,000 pounds per square inch. Enough to crush the ship's hull like an aluminum can.

The *Bowie's* sonar operators had probably heard the implosion over their headphones. Possibly the audio had been recorded. Heller knew the ASW suite's acoustic processors were capable of that, but he was being very careful not to ask. If such a recording existed, he absolutely did not want to hear it.

A voice broke over the tactical net, diverting his thoughts from unwelcome speculation about what the death of a ship might sound like.

"TAO—Air Two. Daniel Boone has visual ident."

Air Two was the secondary aircraft detachment, in charge of operating and maintaining the ship's trio of MQ-8B Fire Scout Unmanned Aerial Vehicles. In honor of the 'Scout' designation, the UAV team had named each of the three helicopter-style drones for famous explorers: *Daniel Boone*, *Magellan*, and *Marco Polo*.

Currently, Daniel Boone was overflying the area where the Motor Vessel *Lecticula* had gone down, searching for survivors (or bodies). The report of "visual ident" meant that the drone's chin-mounted camera had spotted something worth looking at.

This morning, the Tactical Action Officer was Lieutenant Amy Faulk. She keyed her mike. "TAO, aye. Calling it up now."

She tapped a sequence of soft-keys on her console and the video feed from the Fire Scout temporarily displaced the view from topside camera #5. On the big display monitor, a metal drum floated nearly awash in the waves. Clinging to it were two men, both visibly nearing the end of their strength reserves. One wore a camouflage uniform jacket, and the other appeared to be dressed in civilian attire. Presumably a member of the North Korean commando team, and one of the ship's crew.

Watching the screen, Heller knew what he was supposed to do next. He was *supposed* to dispatch a boat with a SAR swimmer, to pluck these survivors from the water.

Under Article 16 of the Hague Conventions, he was obligated to save their lives, even though they were enemy combatants. He was expected to ignore the fact that they'd been smuggling nuclear missiles into Cuba to threaten U.S. cities.

Heller wanted to shoot the bastards. Instead, the law required him to rescue their sorry asses.

The video feed bobbed and jostled slightly as the Fire Scout's stabilized camera did its best to compensate for sporadic gusts of wind.

Heller was sorely tempted to leave the enemy survivors to fend for themselves. There was a sort of loophole in Article 16 that might help him get away with it. Something about only being required to render aid '*so far as military interests permit.'*

Well USS *Bowie* did have other military interests: the SAR effort surrounding the *Mahan* for one, and the ongoing blockade mission for another. He could make a reasonable argument that his current duties did not allow time for rescuing survivors from an enemy vessel.

If he did that, he was sure that his crew would back him up. He was confident that they would confirm his story, and allow him to get away with exploiting the ambiguous language of Article 16.

And that, he realized, was precisely why he couldn't go through with it. He was commanding officer of a United States warship. It was not his job to look for escape clauses in the law. That kind of horseshit was the province of tax lawyers and shady politicians.

Leadership wasn't just about making decisions and issuing orders. It was also about setting an example. Doing the right thing, even when your gut was screaming at you to do something very, *very* different.

On the display screen, the man in the camouflage jacket raised his head and tilted his face toward the sound of the drone's rotors. He lifted one hand in a halfhearted wave.

Heller looked around and caught the TAO's eye. "Let's get a SAR swimmer and an armed detail in boat number two. I also want a security team and a Corpsman standing by on the boat deck."

He turned back to the display screen. "And hurry. I don't know how much longer those guys can hold on."

CHAPTER 23

OFFICE OF NAVAL INTELLIGENCE
FARRAGUT TECHNICAL ANALYSIS CENTER
SUITLAND, MARYLAND
THURSDAY; 26 FEBRUARY
1309 hours (1:09 PM)
TIME ZONE -5 'ROMEO'

"How do you know they haven't done it?" Jerry Catlin asked.

Seated on the other side of the break room table, Martin Quinn rolled his eyes. "Because it's fucking impossible."

"I've seen the tracking data," Catlin said, "and so have you. And I know you've heard the recordings. Something is raising holy hell in the Caribbean. If that's not a supercavitating submarine, then what *is* it?"

Quinn pulled a six-inch Turkey Italiano Melt from a plastic Subway bag. "I never said I know what it *is*," he said. "I only know what it *isn't*."

Catlin unwrapped his own sandwich: homemade tuna on wheat, sweet pickle relish and extra mayo. "You're really that sure? You have no idea what they're dealing with down there, but you're absolutely positive that it can't be a supercav?"

Quinn removed the top layer of bread from his Turkey Melt and started picking out black olives, eating them as quickly as they were located. "Someone keeps stealing my Dr. Peppers out of the fridge," he said. "Could be you. Might be that new guy, the tall one from Material Sciences. I wouldn't rule out Gina Z., for that matter. She guzzles soda as fast as I do, and she never carries change for the vending machines. The point is... I have no idea who's been raiding my Dr. Pepper stash. But I feel pretty safe in eliminating Scooby Doo from my list of suspects."

"Because he doesn't exist?"

Finished with the post-mortem on his lunch, Quinn reassembled the now olive-free sandwich. "Exactamundo."

"Faulty analogy," Catlin said. "By your logic, something that doesn't exist at one point in time could never come into existence at a later date."

Quinn chewed and swallowed a mouthful of Turkey Melt. "So Scooby might be *real* some day? There could be a no-shit talking dog who cruises around in a van solving mysteries? Old Man Witherspoon better get busy on his werewolf mask; Scooby and Shaggy are coming to town!"

"Don't be an ass-hat," Catlin said. "Of *course* I don't expect fictional characters to manifest in reality. That's just stupid. Though, now that you mention it, I wouldn't mind meeting up with a real life version of Velma."

"You mean Daphne."

"No, I mean Velma. I've got a thing about smart women."

"She's jailbait," Quinn said in a taunting tone.

Catlin shook his head. "Are you blind? Velma is college age. Early twenties. Nineteen at the very youngest."

"Nope. Check your facts," said Quinn. "According to Hanna-Barbera, Velma is fifteen years old. Daphne is sixteen. Fred and the Shagster are both seventeen. They're all supposed to be high school juniors."

Catlin stared at his coworker. "Why do you even *know* that?"

"Google is your friend," Quinn said, and tore off another bite of Turkey Melt.

"Isn't it kind of creepy that you've taken the time to research the ages of animated characters?"

"I'm creepy?" Quinn asked. "I hate to point out the obvious, but you're the one with a fetish for cartoon jailbait."

Catlin blinked several times. "You've got me sidetracked. What was I talking about?"

"Damned if I know," said Quinn. "I never know what you're talking about. But you don't usually know what you're talking about either, so I guess that makes us even."

"We were discussing your faulty logic," Catlin said.

"You said my analogy was faulty. You have yet to cast aspersions on my logic, which is fortunate for you, because my logic is bulletproof."

"Let's peel the onion and find out," said Catlin. "If I understand what you've been saying, there can't possibly be a supercavitating submarine in the Caribbean, because there's no such thing."

"That's about the size of it."

"How do you know there's no such thing?"

"Because it's fucking impossible," Quinn said.

Catlin paused between bites of his tuna on wheat. "Which brings us back to where we started."

"What's your point?"

"Your argument is circular, but never mind. What makes you think a supercav sub is impossible? We have absolute proof that the underlying concept works, from torpedoes like the Russian Shkval and the German

Barracuda. The U.S. even had a working prototype of a supercav torpedo, but the program got scrapped when the Navy decided to concentrate on the Mark-48 ADCAP. Seems like only a matter of time until somebody figures out how to scale the technology up to larger platforms."

The last of his sandwich gone, Quinn balled up the paper wrapper and stuffed it back into the plastic Subway bag. "Ever hear of the Avrocar?"

"No. I don't think so."

"Google it sometime, when you're not drooling over pictures of underage cartoon girls. It was a serious attempt to build a jet-propelled flying saucer for use in combat. Top Secret project at the time, but it's declassified now. A Canadian aerospace company, under contract to the U.S. Air Force."

"And?"

"And the powered scale models zoomed around like over-caffeinated Frisbees. Full thumbs-up in the proof of concept department. Then they built one at full scale."

"It didn't fly?"

"That depends on what you mean by flying," Quinn said. "It was designed to reach high altitudes at supersonic speeds. Instead, it wallowed three or four feet off the ground, completely unstable, at about the speed of a bicycle."

"You're saying not everything is scalable?"

Quinn stood up. "Exactamundo, my friend. Not everything is scalable. And if a supercav sub *does* turn out to be possible, we'll be the ones doing it. Or the Germans. Maybe the Swedes. They've done some pretty cool shit with their *Gotland* class boats. But not the North Koreans. They haven't got the R&D smarts, the technical sophistication, or the industrial infrastructure. It'd be like building the Starship *Enterprise* in Tajikistan. Not fucking happening."

"People were saying the same thing about North Korean ICBMs not too long ago," said Catlin. "They weren't supposed to have the technical knowhow to build missiles with intercontinental range. Then one day, they lofted a Hwasong-14 into the Sea of Japan. Big surprise to everybody. Same thing with miniaturized warheads. We were absolutely certain they couldn't do that stuff, right up until they *did*."

"Yeah, but they weren't inventing the core technology," said Quinn. "They could copy from our ICBM and warhead designs, and Russian designs, and Chinese designs, and whatever they could beg, borrow, or steal. But they *can't* copy somebody else's supercav design, because no one has ever built a supercavitating submarine."

Without waiting for a reply, he made a basketball-style toss with his lunch trash, dropping the wad of paper and plastic into the open waste can. A perfect two-pointer. And then he was out the door.

With Quinn gone, Catlin—a more methodical eater—continued to work slowly on his tuna sandwich. He would Google the Avrocar thing (and Velma's age), in case Quinn was yanking his chain again.

But even if Quinn was right about the failed flying saucer program, that didn't justify a knee-jerk dismissal of supercav technology. There might be a way to make it work. There almost certainly *was* a way to make it work, as the crew of USS *Mahan* had already discovered.

He pulled out a mechanical pencil and started doodling on his paper lunch sack. If he wanted to build a supercavitating submarine propulsion system, what would his design look like?

He was absently outlining a triangle when it occurred to him that he had unconsciously asked himself the wrong question.

The correct question was this....

If a North Korean engineer—with North Korean training, North Korean technical resources, and North Korean cultural biases—wanted to build such a submarine, what would *that* design look like?

Catlin erased the triangle and began to sketch in earnest.

CHAPTER 24

WHITE HOUSE
PRESIDENT'S STUDY
WASHINGTON, DC
THURSDAY; 26 FEBRUARY
4:48 PM EST

Secretary of Homeland Security Fernando Salamanca shook his head. "This blackout is a demonstration of force, Mr. President. Not intended to cause us serious damage."

"I'm not sure I can agree with that," said National Security Advisor Frank Cerney. "I'll grant you that the physical destruction to infrastructure is relatively minor, but the damage to national security is completely off the charts."

The president nodded. "I have to go with Frank on this one. The North Koreans have pulled the plug on the capital city of the United States, and everybody knows it. At the top of the hour, CNN is running coverage of the three families that froze to death in Congress Heights and Washington Highlands. At the bottom of the hour, the story shifts back to that elderly couple who asphyxiated trying to heat their apartment in Knox Hill with a charcoal grill. In between, the coverage alternates between footage of DC residents burning furniture in the streets to stay warm, and cyber security experts announcing that Kim Yong-nam can wipe out the entire U.S. power grid with the press of a button. If the CNN polls are anything to go by, about a third of the people in this country are ready to run for Canada, and another third are buying up ammunition and digging in for World War III."

"What about the other third?" Secretary Salamanca asked.

President Bradley gave him a grim smile. "The other third are convinced that this entire situation is a government hoax, perpetrated as a pretense for declaring martial law, suspending constitutional protections, and turning over control to the new world order."

"I'm leaning toward the Canada option," Salamanca said.

"So am I," said the president. "But all kidding aside, people are terrified. They're losing confidence in our ability to defend them against unexpected threats. All of a sudden, North Korea is looking less like the punch line of a joke and more like the harbinger of doom."

"We can hardly blame the public for being afraid," the national security advisor said. "Have you seen what Fox News is running?"

"I think I missed that," the president said. "I usually prefer to get my news from other sources."

"Well, the boys at Fox are stirring the pot pretty hard," said the national security advisor. "A bunch of think-tankers backed up by a retired Army colonel, speculating about which of our cities and towns are within striking distance of warheads launched from Cuba. Lots of flashy graphics with estimated fallout footprints, intercut with CGI animations of nuclear fireballs."

The president nodded. "How good is their speculation?"

"Not too far off from the Pentagon's estimates. Fox is basically drawing an arc from San Antonio to Virginia Beach, and counting everything southeast of that curve as a potential mushroom cloud."

"So the pundits are assuming the missiles are either Rodong-2 series, or something with similar characteristics," said Secretary Salamanca. "About what my people and DoD have been figuring. That makes the potential target area all of Florida, Georgia, Alabama, Mississippi, Louisiana, Tennessee, South Carolina, and North Carolina—along with half of Texas, most of Arkansas, Kentucky, and Virginia—as well as portions of five other states. Not to mention a big slice of Mexico, if we're not the only country on the target list."

"DIA recommends that we assume a twenty percent improvement in flight and payload performance over the stock Rodong configuration," said the national security advisor. "Just to make sure the North Koreans don't surprise us by exceeding our expectations."

"They've already done that," the president said.

No one pointed out the obvious. As described by the national security advisor, the expanded danger area put Washington DC squarely within striking range of the missiles.

The president turned his chair and looked out the windows at the lengthening shadows. Sunset was less than an hour away and—except for the emergency shelters and facilities supplied by backup generators—the city was in for another night of darkness and deadly cold.

"Tell me where we are with recovery operations and emergency relief efforts," he said.

Just as the secretary of homeland defense was mentally shifting gears, there was a quiet knock at the door. White House Chief of Staff Jacqueline

Mayfield let herself into the president's study. "I apologize for the interruption, Mr. President, but you need to see this."

She picked up a remote and pressed the power button for a small television tucked between family photos on a side table. The screen flared to life with the recap of a soccer match. She tapped in a channel selection.

The soccer pitch gave way to the MSNBC studio, the news desk covered by that anchorman in his late forties, the one with the movie star face and the sonorous pipe organ voice. Oliver Somebody—whose ageless features and slightly graying temples contrived to straddle the divide between the under-thirty and over-forty demographics. The network tended to trot him out for any story with the markings of an emerging international political crisis.

To the anchorman's left, an animated graphic depicted a silhouette map of North Korea, overlaid with footage of marching troop formations and fiery missile launches. Oliver Somebody's lips were moving, but no sound came out; the television speakers were muted.

After five seconds or so, the chief of staff manipulated the remote, unmuting the sound. "Here. They're running it again."

The scene cut to video of Kim Yong-nam standing at a podium on the granite steps of the Mansudae Assembly Hall in Pyongyang. Behind the Supreme Leader were four men in North Korean military uniforms, each one wearing more medals, ribbons, and badges than a platoon of decorated combat Marines. At the bottom of the screen, the words '*North Korean Ultimatum*' shared the crawl banner with the MSNBC logo.

Speaking in Korean, Kim's voice was dialed down to a murmur, to bring the audio of the network's English translation into greater prominence. The result was not unlike a poorly dubbed martial arts movie, but the interpreter's tone was ominous enough to forestall any sense of amusement.

On the screen, Kim stood with his hands clasped behind his back, in unconscious (or perhaps conscious) imitation of the long-dead chairman of the Chinese Communist Party, Mao Tse-Tung.

"Officers and men of the three services and the strategic rocket forces of the heroic Korean People's Army. Officers and men of the Korean People's Internal Security Forces. Members of the Worker-Peasant Red Guards and Young Red Guards. Respected citizens of Pyongyang, Party members, and other working people across the country. Compatriots in South Korea and abroad. Comrades and friends."

"Today, with a great national pride and dignity, in noblest respect and infinite glory to the great Comrade Kim Il-sung who founded our glorious Party, I have the honor to finally and truly reveal the indomitable strength and might of the Workers' Party of Korea."

There was a swell of cheering from an unseen crowd. Kim waited for it to die down.

"We have labored long and patiently to achieve peace on the Korean Peninsula, but invasive outsiders and provocateurs have continued to threaten our nation, our people, and our way of life. They have attacked our economy with illegal sanctions, blocking our trade with the nations of the world, and intimidating the many countries who would eagerly step forward to be our allies. They have endangered our security by arming our enemies, and by raising our South Korean comrades in false rebellion against the People's State and the followers of Juche."

The secretary of homeland security crossed his arms. "What exactly are we looking for? Sounds like the usual Kim Dynasty bluster to me."

The chief of staff held up a hand. "Wait for it...."

In the background, Kim Yong-nam's voice was gaining in volume. His rising agitation played counterpoint to the calm intonations of MSNBC's interpreter.

"The peaceful people of the Democratic People's Republic of Korea have accepted the insults and crimes of our enemies for long enough! As of this moment, the transgressions against us will END!" The last word was a shout.

Kim was ranting now, hands appearing from behind his back to slam the top of the podium.

"We will no longer tolerate the illegal embargos against our people! We will no longer allow imperialist aggressions to threaten our sovereignty and the security of our borders! We will no longer permit our brothers in the south to be separated from the one true Korea!"

The chief of staff nodded toward the screen. "Here it comes...."

"Our nuclear missiles are now aimed at the hearts of our foulest and most pernicious enemy," the translator said on Kim's behalf. "If our rightful demands are not met, we will burn the United States into a lifeless radioactive cinder. We will wage a merciless war of justice using the weapons Americans fear above all else!"

Again, the unseen crowd cheered wildly. Again, the Supreme Leader waited for the fervor of his listeners to abate.

"We have already struck the first blows against our insidious adversary. Their capital city lies powerless and dark. We stand poised to spread that same darkness throughout every corner of their lands. Our invincible weapons have wrought destruction on the American Navy. We will continue to demolish American ships until the sailors of the enemy fleet throw off the chains of their criminal masters, and join in our cause of righteousness."

"These things will not happen in some far off future. They are not things that *may* happen. They are actions already taken and blood already spilled. We wait no longer for justice. It will be surrendered into our hands without delay, or we will tear it from the dying fingers of those who are foolish and corrupt enough to oppose us."

"Here comes the clincher," said the chief of staff.

The MSNBC interpreter continued. "To this end, I demand the permanent withdrawal of all American military forces from Korean soil. All banks and financial institutions holding accounts on behalf of South Korean citizens, organizations, companies, or officials will immediately transfer those assets to the care of the legitimate government of Korea for protection and control. All economic sanctions, embargoes, and other wrongful restrictions imposed against the Democratic People's Republic of Korea will be lifted. And the United States will take no actions of any sort to hinder the reunification of the Korean peoples, whether that happy objective is accomplished peacefully, or by the use of necessary and justified force to repatriate our misguided comrades."

"Well, at least he's not asking for anything unreasonable," the national security advisor said.

The president waved him to silence.

On the television, Kim's hand went to the right side of his head, two fingers pressing the area above his ear—perhaps in a pantomime gesture of profound thought—or perhaps to massage away a transient twinge of discomfort.

The interpreter spoke again. "As Great Russia is reclaiming the peoples and territories of Crimea, we now reclaim our own stolen peoples and territories. These things will all happen, with the willing assistance of our enemies, or over the smoldering ashes of their remains. The Workers' Party of Korea will continue toward the bright future that is the destiny of our great nation."

Kim Yong-nam's words again rose to a shout. "Listen to my words, people of America! You will step aside now, or the world will see you burn!"

The North Korean leader tilted his head in a minimal bow, and the roar of the crowd grew to compete with the last words of the English translation.

The camera cut back to the MSNBC news desk, where handsome Oliver Somebody began his follow-up commentary.

The chief of staff tapped the power button and the television screen went dark. "That's all we have so far, Kim's demands and his threat to nuke us into the Stone Age."

The secretary of homeland defense shook his head. "The Kim family's been threatening to destroy the United States since the nineteen-fifties. How is this any different?"

"It's *different*," said the president. "They might actually be able to do it this time. Knock out the Eastern U.S. with intermediate-range nukes from Cuba. Eliminate most of our government—present company included—along with the pentagon and about eighty percent of our military command and control structure. Then, light up the West Coast with ICBMs, and America goes down for the count."

He continued to stare at the television, as though the darkened screen had further secrets to reveal. "Trust me," he said. "This time is different."

CHAPTER 25

YN3 Philip Ahn was rethinking the helicopter thing. Helos looked so fucking cool in the movies and on the cop shows. Gray or camo war machines owning the sky; transporting Spec Ops teams of Navy SEALs, or Army Rangers, or Marine Force Recon units to secret insertion points for badass covert raids and firefights.

Nothing in the movies hinted at how *loud* the damn things were, how badly they vibrated your kidneys, or how nauseously unpleasant their crawly sideways motions could be.

Then there was the smell. Hot metal, mixed with lubricating oil, burning kerosene, and the unavoidable odors of human bodies stewing in an enclosed capsule.

The flight was entering its third hour, and the pizza Phil had scarfed down for lunch was not riding well in his stomach. He needed to pee. He almost needed to puke. But most of all, he needed to get the fuck out of this whirling, shrieking, rattling nightmare of an aircraft.

With all fantasies of Special Operations badassery now thoroughly squelched, he turned his thoughts back to wondering why he was here.

He was a Yeoman, for God's sake. A pencil pusher. As some of the more active Coast Guard ratings liked to joke, a *Xerographer's Mate*. So what was he doing in a helicopter over the open ocean? And why wouldn't anyone tell him anything?

The helo had flown directly through Cuban airspace, straight over the island, with no delays for permission and no interference from local military or police. Someone had pulled serious diplomatic strings to make that happen. Who had that kind of political horsepower? And why were they wasting it to fly a junior Coastie paper shuffler out to a Navy ship?

With the North Korean mess going on, it was possible that the Navy

108

needed an interpreter who could speak Korean. He fit the bill for that, more or less. His parents—now naturalized American citizens—had both grown up in Seoul before immigrating to the states in their early twenties. Phil and his two older sisters had been raised in a household where English and Korean were spoken in fairly equal measures. But he had never put serious effort into mastering the language of the country his parents had left behind.

He could usually get his ideas across in Korean and he understood the language more clearly than he spoke it. That didn't make him fluent by any stretch of the imagination, though. As his mother liked to point out, his vocabulary and grammar were weaker than they should have been, and his pronunciation was (if anything) weaker still.

If the Navy needed someone to translate, they could easily have chosen someone better suited than he was. That couldn't be what they wanted, anyway. The Navy had their own interpreters. There was no reason for them to requisition a Coast Guard YN3 who sort of spoke the language.

As he was racking his brain for alternatives, the monotonous thunder of the rotors changed in some indefinable way. He felt a sinking elevator sensation in the pit of his stomach.

He leaned forward in his seat and strained to look past the heads and shoulders of the pilots. The helo was dropping now, the waves coming up much faster than seemed reasonable or safe.

Then he caught sight of the ship, and it looked small. *Really* small. The flight deck seemed to be the size of his fingernail. And it was moving. A lot. Bobbing. Rolling.

Maybe that would be enough to abort the landing. Maybe the pilots would take one look at the tiny unstable flight deck, and turn back for the Coast Guard station at Key West. Get somebody else to handle whatever they'd brought him out here to do.

But the pilots showed no sign of turning back. They didn't even seem to be concerned. The helicopter continued to drop toward the ship, and the pizza in Phil's stomach announced an entirely new level of unhappiness.

He clamped his eyes shut and recognized instantly that it only magnified his queasiness. He settled for staring at his boots instead. The toe of the left one had picked up a scuff. He'd have to find some polish and buff it out, assuming that he survived the next few minutes.

Even if the circus acrobat landing didn't kill him, he'd be aboard a U.S. Navy destroyer, in the same stretch of the Caribbean where the other destroyer had been blown up. According to internet buzz (and what little he'd seen of the news), the Navy was getting its ass kicked down here by some kind of killer North Korean rocket sub. Not the type of thing he wanted to get involved in if he had any say in the matter. Which, of course, he didn't.

It occurred to him that he might actually be flying toward the scene of his death, either by helo crash, or getting blasted into dog food by an enemy super weapon. The thought pissed him off. He had plans for Saturday night with that little tourist hottie from The Lazy Gecko. If his weekend was going to be interrupted by violent dismemberment, he at least wanted to know what the fuck he would be dying for.

Eyes still focused on his boots, he wasn't prepared for the jolt that shot up his spine when the landing gear hit the deck. The pitch of the helo's engines changed dramatically and he felt a microsecond of panic. Then his brain processed the available clues and decided that the helicopter was down. He wasn't dead yet. That was a good sign.

Two minutes later, after the obligatory head-bowed dash under spinning rotor blades, he was through a watertight door and into the destroyer's aft starboard passageway.

A Navy lieutenant was there to meet him. They were indoors and not wearing covers, so Phil decided that saluting would not be necessary. Or would it? Maybe the Navy's rules on that sort of thing were different from the Coast Guard's. Could be that he was expected to pop tall and snap out a salute.

Instead, he dredged up the only thing that seemed to fit the occasion. "Request permission to come aboard, sir."

The lieutenant grinned. "Granted. It isn't like we have much choice, since you're already here." He gave Phil a rapid visual inspection, taking in the Coast Guard sailor's wrinkled blue Operational Dress Uniform and the sickly look that probably lingered on his face. "Rough flight?"

"Seemed like it to me, sir. But maybe helos are always like that."

"I'll take your word for it," the lieutenant said. "I refuse to fly in anything that has to beat the air into submission."

It was an old joke. Phil laughed anyway. It never hurt to let officers think they were clever.

The lieutenant turned and starting walking toward the forward end of the ship.

Phil followed a few steps behind. "If you don't mind my asking, sir, where are we going?"

"The Admin Office," the lieutenant said over his shoulder. "You have some paperwork to take care of."

That took Phil by surprise. The Admin Office? Had the Navy really dragged him out of Key West to shuffle papers in the middle of the ocean? They couldn't possibly be *that* short of Yeomen. There had to be something more to this.

"Uh.... What kind of paperwork, sir?"

"We're upgrading your security clearance to Top Secret," the lieutenant said. "So you'll basically be signing away your birthday, your firstborn son, all the usual stuff."

Phil nearly stopped in his tracks. "I think you've got the wrong guy, sir. I'm not eligible for TS. My parents were born in a foreign country, and I've never had the required background investigation."

"It's a special interim clearance," the lieutenant said. "Requested by Commander Atlantic Fleet, with expedited approval by Defense Security Service. A one-time deal. Short-term access, but you'll be permanently barred from disclosing any of the information you're about to receive. At least until it all gets declassified, which probably won't happen in your lifetime."

This time, Phil did stop. "Lieutenant? You understand that I'm a third class Yeoman, right? My qualifications include typing up the Plan of the Day and changing the toner in the Xerox machine. Sometimes I manage to file things in the right drawer. Nobody in his right mind would give me Top Secret information."

The lieutenant checked the passageway in both directions, stepped close, and lowered his voice. "Petty Officer Ahn, you're going to be our interpreter. We need someone who speaks Korean."

Phil made a concentrated effort not to groan. "I hate to disappoint you, sir, but my Korean sucks. I was never what you would consider fluent to begin with, and I pretty much let it slide when I left home for boot camp."

"We know that," said the lieutenant. "But half a loaf is better than none, and you're the best we could do on short notice."

"Doesn't the Navy have translators? I mean *real* translators?"

The lieutenant nodded. "There was a Korean interpreter aboard USS *Mahan*. If he survived the sinking of his ship, we haven't found him yet. The Navy's flying out two more from Defense Language Institute in California. They touch down at Naval Air Station Key West in about three hours. There's a helo standing by to bring them out our way. In the meantime, we start with you. Just do the best you can."

Phil nodded. "Aye-aye, sir. Who am I going to be talking to?"

The lieutenant started walking again. "Let's go knock out your clearance paperwork. Once you're nice and legal, we'll tell you as much as we can."

CHAPTER 26

There was a soft tap at the door.

National Security Advisor Frank Cerney looked up from the stack of briefing folders on his desk. "Come in."

The door opened and the deputy national security advisor, William Snowcroft, poked his head into the office. "Do you have a second, sir?"

Cerney beckoned for the man to enter. "Sure, Bill. What have you got?"

Snowcroft came into the office and closed the door. Instead of taking a seat, he leaned against the doorframe. "Remember the interpreter we sent to talk to the Korean prisoners aboard USS *Bowie*? The kid we borrowed from the Coast Guard? Well it looks like he might be on to something."

Cerney nodded. "Keep talking."

"The commando we captured is a Major Ri Kyong-su, North Korean Maritime Special Operations Force. He was the officer in charge of the detail protecting the ship and the missiles. Snake-eater type. Probably knows fifteen ways to kill you with your own shoelaces."

"I'll try to keep my feet out of his way," Cerney mumbled. "And I'm assuming that Major Snake-eater hasn't tried to murder our interpreter with footwear."

"No, sir. In fact, he seems to be willing to talk."

Cerney sat back in his chair. "*Seems* to be? Meaning that he hasn't started talking yet?"

"He claims to have important information to divulge," Snowcroft said, "but he won't talk unless we agree to certain conditions."

"What kind of conditions?"

"He's asking for asylum in the U.S.," Snowcroft said. "Protection and citizenship for himself, his wife, his two-year-old daughter, and his sister.

112

Oh, and we have to teach them all English."

"I take it they're all still in North Korea?"

Snowcroft nodded.

Cerney snorted. "He doesn't want much, does he? All we have to do is penetrate the territory of a sovereign nation, kidnap two women and a child who don't know we're coming—and who, I might add, have no reason whatsoever to trust us—then spirit them quietly away to the land of Wal-Mart and Chicken McNuggets."

"We don't have to accept his terms," Snowcroft said.

"You're right about that," said Cerney. "Why are we even having this conversation? What do we think this guy knows?"

"This was his second voyage to Cuba, so he's got the delivery protocols mapped out pretty well. Also, he says that all of the commando teams were trained at the same time, and that all of the shipments were identical. He knows how many missiles were carried by each ship and what kind they are. He can tell us how many missile sites there are, how they're supposed to be laid out, and how they're manned."

"Can he pinpoint the locations?"

"No. Evidently, that information was only shared with the missile crews. But at least he can tell us the scope of the threat, and let us know how many sites we're going to have to hit."

Cerney shook his head. "Not good enough. Granted, that's all useful information, but it's hardly enough to justify an international snatch job."

"There is one more thing," Snowcroft said. "Major Ri claims to know something about Kim Yong-nam."

"Something? What the hell does that mean?"

"He's not very forthcoming with the details, but he says that it's big. Enormous. The sort of thing that will fundamentally transform our understanding of Kim Yong-nam's strategic mindset. And it will supposedly give us insight into what the whole Cuba thing is about."

"Sounds like this guy is trying to blow smoke up our butts," Cerney said. "How would a common soldier know secrets about the Supreme Leader?"

"He's not a common soldier. He's Special Forces. North Korea's version of a Navy SEAL."

"Fine," said Cerney. "But how many of our SEALs are privy to secret knowledge about the president?"

"He says it's not something he learned through military channels. Whatever it is, he found out from his sister."

"His sister? And where did *she* get it from?"

"We don't know."

"Have we asked?"

Snowcroft nodded. "Of course. Several times."

"No answer?"

"No answer. The sister's method of access is supposedly part of the big secret."

Cerney's fingers began to fiddle with his necktie. "What about the other Korean prisoner? Is he talking?"

"Not at all. Not even name, rank, and serial number. Major Ri says the man is a low level maintenance worker from the ship's crew, but the prisoner won't even confirm that much. As far as we can tell, he hasn't spoken a word since he was captured."

"Loyalty to the fatherland?"

Snowcroft shrugged. "Could be. Or fear. He's probably got a pretty good idea of what his government will do if he talks to us."

"And all of this is coming to us through the Coast Guard sailor, right? The kid whose Korean is a bit dodgy?"

"Yes, sir. But Petty Officer Ahn's facility with Korean appears to be returning more quickly than he expected. He's having very little trouble communicating with Major Ri."

"I'm not inclined to trust a twenty-two-year-old kid's assessment of his own performance," said Cerney. "Not when the stakes are this high."

"You wanted an interpreter on scene as quickly as possible, said Snowcroft, "and Petty Officer Ahn was the closest asset we could tap. The team from Defense Language Institute should be landing at Key West in the next few minutes. From there, it's another three hours by helicopter to the USS *Bowie*."

"So we're looking at midnight before the professional interpreters even meet with the prisoner?"

"Something like that."

Cerney fell silent, his fingers still fidgeting with the necktie. After thirty seconds or so, he sat up straight in his chair. "We're going to leave this on the back burner until we hear from the real interpreters."

"What if it's time sensitive?"

"If there was a timing issue, our North Korean major would have made that part of the discussion, to pressure us into moving quickly. I think we can afford to wait a few more hours. In any case, I can't see taking this to the president until we know for sure what the prisoner is actually saying to us."

"In other words, we wait?"

Cerney nodded. "We wait."

CHAPTER 27

FOXY ROXY
ATLANTIC OCEAN, NORTH OF GUARDALAVACA, CUBA
THURSDAY; 26 FEBRUARY
9:03 PM
TIME ZONE -5 'ROMEO'

Cassy Clark wasn't happy about the west wind they were sailing into. The trade winds in this region were almost always out of the northeast. Any major deviation from that pattern was usually a sign of bad weather in the offing.

But the night sky was cloudless: the stars bright and unwavering. The swells were gentle, with no whitecaps under a moon waxing toward gibbous. None of the usual signs of a coming storm, except for the unseasonal wind direction.

Even so, she was tempted to fire up the single-sideband radio and try for a weather broadcast. She'd have to talk it over with Jon first, though. For all of his wonderful qualities, her hubby had more than a few obsessions, and one of them was battery power. He hoarded electricity like it couldn't be replaced, as though the wind generator at the top of the mast and the boat's diesel engine were in imminent danger of simultaneous failure. As though dead batteries in some way equated to mortal danger, despite the fact that electricity wasn't actually necessary to live comfortably on the boat.

Their food was canned, and didn't actually require cooking if the propane tank for the stove ran out. The reverse-osmosis water filter could be pumped by hand. The compass was magnetic. On the boat, electricity was a great convenience, but everything vital to their survival could be operated without it.

Jon knew all of that, and yet he couldn't stop treating electrical power like a life-or-death resource. Cassy sometimes wondered if he had begun to subconsciously associate electricity with ammunition.

She still didn't know everything about his last firefight: the one that had wiped out so much of his unit. Uncovering the hidden details—the

115

parts Jon never wanted to think about—might take Cassy years of gentle coaxing, assuming that he *ever* loosened up enough to talk about them. But she knew one crucial part of the story, because it surfaced during the worst of her husband's nightmares. Pinned down by superior firepower, Jon's unit had run low on ammo. Jon himself had run out completely.

Cassy had often tried to picture what that must have been like—to load your last magazine in the middle of a desperate battle—to feel the last of your rounds ticking away, one by one. Knowing that the Marines around you were caught in that same dismal countdown, their own final magazines depleting one precious bullet at a time while the enemy continued to spray fusillades of deadly fire. Waiting for that inevitable instant when your M-4 carbine locked on an empty chamber.

Cassy didn't know what feelings might course through the hearts of combat trained Marines in that circumstance, but all she could imagine were despair, blind panic, and a crushing sense of hopelessness.

And maybe that's what electrical power was to Jon. Something he could stockpile. A resource that he could squirrel away and protect. A reserve that wouldn't deplete itself when he needed it, the way the last of his ammunition had finally run out.

Maybe that was a stupid guess. Maybe the obsession had nothing to do with ammunition or Jon's final battle. But the source was somewhere back in Afghanistan; Cassy was sure of that. And one of these days, she hoped to have some luck in soothing that particular fear.

In the meantime, she'd hold off on using the radio unless she spotted signs of impending weather. She would concentrate on her sailing and ignore the implied threat of the strange west wind.

At the moment, the *Foxy Roxy* was close-hauled on a starboard tack, but Cassy was thinking about bringing the bow a degree or two closer to the wind. She checked the inhaul, factored the tension against the gentle pull of the helm, and decided to leave the old sailboat right in her current groove. Maybe another half hour on this leg, and then it would be time for a tack to port.

Jon would be up to relieve her at about nine-thirty, so she might leave the tack for him. He was already awake. She could hear him moving around below decks—getting dressed, making coffee, preparing for his shift on the helm.

They were pleasantly familiar sounds. Part of the now comfortable pattern of life on the boat. The clank of the metal coffee pot. The zip and shuffle of feet finding their way into khaki trouser legs. The quiet click of Roxy's claws on the deck as she observed the minor flurry of activity like a canine overseer. An occasional yawn from Jon as he shook off sleep and brought his mind and body up to speed.

But tonight Cassy heard sounds that were not part of the usual pattern. A yip of pain or surprise from Roxy, followed by frantic thrashing and the sound of a falling body. Then a string of curses from Jon, more confused in tone than angry.

Cassy leaned toward the open companionway. "You okay, honey?"

Jon didn't answer immediately.

Cassy raised her voice a notch. "Jonnie, is everything okay?"

"I think so," he said. "Give me a second." He sounded hesitant. Puzzled.

Without stopping to think, Cassy released the helm. She was vaguely aware of the wheel turning without the pressure of her hand, the bow coming about into the wind, the old boat starting to lose way. She didn't care. She was through the companionway and down the three steps into the cabin before she even realized that she was moving.

Jon was sitting on the deck with his back against the galley cabinets, rubbing his eyes while Roxy sniffed around him with obvious concern.

Cassy dropped to her knees and put her hands on his shoulders. "Talk to me, Jonnie. Tell me what's wrong."

Jon's hands came away from his face and he began blinking furiously. "Can't see very well. My vision is blurry. Purple spots in front of my eyes."

Cassy turned his face toward her own and tried to get a good look at his pupils between blinks. She couldn't tell much without an ophthalmoscope. "Has this been going on since the blast?"

Jon nodded. "Yeah, but not this bad."

"And you didn't bother to tell me?"

"I didn't want to worry you."

She sighed and slapped at his shoulder. "You don't hide things from me, Jon. I thought we had a deal about that."

"We do," Jon said softly.

"Then why didn't you tell me?"

"I didn't want you to overreact."

Cassy shook her head. "I swear to God, if I didn't love you so much, I'd throw your sorry ass overboard."

"I outweigh you by ninety pounds."

"More like eighty-five," Cassy said. "You think I never learned how to move patients who were twice my weight?"

Jon half-smiled. "There's a difference between a cooperative patient and an uncooperative Marine."

She swatted at his shoulder again. "What makes you think you'd be conscious at the time, asshole?"

Before he could respond, she stood up. "Let's get you back to bed."

"It's my turn on the helm," Jon said.

"Not anymore, it isn't. You are now officially out of the watch rotation, Mr. Jarhead. Doc's orders."

"You can't single-hand it all the way to Key West."

"We're not going to Key West," Cassy said. "Change in plans. I'm turning this tub around, and we're heading to Guantanamo."

"That's the wrong direction," Jon said. "Anyway, they won't let us in. Gitmo is not an open base."

"You don't have a vote in this," said Cassy.

"Since when?"

"Since you were put on the sick list. And they *will* let us in. A Bronze Star Marine with a medical emergency? We'll get in alright. Leave it to me."

"Key West is—"

Cassy cut him off. "Key West is more than twice as far away and I'm not waiting that long to get you to a doctor."

"I'll be fine," said Jon.

"I know," Cassy said. "Because I'm taking you to the nearest doctor. That leaves Key West off the list."

Jon sighed. "You are one stubborn woman."

"True," Cassy said, "but my husband tells me that I'm also cute, so it more or less balances out."

"I don't remember ever saying that you were cute. I'm fairly certain that I said *beautiful*."

"Same thing," Cassy said.

"No it isn't. Beautiful is way better than cute."

"I suppose," said Cassy. "But I can't exactly take your word for it. You're practically blind as a bat."

"Bats aren't blind. That's a myth. And I'm definitely not too blind to spank you."

Cassy snorted. "Give it your best shot, Marine. Then you can explain to the doctor at Guantanamo how you screwed up your eyesight *and* broke both of your arms."

Jon laughed. "I love you."

"I know," Cassy said. "That's why I'm not throwing you overboard."

CHAPTER 28

"Let me see if I've got this straight," President Bradley said. "This North Korean major gives us every impression that he wants to talk, and then he suddenly clams up?"

National Security Advisor Frank Cerney shook his head. "Not quite, Mr. President. Major Ri is talking, but he refuses to speak to our trained interpreters."

"Which leaves us where?"

"We're still in business; it's just not happening the way we planned. Major Ri is willing to work with Petty Officer Philip Ahn, the Coast Guard sailor we sent ahead to start the initial dialogue."

"He'll talk to the amateur, but not to the professionals?"

"That's right, sir."

"Do we know why?"

Cerney's fingers rose toward his necktie; then he seemed to catch himself and lowered his hands. "Petty Officer Ahn is of Korean descent, so it's possible that Major Ri finds him easier to trust. It's also possible that the professional interpreters come off as a little bit *too* professional."

"Meaning that the major suspects them of being CIA?"

"Could be. Or he might believe that an amateur is more likely to let something slip during their conversations."

"Should we be worried about that?"

"No, Mr. President. Petty Officer Ahn doesn't know anything that would be of use to the North Koreans, or to the prisoner. We jacked up his clearance in case Major Ri happens to blurt out something sensitive, but Ahn has never been given access to any information pertaining to national security."

"So our only real worry in using the Coast Guard kid is the danger of

119

mistranslation?"

"That's correct, sir, but the risk should be minimal. The trained interpreters will review recordings of every session. If Petty Officer Ahn makes a mistake, they'll catch it."

"I suppose that'll have to be good enough," said the president. "What about Major Ri's big secret? Do we know any more about that?"

Cerney shook his head. "The topic is off limits until we promise to meet his terms."

"He's ready to take our word for it? We're the Imperialist American Aggressors—the enemies of all good and right thinking people—and he's willing to trust us?"

"So he says, Mr. President. The moment we agree to do what he wants, he starts talking."

"Why would he take a chance like that? He has no way to be sure we'll honor our end of the bargain."

The national security advisor said nothing.

"It's hope," said the president. "That's the only thing I can think of. Major Ri doesn't know that we'll deal with him honorably. He doesn't know that America will be a good place for his family. He's trusting in the hope that our government will be more honest than his government. That our way of life will be better than the one he's leaving behind."

Another half minute of silence passed before the president spoke again. "Send the word to Petty Officer Ahn. We accept Major Ri's terms. He has the personal promise of the President of the United States."

"Sir, that's going to be a tough promise to keep."

"I'm aware of that," the president said. "But we're going to keep it, Frank. Do I make myself clear on that? We *are* going to keep it.

CHAPTER 29

OFFICE OF NAVAL INTELLIGENCE
FARRAGUT TECHNICAL ANALYSIS CENTER
SUITLAND, MARYLAND
FRIDAY; 27 FEBRUARY
1246 hours (12:46 PM)
TIME ZONE -5 'ROMEO'

Jerry Catlin plopped into the chair across from Martin Quinn and deposited a much-reused paper lunch bag on the break table. "I figured out how they did it."

Quinn chewed for a couple of seconds, and then swallowed a mouthful of bacon cheeseburger. "Don't tell me.... I've got this one.... In the library with the candlestick. Am I right?"

"Alright," Catlin said, "I didn't *actually* figure out how they did it. I just figured out how *I* would do it, if I was in their position."

Quinn wiped his lips with a Burger King napkin. "I assume you realize that you've started this conversation in the middle. Can we back up to the part where you tell me what the hell we're talking about?"

Catlin unrolled the top of the paper bag and pulled out a homemade sandwich: ham and Swiss on wheat, with spicy mustard. "The North Korean supercav. We talked about it yesterday. I figured out how they made it work. Or at least how they *could* have made it work."

"Oh, we're back to that? I already told you. Can't be done. It's impossible."

"Not for them," Catlin said. "I agree that it's impossible for us, but not for North Korea."

The bacon cheeseburger paused midway to Quinn's mouth. "Want to run that by me again? A bunch of third world nut jobs have better technology than we do?"

Catlin finished his first bite of sandwich. "Not better. Just different. It's not a level playing field, Martin. This is one of those cases where they have the advantages."

"Such as?"

"They don't have to deal with the kind of environmental restrictions we face," Catlin said. "Same thing for human safety."

"Granted. So what?"

"That lack of regulatory oversight gives North Korean engineers options that we don't have."

"Meaning what, exactly?"

Catlin worked through another bite of sandwich before continuing. "Imagine this," he said. "You've been tasked to design a supercavitating submarine propulsion system, and all of the usual restrictions are taken away. Your bosses don't care if your design pollutes the ocean. They don't care about long term health effects on the crew, as long as the sub is operational for the duration of the mission."

"The bosses might not care, but the crew would never go for it."

"Not one of *our* crews," said Catlin. "I'll give you that much. But a North Korean crew wouldn't have the kind of technical background that our sailors bring to the table. Plus, they're raised in a culture that likes to kill off people who question the wisdom and benevolence of their leaders."

"Try to imagine what it would be like," he said. "You can cut corners on reactor shielding, eliminate protective mechanisms, minimize safety margins, and utilize technical solutions that are hazardous or even lethal in the long run. Nobody gives a shit if the sailors all keel over dead after their mission is complete. Emphysema, silicosis, lead poisoning, radiation exposure, toxic encephalopathy, or the galloping fucking never-get-overs. Whatever. No EPA monitoring for environmental contamination. No OSHA looking down your neck. No attorneys lining up to sue your ass off when the crew members start dropping like flies. What kind of propulsion system could you design if you didn't have to worry about any of that crap?"

Quinn shrugged. "I'd have to think about it."

Catlin reached into his shirt pocket and pulled out a folded piece of graph paper. He unfolded it and smoothed it out on the table top. It was a pencil sketch marked up with numerous formulas and notations. "I *have* been thinking about it," he said. "And it damned well *is* possible."

CHAPTER 30

The transporter erector launcher was stationed in a clearing about sixty meters west of a winding forest road. The ruts left in the soft soil by the vehicle's ten massive tires had been carefully covered up, and the displaced foliage had been replaced for the first few meters, to make the departure point from the road difficult to spot. Not that the road was heavily trafficked.

Like all of the launch sites, this one had been chosen with the help of Rafael Garriga, General de Ejército of the Cuban Revolutionary Armed Forces. It was an area rarely travelled by the locals, and the vehicle's woodland camouflage job blended in fairly well with the forest undergrowth.

If a random passerby happened to catch sight of the big machine, the Cuban populace had long ago learned that it was not healthy to pry into the dealings of the military. In the unlikely event that anyone was foolish enough to leave the road and investigate, they'd come face to face with heavily-armed North Korean soldiers.

At the moment, there were no locals within several kilometers of the site. No one but the missile crew heard the four minute succession of hydraulic whines and mechanical groans as the vehicle's erector arm lifted the missile out of its horizontal cradle and elevated it to the upright firing position.

Then the fueling process began. A pump whirred into action, slowly transferring 9,200 kilograms of red fuming nitric acid from a reservoir inside the vehicle to the missile's oxidizer tank. When this transfer was 70% complete, a second pump cycled on line, sending 3,700 kilograms of unsymmetrical dimethylhydrazine coursing into the missile's fuel tank.

The fueling operation took almost exactly an hour, and the three man missile crew used the time to pack up their gear and prepare their three Chinese-built Haojin dirt bikes for a quick departure. By the time anyone came to investigate the source of the launch, the Korean soldiers would be well out of the area, on their way to another missile site.

Five minutes before the scheduled launch time, Lieutenant Jo Ju-won, the officer in charge of the missile crew, unlatched the lid of the firing control module and engaged the power breaker. Tethered to the main circuit bus of the launcher vehicle by a long black electrical cable, the module was a rectangular steel-skinned box, about a third of a meter on a side, painted in the same woodland camouflage scheme as the rest of the mission equipment. Like the vehicle itself, the module was much sturdier than it needed to be—the product of a brute force engineering ethic that had fallen out of use in western countries by the start of the nineteen-sixties.

The electronics in the module took a couple of minutes to warm up, but the lieutenant had allowed time for that. Finally, the double row of status lamps began flipping from red to green as various components of the missile and launcher reported themselves ready.

The final lamp, *Warhead Pre-Arming Complete*, seemed to be taking much longer than usual—as if the weapon was trying to decide whether or not to take part in the coming mission of destruction.

Ten seconds passed, and then twenty more. The lamp remained stubbornly red.

Lieutenant Jo was now faced with a dilemma....

He could override the warning and proceed with the launch, trusting to luck that the malfunction was in the status lamp wiring rather than the warhead. If he was wrong, the missile would arrive on target unarmed and his government would likely attribute the failure to incompetence on his part, or maybe even sabotage. In either case, his life would be forfeit.

Alternately, he could shut the missile and launcher systems down, and then power them back up in the hopes that the balky circuit or component would reset itself. He would miss the planned launch window by a few minutes, but surely an effective attack was more important than a timely one.

Or *was* it? He had been given a precise launch window, timed to the second. What if other events were dependent on the timing of this attack? What if a delayed launch caused the failure of some critical plan? Again, his life would be forfeit, but that wasn't the important thing. He would let down the People's Army, and possibly even embarrass the Supreme Leader. The very thought made him feel unworthy to live.

The seconds continued their relentless march and Jo was no closer to knowing what to do. He had two courses of action, both of which seemed to lead toward disaster.

The launch window was now less than ninety seconds away. He had to do something. Anything.

He laid his finger on the *override* switch. An instant before he pressed the switch, the final status lamp flicked from red to green. The warhead had decided to cooperate after all.

Lieutenant Jo shifted his finger to the *launch* button and watched the last minute trickle away. Sixty seconds.... Forty.... Twenty....

Five seconds later he pressed the button, dropped the firing module, and ran for the dirt bikes.

The firing module cable was designed to be long enough to put the operator outside the thermal and overpressure area of the missile's launch footprint. As an added precaution, the ignition sequence had a built-in fifteen second timer, allowing the operator to move farther away from the missile's exhaust zone.

Jo didn't waste a single one of those precious seconds. He was on his bike, weaving through the underbrush when the Rodong-2 missile belched fire and blasted through the opening in the forest canopy on its way to the sky.

Despite the glitch, the launch had gone off exactly on schedule. Even as the three Korean soldiers were turning left on the road, the exhaust trail of the missile was curving northwest, toward its target on the American mainland.

CHAPTER 31

President Bradley broke away from his Secret Service detail at the elevator, and hurried through the open blast doors into the PEOC. He spoke to the only person he saw, an Army major who was tapping the screen of a tablet computer. "Have we identified the target?"

The major wrenched his gaze away from the tablet and snapped to attention. "Sorry, sir! I didn't see you come in."

"At ease," said the president. "Do we know where it's headed?"

The officer's posture became marginally less rigid. "Not yet, sir. NORAD confirms that the launch point was in eastern Cuba, and the missile is following a depressed trajectory optimized for STOF. They're calculating the impact footprint now."

"STOF?"

"Short-time-of-flight," the major said.

"*How* short?"

"That depends on the range to the target location, sir, as well as any last-second warhead maneuvers during the descent phase."

"Give me worst case."

"Intel assumes that the missiles are either Rodong-2 series, or something with similar performance characteristics. If their assessment is accurate, the flight time for a depressed trajectory shot could be less than seven minutes."

President Bradley's gaze shifted to the wall-sized video display. The screen was dark. "Meaning that the missile could reach its target any time now."

"Affirmative, sir."

Following the president's eye, the major raised his tablet and studied the available menu options. "My apologies, Mr. President. We weren't

126

prepared for your arrival. We just received the launch alert a couple of minutes ago. The operations staff are on their way down now."

He made two additional taps on the tablet's glass interface surface. The video wall flickered on, the giant screen depicting a geographic display of Cuba and the eastern United States.

The missile trajectory appeared as a curving red line running from the eastern end of Cuba to a point about a hundred miles west of Macon, Georgia. There, the solid line split into a triangular area of translucent red, with its westernmost corner near Corinth, Mississippi and its easternmost corner touching Knoxville, Tennessee.

This was the target zone, and the warhead could strike anywhere within its borders. The triangle enclosed about fifteen percent of Georgia, the upper third of Alabama, the entire central region of Tennessee, and a tiny sliver of Mississippi. The weapon's impact footprint encompassed Atlanta, Huntsville, Chattanooga, Nashville, Knoxville, and many smaller cities and towns.

In some way that President Bradley would never be able to describe, seeing the symbology on the screen brought home the reality of the situation. This was not a training scenario or a theoretical exercise. This was death, screaming out of the stratosphere at some multiple of the speed of sound, hurtling toward the inhabitants of a city still not identified. At this very instant, an unknown number of American citizens were thinking their final thoughts, speaking their final words, taking their final breaths. Some of them would be outside right now, looking up at the sky, watching the streak of incandescent plasma as a nuclear bomb plummeted out of the heavens toward a rendezvous with destruction.

On the huge display screen, the red line grew steadily longer and the target zone shrank by a corresponding amount as the geometries of terminal flight reduced the size of the area where the warhead might fall.

"What about interceptors?" the president asked. He recognized the tremor in his own voice, and made a deliberate effort to steady it. "Is there any possibility of shooting that thing down?"

"Negative, sir. The flight time isn't long enough. Interceptors from our West Coast BMD sites have no chance of engaging before the missile reaches target."

The major didn't have to say the next part. There *were* no East Coast Ballistic Missile Defense sites. The Pentagon had done studies on five locations for possible installations, but the bases had never gone beyond the exploratory planning stages. All of America's probable nuclear adversaries were west of California. No one in government or the military had foreseen the possibility of a second Cuban Missile Crisis.

"What about Patriot batteries?" the president asked hopefully.

"Not for anything in the target zone," the major said. "There are Patriot sites covering some of the major cities. Also, there are Navy BMD ships positioned to protect certain cities in coastal regions."

"Such as Washington, DC."

The major nodded. "Affirmative, sir. We're well covered here."

That last remark was probably intended to be comforting, but it wasn't. The government was sitting cozy under a missile shield that didn't extend to the ordinary public. The people inside the shrinking red triangle on the display screen had no such protection. In a few more seconds, some of them were going to be blasted to radioactive cinders.

The trajectory line on the screen was still growing longer, the impact footprint still getting smaller. It enclosed only one city now: Franklin, Tennessee—the three sides continuing to narrow in on what was clearly the target.

Chaz wanted to do something. Help those people. Stop this from happening. But presidential authority holds no sway over the law of gravity, or the physics of inertia. There was no order he could give; no switch he could throw; no policy he could enact that would make the slightest shred of difference.

The triangle shrank to nothing, and the red line completed the last section of its arc. The missile had reached its target.

As if on cue, the elevator doors opened, disgorging a group of military and civilian personnel who all scurried for their respective duty stations within the operations room. The attack was over, but the staff of the PEOC had arrived.

CHAPTER 32

As usual, eleven-year-old Stevie Bishop trailed a dozen paces behind his father and older sister as they left the warmth of the heated Macy's store to brave the winter winds of the parking lot. Stevie was always lagging behind. He was an ambler. A slow-footed world-watcher, moseying through life at the leisurely tempo dictated by his roving eyes and his insatiable curiosity.

Dad and Tiffany were already off the sidewalk and threading through the light mall traffic before Stevie rambled out the exit doors. Without looking back, Dad spoke over his shoulder. "Get a move on, Stevie. We haven't got all day."

That proclamation had been issued at least a thousand times in Stevie's memory, by parents, teachers, siblings, and even friends. It had been ignored just as often. Stevie Bishop moved at the speed of Stevie Bishop. No faster, and no slower.

He checked both ways for traffic and then started across the asphalt. He glanced left and saw two women standing next to a silver Volvo, both of them staring up at the sky. He glanced right. More people standing outside of their cars, faces turned upward.

He ambled the last few feet to get out of the traffic lanes, and then stopped and looked up.

There was a glowing line across the gray February clouds. A streak of radiant smoke, curving downward toward the Earth like a giant meteor or something.

Stevie broke into one of his rare trots, closing the distance on Dad and Tiffany. "Dad! Are you seeing this?"

But Dad was too busy looking for the car to pay attention. Tiffany's focus was welded to the screen of her iPhone; texting, or snapchatting, or whatever.

Stevie ran up behind Dad and grabbed his elbow. "Dad! Look up!"

Dad turned back with an exasperated expression. "Stevie, for God's sake—"

Stevie jabbed a finger repeatedly toward the sky. "Up, Dad! Look up! *Now!*"

His father sighed heavily and turned his face upward. Then he caught sight of it. "Good Lord! What *is* that?"

The trail of glowing smoke was much closer now, and *much* larger. There was still not a sound from it. The strange spectacle was utterly silent.

"It's moving faster than the speed of sound," Stevie said—his Fifth Grade Science finally coming in handy. "The noise is all following behind it. We won't hear anything until it passes."

He was wrong for two reasons. First, the meteor thing wasn't *going* to pass. It was coming straight down toward them. Second, there *was* something to hear after all. Tiffany looked up from her iPhone and screamed.

Then the shockwave and fireball hit. The boy named Stevie Bishop felt the briefest imaginable flair of pain, and everything was gone.

CHAPTER 33

SWIFT, SILENT, AND LETHAL:
A DEVELOPMENTAL HISTORY OF THE ATTACK SUBMARINE

(Excerpted from working notes presented to the National Institute for Strategic Analysis. Reprinted by permission of the author, David M. Hardy, Ph.D.)

In 1775, David Bushnell, an engineer trained at Yale College, built a one-man attack submarine which he dubbed the *Turtle*. Constructed from curved oak planks strengthened by iron bands, the vessel's hull resembled a wooden peach.

Bushnell equipped the *Turtle* with a hand-operated propeller for horizontal propulsion, and one mounted vertically for minor depth adjustments. The primary depth control mechanism consisted of ballast tanks which could be filled or emptied by hand-pumps. With a few refinements, his pump and ballast tank concept remains in use aboard modern submarines.

The following year, after the American colonies declared independence from Britain, his little submarine was put to the test.

British warships had blockaded New York harbor, giving them control of the Hudson River Valley and dividing colonial forces. The newly-formed United States of America had no navy to challenge the British fleet and the tactical situation was desperate. If the blockade remained unbroken, the revolution was in danger of failure.

Bushnell had designed his submarine for just such an eventuality. With the help of fellow Yale graduate Phineas Pratt, he created an underwater bomb with a clockwork detonator, to be carried by the *Turtle*. By current standards, this new weapon would be considered a limpet mine, but Bushnell called it a *torpedo*—in honor of a harmless-looking (but lethal) cousin of the stingray.

Ezra Lee, a sergeant in the Continental Army, climbed into the submarine shortly after midnight on September 7, 1776, and submerged beneath the waters of New York harbor.

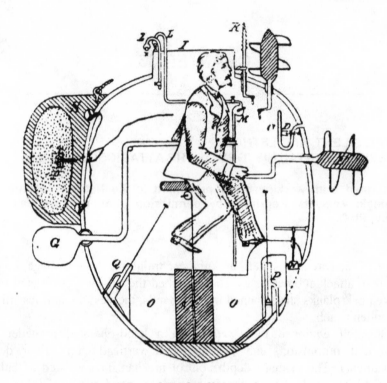

David Bushnell's Turtle

His target was HMS *Eagle*, the flagship of the British fleet, commanded by Admiral Lord Richard Howe.

Sergeant Lee's orders were to sneak below the hull of the *Eagle*, attach the torpedo to the ship's bottom using a crank-style auger, then retreat to a safe distance before the clockwork timer detonated the explosive.

The plan was approved by General George Washington, who referred to the *Turtle* as the '*infernal machine.*' Though he saw little chance of success, Washington was willing to try anything to break the blockade.

Working by the glow of bioluminescent moss surrounding the compass and depth gauge, Ezra Lee maneuvered the *Turtle* beneath HMS *Eagle*. He cranked the auger but he couldn't penetrate the planking of the British ship.

After several minutes of rest, he tried again. His second attempt was no more successful than the first.

With his air supply running low, Lee pumped out the ballast tanks shortly after the *Turtle* was clear of the *Eagle's* hull. He probably hoped that his tiny craft would be hidden by the darkness. If so, his plan didn't work. British lookouts spotted the strange vessel and deployed a longboat to chase it down.

Realizing that the boat would overtake him, Lee jettisoned the torpedo and the *Turtle* gained enough of a lead to disappear into the darkness. Lee made it to shore, glad to be alive but disappointed by the failure of his mission.

But Bushnell's invention wasn't done yet. Detaching the torpedo had activated the weapon's clockwork timer. The discarded bomb lay on the harbor bottom, just fifty yards from HMS *Eagle*.

When the timer expired, the explosive charge detonated. The blast lit the harbor like underwater lightning.

Admiral Howe was understandably concerned by a massive explosion so close to his flagship. Caution outweighed his desire to maintain the blockade. He ordered his fleet to head for open sea.

Without damaging a single enemy ship, the *infernal machine* had achieved an important naval victory.

In 1797, the American inventor Robert Fulton offered to build a submarine for France to use against British warships. In a letter to the French government, he described the proposed vessel as: "*A Mechanical Nautilus. A Machine which flatters me with much hope of being able to annihilate their navy.*"

Fulton's intent was to build and operate the submarine at his own expense, in exchange for which he would receive payment for each British ship he destroyed. After two years of delays, his offer was accepted. He proceeded with construction of the submarine *Nautilus*.

Similar in concept to Bushnell's *Turtle*, the *Nautilus* had a longer hull form and a significantly larger propeller. Fulton's submarine was also equipped with a sail for maneuvering on the surface, as well as a lengthy ventilation tube which allowed the crew to receive fresh air while submerged.

The *Nautilus* made several successful test voyages, reaching depths of up to twenty-five feet, dive durations of nearly six hours, and a submerged speed of about four knots. The French Navy was impressed.

Unfortunately for Fulton, the *Nautilus* never managed to conduct an attack. British ships were able to spot the approaching submarine and avoid contact.

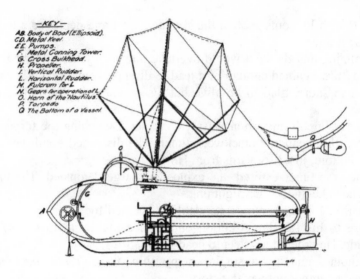

Robert Fulton's Nautilus

After a number of failed engagements, the French government backed out of the agreement. Speaking to Fulton, an officer of Ministère de la Marine said, *"Go, sir. Your invention is fine for the Algerians or corsairs, but be advised that France has not yet abandoned the ocean."*

When it became clear that no other governments were interested in a similar arrangement, Fulton had the *Nautilus* broken up for scrap.

The next attempts to use submarines in combat came during the War of 1812 when the United States deployed two submersibles against the British Navy.

The first attack took place during the week of June 14, 1814 in the waters off New London, Connecticut. A semisubmersible torpedo boat manned by nine American sailors attempted to ram a spar-torpedo into the hull of a British warship. The name of the target ship and other details are not recorded.

The semisubmersible ran aground near Long Island, and was destroyed by the British Navy. Eight of the American sailors swam to shore. The ninth man drowned during the swim.

The next attack occurred a few weeks later, also in New London Harbor. The vessel in this case was a fully submersible submarine, built and operated by Connecticut inventor Silas Clowden Halsey.

The only recorded details of the submarine's design come from a sketch in the notebook of industrialist and gun manufacturer Samuel Colt. Except for the elongated hull, air tube, and variations in configuration, the design appears similar to David Bushnell's *Turtle* from the American Revolution.

A letter from U.S. Navy Commodore Stephen Decatur indicates that the British fleet had warning of the attack, and may have taken action to destroy the submarine.

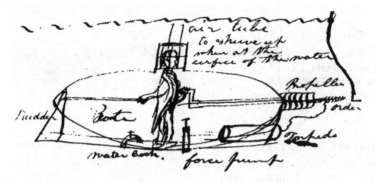

Samuel Colt sketch of Silas Clowden Halsey's submarine

There are no recorded accounts of the engagement, if one occurred. The only established fact is that Halsey didn't return from his mission.

We'll likely never know whether he was killed by enemy fire or dragged to the bottom and drowned by some mechanical failure. History remembers Halsey as the first submarine sailor to die in the line of duty.

He would not be the last.

CHAPTER 34

President Bradley looked up from the short briefing sheet. "Are we absolutely certain that it wasn't nuclear?"

The national security advisor nodded. "As near certain as we can be this soon after the attack, sir."

"Meaning there's room for doubt," the president said.

Cerney nearly shook his head, but caught himself. "Not *much* room, sir. We may not have conclusive proof yet, but the initial evidence all points to conventional explosives."

"And what evidence have we got?"

"Four primary indicators," Cerney said. "First, the damage radius was much too small for even a minimum yield nuclear weapon. Second, a nuclear ground burst gives off a particular type of seismic shock that didn't occur during this attack. Third, Homeland Security offers funding to first responder units who want to purchase chemical, biological, or radiological testing equipment. We got lucky and the local fire department had a handheld survey meter taking up shelf space in the Chief's office. They report only normal background radiation at the blast site."

"That's only three things," the president said. "You said there were *four*."

"Number four is the easy one," said Cerney. "No mushroom cloud."

"Then we're certain it wasn't nuclear?" asked the president.

"*Nearly* certain," Cerney said.

"What will it take for us to be *completely* certain?"

"There's some kind of test for xenon isotopes that's considered absolutely definitive."

"But in the absence of that, we're as sure as we can be?"

"Yes, Mr. President."

"This is a hell of a thing to be *nearly* certain about," the president said. "What about casualty reports? Do we have any numbers?"

"No, sir, but I can tell you it's not going to be pretty. The point of impact was in the parking lot of the Coolsprings Galleria shopping mall. The blast area overlaps the mall buildings, about a fifty-yard swath of Interstate 65—in both directions—and a sizeable section of the parking lot itself. About half of the mall buildings were collapsed by the explosion, and the other half are in flames. Between shoppers, mall employees, and drivers on the freeway, the number of casualties is going to be off the scale. We could easily be looking at two or three times the body count of 9/11."

President Bradley tried to keep his features impassive, to mask the growing sense of shock that threatened to overwhelm him. Thousands of deaths from a single conventional missile attack? How was that even possible? How was *any* of this possible?

North Korea had somehow gone from a pathetic kindergarten bully to a dire and immediate nuclear threat. As little as a week earlier, the idea of such a tectonic shift in the balance of power would have been laughable. But—some uncounted number of bodies later—no one was laughing, except (possibly) Kim Yong-nam and his puppet government.

"We have to hit them," said a baritone voice. "We have to hit them *hard*; and we have to hit them *now*."

The president turned to see General Boosalis, Chairman of the Joint Chiefs of Staff, crossing the operations room on an intercept course.

"Exactly which 'them' are you talking about?" the president asked. "The missile sites? Or the North Koreans?"

The general stopped when he reached easy conversation distance. "Both, Mr. President. We need to hammer those missile sites for obvious reasons. And we have to retaliate against North Korea because what they've done is an act of war, and because no one can be allowed to massacre American citizens and get away with it."

"I'm with you on all counts," said the president. "The question is: how do we hit *either* set of targets without getting a few dozen of our own cities nuked in the process? We can't retaliate against North Korea while an unknown number of nuclear warheads are pointed at our collective foreheads. And we can't call in a strike on the missile sites until we know how many there are, and *where* they are."

The general nodded. "That just about sums up the opinions of the Joint Chiefs, sir."

"Wonderful," the president said. "We may be getting our asses kicked by a third world maniac, but at least we've got consensus."

"We are making some progress," said the national security advisor. "Between satellite coverage and high altitude surveillance drones, we believe we've identified two of the missile sites. Possibly three."

The president raised his voice. "*Possibly* three? Meaning we're pretty *sure* it's a nuclear missile site, and not some local bootleggers cooking rum in a sugarcane barn? This is a friendly country we're talking about. I can't launch strikes against *possible* missile sites. We've got to have hard data."

"We need boots on the ground," the general said. "To verify targets before we call for strikes."

President Bradley shook his head. "If I try to put troops into Cuba, Kim Yong-nam is going find out in about five seconds. And about two seconds after that, he's going to start pushing buttons."

"I wasn't thinking of a new deployment," said the general. "We've already got troops in Cuba. The Marine Corps Security Force Company out of Naval Station Guantanamo."

The national security advisor looked doubtful. "Are those guys trained for this kind of thing? We can't afford to screw this up."

The general smiled. "Recon is part of their training, sir. And these are hardcore Marines. They'll get the job done."

"I need to talk to State," said the president. "We'll have to clear this with President Diaz-Canel through diplomatic channels."

"That's your privilege, Mr. President," said General Boosalis, "but I wouldn't recommend it."

"Why not? We're not dealing with Fidel or Raúl Castro anymore. The new administration is approachable and reasonable."

The general was slow in answering. "I'll tell you why I'm concerned. Because the North Koreans could not have mounted an operation this large without help from someone powerful in the Cuban government or military."

The president's eyebrows went up. "You're suggesting that President Diaz-Canel had a hand in this?"

"Not at all, sir," the general said. "In fact, I'd consider that unlikely. I don't think he would deliberately invite U.S. nuclear retaliation against his country. But it's got to be somebody near the top. Someone with enough pull to facilitate North Korea's plans, and then keep it quiet. If that person gets word of what we're doing, he'll alert Kim Yong-nam, and the jig will be up."

"In other words," the national security advisor said, "you're asking the president to authorize covert military operations in a friendly country, without bothering to notify the national government?"

General Boosalis made a palms-up gesture. "Well, when you put it that way, it doesn't sound very good."

"No," said President Bradley. "It doesn't sound good at all."

CHAPTER 35

USS BOWIE (DDG-141)
CARIBBEAN SEA, NORTH OF CAYMAN BRAC ISLAND
FRIDAY; 27 FEBRUARY
1741 hours (5:41 PM)
TIME ZONE -5 'ROMEO'

There was a tap at the door, and YN3 Ahn poked his head timidly into the wardroom.

Captain Heller motioned for the yeoman to enter. Ahn did so, followed by the two interpreters from Defense Language Institute, CTI1 Julia Cerroni, and CTI2 Hector Nash.

Ahn stopped a few feet short of the long dining table, at a position directly across from where the captain was seated. The junior petty officer's body began its usual routine of subtle posture changes as he unconsciously searched for the proper balance between the formal rigidity of standing at attention, and the relaxed bearing of standing at-ease.

YN3 Ahn was always jittery when he found himself in the sections of the ship designated as 'officer's country.' By contrast, the more seasoned petty officers from DLI usually had a more relaxed demeanor. The nature of their job made them frequent visitors to officer's country, and they were accustomed to dealing with senior leadership. But today, they seemed just as antsy as the junior yeoman.

No.... This didn't look like nervousness. It looked like shock. All three sailors wore expressions of startled incredulity, as if they'd witnessed something horrifying and not quite believable.

"You look like you've just had front row seats for the end of the world," said Heller.

No one laughed, and no one spoke.

"Alright," Heller said, "let's try this again. I'm assuming that you have something to report?"

Ahn nodded dully. "Yes, sir. Sorry, Captain. It's...." His voice trailed off into silence.

Captain Heller waited, but the sailor didn't continue. That was odd enough. But the other two interpreters were not stepping in to pick up the thread of the dropped report, and that was even stranger. They really did look like they'd seen the devil. Or something worse.

Heller raised his eyebrows. "Eventually, somebody is going to have to say something. Or am I going to have to bring in a mind reader to find out whatever it is that you're not telling me?"

"Sorry, Captain," Ahn said again. "It's just that we.... That is—"

"He's got cancer!" said CTI1 Cerroni in a tone that held none of her usual professionalism. "In his brain. And it's killing him."

Heller held up a palm. "Hold on a second," he said. "*Who's* got cancer? You mean Petty Officer Ahn?"

Ahn shook his head. "Not me, sir. Kim Yong-nam. He's got a brain tumor. Malignant. About the size of a golf ball. And it's terminal."

"Let's back up a little bit," said Heller. "How do you know this? Did you catch a CNN report that I missed?"

"Major Ri told us," said Cerroni. "Or he told Petty Officer Ahn, and we were monitoring."

"This is the thing about Ri's sister," Ahn said. "Remember there was supposed to be some kind of big secret about her? That thing he wouldn't tell us until the government met his terms? Well this is it."

"Her name is Ri Su-mi," said CTI2 Nash. "She's a nurse. She works at Bonghwa Clinic, which—according to Major Ri—is where the absolute cream of the North Korean elite are treated. Ri thinks it might be the only modern medical facility in his whole country, and it's restricted to eight or ten patients. Maybe not even that many. So naturally that's where the Supreme Leader goes for medical care."

"She's been assisting the French doctor brought in to treat him," said YN3 Ahn. "Major Ri claims that his sister has personally seen the test results, along with the x-rays, or CAT scans, or whatever they've got over there. She also overheard the doctor discussing the diagnosis with Kim's personal interpreter. In fact, she overheard a lot of stuff. The cancer is late stage, highly aggressive, and completely inoperable. It's already into his spinal cord, and it's spreading through his central nervous system like wildfire."

"He's got a few weeks before the effects really start to show," said CTI1 Cerroni. "Five or six months after that, it kills him."

"Some people might be inclined to call that *good* news," Captain Heller said.

"I know what you mean, sir," said Ahn. "I'd probably feel that way myself. But Major Ri tells us that Kim Yong-nam is really cranking up the propaganda at home. He has publically sworn a personal oath as Supreme

Leader that North and South Korea will be reunified before the next
Victory Day celebration, and that's July twenty-seventh. Only five months
from now."

"He's being medicated for pain," Petty Officer Nash said, "but Ri's
sister doesn't know if the drugs are powerful enough to influence his
thinking. She also doesn't know whether or not the tumor could be
affecting his mental stability."

Heller sat without speaking for several seconds, trying to process the
idea that Kim Yong-nam's decision-making processes might be clouded
by drugs, or entirely unhinged by organic deterioration of his brain. Even
assuming that Kim was somehow playing with a full deck, the man would
be in his grave before the coming summer gave way to autumn.

Risk a nuclear confrontation with his American enemies? Why the hell
shouldn't he?

If Kim won the showdown, he would be elevated to a god in the minds
of his people. His would be an unsurpassable legacy as the man who
reunited his divided country, and made a world superpower bow to his
will.

If America refused to submit and the showdown devolved into a
nuclear shootout, he'd go out in a literal blaze of glory—dying only a few
weeks (or months) before the cancer finished him off.

Kim Yong-nam had nothing to lose. Not a single damned thing. In a
career touched by many moments of danger, that was the most terrifying
thought that had ever entered Zachary Heller's mind.

He blinked, and realized that the interpreters were not finished
rendering their reports.

"Major Ri gave us the rest too," said Ahn. "Everything he promised.
There was a single launcher with a conventional warhead, for a one-time
demonstration of force. I guess we already know about that one. The real
weapons are twenty-four modified Rodong-2 missiles with nuclear
warheads. Ri doesn't know the yield ratings. Six missiles per site, for a
total of four launch sites. There were supposed to be two more launch
sites, but one of the delivery ships blew itself up, and we sank the other
one."

Ahn held out a steno pad. "We've got the details all written down, sir.
If we get him a map, Major Ri has got a rough idea of where the launch
sites are hidden."

Captain Heller reached across the table and accepted the offered pad.
"Good work, all of you. I'm going to sit you down with the Operations
Officer and have you draft a formal report. It'll go out Top Secret. And I
shouldn't need to remind you that everything we've just talked about is

also TS. None of you are to breathe a word of this to anyone except me, the XO, or the Ops Officer. That's an order."

The sailors nodded in unison. "Aye-aye, sir!"

Heller dismissed them.

As the three interpreters exited the wardroom, he sat back in his chair. The intelligence community would have to figure out some way to confirm Major Ri's story, but Heller already found himself believing it. He could sense the truth of it in some instinctive way. His subconscious mind was already reevaluating countless ideas and suppositions in light of this new information.

Drugs, brain damage, or the specter of impending death. It didn't really matter which of those factors was driving Kim Yong-nam's actions. Possibly a combination of all three. Regardless of his motivations, he was clearly prepared to play this out to the very end.

Kim would get what he wanted, or the son of a bitch would literally watch the world burn.

CHAPTER 36

PENTAGON
ARLINGTON, VIRGINIA
FRIDAY; 27 FEBRUARY
7:28 PM EST

Secretary of Defense Mary O'Neil-Broerman sat at her desk, rereading a transcript of the latest interview with Major Ri Kyong-su. She'd been through the Top Secret document three times already, along with the accompanying quick-look assessment from the Office of Naval Intelligence.

Nestled in a bookcase across from her desk, a flat screen TV was playing with the sound turned down. The display was divided into quarters, showing feeds from CNN, MSNBC, Fox, and CBSN. All of them were focused on the destroyed shopping mall in Tennessee, with particular emphasis on the still-rising body count.

Periodically, there would be cuts to footage of Interstate 10, 20, 40, or 70, showing gridlocked westbound traffic as people tried to migrate out of the predicted target footprint of the North Korean missiles. Just the more timid souls, so far. The public wasn't panicking yet, but it wouldn't take much to push some of them over the edge.

Mary was mostly ignoring the television, glancing up only sporadically to check for new developments in the lead story. Once an hour or so, she'd unmute each channel for a couple of minutes, to find out what the endless parade of armchair quarterbacks were blathering on about.

So far, the rhetoric was predictably partisan. The left-leaning pundits were calling for an emergency session of the United Nations Security Council, as though a room full of UN diplomats could somehow vote two-dozen nuclear warheads out of existence. The right-leaners were demanding immediate military action against North Korea, with a few of the hotheads already advocating nuclear strikes against Pyongyang. Like the liberal "experts," the conservative pundits offered no suggestions for dealing with the nukes in Cuba. Was everyone hoping that those missiles would quietly evaporate?

The senior senator from Nebraska had provided a bit of comic relief an hour earlier by trying to reframe the missile crisis as an argument against gun control. His logic on that had been a bit hard to follow. Maybe he figured Americans would need their guns, in case some sneaky North Koreans decided to swim ninety miles to Key West and deliver the nuclear warheads by-hand.

The senator was on the screen again now, but Mary wasn't watching him. She had eyes only for the transcript. The document contained little (if any) ambiguity, but her mind insisted on searching for a loophole in the now-familiar sentences: some alternative interpretation that didn't pit the United States against a dying megalomaniac with no reason to shy away from a potential nuclear holocaust.

This was where the concept of strategic deterrence broke down. A nuclear balance of power could only be maintained when both sides were afraid to risk total annihilation. But what happened when fear was removed from the equation? The combined megatonnage of the American arsenal lost all relevance against an enemy who could not be intimidated into keeping his finger off the big red button.

If this Major Ri was telling the truth, it was possible—even likely—that Kim Yong-nam didn't care if his actions ended up provoking World War III. The crazy asshole might actually be excited by the prospect. A final middle-finger salute to the planet he was so soon to depart.

Of course, none of this was intended to be "actionable intelligence." Until Major Ri's claims were either corroborated or disproven, the transcript was supposed to be treated as an abstract hypothetical, if that was the proper term. But Mary had read the damned thing, and she could see no way to disconnect the implications from her decision-making processes.

By now, President Bradley had seen the transcript too. Surely he wouldn't be able to disregard the information anymore than Mary had. And why should they disregard it? That would be foolish, and potentially fatal.

If they acted on the assumption that Kim was dying (and therefore not afraid of nuclear confrontation), the worst possible outcome would be an overestimation of his willingness to escalate. Conversely, if they ignored the unconfirmed report of terminal cancer, they could easily underestimate Kim's readiness to go nuclear. The worst possible outcome of *that* would be millions—or tens of millions—of dead American citizens.

Mary closed the transcript folder. The whole "actionable intelligence" thing was a load of crap. This was a complete no-brainer.

The only possible course of action was to treat Major Ri's story as true until (and unless) it was proven to be false. Anything else would be risking the unthinkable.

As much as she hated the idea, that put Kim Yong-nam in the driver's seat, right where the bastard wanted to be.

CHAPTER 37

HARBOR SECURITY BOAT (HSB-10)
NAVAL STATION GUANTANAMO BAY, CUBA
SATURDAY; 28 FEBRUARY
1027 hours (10:27 AM)
TIME ZONE -5 'ROMEO'

MA2 Douglas T. Hightower throttled back the twin Honda outboards and allowed the 27-foot security boat to glide into position off the starboard bow of the incoming sailboat. Aft of the deckhouse, MA3 Chester "Moose" Nolan, had the M240-N locked and loaded on the port side mount, ready to kick ass if the sailboat turned out to be a threat.

The big Alabama lunk was one scary-looking dude, able to intimidate most troublemakers into toeing the line, even without a 7.62mm machine gun for emphasis.

Not that the sailboat was showing much in the way of danger signs, apart from turning out of the harbor shipping lane. Just an old fiberglass sloop with her sails furled, putting along at three or four knots on what was probably an underpowered inboard diesel.

This was more likely to be a navigational error than an actual threat. The blonde woman at the helm looked like a vacationer. Probably a beach bimbo out of Miami, with too much boat and not enough sense. She might not even know what the buoy markers were for.

Hightower unclipped the radio mike from the console and cleared his throat, summoning up his best hard-ass voice for the initial challenge.

The woman on the sailboat lifted her own microphone and beat him to the punch. "Harbor Security Boat One-Zero, this is civilian sailboat *Foxy Roxy*, hailing you on channel one-four."

Surprised by this reversal in the order of things, Hightower was slow to respond.

The woman filled the silence by repeating her call. "Harbor Security Boat One-Zero, this is civilian sailboat *Foxy Roxy*, hailing you on channel one-four. Do you read?"

Hightower keyed his mike. "This is Harbor Security Boat One-Zero.

You're entering the restricted waters of a U.S. military facility. You are ordered to change course and return to the civilian traffic lane."

The sailboat continued on its plodding course toward the naval station piers. "Negative," said the woman. "This is First Class Hospital Corpsman Cassandra Clark. I'm en route to the base hospital with a patient in need of treatment. There are two persons and one canine aboard. No weapons, no contraband, and no hostile intent."

Hightower hesitated again. He'd been trained for a lot of different force protection scenarios, but this one didn't fit into any of the usual categories.

He resorted to repeating his challenge. "You're entering the restricted waters of a U.S. military facility. You are ordered to change course and return to the civilian traffic lane."

"I heard you the first time," the woman replied, "and I told you; that's not happening."

Hightower keyed his mike again. "This is not an authorized point of entry to the naval station."

The woman's voice carried a tone of exasperation. "In case you haven't noticed, I'm on a sailboat. It's not like I can drive through the front gate."

"I'm sorry, Lady" Hightower said, "but you can't come in this way either."

"Let's knock off the '*Lady*' business," said the woman. "If you need stitches or Motrin, you can call me '*Doc*.' Otherwise, I answer to 'HM1' or 'Petty Officer Clark.'"

Moose Nolan, who could hear the radio through the open door of the deckhouse, made a strangled sound that might have been a laugh disguised as a cough.

Hightower would have a talk with that dumbass redneck, but that would be later—after Boat Girl and her smart mouth had been taken care of. If Hightower had anything to say about it, that bitch was going to see the inside of a detainment cell.

The woman raised an arm and her voice came over the radio again. "Can you see what I've got in my hand? This is a Common Access Card with the Navy emblem on it. The same DoD-issue ID you're carrying in your wallet right now."

Hightower ignored her. He switched radio channels to call for backup.

⚓ ⚓ ⚓

An hour and a half later, Hightower was writing the preliminary apprehension report while Boat Girl sat on a wooden bench in the outer office of the Security Department with her hands zip-tied behind her back.

It was all Hightower could do to keep the grin off his face.

The woman's ID had checked out. She really was a First Class Hospital Corpsman, in the Navy Reserve. Like that counted for something. Trying to get onto *his* base illegally. Ignoring *his* authority. Busting *his* balls. Waving her weekend warrior ID card like it was some kind of free pass.

Well the bitch was in Gitmo now, and that stateside political horseshit didn't play down here, as she was already finding out.

Her husband (a big bastard) was at the hospital, with two MPs standing at his elbows. Getting his eyes checked out. *That* was the fucking medical emergency? The dude was seeing spots? Boo-fucking-hoo.... What a pussy!

They were both gonna get the book thrown at them; Hightower was sure about that. National security. Illegal immigration. Navy Regs. Maybe even the Homeland Security Act.

The hand of military justice was going to reach out and pop them like a couple of zits. Hightower was contemplating the idea with satisfaction when an inner door opened and a man walked into the room.

Something about the newcomer's posture and stride caused Hightower to glance up from his work. He caught sight of eagle collar insignias, and realized that it was a colonel.

Once again, Boat Girl beat him to the punch. She was on her feet, calling out '*attention on deck!*' before Hightower could react.

Hands zip-tied behind her back, the woman couldn't come to true attention, but she was clearly giving it a solid try.

Hightower got a better look at the officer. It was Colonel Dawkins, CO of the Marine Corps Security Force Company. A serious bigwig on a base as small as Gitmo.

The colonel stalked past with an absent nod. "As you were."

Hightower relaxed, his focus already returning to the half-completed apprehension report when the colonel stopped and turned back to stare at Boat Girl.

"Doc Wilson? Is that you?"

Hightower saw the change in Boat Girl's face as she recognized the officer.

"Uh... yes, sir," she said. "I'm still me! But it's Doc Clark these days."

Colonel Dawkins shifted his gaze to Hightower with an uncharacteristic air of amusement. "Afternoon, MA2. Do you know this woman?"

Hightower nodded cautiously. "Affirmative, sir. She's my detainee."

The colonel's eyebrows drew together and he looked back to Boat Girl, taking in her zip-tied wrists for the first time.

"Detainee? What's the story here, Doc? What have they got you for?"

"It's a long and ugly list, sir," the woman said. "Squeezing the Charmin. Mopery and dopery on the high seas. Loitering with intent to gawk. And they suspect me of voting Democrat in the last election."

The Marine officer's granite-hard features took on an expression of quiet curiosity, and Hightower felt stirrings of unease somewhere deep in his stomach.

"Seriously, Doc," the colonel said, "what kind of trouble have you got yourself into?"

"Unauthorized entry to the base, sir. My husband had an accident. I was trying to get him to the hospital."

The colonel nodded. "You still married to the Jughead who got his ass shot off at Panjwayi?"

"Yes, sir. But he's still got some of his ass left. Most of it, actually."

"He got the Silver Star for that, right?"

Boat Girl shook her head. "His platoon commander put him in for the Silver, but it got downgraded to Bronze."

The colonel's face went hard again. "God help me, but I do hate that shit. Your man whips seven kinds of butt for the Corps and spills three pints of blood in the process. Then some rear echelon chair warrior pisses all over the award write-up, and a bona fide combat hero gets the shaft."

"They *did* give him the Purple Heart."

Colonel Dawkins waived a dismissive hand. "Come on, Doc, *I* got the Purple Heart—for a scratch that barely needed a Band-Aid."

"It was more than a scratch, sir," Boat Girl said. "I put about thirty staples in you myself, and I didn't do any of the big parts."

Hightower's unease was quickly morphing into something closer to dread. This woman was a war buddy of the senior Marine officer in Cuba? What were the fucking odds?

"It was a scratch," the colonel said. "Nothing like what your boy got. Speaking of which.... What kind of accident? Nothing too serious, I hope."

"Flash blindness," Boat Girl said. "Maybe retinal burns. We were sailing south of the island when the nuke went off. Jon caught some of the flash."

Colonel Dawkins grimaced. "You think it's permanent?"

"I don't know, sir. That's why I had to get him to the hospital."

Hightower felt his mouth get the better of him. "It's nothing serious, Colonel. Not an emergency. Just spots in front of his eyes. Like when you accidentally look at the sun for a second."

The colonel rewarded Hightower with a look that would freeze water. "I've seen the Doc here clamp off a femoral artery with her bare fingers, while the Marine who owned it was screaming for Jesus. Saved that

Jughead's life, *and* his leg. So—unless you've got some advanced medical training that I don't know about—I'm inclined to give HM1 Clark's diagnosis a tad more weight than yours. I assume you don't have a problem with that?"

Hightower shook his head miserably. "No, sir. Of course not, sir."

"Good," the colonel said. "Glad we got that settled. Now, tell me about this illegal entry to the base.... Did HM1 Clark identify herself as a U.S. Navy petty officer?"

The flicker of dread in Hightower's stomach was solidifying into a knot of pure panic. "Uh... yes, sir."

"Did she produce a DoD-issued ID card?"

Hightower was finding it hard to speak now. "Yes, sir...."

"Did she indicate that she was transporting a patient to the Navy hospital for treatment?" The question was delivered with a calm that was almost deadly in its intensity.

How was this happening? How the fuck was this happening? The bitch had tried to put one over on Hightower. Smart mouth, trying to sidestep his authority. Trying to push him around on his own turf.... How in the name of holy fuck was this happening?

"I'm sorry," the colonel said. "I didn't catch that."

It was all Hightower could do to form the words. "Yes, sir."

The colonel nodded. "I see. Then maybe you can tell me why the best Fleet Marine Force Corpsman I've ever served with is standing here zip-tied like a fucking terrorist?"

Hightower's tongue was suddenly and completely dry. "It's... uh... It's... kind of a long story, sir."

"I'll just bet it is," said Colonel Dawkins. "And I can't *wait* to hear it."

CHAPTER 38

USS BOWIE (DDG-141)
CARIBBEAN SEA, NORTHEAST OF GRAND CAYMAN ISLAND
SATURDAY; 28 FEBRUARY
1417 hours (2:17 PM)
TIME ZONE -5 'ROMEO'

There was something going on in the port quarter of the array.

The aft towed array operator, STG2 Denisha Jenkins, edged forward in her chair and scrutinized her upper display more closely. The AN/TB-37U Multi-Function Towed Array was in passive mode now, the string of transducer/hydrophone modules sliding silently through the water at the end of their tow cable, trailing a thousand yards behind the ship like the tail of a kite.

Denisha's upper screen was currently showing an A-BAB display. Short for All-Beams/All-Bands, A-BAB was intended as a real-time summary of acoustic contacts, cramming every frequency detected by the array into a single visual presentation.

It was an article of faith with most sonar techs that A-BAB was worthless: the brainchild of an overeager Lockheed Martin development team who had continued charging ahead (and—no doubt—charging Uncle Sam) long after it became clear that their brilliant concept was a steaming dog turd.

When Denisha had taken the operator's course, the instructors had spent less than ten minutes demonstrating the A-BAB format. The more politically correct of them referred to A-BAB as the *'Grab Bag'* or the *'Trash Can.'* Some of the less reserved instructors preferred the term *'Ass Rag.'* No matter which label they used, the instructors unanimously considered A-BAB to be a complete waste of time.

The format *was* hard to read; Denisha couldn't argue with that. The chaotic false-color display looked like a bucket of confetti under attack by a leaf blower. A riot of colored dots shifting rapidly and continually, with no discernible pattern or meaning.

But the display wasn't meaningless to Denisha. A-BAB communicated information to her in a way that she could never explain—not even to herself.

The other STs had given her all kinds of shit when she'd first started using A-BAB, but the laughter and the ribbing had stopped a long time ago. Somehow, Denisha's mental wiring allowed her to extract contact cues from a display format that no one else could read. The mechanics of the extraction process were a mystery to her. She had no idea what her brain might be reacting to in the visual turmoil of A-BAB, and she'd given up trying to figure it out. All she knew was that the display worked for her sometimes.

And it was working for her *now*....

There was something going on in the port quarter of the array. She wasn't sure what yet, but she had an instinctive certainty that it wasn't ambient noise.

Denisha's fingers danced across the soft-keys and icons of her lower screen, calling up five adjacent beams focused on the area of the "something." The acoustic data took a minute or so to populate—frequencies appearing first as pinpoints, then elongating into vertical lines as new information at the top of each beam pushed older information downward. It was a classic "waterfall" style display, with the most current contact data at the top, the oldest data on bottom, and the area between illustrating changes to the various frequencies over-time.

This new contact—and Denisha had little doubt that it *was* a contact—was showing four clear freq lines, six more that were much fainter, and several others that we so weak she could barely make them out.

Denisha studied the pattern of tonals. The grouping looked familiar. There were no alerts from the system's automated threat library, so the contact wasn't anything that the classification algorithm expected to see operating in this area.

She rolled her cursor to the brightest tonal line and set a marker. This created an attached callout box, with tiny digits showing the actual frequency value to the nearest tenth of a Hertz. She quickly worked her way through all of the lines, progressing from strongest to weakest. When she was finished, her screen contained markers with numerical values for every visible freq in the contact's acoustic signature.

A tap of a soft-key captured and stored her current screen image, in case the contact suddenly faded, as they were prone to do.

That done, she began sorting through a different threat library—the one between her ears. Maybe not as fast or fancy as Lockheed Martin's software version, but capable of making intuitive associations that no system application could equal. (Not yet, anyway.)

And Denisha's mental threat library had seen this grouping of tonals before. Or something very similar.

It almost looked like.... No.... It couldn't be.... Not *here*. Besides, those boats were all retired, weren't they?

She turned the idea over in her mind for another ten seconds, and then looked around for the Sonar Supervisor, STG1 Wyatt.

He was standing near the compartment's tiny work desk, discussing something with Chief Scott.

Denisha lifted a hand. "Hey, Supe. Got a second?"

Wyatt met her eyes. "Sure. What's up?"

"You remember the old Chinese *Han* class attack subs? They've all been scrapped, right?"

Wyatt responded with a one-sided shrug. "There might still be a couple of them on China's active rolls. Probably don't get much sea time, though. Why do you ask?"

Denisha turned back to her lower display. "I could be wrong, but I think I'm tracking one now."

This brought a frown from Wyatt. He started to respond, but Chief Scott was already moving toward Denisha's console. Wyatt took a couple of long steps to catch up.

With the Sonar Supervisor standing over her right shoulder and the chief standing over her left, Denisha pointed to a pattern of tonals on the screen. "Look at the AC power structure."

She moved her finger to the right. "And this would be the reactor coolant pump."

Her finger shifted to a cluster of weak and fuzzy frequency lines. "Don't these kind of resemble that weird heat-exchanger rumble you get from a *Han* class?"

Wyatt and Chief Scott were both nodding thoughtfully.

"Not a spot-on match," said the chief. "But that *does* look a lot like the plant noise from a *Han*."

"Since when does China deploy attack subs to the Caribbean?" Wyatt asked.

"I don't think it's really a *Han*," said the chief. "It's missing some of the harmonics we should be seeing, plus it's got a few extra tonals down in the lower freqs."

"Alright," said Wyatt, "but if it's not a *Han*, what does that make it?"

Chief Scott thought for a couple of seconds before answering. "Unknown nuclear submarine. Possibly Asian construction. That's the closest I can get to a concrete classification."

"*Hey*...." Denisha said slowly. "This might be our North Korean supercav.... What if this is what that thing looks like when it's not tearing up the ocean at three-hundred knots?"

"You may be right," said the chief. "But even if you're not, there's only one friendly sub in the blockade zone, and this is definitely *not* the *Albany*."

STG1 Wyatt reached for the 29MC microphone. "You want me to call it away, Chief?"

The chief nodded. "Do it."

Wyatt pressed the mike button. When he spoke, his voice was heard over speakers in Combat Information Center, the bridge, and the CO's and XO's staterooms. "All Stations—Sonar has passive narrowband contact off the port quarter! Bearing one-seven-five! Initial classification: POSS-SUB, confidence level high!"

The antisubmarine warfare team went into action before he finished speaking.

The first sub engagement had been a complete (and rather nasty) surprise. It had come during blockade operations, when the *Bowie's* watch standers had expected only surface action. The unprepared crew had scrambled to assemble an ASW team on the fly.

That mistake would not be repeated. Since the earlier encounter, the ship had been operating continually at Condition Two-AS, with two full antisubmarine warfare teams working in alternating watch shifts.

Team Two-AS Gold was on watch now, and the Undersea Warfare Evaluator spoke over the tactical net no more than ten seconds after the initial contact report. "All Stations—USWE. Bearing is clear. No surface tracks within forty degrees of one-seven-five. Contact is now designated as *Gremlin Zero-One*. Break. UB—USWE. Target *Gremlin Zero-One* with Anvil. Let me know when you have a firing solution. Break. TAO—USWE. Request permission to set Helo Ready-Five. Request batteries released."

Lieutenant Amy Faulk was back in the Tactical Action Officer's seat today. Her response came over the net almost immediately. "USWE—TAO. You have permission to set Helo Ready-Five. Stand by on your request for batteries released."

The delay was normal operating procedure. Per Captain Heller's standing orders, any Tactical Action Officer was authorized to fire defensive weapons at his or her own discretion, provided that the ship was being directly threatened. But the submarine contact had not (so far) made any overtly threatening moves. Consequently, an ASROC launch against *Gremlin Zero-One* would count as an *offensive* attack. To do that, the TAO needed authorization from the captain, who would already be on his way to CIC by now.

While they were waiting for permission to filter back down the chain of command, the ASW team had plenty to keep them busy. Out on the flight deck, the helo detachment would be prepping *Sky Wolf* to get airborne on five minutes' notice. The rest of the team was working toward a fire control solution.

Denisha already had the contact fully locked and tagged. With every refresh cycle of the acoustic processors, updated bearing and frequency data were automatically transmitted to the Underwater Battery Fire Control System, which was already working the problem.

An ASW fire control solution is composed of four critical variables, which combine to identify a submarine's position and movement through the water. Those variables are bearing, range, course, and speed.

The bearing of *Gremlin Zero-One* was already a known value. It was being tracked in real-time by Denisha and the towed array. The remaining three variables were still undetermined.

By comparing miniscule changes in the data stream from Denisha's console, the fire control computer—under the watchful guidance of the UB operator—could use bearing rate and Doppler shift to calculate the three unknown variables, and "solve" the fire control problem.

If the resulting estimates were accurate enough, a weapon fired at the sub would have a good chance of hitting its target. If any of the estimates were too far off the mark, the weapon would miss and the submarine would counterattack. Because *Gremlin Zero-One* was probably the North Korean mystery sub, the *Bowie* could end up running from the same kind of supercav torpedoes that had killed the USS *Mahan*.

The bitch of it was, you could never really tell how accurate your fire control solution was. The only way to find out for sure was to launch a weapon and see how the dice rolled. If you got a hit, you knew your solution must have been pretty good. If you found yourself floating in a burning oil slick with half of your internal organs gone, maybe the fire control solution hadn't been so great.

Denisha knew she should be afraid. Her own death might be only minutes away. The contact on her screen could be the last thing she ever saw. By all rights, she should be shitting her pants right now. But fear—if she felt any at all—was way down on her list of priorities.

You couldn't run from a Shkval, or whatever those fucking rocket torpedoes were. They had a speed advantage of like two-hundred knots. If they came after you, there wasn't a damned thing you could do, so there wasn't much point in worrying. Besides, she was too pissed off to be scared.

Bernadette Tompkins from North Philly had been aboard the *Mahan*. "Bernie" had been a boot camp buddy who (just like Denisha) had joined the Navy to get out of a bad neighborhood and build a new life.

Teddy Hicks from Sonar A-School had been on the *Mahan* too. He'd been a tall quiet boy, with big hands and a shy smile.

Bernie and Teddy hadn't been family, or even close friends, but they had meant something to Denisha. She had cared about them. And now they were dead.

Neither one had made it out of the *Mahan* alive. Denisha couldn't stop thinking about that, wondering what it must have been like.

Had the end been fast and painless? The quick hammer blow of the big explosion and then nothing? Or had it been a prolonged nightmare of terror and pain? Trapped and bleeding in the powerless wreck of the sinking destroyer—scrabbling in the dark to find air pockets as the water rushed in through every crack, every hole, every broken seal. Fighting for ten more seconds of breath. Five more.... *One* more.... Pleading with a god who either didn't exist, or couldn't be bothered to answer the prayers of people who actually needed him.

None of these thoughts awoke fear in Denisha's mind. Instead, they stoked the fires of her anger, and strengthened her determination to kill the submarine that had destroyed the *Mahan*.

She wished the chief and the Sonar Supe would stop hovering behind her chair, but she couldn't realistically expect them to go anywhere else. For the next several minutes, her display screens were the center of the universe.

"Contact isn't maneuvering," observed Wyatt. "Probably finalizing his own firing solution. Getting ready to blow us away."

Chief Scott nodded. "That's one of the hard parts of being a sub hunter. You never know how close the other guy is to pulling the trigger."

Denisha kept her eyes on the contact and tried to ignore the conversation taking place behind her.

The target was showing slow left bearing drift, gradually moving toward the aft end of the array. She recentered her display to shift the submarine back to the middle of the screen. She considered tweaking the processor thresholds to bring some of the weaker frequencies into greater prominence, but decided not to press her luck.

That was a core rule of ASW: if you've got a solid track, don't fuck with anything unnecessarily. Many a contact had been lost by busy-bee operators trying to fine-tune something that could have been left alone.

She was only half-listening when Captain Heller issued the 'batteries released' command over the net. The USWE now had permission to attack the target as soon as UB got the firing solution nailed down.

Denisha stole a glance at the system clock just as the bridge was announcing flight quarters over the 1MC speakers. *Sky Wolf* would be launching any minute. It would fly out there and kill the sub at a distance.

This happy thought was interrupted by the realization that one of her markers had disappeared from the display. The associated frequency line had vanished as well—fading into the salt-and-pepper speckles that represented the ocean's ambient noise levels.

The other freqs were starting to fade as well. Damn!

Denisha tried to keep the annoyance out of her voice. "Heads-up, Supe. We're losing this guy."

STG1 Wyatt broke off whatever he had been saying to the chief. "Say again?"

"*Gremlin Zero-One*," said Denisha. "Target strength is dropping below background noise. We're losing him."

"Well get him back!" Wyatt snapped.

Then, recognizing that the demand was as unrealistic as it was unhelpful, Wyatt quickly modified his tone. "Try lowering the signal bias on your processor thresholds. See if you can dial him back in."

Denisha didn't need anyone to tell her that. She was already doing it. She had the necessary menus open on the upper display, and she was calling up the slider bars and signal curves to adjust processor sensitivity.

Wyatt started to point toward the screen, but the chief waved him away. "She knows what she's doing. You better warn the USWE."

Wyatt nodded and keyed his mike. "USWE—Sonar. Be advised, signal strength for *Gremlin Zero-One* is dropping rapidly. Contact is weak and fading fast."

The net was silent for a several seconds. This was clearly not welcome news. Finally, the USW Evaluator responded. "Sonar—USWE. Copy your fading contact. Break. ASTAC—USWE. How long before we can launch the helo?"

"USWE—ASTAC. *Sky Wolf* can be up in approximately three minutes."

"USWE, aye. I don't think we have that kind of time. Break. UB—USWE. How's your fire control solution?"

"USWE—UB. I've got a rough solution. Target is near the outer edge of the range envelope for Anvils. Estimated contact course is one-six-four. Estimated speed ten knots. Low confidence."

"UB—USWE. I copy one-six-four at ten knots. Low confidence. Stand by."

Denisha's frustration mounted as tonal markers vanished from her screen one after another. Adjusting the processor thresholds wasn't helping. Neither was anything else on her extensive list of tricks. The contact was all but gone now.

"If we're gonna shoot," she said, "we'd better do it soon."

"The TAO and Evaluator will be talking it over with the skipper now," said Chief Scott. "Considering how badly we got mauled the last time around, they're probably not too eager to start lobbing ordnance without a decent firing solution."

"What if we don't find him again?" asked Wyatt.

"There are worse things that could happen," said the chief. "Like getting two or three supercav torpedoes up our ass because we jumped the gun on this."

"My last freq just went dark," said Denisha with a sigh. "I have no remaining signals to track."

Wyatt took a quick look at her display and reached for the 29MC microphone. "All Stations—Sonar has lost passive narrowband contact. Last bearing one-five-niner."

He shifted back to the tactical net and pressed his mike button. "USWE—Sonar. We've got enough track data to shoot on a time-late solution. But if we're going to do it, sir, it has to be *now*."

The reply came about ten seconds later. "Sonar—USWE. We are at weapons-hold. We are *not* engaging this contact. I say again, weapons-hold. We are *not* engaging this contact. Return your operators to normal search routines."

The words hit Denisha like a slap in the face. *Normal* search routines? *Normal fucking search routines?* They'd had the bastard square in the crosshairs. All they'd needed to do was hit the goddamned button. Send those North Korean assholes to the bottom of the ocean as an honor guard for Bernadette Tomkins, and Teddy Hicks, and the rest of the dead *Mahan* sailors.

She had a wild impulse to key her mike and tell the USWE to grow some balls and pull the trigger. Finish the fight right fucking now. End it.

But a more rational part of her mind overrode the urge, wisely concluding that a move that stupid would get her pulled out of the watch rotation. Then she'd have no chance to participate in the finding and killing of the enemy submarine.

So she swallowed her anger, called up A-BAB on the upper display again, and resumed the long search.

CHAPTER 39

From: <zachary.heller@navy.mil>
Sent: Saturday, February 28, 6:47 PM
To: <efraim.j.heller@beth_israel_newhaven.org>

Subject: Shabbat Shalom

Abba,

The sun is dipping below the horizon, but the first three stars have yet to show their faces in the sky so I'm not too late to wish you a peaceful Sabbath.

I have to confess that I didn't do a very good job of observing the customs. I didn't light the candles, or read the Torah, or pray. I didn't recite birkat ha-mazon after my meals. (Given how far my eating habits have strayed from the kashrut, that would have been hypocrisy.)

Instead of resting and reflecting, my Shabbat was spent trying to locate and kill a group of complete strangers.

There are obviously gentler and less direct ways of saying that, but when you strip away the euphemisms, that's the kernel of truth beneath the polite words. That's the reality of what I'm doing.

Don't get me wrong; I believe in the mission we've been given, and I'm determined to carry it out. My crew and I are defending our country, as trite as those words have come to sound in this age. We're doing vital work, and it would not be an exaggeration to say that the fates of countless human beings hang in the balance.

But none of those things can alter the fact that I'm trying very hard to end the lives of people I've never even met.

This is a strange profession I've gotten myself into. It's possible to have a thirty-year career and never see ten seconds of combat. It's also possible to die in battle just a couple of months after basic training. A few days ago that happened to some of the younger sailors aboard USS *Mahan*. Actually it happened to nearly everyone on that ship. Close to three hundred people were killed, and every one of those deaths was an incalculable tragedy. Even so, there's something especially dreadful about losing a kid who's not old enough to shave.

I realize that everyone's time on this earth is limited. Sooner or later, the black camel kneels for each of us. But it's such a crime when it happens to someone whose life is only getting started.

Some of my own crew members aren't long out of high school. They're still too naive to accept the truth of their own mortality. Deep down, they believe that death is something that happens to other people.

You know different, Abba, and so do I. No matter how much I want to protect these kids, I have no way to guarantee their lives, much less their innocence.

And I can't see any alternatives to the setup we're using. We can't run the entire Navy with middle-aged sailors, and I wouldn't want to try. We need the wise old goats, and the young up-and-comers, and the core of seasoned ones in-between.

Besides, all those old timers and veteran sailors had to come from somewhere. Every one of them (and I'm not excluding myself) started out fresh-faced and wide-eyed. The path to knowledge and experience must inevitably pass through youth and then leave it behind.

In case you're wondering, I do recognize the contradiction in what I'm saying. Here I sit, bemoaning the deaths of young men and women, even as I'm pouring my thoughts and energy into killing sailors who may not be a day older than my own youngest crew members.

I don't know what to say about that, except to invoke the logic of tribe. My sailors are my people, as the congregants of Temple Beth Israel are your people, and as the citizens of the United States are both your people and mine. The compulsion I feel to protect my sailors is either instinctive, or so deeply ingrained in my social conditioning that it feels like instinct, and it overrides any qualms I have about the youth of enemy sailors.

Sorry, I'm probably not making much sense right now. I really just needed to vent some of my doubts and frustrations, and these are not the kinds of thoughts I can share with anyone on the ship. For my officers and crew, I must always be the captain: a paragon of pure and unruffled confidence, no matter how I'm actually feeling beneath the façade of command.

When you are troubled, you lay your problems at the feet of El Shaddai. My connections at the front office are not as good as yours, so I lay my problems at the feet of my father instead. Of the two of us, I count myself as the luckier man. Your questions and confessions may be heard by a higher power, but mine are answered with compassion and wisdom.

Thank you, as always, for listening without judging. For guiding me without trying to control me. For finding it in your heart to be proud of me, despite the many disappointments I have caused you.

I love you, Abba.

Shalom Aleikhem.
Zach

CHAPTER 40

Secretary of Defense Mary O'Neil-Broerman rested her head against the window of the Pentagon limousine, eyes only half focused as the buildings of Georgetown University slid past at the edge of her vision. She would be home before 10:00 p.m. for the first time since that Coast Guard boarding team had gotten their tails shot off trying to inspect a North Korean freighter.

The Georgetown campus was well lit. Mary tried not to think about the speed with which electricity had been restored to this area, while families in some of the Ward 7 and Ward 8 neighborhoods were still shivering in the dark.

There was an unpleasant negative symmetry in that. The people who were best equipped to survive an extended blackout were also imbued with sufficient clout to guarantee that their electricity was restored quickly. It was the people without fireplaces and well stocked pantries who languished at the bottom of the priority list.

Power was back on in nearly all parts of the city, and the few remaining blacked out areas now had functioning emergency shelters and portable generators to help the locals ride out what should (hopefully) be the last night of the outage. Even so, it was difficult not to notice that the last neighborhoods to receive assistance just happened to coincide with the lowest per capita incomes in the district.

The divide between the *haves* and the *have nots* had always been well defined in DC, but an infrastructure failure of this magnitude could bring the inequities of the system into uncomfortable clarity.

Mary wondered—not for the first time—if there was something she should be doing to improve the lives of less fortunate people. But smarter minds than hers had been wrestling with the problem for centuries, without much evidence of tangible success. And she had a big enough job trying to protect the American people (rich and poor alike) from outside enemies,

163

such as a couple of dozen nuclear warheads parked just south of the Florida Keys.

For all its truth, that felt like the sort of easy-out answer that she hated. Just another way of saying, '*if it's not my job, it's not my problem.*' But poverty and social inequalities were everybody's problem, weren't they?

Her thoughts were interrupted by a buzz from the limo's STE phone.

She picked up the handset, clicked the crypto card into the slot, and pressed the 'Secure' button.

Following a brief warble of synchronizing encryption, a voice came on the line. "Madame Secretary, this is Lieutenant Colonel Maxwell, the NMCC Communications Officer of the Watch."

Mary closed her eyes. She was no stranger to nighttime calls from the National Military Command Center, and not one of them had ever been good news.

"Good evening, Colonel. What can I do for you?"

"Ma'am, Kim Yong-nam is making another proclamation right now. It's being carried live by all the major networks as a breaking story. You're going to want to find a television as quickly as possible. Either that, or I can have the Signals Office cross-feed the video to your cell phone."

"Give me the quick and dirty," Mary said. "I'm not going to watch it on a screen the size of a postage stamp."

"Ma'am, the short of is that he's giving us a deadline. The president has one week to publically agree to the whole laundry list of demands. Withdraw our troops from Korea; turn over South Korean assets held in U.S. banks; lift all sanctions and embargoes. Everything."

"Did he give us a drop dead date, so to speak?"

"Twelve noon, Korean local time, on Sunday the eighth of March. If the president doesn't make a binding public commitment before then, the warheads start flying."

"Not one thing on that list is within the scope of presidential power," said Mary. "Apparently, Mr. Kim doesn't understand how our system of government works."

"Kim is a dictator," said Maxwell. "He probably thinks the president can strong-arm Congress and the courts into submission."

"Maybe," said Mary. "Or maybe he knows we can't meet his demands, and he just wants an excuse to nuke us from Hell to breakfast."

"Could be, Madam Secretary. Either way you figure it, we're on a countdown now."

"Understood," said Mary. "Thanks for the report, Colonel. I'll check in with NMCC after I've had a chance to touch base with the national security advisor."

She hung up the phone and tapped on the glass of the partition to the driver's compartment.

When the driver met her eyes in the rearview mirror, she made a circling motion in the air with her finger. Turn it around. Back to the office.

So much for making it home before ten.

⚓ ⚓ ⚓

Cuban Revolutionary Armed Forces Headquarters:

General Garriga locked his office door and turned up the volume of the phonograph. The pop and hiss of old bolero music swelled to fill the room as he walked quietly back to his desk.

Seated in his chair, he retrieved the metal lock box from behind the humidor and rum bottle in the lower left desk drawer, and twisted the combination dial through the necessary pattern to unlock the lid.

He went through the rigmarole for powering up the satellite phone, synchronizing the encryption, and punching in the phone number.

As usual, his North Korean contact took eight or more rings to answer. Also as usual, the man began with his familiar complaint. "I've asked you to only call at the agreed-upon time! We have the schedule for reasons of security."

"It's your schedule that I want to talk about," Garriga said.

There was a pause before the other man responded. "You have a problem with our scheduled time for calls?"

"No," said Garriga. "I mean your *other* schedule. The one your Supreme Leader just announced to the world."

The Korean's voice was cautious now. "What about it?"

"This is not what I agreed to!" snapped Garriga. "You promised me action. Your country was going to rain fire and death on the heads of the Americans! Burn their cities to the ground!"

"And so we will," said the Korean.

"Then why are you issuing deadlines? This is supposed to be the apocalypse for those murdering capitalists, not a diplomatic negotiation. Where is the destruction that you talked about?"

"The destruction is coming," said the Korean. "Everything we have promised will happen. But first, the world must see the unbeatable American superpower kneel before the very nations they have pissed on. They treat my country like a leper, and they treat yours like a tiny lapdog—finally allowed into the dining hall to prance, and caper, and beg for scraps from the hand of the master."

The anger in the Korean's voice was obvious now, and still rising. "The world will see America grovel. And *then*, we will destroy them."

"When?" demanded Garriga. "How much longer do I have to wait?"

But he was talking into a dead phone. The North Korean had terminated the connection.

CHAPTER 41

WALMART NEIGHBORHOOD MARKET
NORTH UNIVERSITY DRIVE
CORAL SPRINGS, FLORIDA
SATURDAY; 28 FEBRUARY
10:37 PM EST

Gracie Hopkirk slid the barcode for the twentieth can of beans past the laser doohickey and waited for the bleep of a successful scan. The register was behaving itself for once, and a good thing too. This customer had two shopping carts piled high, and the guy behind him had three.

What in the world did anybody need with twenty cans of beans on a Saturday night? More than twenty, because the guy was still piling them on the belt.

Beans. Corn. Peas. Soup. SpaghettiOs. Carrots. Sardines. Potatoes. Mixed veggies. Peaches. Pears. Those little meat sausage things that nobody likes. Gallon jugs of water. Powdered baby formula. Everything in cans or plastic bottles. Nothing from the refrigerated or freezer sections, and nothing perishable. Not even bread or milk.

The man's second cart was loaded with non-food stuff. Bundles of disposable diapers. Four flashlights and six kinds of batteries. Baby wipes. Paper plates and plastic utensils. Bottles of hydrogen peroxide and boxes of gauze. Three first aid kits. At least two bottles of every over-the-counter pain killer in the store.

Gracie took a quick glance at the next guy's haul and saw the same general sorts of stuff, minus the diapers. Canned goods. Water. Aspirin. Motrin. Tylenol. Bandages. Like he was shopping from the same kind of list, but he didn't have any babies to worry about.

There were two more people joining the line now, both with more than one cart in tow.

Gracie had never seen anything like it before. This store was usually a ghost town after ten. Where were these people coming from, and why did they all look so jittery? Almost frightened....

She kept powering through the items on the belt, bagging them as she went, and passing each filled sack back to the customer. As she worked, she could hear the automatic doors opening and closing behind her. More people coming in. A *lot* of them.

And the line at her register was getting longer. Still grabbing and scanning with her left hand, she snagged the intercom phone out of its cradle and hit the call button. "This is Register Four. We need backup checkers to the front, please."

The doors kept opening, more people streaming in. Everybody moving quickly, stuffing things into carts almost without looking. Like they thought the store was going to run out.

That's when it hit Gracie that the store really *was* going to run out. At the rate things were going, the shelves would be empty in an hour. Nothing left but bread, produce, and the perishables from the cooler sections.

The first customer was done now, fiddling with the chip reader for his credit card.

Gracie figured it couldn't hurt to ask. "People are stocking up pretty hard. Was there a hurricane warning on the news, or something?"

"Road trip," said the customer absently. Like his mind was already somewhere else.

"Where are you headed?"

"West," said the man. And he started his carts toward the front doors. "As far west as possible."

Gracie watched him go as the next customer started loading the belt.

People were still pouring into the store.

⚓ ⚓ ⚓

Blairsville, Georgia:

While Darryl Tanner was bolting the upper hatch and checking the air seals, Jeanette was down in the shelter tucking Molly and Evan into their bunks.

The Tanners had practiced the drill often enough that the kids were getting good at it. They could be roused from a sound sleep, zombie shuffled the eighteen yards from the back door of the house to the tool shed, and be carried down the entrance shaft into the shelter—all without fully regaining consciousness.

Jeanette was in charge of herding the kids. Darryl was responsible for hiding the Jeep in the pine thicket behind the house, buttoning down the hatch, and taking the final steps to conceal the entrance.

He'd built a pretty cool cable rig for that. It rolled an old lawnmower right over the top of the hatch, hiding it from anybody nosey enough to take a look in the shed. If any hostiles showed up and started seriously poking around, the shed had a few surprises in store—some of which had their own tripwires, and some of which could be triggered by remote from down in the shelter.

No one in the Tanner family ever called it the shelter, of course. That word was an absolute no-no. Not much point in having a secret hidey-hole if your kids could blab about it in kindergarten class.

To prevent just that sort of lapse in security, Darryl and Jeanette always referred to the shelter as the "family room." That way, if Evan or Molly *did* happen to let something slip about their late night emergency drills, any mention of sleeping in the *family room* would encourage images of happy children napping on sofas while the Disney channel played at low volume on television.

The "family room" was a 10x20 galvanized corrugated pipe style unit, built by Atlas Survival Shelters, and buried fifteen feet underground. Darryl would have preferred the 10x26 unit, but the cost difference was more than $20,000, and the "home improvement loan" that had financed the installation just couldn't be stretched that far. Besides, the 20-foot unit was adequate for his little family.

When he got to the bottom of the entrance shaft, he checked his watch. They had made decent time tonight. Everyone in and locked down less than twelve minutes after he had given the signal. A couple of minutes over his ideal time, but not bad at all.

Jeanette had Fox News going on the little flat screen with the sound muted when Darryl got to the seating area.

He sat on the narrow couch next to her. "Anything new?"

She shook her head. "Not yet. They're rehashing the ultimatum."

"We should take turns keeping an eye on the coverage," Darryl said. "I'm good for a couple of hours if you want to sleep the first shift."

"Can you tell me what you're thinking, Honey?" Jeanette asked. "You know I'm not doubting your judgment. If you say it's time to hunker down, we hunker down. But Kim Young-what's-his-name gave the government a week to meet his demands. We should have at least a few days before things get dangerous, don't you think?"

"Maybe," said Darryl. "Unless that lying commie changes his mind. Or unless *our* boys decide to take out his missiles ahead of time. If the pentagon starts bombing military targets in North Korea, Kim is gonna fire off his nukes. You can bet your last dollar on that. Same thing if we go after those launch sites in Cuba. We start hitting his missile launchers; he starts handing out the mushroom clouds. And we—the common people who don't get to listen in on the classified pentagon briefings—won't be warned ahead of time when the apple cart's gonna get kicked over. We won't find out until the ordnance is already in the air."

Jeanette nodded once. "I can see that. But you don't think all that's going to take two or three days?"

"We might have three days," said Darryl. "Or even four. Depends on how close our forces are to being ready to strike. Then again, our boys might open up a can of whup-ass on North Korea about an hour or so from now. We'll be up in our beds, sleeping like babies. Never even know when the lid comes off the pot."

He reached out and touched Jeanette's cheek. "I'm overcautious. I'll admit that. But I'd rather have our kids down here a week too early than five minutes too late."

Jeanette nodded again. "You're right, Honey. Better safe than sorry."

"Better safe than sorry," Darryl echoed. "Now, you go get some sleep, Pretty Lady. I'll wake you up in a few hours, when it's your turn to keep the watch."

Jeanette gave him a tired smile and stood up to make her way to the bunk beds.

Darryl settled into the couch and watched the repeating images from the Fox News coverage. He had taken every precaution he could think of. With the lights off, doors locked, and vehicle gone, the house should seem deserted if any intruders came looking. The entrance was hidden, and—with the nearest neighbors more than a mile away—he was pretty sure that he'd managed to keep the installation of the shelter a secret. His family was as well protected as he could arrange.

Now came the waiting.

⚓ ⚓ ⚓

Wake Forest University, Winston-Salem, North Carolina:

Mendy Bobbitt held the Android tight against her ear and tried not to let too much frustration come through in her tone of voice. "Dad, for the fiftieth time, I'm *fine*. The news is mostly fear mongering. You've been telling me that for years. And even if North Korea decides to do something stupid, Winston-Salem is not on *anybody's* target list."

"What about military bases in the area?" her father asked. "You don't have to be the target. Sometimes it's enough to be *near* the target."

"There's a piddly little Army Reserve unit," said Mendy. "And a National Guard Center that nobody would waste two shotgun shells on. Nobody is pointing nuclear weapons at this place."

"I don't care. You need to come home."

"Dad, I'm twenty years old. All grown up now. But every time there's a tornado alert or a flood warning in North Carolina, you want me to scurry back to Nebraska."

"There's nothing wrong with Nebraska," he said.

"I know that," said Mendy. "Nebraska is fine. In fact, it's better than fine. It's wonderful. And I love going home. But I've got midterms on Monday, and I can't do them from Cedar Bluffs."

"Maybe you can get a retake."

"What am I going to use for a justification? North Korea was making crazy threats? Those knuckleheads are *always* threatening to burn down the world. I don't think my professors are going to regard that as a valid excuse."

"There was that shopping mall," her dad said. "The one in Alabama that got hit by a missile."

Mendy could feel a headache starting. "That was Tennessee, Dad. Nowhere close to me. And I promise to stay away from shopping malls until after midterms, okay?"

Survival Net Forum

Whether you're digging in or bugging out, we're your #1 site for Survival Planning.

Online Now: 154 Registered Users / 71 Visitors / 3 Moderators

---

Guest 003568

    Rank: Newb
    Posts: 1

Topic: Is it time to run?

    Watching the News tonight and this North Korean deadline thing is scaring the crap out of me. I live in southern Kentucky. Should I think about moving my family? If so, how far should we go to be safe?

Dirt Weasel

Rank: Old Hand

Posts: 923

Topic: Re: Is it time to run?

I'm more of a gear-up and burrow down kind of guy. My best advice is usually to prepare in advance and fortify your position to ride out the trouble. But it's a might late to start prepping for this one. If you're gonna run, better do it quick. The closer we get to the NK deadline, the more jammed the freeways are going to be.

How far? Assuming that the maps on Fox and CNN are even close to accurate, you shouldn't slow down till you're west of Missouri. That's my two cents.

Keep your powder dry, your aim steady, and trust the Almighty to see you through.

Shadow Master

Rank: Old Hand

Posts: 876

Topic: Re: Is it time to run?

No point in running. This whole thing is Fake News. Another false flag operation, just like 9/11. Your "democratically elected" government creating a phony emergency to justify lining the pockets of the military industrial complex.

Wake up! The masterminds of this threat aren't in North Korea. They're in Washington.

Jet fuel can't melt steel beams and North Korean missiles can't fly.

*** THIS POST FLAGGED FOR MODERATOR REVIEW ***

Guest 003592

Rank: Newb

Posts: 1

Topic: Beautiful Russian women want to marry you!

Text Deleted. Text Deleted. Text Deleted. Text Deleted. Text Deleted. Text Deleted. Text Deleted. Text Deleted. Text Deleted. Text Deleted. Text Deleted. Text Deleted. Text Deleted. Text Deleted. Text Deleted. Text Deleted.

*** THIS POST REMOVED BY MODERATOR ***

Steel Worker

> Rank: Journeyman
> Posts: 239

Topic: Re: Is it time to run?

> I agree with Dirt Weasel. Better to fort-up than to evac. But if you're gonna haul ass, do it now.
>
> The farther west, the better.

Guest 003609

> Rank: Newb
> Posts: 1

Topic: Re: Is it time to run?

> Another Newb here, like Guest 003592, only I can't run. My daughter is in the hospital and I'm not leaving without her. Should I be buying a gun?

Steel Worker

> Rank: Journeyman
> Posts: 240

Topic: Re: Is it time to run?

> Only buy a gun if you know how to handle one. Otherwise you're as dangerous to your friends as you are to your enemies.

⚓ ⚓ ⚓

Shreveport, Louisiana:

Leila Atwood switched off the news broadcast and turned to Neal. "We should send the kids to stay with your mom, until this North Korea thing works itself out."

Neal, who was clearly no less spooked than Leila, nodded. "I think you're right. We should get them well away from here, in case things start happening."

He stood up. "I'll call Mom and get things moving on her end. You can start looking at flights to San Diego."

"Delta?"

"Any airline that's not a puddle jumper," said Neal. "Don't worry about frequent flier miles. And let's try for non-stop if we can get it. A lot of frightened people are going to be flying west right about now, and we don't want to risk the kids getting bumped off an overbooked connecting flight in Podunk, Iowa."

Leila stood as well. "Good point."

The Atwoods exchanged a quick hug and then went to carry out their separate tasks. With a little luck, they could have their children booked on a westbound flight before the sun came up.

CHAPTER 42

STEEL WIND (KANG CHUL POONG)
CARIBBEAN SEA, WEST OF GRAND CAYMAN ISLAND
SUNDAY; 01 MARCH
0314 hours (3:14 AM)
TIME ZONE -5 'ROMEO'

Hwa Yong-mu shifted in his command chair and swallowed a mouthful of copper-tasting saliva. His gums were bleeding again. Not as badly as last time, but he would have to take care not to show his teeth until the moment of weakness had passed.

He fought a compulsion to lick his lips, to wipe away any telltale traces of his body's betrayal. The urge to scratch his head was nearly as powerful, but he had learned the hard way that unnecessary contact with his scalp tended to make more of his hair fall out.

Everyone aboard the *Steel Wind* wore severely short haircuts, to make the loss of hair less obvious. But even when the length was only a few millimeters, the shed follicles could gather on the shoulders and collar of a man's uniform, where they detracted from his military appearance.

None of the physiological reactions were unexpected. Hwa and his crew had been exhaustively briefed by a team of doctor-researchers who were specialists in the symptoms of low-level radiation exposure. The charts and evidence were quite clear—as long as everyone took their pills, monitored their contamination badges, slept under the foil blankets, and followed the other precautions—they could be successfully treated and returned to perfect health at the end of the voyage.

In the meantime, a few physical debilities were an acceptable price for carrying out the vital mission entrusted to Hwa and his men. Or so he told himself whenever his body revealed some new sign of fragility.

That didn't stop a troublesome little voice in his mind from wondering if all of the wondrous safeguards might be counterfeit. The pills, the foil blankets, the restorative skin ointments, and the other things, were supposedly the products of miraculous scientific breakthroughs, known only to a small number of North Korean doctors and researchers. But what

175

if it was all fakery? What if the only purpose of the preventive measures was to quell the doubts of the crew as each man's body reacted to the inevitable consequences of radiation bombardment?

Sometimes as he lay in his cramped bunk trying to sleep, Hwa couldn't stop going over the math in his head. The submerged displacement of the *Steel Wind* was only 502 tons. That small a vessel could not possibly support the kind of 100-ton radiation shield carried by most nuclear submarines. So the *Steel Wind* had been outfitted with a high-tech laminate radiation barrier that only weighed four tons. Alternating layers of carbide and oxide ceramics, interleaved with micro-thin films of lead and tungsten foil. It was supposed to be a nearly mystical combination, allowing the supercavitating submarine to use just four percent of the usual shielding mass, with only a minimal increase in overall exposure.

What if the increase wasn't minimal? What if the accumulation over the length of the mission was enough to permanently damage the health of Hwa and his crew? Or even kill them?

That wasn't possible, was it? Everyone aboard the *Steel Wind* wore a contamination badge, which darkened in response to contact with harmful radiation. There was an official medical chart for interpreting the badges: with white for no exposure, light gray for minimal exposure, followed by darker grays shading toward black, where the cumulative dosage became a serious threat to health.

The colors of all fourteen badges were scrupulously examined and recorded every day, with a written report to Hwa as the submarine's commanding officer. True, the badges were gradually growing darker, but that was expected to happen as exposure accumulated over the length of the voyage. So far, they were all toward the light gray end of the scale, well within acceptable tolerances for human health.

But Hwa's troublesome internal voice had reservations about the badges as well. It was possible that those trusted monitors of safety were nothing more than swatches of chemically treated cardboard that darkened slowly over time. The progressive changes in color might have no relationship whatsoever to actual radiation exposure.

Hwa Yong-mu did everything in his power to suppress these thoughts. Misgivings of this type were not worthy of an officer in the Korean People's Navy, or a citizen of the Democratic People's Republic.

His rank was *chungjwa*, the North Korean equivalent of commander, and he was young to have risen so high—and to have been entrusted with so vital a mission.

Perhaps his youthfulness was a flaw in his character. Perhaps a more seasoned officer would have the fortitude to purge himself of impure thoughts.

But Hwa refused to believe that. He was a loyal follower of the Supreme Leader. He had reread *Juche sasang e daehayeo*, Kim Jong-il's masterful treatise on North Korean socialism, until he could recite entire chapters from memory. He was a faithful believer and a fervent patriot of the fatherland.

So why did these shameful questions continue to plague his mind? His men were not afflicted by such reprehensible suspicions. Or *were* they?

Occasionally Hwa thought he spotted something furtive in the eyes of one of crew member or another, unless that was more trickery from his imagination.

With an effort of will, he dragged his attention back to the mission, away from the self-reinforcing circle of dark thoughts.

There was a job to do: one that required his complete concentration, whether or not the insidious voice inside his head was right.

He swiveled his chair to regard the attack station less than two meters away. The Weapons Officer was putting the final touches on the current firing solution. Passive bearing fixes continued to stream in from sonar. Two weapons were prepped and waiting in their tubes. One would be sufficient, but no submariner ever willingly passed up an opportunity to prepare for the unplanned.

The target was an American warship, identifiable by acoustic frequencies from its General Electric LM2500 gas turbine engines. Hwa's sonar operators had not been able to narrow the signature down to a particular hull, or even make a positive determination of the ship's class, but the contact was definitely a combatant.

He didn't care whether it was a cruiser, a destroyer, or a frigate. His mission was to shatter the illegal imperialist blockade, sending every enemy vessel to the bottom.

He secretly hoped to catch an aircraft carrier in his sights, to become the first military commander since 1945 to sink a U.S. Navy flattop in combat. But whether or not fate ever permitted him such an honor, he would see this job through to the end.

Bleeding gums or not; shameful inner voices or not; he would destroy any American ship that came within range of his supercavitating torpedoes.

The Weapons Officer looked up from the attack station and gave Hwa a nod. The firing solution was locked in.

Hwa swallowed another mouthful of blood and returned the nod.

Time for the kill.

CHAPTER 43

USS WALTER W. WINTERBURN (DDG-132)
CARIBBEAN SEA, WEST OF GRAND CAYMAN ISLAND
SUNDAY; 01 MARCH
0317 hours (3:17 AM)
TIME ZONE -5 'ROMEO'

United States Navy warships never sleep. From well before the fanfare and flag waving of her commissioning ceremonies until the moment she's stricken from the service registry, every U.S. combatant vessel hums with unceasing activity.

At sea, tied to a pier, or lying in the cradle of a shipyard dry dock, her decks, passageways, and compartments are alive with officers and sailors. Sometimes the activity is readily apparent, as crewmembers go about the business of maintenance, training, cleaning, and conducting combat or non-combat operations. Other times, the action is more subdued and less obvious. But even cruising late at night during those rare intervals when most of the world considers itself to be in a state of peace, at least twenty percent of a warship's crew is awake and working. Standing watch on the bridge, in the engineering spaces, at the damage control consoles, at the radar displays and other sensors in CIC and Sonar Control. Roving watch personnel, patrolling for signs of fire, flooding, and security threats. A continual pulse of wakeful attention that ebbs and flows, but never stops.

USS *Walter W. Winterburn* was no exception to the principle. At a little after 3:00 a.m., while two-thirds of her crewmembers lay resting in their bunks, more than a hundred men and women were awake and on duty. Collectively, their job was to guard the ship and protect sleeping shipmates from harm.

Keeping the watch is a practice that predates most other functions of human civilization. Long before the discovery of fire or the earliest tools, Australopithecus (or some equally remote ancestor of man) had undoubtedly learned the importance of standing guard against hostile bands of fellow hominids and the predators of the night.

It's a sacred trust that remains as crucial to modern life as it was at the dawn of humanity—although many people today have only a hazy awareness of the men and women who are sworn to protect them from harm.

The Mid Watch team of the USS *Winterburn* knew their jobs and they kept the ancient tradition with all the care and solemnity that such a vital responsibility demands. They did not shirk from their duties. Nor did they lack in skill or diligence.

Unfortunately, skill and diligence are not always enough. Sometimes, luck outweighs the best of intentions and preparations.

Fortune was not with the *Winterburn* in the pre-dawn hours of March the first. The ship's initial bit of bad luck took the form of simple refractive physics. The thermal profile of the ocean created a refraction zone that bent sound energy away from the destroyer's acoustic sensors, sending all possible target signals into deeper water where they could not be detected.

Not a trace of the approaching submarine appeared on any display screen in *Winterburn's* Sonar Control. There was never a single moment in which the Mid Watch sonar team could have spotted the imminent threat. There was no opportunity for them to take the appropriate actions.

Their first clue was also their final one: the sudden detection of hydrophone effects off the port stern. Unlike the deep and quiet running submarine, this new sonar contact was incredibly loud—blasting across the broadband and narrowband displays like a runaway rocket. And that's exactly what it was.

The Sonar Supervisor quickly identified the blaring acoustic signature as a supercav torpedo. His hasty classification was absolutely correct and of no tactical use whatsoever. It was already too late. The incoming weapon was too close and *much* too fast.

The end came in seconds.

Guided into position by a GOLIS internal navigation system (Go-Onto-Location-in-Space), the torpedo reached a preprogrammed waypoint beneath the keel of its target. The final arming criterion for the warhead was satisfied. Two hundred twenty-five kilograms of plasticized RDX detonated with a destructive force more than one and a half times as powerful as an equal mass of TNT.

USS *Walter W. Winterburn's* second bit of bad luck was even more deadly than the first. The epicenter of the exploding warhead happened to be directly below the forward ammunition magazine.

The *Winterburn* was not merely devastated. She was obliterated.

When the reverberations of the shockwave had subsided and the last droplets of spray had fallen back to the wave tops, all that remained of the

9,200 ton destroyer was a spreading oil slick and a field of thinly scattered debris floating under the stars.

United States Navy warships never sleep.

But sometimes they die.

CHAPTER 44

A poke in the ribs jolted National Security Advisor Frank Cerney out of his first decent sleep in nearly a week. He swatted drowsily at the intruding hand, but the poking assault was renewed.

"Wake up, Batman," Heather said in his ear. "Your double-secret bat phone is ringing."

"Tell 'em I quit," Cerney groaned. "Better yet... tell 'em I'm dead."

Heather poked his ribs again. "*You* tell them, Hubby Dear. Lowly wives do not speak on the bat phone."

Frank's response was preempted by another string of low beeps from the secure telephone unit on the bedside table.

He groaned and fumbled the handset out of the cradle, nearly dropping it before he could align receiver to ear. "Cerney."

The voice on the other end was crisp and wide awake. "Good morning, sir. This is Lieutenant Colonel Buchanan, the Sit Room Duty Officer. Sorry to disturb you so early, but we're going to need you in the Situation Room."

"Give me the two-cent version," Frank said, "and let's keep it unclassified because I'm too cross-eyed to diddle this phone into secure mode."

"There's been another naval engagement, sir."

"I take it that things didn't go well for our team?" Frank asked.

"No, sir," the Duty Officer said. "Things didn't go well at all."

Frank rubbed his eyes. "I'll be on my way as soon as I can get some pants on," he said. "Make sure there's coffee."

He returned the handset to the cradle and sat up on the edge of the bed, looking over his shoulder to tell Heather about the abrupt cancellation of their plans for a lazy Sunday morning.

She was already burrowed under the comforter and snoring softly. He'd

181

leave a note instead and call her later in the morning if he could.

His eyes traced the curve of her cheek and the tangled mass of her red-gold hair, faintly visible in the feeble illumination of the bedside clock. Listening to the gentle rhythm of her breathing, he wondered for the millionth time what he had done to deserve the love of this woman.

He stood there for perhaps a minute, reluctant to look away from his sleeping wife. Then he blinked, sighed, and shuffled toward the bathroom to wash up.

⚓ ⚓ ⚓

White House Situation Room:

The Frank Cerney who straggled into the Sit Room forty minutes later was not a good match for the photo on his security badge. The man pictured on the badge was nattily turned out, with a charcoal Armani suit and a perfect Double Windsor in his striped Princeton necktie.

This alternate version of the national security advisor was bleary-eyed and pasty of complexion. His hair was badly combed, his shave was spotty, and his necktie was askew.

The Situation Room Duty Officer, Lieutenant Colonel Buchanan, met him at the door with a cup of coffee. "No disrespect intended, sir, but you look like death on a cracker."

Frank accepted the coffee and downed about half of the steaming liquid in two large gulps. "This better not be decaf," he said. "I don't have the strength to kill you, but I can drool on your shoes and cry a lot."

The Duty Officer smiled. "I wouldn't give decaf to my worst enemy, sir."

Frank chugged down the second half of the coffee and found a seat at the empty conference table.

"Okay," he said. "I've got some brain cells coming on line. So what have we got?"

"My team is putting together some visuals for briefing the president," said Buchanan. "But they're not ready to look at yet."

"I don't need a dog and pony show," Frank said. "Just tell me why you got me out of bed."

"We think we've lost a guided missile destroyer down in the blockade zone."

The qualifying word in that sentence caught Frank's attention. "We *think* we lost a ship? Isn't that sort of a binary solution set? Either we've lost one, or we haven't, right?"

"At the moment, Fourth Fleet is calling it a *probable* loss," the Duty

Officer said. "No absolute proof, but that's where the indicators are pointing."

Frank regarded the now-empty coffee cup with a doleful eye. "Alright. Spell it out for me."

"The ship in question is the USS *Walter W. Winterburn*, an *Arleigh Burke* class missile shooter out of Mayport, Florida, assigned to blockade duty south of Cuba. She was last located about thirty nautical miles west of Grand Cayman. At zero-three-eighteen hours local time, the ship reported an incoming torpedo over Navy Red and the fleet tactical nets. Based on speed and acoustic characteristics, their initial classification listed the weapon as a probable supercav."

"And?"

"And that was the *Winterburn's* final communication. The ship went silent on all radio channels, dropped off of the tactical networks, and disappeared from radar. She's also not showing up on satellite imagery. SOUTHCOM has already managed to divert a high-altitude surveillance drone to the area. It picked up some infrared footage of floating debris, but not even much of that. No survivors spotted, and no sign of the ship. Just a big empty place where a U.S. Navy destroyer used to be."

"Our North Korean super sub again?" Frank asked.

"That's SOUTHCOM's prime suspect," the Duty Officer said. "Unless there are *two* hostile units down there with supercavitating weapons."

Frank nodded. "What else are we doing about this?"

"There are three P-8 Poseidon's en route to the area of interest. One assigned to search for the *Winterburn*, and the others to hunt for the enemy sub. And the *Harry S. Truman* Strike Group is steaming northwest to get within helo range. When they're close enough, they'll launch SH-60s for search and rescue."

Frank's bleary eyes were suddenly wide open. "Hang on a sec.... We've got an aircraft carrier moving *toward* this killer submarine?"

"Yes, sir. SOUTHCOM needs the air resources for SAR and ASW. Nobody's got more of that than a carrier strike group."

"Is the president in the loop on this?" Frank asked.

"I'm not sure, sir," the Duty Officer said.

"Well we need to find out, and pretty damned fast. If he doesn't know, we have to tell him immediately."

"We were planning to wait until the briefing materials were—"

"Forget about the brief!" Frank snapped. "We've got a nuclear aircraft carrier steaming blindly toward an unknown threat that's already killed two of our warships."

"Not blindly, sir," the Duty Officer said. "The *Truman* is protected by escort ships with sonar, ASW helos, and two fast attack subs in associative support."

"All of which are armed with conventional torpedoes," Frank said, "just like USS *Mahan* was, and you know what happened to her."

He sat up straighter in his chair. "Have you seen the post-mission analysis of that engagement, Colonel? The *Mahan* dropped an ASROC right in the sweet spot, maybe fifty or sixty yards off the target's bow. You couldn't ask for a cleaner shot. By the time that weapon got up to speed, the sub was already outside of the attack envelope. It blew past like that ASROC was tied to an anchor. And about thirty seconds later, the *Mahan* was blasted out of the water."

The Duty Officer seemed about to respond, but Frank cut him off. "I don't care how many antisubmarine warfare assets the *Truman* has. If they're depending on ordinary torpedoes to stop a supercav submarine, then they're basically defenseless. Which means that we're sending an aircraft carrier strike group—the ultimate symbol of American military power projection—into a fucking meat grinder. We couldn't give Kim Yong-nam a bigger birthday present if we offered him the keys to the White House."

Frank leaned across the conference table and reached for the nearest telephone. "You've got two minutes to get your ducks in a row, Colonel. I'm waking up the president."

CHAPTER 45

//TTTTTTTTTT//
//TOP SECRET//
//FLASH//FLASH//FLASH//
//011148Z MAR//

FM   USSOUTHCOM//
TO   CARSTRKGRU EIGHT//
INFO COMFOURTHFLEET//

SUBJ/CHANGE IN TASKING/IMMEDIATE EXECUTE//

REF/A/RMG/USSOUTHCOM/011023Z MAR//

NARR/REF A IS SAR AND ASW TASKING ISSUED BY U.S.
SOUTHERN COMMAND FOLLOWING 010818Z MAR ATTACK ON
USS WALTER W. WINTERBURN IN CARIBBEAN SEA.//

1. (SECR) REF A IS CANCELLED AND RESCINDED.

2. (TS) HOSTILE SUPERCAVITATING SUBMARINE
OPERATING IN CARIBBEAN BLOCKADE ZONE HAS
DEMONSTRATED SUSTAINED SPEEDS EXCEEDING THREE-
HUNDRED (300) KNOTS. SUCCESSFUL ENGAGEMENT OF THIS
CONTACT USING CURRENT U.S. INVENTORY ASW WEAPONS
IS CONSIDERED HIGHLY UNLIKELY, DUE TO EXTREME
SPEED DISADVANTAGE.

3. (TS) BY PRESIDENTIAL ORDER, USS HARRY S. TRUMAN
AND ALL SURFACE AND SUBSURFACE ASSETS ATTACHED TO
CARRIER STRIKE GROUP EIGHT ARE DIRECTED TO
WITHDRAW AT BEST AVAILABLE SPEED, AND REMAIN AT
LEAST ONE-HUNDRED (100) NAUTICAL MILES EAST OF
LONGITUDE 75W.

4. (TS) STRIKE GROUP AIR ASSETS MAY OPERATE WEST
OF LONGITUDE 75W, AS REQUIRED FOR DEFENSIVE
DEPLOYMENTS AND OPERATIONAL MISSION PARAMETERS.

SUBJECT TO CURRENT RULES OF ENGAGEMENT, STRIKE
GROUP AIRCRAFT MAY CONDUCT OR SUPPORT ASW
OPERATIONS WEST OF LONGITUDE 75W, BUT NO SURFACE
OR SUBSURFACE VESSELS FROM CARSTRKGRU EIGHT WILL
ACCOMPANY THEM.

5. (TS) IF THE SUPERCAVITATING SUBMARINE CONTACT
IS DETECTED EAST OF LONGITUDE 75W, USS HARRY S.
TRUMAN AND ALL ATTACHED SURFACE AND SUBSURFACE
ASSETS ARE ORDERED TO BREAK OFF CONTACT, AVOID
DIRECT ENGAGEMENT, AND WITHDRAW TO A SAFE AREA AS
DETERMINED BY THE TACTICAL SITUATION.

6. (SECR) COMFOURTHFLEET WILL ISSUE ADDITIONAL
ORDERS AND AMPLIFYING INTELLIGENCE.

7. (SECR) IMMEDIATE ACKNOWLEDGEMENT OF THIS ORDER
IS REQUIRED.

8. (UNCL) ADMIRAL COOK SENDS.

//011148Z MAR//
//FLASH//FLASH//FLASH//
//TOP SECRET//
//TTTTTTTTTT//

USS HARRY S. TRUMAN (CVN-75)
CARIBBEAN SEA, SOUTHEAST OF JAMAICA
SUNDAY; 01 MARCH
0651 hours (6:51 AM)
TIME ZONE -5 'ROMEO'

Admiral Carey Hatcher swished his razor in the sink to rinse away the accumulated shaving cream. As he tapped away the excess water he inspected his reflection in the stainless steel mirror for any stray stubble.

He was going after a triangular patch under his left ear when there was a rap at the door of his stateroom. He toweled his chin, reached for a khaki shirt, and took the three steps necessary to exit the head and reenter his stateroom. "Come."

The outer door opened and in walked Hatcher's new flag lieutenant, Leonard Olson, carrying a white folder bordered with red diagonal stripes.

Hatcher reached for the folder. "Morning, Len. What have you got there?"

"Flash traffic, sir. Immediate execute."

"Bad news?"

The lieutenant nodded. "Yes, sir."

Hatcher accepted the folder without opening it. "If you're going to get anywhere as an officer, Len, you've got to work on that poker face. You're broadcasting frustration and uncertainty on every frequency known to man. It's in your eyes. It's in the set of your spine. It's in your tone of voice. The dumbest seaman deuce in the Navy can spot that kind of thing from a thousand yards away, and it scares them silly. Remember, your subordinates—especially the junior enlisted personnel—look to you for calm and rational self-assurance. I don't care how badly the shit is hitting the fan, you *never* let your people see doubt, or fear, or disappointment on your face. You can piss your pants in the privacy of your stateroom if you have to, but when you're out among the crew, *none* of that shows. Not ever. Understood?"

The lieutenant squared his shoulders and made a visible effort to take control of his demeanor. "Understood, sir."

Admiral Hatcher flipped open the folder, peeled back the cover sheet, and skimmed the Top Secret message. When he reached the end, he slowed down and read through the document a second time at a more deliberate pace—supremely aware of the guidance he'd just foisted on this young officer.

Withdraw? They were ordering him to *withdraw* from a combat zone? United States aircraft carriers didn't run away from danger. They ran *toward* the danger. That's what they were fucking *built* for!

He wanted to shout. He wanted to punch the bulkhead, break things, and hurl obscenities against the gods for allowing such an injustice to occur. He might have given into the impulse if his own words were not still echoing in his ears. Injustice or not, he couldn't bring himself to contradict his own advice so quickly and so blatantly.

He inhaled slowly and quietly; then exhaled even more slowly, doing his best to vent his rising anger instead of voicing it.

"You're right," he said, "this *is* bad news. But we don't get to choose our orders. Sometimes we're bound to get the short end of the stick."

He closed the folder and tucked it under his arm. "Please locate the commanding officer; give her my compliments, and invite her to drop by my stateroom at her earliest convenience."

Lieutenant Olson nodded. "Aye-aye, sir!" He executed a brisk about-face and exited the stateroom with a lively stride that gave no hint of the disappointing news he was carrying.

When the door was safely closed behind the departing officer, Hatcher threw the striped folder across the room. The offending conglomeration of paper and cardboard tumbled and fluttered through the air until it smacked into the far bulkhead and fell to the deck.

Hatcher stalked over to it, prepared to grind the damned thing into the carpet. Son of a bitch.... Son of a *bitch*.... Son of a *BITCH!*

Presidential order? What kind of horseshit was that? Some gutless idiot had whispered cowardly nonsense into the president's ear, and the fool had eaten it up. Now a United States Navy strike group was running away from the North Koreans.

Not the Russians. Not the Chinese. *The North fucking Koreans!*

Of all the scenarios he had ever planned for, not one had involved yielding the seas to a flyspeck of a country that could barely make electricity.

He didn't stomp the folder into the deck, as much as he was tempted to. Instead, he picked it up, straightened the wrinkled pages, and laid the somewhat restored assemblage on his desk.

Then he walked back into the head to finish shaving.

CHAPTER 46

MARINE CORPS SECURITY FORCE COMPANY
NAVAL STATION GUANTANAMO BAY, CUBA
SUNDAY; 01 MARCH
0934 hours (9:34 AM)
TIME ZONE -5 'ROMEO'

Colonel Dawkins ushered Jon and Cassy Clark into his office and waved them toward a pair of overstuffed leather armchairs. "Come on in, Doc. Mr. Clark. Make yourselves at home."

The Clarks took the offered seats, but neither of them looked the least bit comfortable, despite the plush furnishings and the colonel's easy-going manner.

Dawkins dropped into a seat across from the couple and smiled. "Seriously, Doc, take a load off. You too, Mr. Clark. If you were still in the Corps, I'd say *at-ease*. Now that you're one of those lazy civilian-types, I'll just tell you to chill out. Put your feet up. Scratch your ass. Whatever it is you do to relax."

His playful tone seemed to have the desired effect. Both Clarks allowed their body postures to unwind and their facial expressions to loosen up.

"I know you got a shitty welcome to the base," Dawkins said, "but we've got that all straightened out. Neither one of you is in any trouble and nobody's mad at you."

"I'm not so sure about that last part," Cassy said. "The MA2 who arrested us is probably ready to shoot us on sight."

The colonel's smile widened to a grin that wouldn't have looked out of place on a shark. "I wouldn't worry too much about Petty Officer Hightower. I believe his attitude has been sufficiently adjusted. If he needs additional counseling, I'll see to it personally."

"But I didn't bring you here to talk about your immigration status," he said. "I've got something I want to kick around with both of you."

He looked directly at Jon. "Before we get into that, what's going on with your eyeballs? Are those Spiderman goggles gonna fix you up? Or does the Corps need to issue you some new peepers?"

Jon was wearing disposable sunglasses, smoked one-piece plastic that wrapped around his temples like the stylized mask of a b-grade comic book superhero.

"These should do me just fine," he said. "Plus about twenty-five kinds of goop to put in my eyes. Also, the doctor told me not to stare at any more nuclear explosions for at least a week."

Cassy shoved at his shoulder. "*Three* kinds of eyedrops. A mydriatic to paralyze the ciliary muscles and let the corneas heal, a topical antibiotic to prevent infection, and Prednisolone to reduce inflammation and avoid scarring."

"But his eyes are going to be okay?" the colonel asked.

"They'll be fine," Cassy said, "if he takes his meds and follows the doctor's orders." She nudged his shoulder again. "And you *are* gonna do that, aren't you, Jonnie?"

Her husband nodded. "Yes, Doc."

Cassy smiled. "See? Marines *can* be trained."

"I wouldn't go that far," Colonel Dawkins said. "But most of us have enough brain cells not to argue with the people who are trying to keep us alive."

"That's all a Corpsman can ask for, sir," Cassy said. "We don't insist on *smart* Jarheads, but we do like for them to be *alive* if at all possible."

"We generally try to accommodate you on that," said the colonel, "but things don't always work out according to plan."

His voice took on a more serious tone. "And that's pretty much why I asked you to come here."

The Clarks waited for him to continue.

"What I'm about to tell you is highly classified," the colonel said. "Your security clearance is no longer active, Mr. Clark, and there's not enough time to renew it. Doc, your clearance is currently active, but it's not high enough for this discussion, and there is no time to upgrade."

Jon and Cassy exchanged glances. Clearly they were becoming more puzzled by the second.

"Ordinarily, that would put this little plan at a complete standstill," said Colonel Dawkins. "We can't usually bypass the legal and administrative hurdles for granting access to classified information. But this is not an ordinary situation."

He paused until he had a nod of understanding from both of them.

"We can't just throw Federal Law and military regs out the window," he said. "But—according to my top legal beagle—there's a way to do this, if we apply a *highly* creative interpretation of Executive Order #12968. Apparently there's a loophole somewhere in the fine print for granting temporary access to classified material under what the order refers to as 'extraordinary circumstances'."

The colonel's shark-like grin reappeared. "There are a couple of dozen nukes pointed at U.S. cities, and the man with his thumb on the button is crazier than a shithouse rat. Not to mention a science fiction rocket sub blasting the living fuck out of the Atlantic Fleet. I figure that qualifies as *extraordinary circumstances*. Would you agree?"

Jon and Cassy Clark nodded again, still no closer to understanding what this conversation was leading up to.

"I'm going to ask you to sign some papers in a minute," Colonel Dawkins said, "to take advantage of that loophole. But the papers aren't the important part. The legal consequences if you divulge this material aren't really important either, at least not in the big scheme of things. Here's the important part.... If security on this op is blown, some of my Marines are going to die. That's more or less guaranteed. And if word gets back to the North Koreans, there could be twenty or thirty million dead American citizens to keep my dead Marines company. I need you to both understand that."

Cassy and Jon exchanged another look, and then both nodded again.

"We understand," Jon said. "We don't have a clue what you want us for, but we understand what'll happen if we compromise security."

"Good," the colonel said. He reached for a pair of manila folders on a side table near his chair. "I'm going to need you to sign these before I tell you anything else. Your signatures won't commit you to taking part in the operation we're going to discuss. What they *will* do is make you legally and criminally culpable if you unlawfully disclose any of what you're about to hear."

He held out a folder and an ink pen in each hand.

This time, the Clarks didn't have to exchange a look. Without a word, they reached for the folders and pens.

The paperwork consisted of a single-page acknowledgement form with a signature block at the bottom. Cassy rapidly read through the text and signed in the designated place. Then she read Jon's form aloud to him, to save his eyes from unnecessary strain.

His scrawl on the paper was not aligned with the signature block, but Cassy didn't think anyone would complain.

Colonel Dawkins took back the signed documents and laid them on his desk. "How many people does your sailboat sleep?" he asked.

"She can handle four pretty comfortably," Jon said. "Six with some crowding, if nobody minds getting up close and personal with a dog who farts in her sleep."

"Six is good enough," the colonel said. "Eight would be better, but we can do it with six people."

"Do *what* with six people?" Cassy asked.

Colonel Dawkins leaned back in his chair. "I've got in mind a little sailing vacation. The two of you and four passengers. Six dumb and harmless American tourists, happily bumming around the coast of Cuba in their seaworthy old sailboat."

"With their dog," Jon said.

"Right," said the colonel. "With their dog."

"These four other tourists that'll be sailing with us," Cassy said. "Can we assume they'll be over-muscled Jarhead types? The kind who can do pushups with their eyebrows?"

Colonel Dawkins put on an air of exaggerated innocence. "Are you suggesting that I would deploy a detachment of U.S. Marines to covertly infiltrate our host country? Petty Officer Clark, I'm surprised at you! I would never even *dream* of such a thing."

"Of course not," Cassy said. "So these definitely-not-Jarheads that you're sending.... What exactly will they be doing?"

"Well, that's where the plan starts to get a little crazy," said Colonel Dawkins.

"Where it *starts* to get crazy?"

"Yeah," the colonel said. "It gets a *lot* weirder from here."

CHAPTER 47

USS ALBANY (SSN-753)
CARIBBEAN SEA, SOUTHEAST OF ISLA DE LA JUVENTUD
MONDAY; 02 MARCH
1703 hours (5:03 PM)
TIME ZONE -5 'ROMEO'

Master Chief Ernie Pooler licked a finger and turned a page of his dog-eared paperback. It was a Bantam mass market reissue from the early eighties—the pasteboard cover and spine held together with masking tape; the yellowed pages going brittle with age. The jacket illustration—a bearded seaman in sou'wester and rain slicker silhouetted against a glowering sky—was nearly invisible behind creases and tape patches.

He had a hardcover first edition of the book in his collection at home, and an electronic copy on that e-reader whatsit that his kids had given him for Christmas. But *this* was the one he liked to read. The one that he got lost in.

His eyes found the top of the new page and his mind remained happily submerged in the adventures of young Harvey Cheyne aboard a decrepit fishing schooner in the North Atlantic.

> *Before long he knew where Disko kept the old green-crusted quadrant that they called the "hog-yoke"—under the bed-bag in his bunk. When he 'took the sun, and with the help of "The Old Farmer's" almanac found the latitude, Harvey would jump down into the cabin and scratch the reckoning and date with a nail on the rust of the stove-pipe.*

> *Now, the chief engineer of the liner could have done no more, and no engineer of thirty years' service could have assumed one half of the ancient-mariner air with which Harvey, first careful to spit over the side, made public the schooner's position for that day, and then and not till then relieved Disko of the quadrant. There is an etiquette in all these things.*

193

The words had flowed from Kipling's pen in the century before last, and they had been printed, reprinted, and repackaged so often that even the long-dead author's estate had undoubtedly lost track. But the prose and the story were fresh every time. Renewed with each re-reading in a way that Ernie had never been able to explain or even understand.

In a long and prolific career, Rudyard Kipling had written many books more famous and better received than *Captains Courageous*, but not one of those others held the wonder and majesty found in this simple tale of a boy discovering his manhood at sea. Not as far as Ernie Pooler was concerned, anyway.

It might be an exaggeration to say that Ernie's first reading of the novel at age ten or eleven had inspired him to become a sailor. If books were significant factors in that decision—and they probably were—then *Up Periscope* by Robb White, and *Run Silent, Run Deep* by Edward L. Beach were equally responsible.

But this was the book he read every year: the one that had stuck with him through a life very different from that of Kipling's youthful protagonist.

Ernie's latest visit to the world of Harvey Cheyne ended with a feather light tap on the doorframe of the Goat Locker. The door swung partway open, and the Messenger of the Watch stuck his head through the gap. "Excuse me, COB. The Skipper's asking for you in the Control Room."

"Thanks," Ernie said. 'On my way."

He closed the paperback, slid to the end of the work table's bench-style seat, and stood up—stretching to loosen the kinks in his lower spine.

A quick stop by his rack to tuck the book under his pillow, and then he was out the door, following the messenger up the ladder.

Thirty seconds later, he walked into Control and strode over to the commanding officer. "You wanted to see me, Skipper?"

Captain Townsend looked around and treated Ernie to an evil little smile. "We've got the bastard, COB. Dead to rights."

Before Ernie could respond, the CO turned his head and started issuing orders. "Right ten degrees rudder, steady on course three-one-five. Make turns for fourteen knots."

As soon as the commands were repeated back, the CO continued. "Torpedo Room, Fire Control—Make tubes one and four ready in all respects. Open outer doors."

Again, the orders were acknowledged and carried out.

The Sonar Technician in Ernie made him long to be in the sonar room, watching the operators work their wizardry on the target's acoustic signals. But the Skipper clearly wanted him here in the Control Room.

So Ernie stood where he was, and waited until the commanding officer was facing his way again. "How solid have we got him, sir?"

"It's our boy alright," said the CO. "Plant noise looks like an old Chinese *Han* class without some of the usual harmonics. And he's got a few extra tonals in the lower frequencies. Definitely our guy."

Ernie nodded. That certainly aligned with their previous acoustic signatures from the North Korean sub.

The Skipper turned away again. "Firing point procedures. Weapons Officer, I want swim-out on both fish."

"Weapons Officer, aye. Swim-out on both fish."

The term 'swim-out' referred to an alternate firing mode for the torpedoes. Instead of being forcefully rammed out of the torpedo tubes by columns of piston-driven water pressure, the weapons would spool up their internal turbines and "swim" out of their tubes under their own power.

Though much slower than the standard launch procedure, a swim-out was many times quieter and far less likely to be detected by the target submarine.

All was now in readiness and Ernie felt a tightening of the muscles between his shoulder blades. He had observed or participated in this same sequence of procedures more times than he could count. But always it had been under training conditions. The contact had been an electronically injected computer simulation, or an unmanned mobile target.

This time, the target was a real submarine, crewed by unsimulated people. When Captain Townsend gave the order, actual human beings were going to die. It was a sobering thought, but there wasn't much time to dwell on it.

"Tube one," said the Skipper, "match generated bearings and shoot!"

The instant the order was acknowledged and carried out, the Skipper repeated it for the second torpedo. "Tube four, match generated bearings and shoot!"

There was none of the usual restrained acoustic thunder of a torpedo launch. No surge of rushing water and hiss of compressed air. Just a pair of low rumbles and high pitched whines that quickly faded to inaudibility.

Over the speaker came the Torpedo Room's report. "Tubes one and four, impulse return. Normal launch."

'Impulse return' signaled that the weapons had received and accepted their final package of targeting data. They were functioning normally.

"Make tubes two and three ready in all respects," the Skipper ordered. He was already setting up for his next shots, in case a second salvo was required.

Meanwhile, the pair of Mark-48s in the water swam slowly toward their preprogrammed navigational waypoints, both weapons still connected to the *Albany's* Mark-2 Combat Control System by thin fiber-optic wires that unreeled as the distance increased.

The waypoint for tube one's weapon was fifteen degrees to starboard of the target, currently designated as Master-One. The waypoint for the other weapon was fifteen degrees to port.

When the weapons reached their respective waypoints, the CCS would turn them both toward a carefully calculated lead-angle position near the target's bow, and then let them off the leash. The turbine engines would spin up to full RPMs, and the 48's would close in on the target at maximum attack speed. Or that was the plan, anyway.

The tactic was known as *simultaneous time-on-target*. If it was properly executed, the enemy submarine would suddenly find itself on the wrong end of two close-aboard torpedoes, converging at high speed from opposite directions.

Against any other submarine on the planet, an STOT attack could be devastating. Against a target capable of accelerating to three-hundred knots, its effectiveness was yet to be proven.

The tension between Ernie's shoulder blades ratcheted up a few more notches. If everything went according to plan, an unknown number of North Korean sailors were about to die horribly. If the plan *didn't* come off properly, it might be the *Albany's* sailors who were in for a messy ending.

And there were a *lot* of things that might go wrong. The wires could break on one (or both) of the Mark-48s, kicking the affected weapon automatically into search mode, and alerting the target. Or, slow-swim mode or not, the target might detect the turbine or blade noise of the incoming weapons. Or the target might catch a sniff of *Albany's* acoustic signature, and pump out a couple of supercav torpedoes to get the party started early. *Or....* Ernie could think of at least four or five more ways that the situation could go to shit.

But none of them seemed to be happening. At least not yet.

"How long till our weapons reach their waypoints?" the Skipper asked.

The Weapons Officer checked his screen. "About another six minutes, sir."

No one groaned aloud, which Ernie recognized as a sign of the crew's discipline and the quality of their training. Everyone hated this part of a slow swim attack. Your weapons took an eternity to creep into position, and every tick of the clock announced another endless second in which the engagement could turn against you.

But even slowed to a subjective crawl, time does continue to pass. After what felt like an hour, the weapons were five minutes from their waypoints. An hour after that, they were four minutes away. In another hour they were two minutes away. Then one minute. Then none.

"Go hot on both weapons!" the Skipper ordered.

"Weapons Officer, aye! Both weapons are hot!"

The tension between Ernie's shoulders began to relax a little. Maybe this was actually going to work. Maybe it was....

And *that's* when everything went to hell.

It started with the Sonar Supervisor's voice over the 29MC speakers. "Conn—Sonar. Hydrophone effects off the starboard bow! Bearing three-three-five, correlated to the current bearing of contact Master-One. Initial classification: supercavitating torpedo!"

Captain Townsend began immediately rapping out orders. "Helm, left thirty-degrees rudder! New course two-nine-five! All ahead flank! Diving Officer, make your depth eight-hundred feet! Weapons Officer, launch one noisemaker, and one mobile decoy!"

The deck of the control room tilted forward and to port as USS *Albany* heeled hard into the ordered dive and turn. The maneuver was executed amid a babble of half-shouted acknowledgements. Somewhere in the process, two muffled thumps announced the launch of the ordered countermeasures.

The noisemaker and decoy were not intended for the incoming torpedo, Ernie knew that. Supercavs move so fast that their own hydrodynamic noise makes the effective use of sonar impossible. The enemy supercav would never see the noisemaker or the mobile decoy. The Skipper was deploying the countermeasures to confuse the enemy submarine, in case it was lining the *Albany* up for a second shot.

The Sonar Supervisor's voice came over the 29MC again. "Conn—Sonar. Hydrophone effects now bearing three-three-seven! Master-One is showing pronounced zig!"

The enemy sub was maneuvering, probably pouring on the speed. That was no surprise, with a pair of 48 ADCAPs on its ass.

The important part of the report was the bearing to the incoming torpedo. Three-three-seven meant two degrees of right bearing drift. As a rule, a weapon that's going to hit you will maintain a CBDR alignment, short for *"Constant Bearing, Decreasing Range."* Meaning that the weapon is heading straight toward you and it's getting closer.

The incoming supercav wasn't maintaining constant bearing. It was showing some bearing drift. Not very much. Just a couple of degrees. But *some*.

Was it enough? Ernie didn't know. For an acoustic homing torpedo, two degrees was nowhere near enough bearing drift to cause a miss. For a straight running supercav? *Maybe*.

The 29MC came to life again. "Conn—Sonar. Hydrophone effects bearing three-three-nine!"

Bearing drift was up to four degrees now. Still not a lot, but four was better than two.

Someone started murmuring softly. It took a second or so for Ernie to recognize the quiet tumble of words as a prayer. He didn't look around for the source. He just hoped that the petitioner, whoever he was, had a good relationship with the big guy upstairs. Maybe good enough to get *all* of their asses out of this fix.

The enemy torpedo was close enough now to be heard with their bare ears, a rising jet engine shriek that reverberated through the hull at painful intensity. The sound escalated wildly in volume as the torpedo shot toward them at some ungodly speed.

In mere seconds, the noise reached a roaring ear-splitting crescendo that was as terrifying as it was deafening.

And then it was past, the jet engine wail receding as the enemy weapon reached its closest point of approach and began moving away.

How close had the deadly machine come to the *Albany's* hull? Twenty yards? Ten? Less than that?

The Skipper wasn't distracted by such details. "Sonar—Conn. What's the status of contact Master-One?"

The response lacked the Sonar Supervisor's usual gift for brevity. "Conn—Sonar. Master-One transitioned to supercav mode just a few seconds after our 48s went hot. He's still running north at high speed. I estimate triple digits, but it will take a couple of minutes to work out a decent calculation."

"Conn, aye. Keep a close watch for any sign of a course change. If the contact turns back to reengage, I need to know about it immediately."

"Conn—Sonar. Understood, sir. We'll stay on him, but I don't think he's coming back. We surprised him with our 48s. He's getting as far away from us as possible."

"Conn, aye."

Captain Townsend released his mike button and let out a long and careful breath. He turned toward Ernie with a look of total incredulity on his face, as though he couldn't quite believe that any of them were still alive. "Holy shit, COB, I don't know how we got out of that."

"I don't know either, sir," Ernie said. "But if I had to bet money, I'd say it was the dive that saved our butts."

"I gave about six different orders," the Skipper said. "Why do you think it was the dive that did the trick?"

"Reasonable assumption, sir," said Ernie. "The *Mahan* and the *Winterburn* were *Arleigh Burkes*. Gas turbine propulsion, plenty of speed, and they corner like sports cars. When they detected the incoming supercavs, I figure both ships must have done exactly what we did—kick up to flank, throw the rudder hard over, and dodge like hell. The only difference is, we were able to change position in *three* dimensions. Surface ships can only maneuver in *two*."

"You might be right," the Skipper said, "but I wouldn't want to count on it working twice."

Ernie said nothing.

The Skipper shook his head. "How do we sink this bastard, COB? That's our mission, but I don't have the foggiest notion of how to kill a submarine that can run circles around our fastest weapons."

"I don't know either, sir," said Ernie. He let the second half of his response go unspoken.

'And I have no idea how to keep this fucker from killing us.'

CHAPTER 48

SWIFT, SILENT, AND LETHAL:
A DEVELOPMENTAL HISTORY OF THE ATTACK SUBMARINE

(Excerpted from working notes presented to the National Institute for Strategic Analysis. Reprinted by permission of the author, David M. Hardy, Ph.D.)

In 1832, French engineer Brutus de Villeroi built a submarine, which he dubbed the *Nautilus*, possibly in reference to Fulton's earlier craft.

De Villeroi's *Nautilus* was 10 feet 6 inches long, with a submerged displacement of about six tons. Crewed by three men, she was propelled by "duck-foot paddles." The ballast system consisted of a lever and piston mechanism that's not clearly described in available writings.

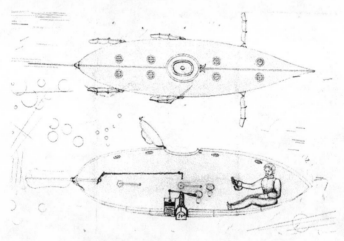

Brutus de Villeroi's Nautilus

The first demonstration occurred on August 13, 1832, off the coast of France. Observing were representatives of the French government, from

200

whom de Villeroi hoped to obtain financial support.

He later demonstrated the *Nautilus* for officials of the Kingdom of the Netherlands, in another failed bid for government backing.

Unable to find patronage in Europe, de Villeroi immigrated to the United States. In May of 1861, he launched a larger submarine, built for salvage operations. The sub was seized by the Philadelphia police as it sailed (half-submerged) up the Delaware River.

The first shots of the American Civil War had been fired only a few weeks earlier. Tensions and suspicions were at fever pitch. Concerned that this unfamiliar vessel might be a Confederate sabotage device, the Philadelphia police asked the U.S. Navy to investigate.

Commander Henry Hoff was dispatched from Naval Station Philadelphia to examine the submarine. Hoff's written report brought Brutus de Villeroi to the attention of senior U.S. Navy leadership, and led to the kind of government patronage he'd been seeking for decades.

On November 1, 1861, he signed a contract with the U.S. Navy to build a submarine for use against Confederate ironclads and other naval targets. Construction was subcontracted to a Philadelphia shipbuilding firm under the supervision of de Villeroi.

The new craft was 30 feet long and 8 feet in diameter, built from riveted iron plating, with thick circular glass ports penetrating the upper deck. Her hull was painted sea green, for camouflage and to minimize corrosion of the iron. Propulsion consisted of sixteen paddles to be operated by eight oarsmen.

Construction was delayed by disputes between de Villeroi and the Navy over modifications to his design. After weeks of arguments, de Villeroi was removed from the project and construction was completed without his supervision.

The unnamed submarine was launched on May 1, 1862, almost five months behind schedule. She was towed to the Navy shipyards at Hampton Roads for sea trials and testing. There, while moored alongside a paddlewheel steamer, the sub was spotted by a local newspaper reporter. He saw the rounded green hull floating with decks awash, and called her the '*Alligator*,' a nickname that stuck.

In August of 1862, the *Alligator* was given a crew and placed under the command of Lieutenant Thomas Selfridge. After a number of tests, Selfridge reported that the submarine was ungainly, underpowered, and "a failure."

The shipyard removed the paddles and replaced them with a screw propeller. This modification increased her speed to four knots, which was considered acceptable for the sub's anticipated duties.

Following a successful test that was observed by President Lincoln, Rear Admiral Samuel du Pont ordered the steamship, USS *Sumter*, to tow the *Alligator* to Port Royal, South Carolina, in preparation for the capture of Charleston.

Nineteenth-century artist's rendering of the Alligator

En route to Port Royal, the *Sumter* encountered bad weather. The *Alligator* sank in the storm, ending her career without a single combat engagement.

South of the Mason-Dixon Line, the Confederacy was working on submarine designs of its own.

In early 1863, private investors in the southern states financed the construction of a submarine known unofficially as the *Fish Boat*. Based on plans drawn up by marine engineers Horace L. Hunley, Baxter Watson and James R. McClintock, the sub was 40 feet long and carried a crew of eight men: seven to turn a hand-cranked propeller shaft, and one to command the vessel and steer.

The main hull was a cylinder formed from riveted iron plating, giving rise to later speculations that the submarine was adapted from a steam boiler. Engineering plans, construction notes, and modern forensic analysis have shown such speculations to be false. The iron cylinder was specifically designed to be a submarine hull.

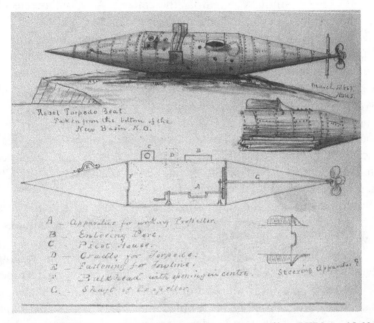

Sketch of the Pioneer by Ensign David M. Stauffer, USN — 1863

The *Fish Boat* was the third attempt by Hunley, Watson, and McClintock to develop an effective attack submarine. Both earlier attempts—the *Pioneer* in 1861, and the *American Diver* in 1862—had ended in failure.

When the *Fish Boat* was launched in July of 1863, its design incorporated lessons learned from the *Pioneer* and *American Diver*. Each end of the new submarine was fitted with ballast tanks that could be flooded or emptied by hand pumps. Additional ballast took the form of iron weights which could be jettisoned in an emergency.

The sub's hull had two watertight hatches, one forward and one aft, atop short conning towers. Each conning tower had portholes for visibility and triangular cutwaters to reduce drag and improve speed through the water. A pair of adjustable diving planes were mounted near the bow, connected to a control lever inside the hull.

Not long after launch, the *Fish Boat* completed her first operational trial, successfully attacking a coal flatboat in Mobile Bay. Afterward, the sub was shipped by rail to Charleston, South Carolina, for additional testing.

Upon arrival, she was commandeered by the Confederate Army and remained under military control thereafter. A Confederate Navy Lieutenant, John A. Payne, volunteered to serve as captain. Seven enlisted sailors from CSS *Chicora* and CSS *Palmetto State* signed on as crew.

On August 29, 1863, as the submarine was running on the surface, Lieutenant Payne accidentally stepped on the lever controlling the diving planes. The sub dove beneath the water with her hatches still open. Payne and two other men escaped the flooding craft, but the other five crewmen drowned.

Some historical accounts maintain that the fatal August 29 accident was caused by the wake of a passing ship, but this is not supported by Lieutenant Payne's report of the event, or by the testimony of Charles Hasker, one of the surviving crew members.

Still convinced that the submarine could operate as a viable weapon, the Confederate Navy raised the *Fish Boat* and returned the unlucky craft to service.

A second crew was recruited in Charleston and began training for combat. Although he was not part of the official crew, on October 15, 1863, Horace Hunley was allowed to assume command of the submarine for a training dive. Possibly the Confederate Navy hoped that Hunley's knowledge as one of the craft's designers might give him special insight into its proper operation. If so, that hope was not well founded. The submarine sank again, and this time there were no survivors.

The Confederate Navy raised the ill-fated craft yet again, recovering the bodies of Horace Hunley and the seven crewmembers.

Hunley was buried with full military ceremonies at Charleston's Magnolia Cemetery. The submarine he had helped design was renamed the *H. L. Hunley* in honor of his work and sacrifice for the Confederacy.

It should be noted that the sub was never formally commissioned. Consequently, the 'CSS' prefix cannot be accurately applied. Sources which refer to the submarine as the CSS *H. L. Hunley* are technically incorrect.

Her potential aside, the *Hunley* had so far proven to be much more dangerous to Confederate sailors than to their Union enemies. With this in mind, General P.G.T. Beauregard, in command of the defense of Charleston, issued orders forbidding further attempts to employ the submarine.

That might have put an end to the *Hunley's* service if it were not for Lieutenant George Dixon, a Confederate Army officer who believed that

the sub could indeed sink Union ships. Dixon requested an audience with
General Beauregard and made a persuasive case for being allowed to take
the submarine into action.

Painting of H. L. Hunley by Conrad Wise Chapman — 1864

The *Hunley* was again readied for service. In view of the submarine's
growing infamy, local sailors were understandably less eager to volunteer
for the third attempt. Lieutenant Dixon's determination was sufficient to
overcome the dark reputation surrounding the vessel, as he did manage to
assemble a crew, although the composition of personnel suggests that the
recruitment process may have been challenging. Instead of southern-born
American sailors, he ended up with a mix of soldiers, sailors, and
European merchant seamen.

On the night of February 17, 1864, after a training period of unknown
duration, Dixon took the *Hunley* into combat. The target was the USS
Housatonic, a sail and steam powered sloop with long-range guns. With
her firepower and speed, the *Housatonic* was the cornerstone of the
Union's blockade of Charleston Harbor. Sinking the sloop might weaken
the Union stranglehold enough to allow Confederate ships to run the
blockade.

At 8:45 p.m., under a bright moon and a calm sea, the *Hunley* made her
approach to the target. A lookout aboard the Union ship spotted the
approaching submarine and raised the alarm. Due to their construction and
positioning, the *Housatonic's* large guns could not be depressed far
enough to bear on the attacking vessel.

The *Hunley's* only weapon was a torpedo mounted to the submarine's
bow by a 16-foot metal spar. At the far end of that spar was a 135-pound

gunpowder bomb with a lanyard style trigger.

By all reports, the attack went perfectly. The *Hunley's* spar rammed into the *Housatonic's* starboard quarter, piercing the hull planking and dislodging the torpedo.

As planned, the *Hunley's* crew reversed the direction of their propeller, backing the submarine away from its wounded quarry. The torpedo remained tethered to the submarine by a 150-foot lanyard attached to the triggering device. When the sub had backed far enough away from the target, the lanyard went taught and pulled the triggering lever.

The torpedo detonated, sending USS *Housatonic* to the bottom of Charleston Harbor with a loss of five lives. Nearly the entire crew of the Union sloop escaped, either by scrambling into the ship's longboats, or by climbing the masts and rigging which extended above the water when the *Housatonic* settled on the shallow bottom.

Tactically, the attack was a success. The target was destroyed, and the most powerful ship in the Union's blockading force was eliminated. As a demonstration-of-concept, the sinking of the USS *Housatonic* proved that a submarine could destroy a fully armed warship.

This realization would go on to spur navies all over the world into action. The attack submarine was no longer a hypothetical exercise. It was real and lethal.

Only one factor detracted from the totality of the Confederate Navy's victory on that February night. The submarine *H. L. Hunley* was sunk with the loss of all hands sometime after carrying out their successful attack.

Although the sub has since been raised and examined by marine archeologists, forensic genealogists, and specialists in a diverse range of scientific fields, the cause of her loss is still unknown.

As of this writing, no one knows what killed Lieutenant George Dixon and the seven men who served under his command. No one knows how or why the *H. L. Hunley* joined her target in death on the bottom of Charleston Harbor.

All that can be said for certain is that this rudimentary Civil War vessel, with her manually operated propeller and her bomb-on-a-pole weapon system, was a harbinger of vastly greater carnage. Her inventors, Horace L. Hunley, Baxter Watson, and James R. McClintock, could have had no possible inkling of what they were unleashing on their unsuspecting world.

CHAPTER 49

"There's coffee on the sideboard," said Captain Heller. "Everybody grab a cup and fix it however you like it."

He was already seated at the wardroom table, a steaming mug positioned within easy reaching distance.

The others followed his recommendation and headed for the coffee urn, lining up (perhaps unconsciously) in order of seniority. The XO, Lieutenant Commander Diane Dubois, went first; followed by the ship's Combat Systems Officer, Lieutenant Boyd Wilkens; then the Undersea Warfare Officer, Ensign Todd Moore; with the sonar chief, STGC(SW) Michael Scott, bringing up the rear.

When all had doctored their cups to match their various preferences, they settled into chairs across the table from the commanding officer.

"First question...." said Heller. "When do we offload our guests?"

The XO stirred her coffee. "OPS has got that all arranged, Captain. We'll be receiving an MH-60S out of GITMO's Leeward Point Field at thirteen-hundred. They're bringing their own guard detachment to escort the prisoners. We'll do a quick hot pump to top off the helo's fuel tanks, and then they'll load up our prisoners and the interpreters. All guests should be off the ship well before fourteen-hundred."

"Good," Heller said. "Next question.... Has everyone read the after-action reports from the *Winterburn* and the *Albany*?"

All four heads nodded.

"Excellent," said Heller. "I thought we could take a few minutes to talk through what we know about all known encounters with the North Korean supercav sub, including our own. Sort of an informal brainstorming exercise, to see if there's anything we've been missing."

He looked across the table at the small group. "Okay, boys and girls, who's got something they want to share with the class?"

After several seconds, Chief Scott raised a finger. "I've been going over what happened with USS *Albany* yesterday, sir. I think it's pretty clear that the Korean submarine was taken by surprise when *Albany's* Mark-48s went hot. Before that moment, the enemy sub made no attempt to maneuver, or to launch weapons."

The assemblage waited for the chief to continue.

"That tells me," Chief Scott said, "that the *Albany* managed to sneak in fairly close without being detected. Not much of a shock, considering how quiet the 688 boats are. It's also consistent with estimated performance characteristics of most North Korean sonar sets. According to the latest Acoustic Intelligence summaries, their most advanced model is three or four generations down from the Chinese Type H/SQC-207, and even that's not anything to write home about."

"We don't know what kind of sonar they're using," said the Combat Systems Officer. "And we don't want to underestimate their capabilities. They've already demonstrated propulsion technologies that are well beyond anything we were expecting. How do we know they haven't made similar breakthroughs with their sonar equipment?"

"That's a possibility, sir," said the chief. "It's also possible that they've acquired high-end sonar gear somewhere on the international market. Maybe a German CSU 90, or a French S-CUBE suite, which is supposed to be pretty shit-hot. But I don't think they've done any of that."

"Why not?" asked the CSO.

"Because they haven't detected *us*," said the chief. "Remember, we tracked this contact on the 22nd of February, before the incident with USS *Mahan*. We saw no sign that it was alerted to our presence. Three days later, the contact fired on the *Mahan*, but it left us alone. We would have been easy pickings right then, but the North Korean sub acted like we weren't even there. Then we tracked the contact again on the 28th. It didn't shoot at us. It didn't maneuver. It didn't make the jump to light speed. It just went on its merry way without noticing us."

"You think that means we're invisible to this guy?" the XO asked.

Chief Scott shook his head. "No, ma'am. Any vessel can be detected under the right acoustic conditions. But we *are* significantly quieter than any of the earlier *Arleigh Burke* flights. I think that means we can probably get in a lot closer than other ships before our acoustic signature creeps above the detection threshold of whatever sonar they're using. Just like the *Albany* did."

Ensign Moore paused with coffee cup half-way to mouth. "Chief, your use of the word 'probably' is not filling me with confidence."

The chief gave his division officer a low-wattage smile. "Best I can do, sir. I could have our team run some counter-detection predictions, based on performance characteristics similar to the Type H/SQC-207 or the Type H/SQ2-262B. But whatever comes out will be an educated guess at best, and we'll still be stuck with *probably*."

"That might not be a bad idea," said the XO. "Run several sets of predictions using various sonar configurations that might plausibly be available to the North Koreans. Then take the worst-case as our assumed counter-detection range. It might come in handy if we're trying to develop tactics for sneaking up on this guy."

"I agree," said Captain Heller. "Which raises the next logical question. If we *can* manage to slip in close to this contact, what are we supposed to do when we get there?"

This led to a period of thoughtful silence, punctuated only by the shuffling of bodies in chairs and occasional sips from one coffee cup or another.

"It's all about the speed differential," said the CSO finally. "We don't have any weapons fast enough to catch this damned submarine. It can outrun Mark-48 ADCAPs. It can outrun our Mark-54s, whether we shoot them over-the-side, or throw them with ASROC. And every air-dropped ASW weapon in our arsenal is built around some variation of the 54, so helos and P-8s are no better off than we are."

"What about non-ASW weapons?" asked Ensign Moore. "How about regular aerial bombs? Get a fix on this guy, and have B-52s drop daisy cutters or bunker busters on his ass until he's just a hole in the water."

"I like how you're thinking," said the XO, "but I'm not sure that's practical. I've seen feasibility studies for a similar tactic in ASW chokepoints like the Strait of Hormuz. The likelihood of success is considered relatively high where the bottom depth is fifty fathoms or less, and the area is topographically enclosed to constrain the explosive force. Under those conditions, you get the shockwave reflecting off the bottom, the water hammer effect, and an overall magnification of destructive power. It doesn't work so well when the water gets deep and the topography opens out. You lose the bottom reverberation, and your shockwave gets bled off by spherical spreading and volume absorption. The probability of a kill falls off pretty rapidly."

"I haven't looked at a bathymetry chart in a while," said Captain Heller, "but I think the average bottom depth in the Caribbean is somewhere around sixteen-hundred fathoms. The topography is wide open. That doesn't sound like a good fit for the carpet bombing idea."

"I guess not, sir," said Ensign Moore.

The captain regarded the junior officer. "Don't let it bug you, Todd. That was a good idea. Definitely out of the box, and that's exactly what we're looking for. It doesn't fit our current tactical situation, but it's precisely the kind of thinking we need, so keep at it."

The ensign nodded. "Will do, sir."

"What about mines?" asked the Combat Systems Officer. "We could lay a minefield somewhere, and then lure the contact into it."

"Same basic problem," the captain said. "Bottom depth. You can't lay moored mines in nearly 10,000 feet of water, and I seriously doubt that SOUTHCOM will risk drifting mines in the Caribbean."

"So we're back to the speed differential," said Chief Scott. "I keep wondering if there's some way we can increase the speed of our weapons. When I say 'we,' I don't mean *us*, obviously. But what about Raytheon? They build the Mark-48 and the Mark-54. Maybe they've got something in R&D—a prototype or something—that can go fast enough to catch this guy. Sacrifice run time to crank the speed way up there. Something like that."

He shrugged. "I'm not a weapons engineer, but there's just *got* to be somebody somewhere working on this kind of thing."

His pronouncement triggered another interval of silence and coffee drinking.

It was a problem that none of them had ever expected to face. They had all studied, and trained, and honed their skills at using the current generation of weapons to maximum effect. Not one of them had ever considered the possibility that their weapons might be inadequate to the task.

Heller suspected that there were similar conversations taking place aboard USS *Albany*, at SOUTHCOM, in the Pentagon, in the White House Situation Room, and probably two dozen other places where military minds gathered to problem solve. He wondered if anyone in any of those other gatherings had the slightest clue of what to do.

His thoughts were interrupted by a strange sound from the least experienced member of the ASW team. He glanced over to see Ensign Moore with an odd look in his eyes.

"Todd? Have you got something?"

The ensign stared into space without responding.

Heller raised his voice a notch and tried again. "Are you still with us, Todd?"

The junior officer's eyes remained unfocused for another few seconds. Then he gave a little twitch and seemed to snap back to reality.

Heller smiled. "Did you take a little vacation there, Mr. Moore?"

The ensign lifted his coffee cup and then sat it back down without taking a drink. "Have you ever heard of a Sea Bat, sir?"

This brought confused looks from everyone at the table. Sea bats were fictional creatures, and a long running gag in the Navy. The stuff of bad practical jokes played on unsuspecting newbies. In a similar vein to mail buoys and relative bearing grease.

Before anyone could ask the ensign to elaborate on this strange turn of subject, he continued without prompting. "I was just thinking, Captain. We're running in circles trying to figure out how to make our weapons go faster. But what if going faster is not the answer? What if the real secret is to go slower? *Much* slower."

"You're going to need to explain that," said the XO.

"I will," said Ensign Moore.

And he did.

CHAPTER 50

Vice Admiral Matthew Cook held up a folder and flapped it in the direction of his Deputy Commander. "Have you seen this, Benny?"

Lieutenant General Benito Herrera eyed the fluttering folder and gave a noncommittal shrug. "I don't have on my soothsayer's hat today, sir. So you'll have to give me a hint regarding which particular '*this*' we're talking about."

"Flash traffic from USS *Bowie*, routed via Fourth Fleet. It's their proposed plan of action for going after that North Korean submarine."

Herrera nodded. "The Sea Bat thing? I've seen it. In fact, that was on my list of things to discuss with you this afternoon."

"Well, discuss away," said the admiral. "What do you think about it?"

"You know me," Herrera said. "I'm just a dumbass Air Force boy. I'm not qualified to render an opinion on all your fancy navular strategeries."

"Belay the dumb-shit routine," said Admiral Cook. "You're the sharpest tactical mind I know, Benny, and I want your opinion on this."

"I'm up in the air about it," said the general. "It's either the stupidest idea I've ever heard, or it's pure gold-plated genius. I honestly can't decide which."

The admiral tossed the folder onto a teetering pile of papers that littered his desk. "Neither can I. But my inclination is to approve the plan. Let them give it a try."

"You might as well, sir" said General Herrera. "Because the one thing we know for sure is that nothing else is working."

212

CHAPTER 51

NORTON DEEPWATER SYSTEMS, INC.
TORRANCE, CALIFORNIA
TUESDAY; 03 MARCH
5:26 PM PST

Rick Kramer almost let the call go to voicemail. He'd already sent his last emails of the workday and his laptop was in the final stages of the Windows shutdown sequence. Fifteen more seconds and he would have been out the door.

But it wasn't his ordinary desk phone that was ringing. It was the *other* phone, the one that belonged to the United States Navy, his company's largest client by far. As Corporate Liaison to the Navy, blowing off the call probably wasn't the smartest move he could make.

He dropped his backpack on the floor and picked up the telephone receiver. "Norton Deepwater, Rick Kramer speaking."

"Afternoon, Rick. Dan here. Sorry to catch you so late in the day, but I'm going to need you to go Secure."

'Dan' was Commander Daniel Dolan of the Naval Undersea Warfare Center in Newport, Rhode Island.

Rick made an effort to keep his voice cheerful and professional. "Will do, Commander. Give me a sec...."

He unlocked the left middle drawer of his desk, reached in and thumbed a six-digit combination into the cipher lock of a steel lockbox that was welded to the bottom of the drawer. The lockbox contained only one item: a Fortezza-Hyper crypto card.

He extracted the small rectangular circuit module and plugged it into a recess in the faceplate of the phone. After a brief string of low-pitched audio tones, the phone's 'SECURE' light winked on.

"We're green," he said.

"Thanks," said Commander Dolan. "I shouldn't need to remind you that this entire conversation will be classified."

"I understand," said Rick. Coming from anyone else, the reminder might have seemed vaguely insulting. They were having the conversation over an encrypted phone line; of *course* it was going to be classified. But he was accustomed to the naval officer's *measure-twice, cut-once* attitude. Commander Dolan was a man who left very little to chance.

"I want to ask about the Sea Bats you're working on for NOAA," the commander said. "You're building them with an acoustic sensor package for tracking marine mammals, right?"

"Yeah," said Rick. "Some of them."

"How many?"

"I don't have an exact figure," Rick said. "I can check the—"

The commander cut him off. "Give me a back-of-the-envelope estimate. We'll figure out exact numbers later."

"Only the ones with acoustic sensor packages?"

"That's right. I'm not interested in other configurations."

Rick considered for a few seconds. "I think it's around a hundred and thirty. Plus or minus ten or so."

"Okay. And how many are already built and ready for use?"

"I'm not sure," Rick said. "The contract calls for a two-phased delivery, and the first consignment isn't due until next month."

"Forget the schedule," Commander Dolan said. "How many are ready to go right now?"

Rick knew the answer to that off the top of his head. "None of them."

The line was silent for a very long time.

When the commander spoke again, the skepticism in his voice came through loud and clear. "*Not one?* You're delivering next month, and you haven't finished assembly on a *single* unit?"

"We've completed assembly on quite a few of them," Rick said. "But they're all still in testing. Not ready for delivery."

"Alright, let's try this again," said the commander. "How many units are in testing?"

Rick racked his brain for the number. "I don't know.... Maybe fifty or sixty?"

"Skip the testing," the commander said. "We don't have time for that. We'll take them as-is. Whatever per-unit cost you negotiated with NOAA, we'll match it, plus a reasonable fee for rush delivery. Crate up every assembled unit, and get them ready for air travel as soon as possible. I'll have our logistics team touch base with you to coordinate the pickup. Also, we'd like to borrow your best engineer for the Sea Bat. Somebody who knows the hardware and software inside and out. We'll be making a few mods to the units, and we need some help to get the details right. Tell them to pack for about a week, warm climate. We'll cover Per Diem, lodging, travel bonuses, and incidentals."

"Hold on just a minute there," Rick said. "I can't authorize this. We don't have a contract with the Navy for Sea Bats, and we *do* have a contract with NOAA. I can't just hand over equipment that belongs to somebody else. Besides, you know the law. This is not how high-dollar procurement works. There are about seventeen federal codes that prohibit you (or us) from doing business this way."

"The legal stuff is the least of our problems," said Commander Dolan. "And don't worry about NOAA; we'll smooth things over with them."

Rick stammered something meaningless, his brain struggling to comprehend how this low-profile project had jumped so wildly off the rails.

The commander was speaking again. "Your CEO is going to get a call from Admiral Cook at U.S. Southern Command in about fifteen minutes. Have him standing by a secure phone. And get your people started on crating up those Sea Bats. I don't mean tomorrow, Rick. I mean now."

There was a click and the green 'SECURE' light went dark.

The commander had hung up the phone.

CHAPTER 52

FOXY ROXY
NORTHEAST OF PUERTO SAMA, CUBA
TUESDAY; 03 MARCH
10:01 PM
TIME ZONE -5 'ROMEO'

"You're starting to luff a bit," Jon said. "Let your helm fall off a couple of degrees."

"I do *not* luff," said Sergeant Olivia Peary. "Especially not with a married man. Mama taught her girls better than that."

Jon chuckled at the lame joke and gestured toward the moonlit headsail. "See where your sail is starting to flap a little? That's called luffing. It means you're steering a tad too close into the wind. Ease the helm off a few degrees to port."

The Marine followed his instruction and the headsail went properly taut again. "What do you do on nights when there's no moon, and you can't see your sails?" she asked.

"You listen for it," Jon said. "And you get to know the feel of your boat. The *Roxy* will tell you all kinds of things, if you speak her language."

"How did you learn all this stuff?" Liv asked.

"My dad taught me," said Jon. "We had an old Catalina 27 when I was a kid. Held together by epoxy, duct tape, and barnacles. As soon as the weather got warm enough, Dad would take us out on the Chesapeake. So I sort of grew up on sailboats."

"And you taught Cassy?"

"Kind of. I showed her a few things. Then she read a couple of books, and—before I knew it—she was giving me a run for my money."

"Well she *is* a squid," said Liv. "Swab jockeys probably get lessons in boot camp or something."

Jon laughed. "Yeah, maybe. But you're picking it up pretty fast too. All of you guys are."

And they were. Except for a touch of queasy stomach from the man they called *Fris*, the four Marines were adjusting to life on the boat with

216

very few hiccoughs. Roxy—the dog, not the boat—had taken a liking to all of them. She didn't mind the crowding, and there was almost always someone close enough to scratch one of her favorite spots.

The Marines looked the part too. They had probably been selected—at least partially—for that very reason. With their suntans, laidback attitudes, and quick smiles, any of the four could pass for Florida boat bums.

Colonel Dawkins (or someone on his staff) had been wise to send two boy-girl pairs instead of four male Marines. Five men and a single woman on a sailboat would have attracted instant attention from any onlookers; but three couples gave the impression of friends on vacation together. Unthreatening, and not worthy of special notice.

The couples bit was an act, of course. Unless they were exceptionally good at concealing their feelings, neither of the Marine pairings had any actual romantic chemistry going on. They put on a convincing act when they were topside and within sight of shore: standing close together, holding hands, and exchanging flirty banter.

All of that stopped below decks, though. When they were out of sight down in the cabin, the playful lovey-dovey stuff vanished and they became four Jarheads on a mission.

Jon was continually fascinated by how their faces changed when they shifted into Jughead mode. Topside, they could be mistaken for a bunch of vacuous and over-privileged college students, spending their parents' money without a care between them. Down below, everything about the four seemed different, from their posture, to the set of their jaws, to the grim determination in their eyes.

Relieved of the need to play airhead tourists, they became visibly harder in affect. They spent most of their time memorizing maps of the Cuban countryside from a ruggedized data tablet, talking over the mission in low tones, or cleaning their weapons. There always seemed to be one or the other of them in the forepeak, where an open stretch of deck provided room for pushups, sit-ups, and crunches.

Jon wondered if his own transitions to Leatherneck mode had been this obvious. Maybe so. When it came time to throw down, you rolled up your sleeves and you put on your warrior face. As he'd heard Gunny Bachman say a hundred times, 'you get hardcore, or you get dead.'

These Marines looked like they knew how to get hardcore. The proof of that could only come when the bullets were flying, but they had all the right earmarks. If they were lucky, they might never find out how they would stand up under real combat conditions.

Jon had finally gotten their names straight, something he'd never been very good at with new people. His lack of skill in this area had not been much of a problem in the Corps, where everyone wore name tags or embroidered name tapes on their uniforms. But these newcomers had come aboard dressed in civies, without a tag or tape in the lot. So putting names with the faces had taken a deliberate effort on Jon's part, one that had eventually paid off.

The tall hatchet-faced man was Staff Sergeant Adam Webb, generally referred to by his last name. Webb was senior in rank, and in charge of the detachment.

Second in command was Sergeant Olivia Peary—vaguely Scandinavian looking, and about an inch shorter than Webb. She answered to Liv.

The shorter man was Corporal Sean Bisbee, who made up in muscle mass what he lacked in height. The others called him *Frisbee*, or just Fris. He had some prankster in him, a tendency that Webb worked to keep under a tight rein. Fris was the one slightly prone to seasickness, which probably also helped with keeping a lid on his practical joking.

The fourth—and smallest—member of the team was Corporal Elvie Lynch. Quiet and lean, with the greyhound musculature of a ballerina, and a thousand-yard stare that could probably kill a man with unshielded eyes. The other Marines called her as *Elf*, although Fris had referred to her as *Kegel* two or three times, until Webb took him aside for a private counseling session.

There was sure to be a story behind the Kegel thing, but Jon wasn't going to ask about it. He'd seen the hardening of Elf's features when the unwelcome nickname was used, and he figured that Fris was at dire risk of having his face kicked in by the female corporal.

Jon didn't doubt that she could do it, either. Fris was taller and more muscular than Elf, but she carried an aura that conveyed a willingness to endure great bodily harm in order to crush her enemies.

None of that was visible when the pair went topside. Out where they were potentially exposed to curious eyes, Elf gave every outward sign of attraction and affection for her make-believe boyfriend. She was clearly able to swallow her feelings and remain in-character. But Fris had better watch his mouth if he wanted to come out of this with all organs intact.

Jon was smiling at the thought when he realized that Liv was talking to him.

"Sorry," he said. "I was off in La La Land."

"Colonel Dawkins says you got the Star," said Liv.

"Classic case of being in the wrong place at the wrong time," Jon said. "And the Corps was handing out Bronzes like jelly beans that day. I was with some Marines who deserved the medal, but I wasn't one of them."

"That's not how Colonel D tells it..."

Jon sighed. "With all due respect to your colonel, he wasn't there. I *was*. And I know what I know."

"If you say so," said Liv. "But Cassy tells pretty much the exact same story."

"I usually try not to contradict my wife," Jon said, "but she wasn't there either. And—let's face it—squids are easily impressed."

"If you say so," Liv said again.

"I should relieve you at the helm," said Jon. "You need to lay below and catch a few hours of sleep. We'll be anchoring off Playa La Playita when the sun comes up. Then Cassy and I will get in some lazy civilian time while you kids go off and do your Marine thing."

"Aye-aye, Captain Bligh," Liv said. "I stand relieved."

Jon took her place at the wheel.

A minute later, she was through the companionway and into the cabin, leaving him alone with sky, and sea, and uninvited thoughts.

CHAPTER 53

Nathan Nguyen took another slug of caramel macchiato and trudged across the concrete apron behind the Navy commander, trying vainly to remember the man's name.

"You must be jet lagged to death," said the commander over his shoulder.

It was Dolan, or Roland, or something that sounded like that. The introductions had happened a little too quickly and Nathan was half asleep.

"Desynchronosis," he said to himself.

The commander flashed an ID card and walked past a pair of armed guards in camouflage uniforms through the partially open door of an unused aircraft hangar. "Could you repeat that? I didn't quite catch it."

Nathan followed into the cool semidarkness of the empty hangar. "Sorry," he muttered. "Talking to myself. Desynchronosis. The technical term for jet lag. It's also known as circadian dysrhythmia, but that usage is falling out of fashion with doctors."

"I didn't know that," said the commander.

And Nathan mentally kicked himself. Why did he have to say *every stupid thing* that popped into his head? These were serious and important people, and he must be coming across like a complete idiot.

The commander continued walking, crossing the open floor toward a steel door flanked by a second pair of guards in the far corner.

"Sorry," said Nathan again. "That's how my mind works. Interesting facts get filed away, and they pop up at random times."

Damn it! He was doing it *again*. Babbling like a moron.

"You must be exhausted," said the commander. "It's only a little after four a.m. by your internal clock. Did you get any sleep on the flight?"

"I don't sleep on aircraft," Nathan said. "Never have. Inner ear thing. Hyperkinesthesia."

Jesus! Was there any way to keep stupid nonsense from coming out of his mouth?

"Sorry to hear that," said the commander. "We may have to get you a coffee IV or something, because we're going to need your brain firing on all cylinders."

By then they had reached the door, and the commander was busy showing ID cards and paperwork to the two guards. Satisfied with whatever was printed on the documents, one of the guards pulled out a black cell phone, hit a speed dial key, and spoke in hushed tones.

After about five seconds, there was a harsh metallic buzzing sound and the steel door swung open on some type of powered actuator arm.

The commander went through, motioning for Nathan to follow.

They were half-way down a short hallway when the heavy door swung shut behind them with the clang of steel-on-steel, followed by a snap of automated deadbolts.

The door at the end of the hall was the ordinary interior sort. No automated opener this time. The commander turned the knob and held the door for Nathan to enter.

The area on the other side might have been a briefing room or a classroom. Several tables were pushed against the back wall and stacked with straight-backed metal office chairs.

Two tables had been left in the middle of the floor as a makeshift work area. On one of them was a partially disassembled Sea Bat glider, its disconnected components arranged in neat rows and carefully labeled. Nearby was a freestanding whiteboard, covered with annotations and rudimentary thumbnail sketches in blue, red, and black dry erase marker.

The other table held several cylindrical devices painted in dull gray or drab green, resembling aerosol cans of various sizes, with extraneous hardware attached. There was also a brick of yellow-green clay, wrapped in faintly greasy-looking translucent paper.

At the Sea Bat table stood two people, a man and a woman, both dressed in powder blue lab coats. At the other table stood a single man in a camouflage uniform.

"Let me introduce you to the team," said the commander. "This is Chief Ruben Goss, he's our EOD expert—"

Nathan was trying to listen, but he couldn't tear his eyes away from the greasy clay brick and the aerosol-looking devices. "Excuse me, are those things explosives?"

"These are mock-ups," said the man in uniform, "for working out the details of form and function. The real explosives come later."

Nathan drained the last of his caramel macchiato and looked around for somewhere to put the cup. There were no trash receptacles in sight, and neither of the tables seemed like a suitable place.

He clutched the cup to his chest like a cherished heirloom. "I'm not quite sure what we're going to be doing here."

"Essentially," said the commander, "the plan is to turn your Sea Bats into antisubmarine weapons."

"I don't understand," Nathan said. "Submarines are fast. These things are slow. I mean *really* slow."

"That's the idea," said the commander.

He glanced down at Nathan's empty cup. "Can we get you some more Starbucks?"

CHAPTER 54

"This is not a bad way to live," Cassy said.

Jon nodded absently without replying.

The shade canvas was rigged and both Clarks were laid out in folding chairs on the deck above the cabin, sipping at cans of Cristal and enjoying the morning breeze. Part of the vacation act: lazy and self-absorbed.

Roxy, who hadn't been briefed on how to behave, was performing splendidly without instruction. At the moment, the Staffordshire Terrier was sprawled in the shade aft of the mast—limbs akimbo—with a relaxed abandon that was almost obscene to witness.

Jon took a pull on his cold Cuban beer, purchased—in true tourist fashion—from three boys in a red-painted plywood boat with an outboard motor built from odds and ends. Even after haggling, the price had probably been about four times the already-inflated rate for Yumas. Still, the beer was good and the delivery had been convenient, so Jon was prepared to accept a touch of friendly price gouging. Besides, the United States Marine Corps was picking up the tab for this trip, so it wasn't his money anyway.

He had no idea how the Marines at GITMO had gotten their hands on the *despacho de navegacion-costera* (coastwise cruising permit) or the *licencia de excepción* (license of exception) that allowed the *Foxy Roxy* to make landfall outside the usual ports of entry. For that matter, he wasn't sure how they'd managed to get the proper passport stamps either. Possibly the U.S. State Department had pulled a few strings, or else someone had dropped a fat bribe on the desk of an official in the Cuban government.

However it had been arranged, the travel documents had been perfectly acceptable to the Guarda Frontera officer who had motored out to meet the

223

sailboat. The man had smiled, examined the papers, scribbled initials in three or four places, and accepted a small gift of cash for his trouble.

This was a rare opportunity, and Jon was sorry that he and Cassy couldn't take advantage of it. They could have gone ashore in the dinghy, browsed the neighborhood shops, and sampled food from street vendors and outdoor restaurants.

But the Marines had taken the dinghy in to the beach, and *they* were the ones playing tourist. Now, they were out among the people of the tiny town, roaming the streets, laughing, snapping selfies, and looking nothing at all like the military scouting detachment they were. Giving no hint that their brightly colored nylon backpacks contained anything more sinister than sunscreen, spare socks, and bottled water.

The plan called for the Marines to split up into pairs after landfall, with each "couple" going its own way to explore the local sights. This division of forces was supposed to make their movements more difficult to track. Both couples would follow arbitrary routes, occasionally bumping into each other when their random wanderings happened to converge at one place or another. Each unscheduled meeting would be marked by feigned surprise, overloud jokes, and high-fives or fist bumps—the typical social rituals of vacationing gringos.

They'd been gone about two and a half hours; playing the part of noisy sightseers the entire time. When Webb decided that they had adequately satisfied the curiosity of the locals, he and Liv would take a leisurely stroll out of town on one of the dirt roads that wound into the countryside. Specifically, the road at the western edge of town, which just happened to lead past a certain wooded area. After they were far enough out of sight to be unobserved, they'd slip quietly off the road and enter the woods.

Elf and Fris would remain in town, moving around and continuing to establish the presence of boisterous wandering tourists.

Jon pushed his Ray-Bans farther up the bridge of his nose and watched a squadron of seagulls ride the updrafts from the narrow strip of shingle beach. He never took the sunglasses off during daylight hours, not even in the cabin or under the shade canvas. His vision was getting better by the hour and the afterimages of the blast were nearly gone, but the Hospital Corpsman in Cassy was never very far from the surface. She'd be all over him in a second if he showed any slackening in his eye care routine.

"You want to be out there with them," she said.

Jon was watching the gulls and only half listening. "Huh?"

"That's where your head is at right now," Cassy said. "Out in the field with the Four Horsemen."

"They're on foot," Jon said.

Cassy scissored a leg sideways and lightly kicked him in the ankle. "Fine, asshole. The Four Pedestrians of the Apocalypse. And you know what I mean. You want to be out there with them."

He shook his head. "Ancient history, Cass. I'm not a Marine anymore, and I have no desire to go back. That's someone else's job now."

"There's no such thing as an ex-Marine," Cassy said. "You were the one who told me that."

Jon took another swallow of the Cristal. The can was sweaty in his hand. The beer was starting to lose its crisp edge. Soon, it would be cool instead of cold. The last of it would be gone before cool gave way to warm.

"Tell me what you're thinking," said Cassy.

Jon lowered the beer can. "I'm thinking... that we should have asked those local boys to bring us some ice."

"No you're not," said Cassy. "In your head, you're out on maneuvers with the Four Pedestrians. You *know* you are."

"Maneuvers are training exercises," said Jon. "What those Marines are doing is real world. Not a simulation. Not an exercise."

This earned him another light kick in the ankle. "Why are you dodging the point?"

"I'm not dodging anything. I don't even know what the point is."

Cassy let her extended leg drop back into the webbing of the lounge chair with exaggerated force. "The point is that you're morphing back into a Jarhead. Just these couple of days around the Four Pedestrians, and you're getting the old taste in your mouth. Don't tell me you're not."

"I'm *not*," Jon said. "*Really* I'm not. That part of my life is over, and I don't want to go back. I've had enough fear and enough pain and enough regret for two lifetimes. Trust me, I don't need any more."

"I know you don't miss the bad parts," Cassy said. "Nobody would miss some of the ugly shit you went through, and remember that I saw a piece of it. At least the aftermath. But I've been watching you since our Jarhead visitors first came aboard. There's still some of Staff Sergeant Clark in you, Jonnie. I can see him. He's in there, doing the seven-count manual of arms inside your head, even if you won't admit it."

"I don't think so," Jon said. "If I was yearning for the old days, I think I'd know it. And I'm not feeling any regrets for what I left behind."

"Not even a little bit?"

"Not even a fraction of a little bit," he said. "None. Not a shred."

But he was lying, and neither one of them knew why.

⚓ ⚓ ⚓

Scout Detachment Alpha:

The unit in Liv Peary's hand was a Rockwell Collins AN/PSN-13 Defense Advanced GPS Receiver (DAGR), known colloquially among America's military services as a "dagger." In standard configuration, daggers were matte green and grey in color, but some clever soul at GITMO had wrapped this one in bright fuchsia neoprene to make it resemble a cell phone. The effectiveness of the deception was somewhat limited by the size of the unit. It was larger than most mobile phones, and significantly thicker than any models on the commercial market, a difference that could best be disguised by keeping the thing out of sight as much as possible.

Real cell phones require communication with cellular service nodes to establish a GPS fix. This unit linked directly to the Global Positioning System satellites, eliminating the need for cell towers, which were not at all common in the less developed parts of Cuba.

The average time-to-fix specification for the unit was listed as under twenty-two seconds. This one could generally sync up and provide a location fix in less than half that time.

Liv got a quick look at the screen, memorized the coordinates, and stuffed the unit back into her pocket. "About five hundred more yards," she said, "then we should think about leaving the road."

She eyed the terrain ahead and did a visual estimate. "Maybe where that tree is with all the red blossoms."

"Sounds good," Webb said.

He was on her left side, matching his pace to hers and holding her hand as they walked. Even out here in the boonies, it was safer to keep up the cuddly tourist act, in case someone in the woods or the cane fields had them in line-of-sight.

As they reached the indicated tree, Liv bent down and pretended to check her shoelaces while Webb took a final look around. "I think we're good," he said.

Liv stood up and the two Marines slipped into the trees and began working their way west.

When they could no longer see the road, they paused to make changes to their clothing. Bright colored outerwear went into their backpacks, and darker more subdued replacements came out. Items that might conceivably be worn by casual travelers, but less visible against the earthy color palette of the forest.

This was a tradeoff that had been discussed at-length with Colonel Dawkins and his planning staff. The sightseer charade was useful for penetrating Cuban territory, and it seemed to be working so far. But the clothing styles and colors necessary to maintain the tourist look were not very suitable for concealment in the wooded areas and cane breaks where the North Korean missile sites were supposedly hidden.

Webb had suggested packing cammies in the backpacks, for use when the scouts got into precisely this situation. But that was another part of the tradeoff. Americans discovered wandering around the backwoods in civies might put on a convincing performance as tourists who had lost their way. If they were caught wearing military camouflage, all semblance of pretense would be lost. Instead of having a chance to potentially talk their way out of the mess, they'd either be arrested or shot, neither of which were options with exciting career opportunities.

Which was how Webb and Liv ended up skulking through the undergrowth of Las Tunas province in clothes that were too conspicuous for their comfort.

They moved slowly and carefully, trying to step either on bare ground, or on leaves that were damp and turning to mulch. The crunch of a dried leaf under foot, or the sound of a snapping twig could carry a long way in the still air under the forest canopy.

When they'd gone a mile or so, Liv located a clearing and took advantage of open sky to grab an updated GPS fix. With the interference of the surrounding trees, the dagger's sync time was considerably longer than twenty-two seconds, but the screen eventually coughed up the current coordinates.

Point Yellow, the estimated position of the missile site, was approximately a half-mile farther in. If the drone surveillance pukes were correct and there *was* a missile site in this area, Webb and Liv could expect to encounter the guard force or missile crew any time now.

They slowed their progress even more, moving with extreme caution, watching and listening before each incremental advance toward the target coordinates.

The orders did not require the scouts to reach the missile site, or even to lay eyes on all of the launchers. Visual identification of a single launch vehicle would be enough. If that couldn't be managed, a positive sighting of uniformed North Korean personnel was a less preferred (but acceptable) substitute, especially if they were seen carrying or operating military hardware. Anything that could confirm the presence of missiles at Point Yellow.

Webb was working his way around the bole of a cottonwood tree when Liv laid a hand on his wrist to still him.

He froze immediately, trying his best to breathe without any sound at all.

When Liv knew that she had his attention, she pointed toward something about five degrees right of their line of advance.

Webb scanned the indicated direction for several seconds before he spotted it. A dark greenish black shape on the far side of a thicket of bushes. The thing was mostly obscured by leaves, but it was large and appeared to be made of metal.

His first thought was a launcher truck, one of the transporter erector vehicles they'd seen images of in the mission briefing. And maybe that's what it was, but his team hadn't been deployed to report on *maybes*.

He wanted to move in closer, get a better look, and a positive ID for whatever the thing was. A year or two earlier, he might have done that, and let his desire for personal involvement get in the way of making the right tactical decision. He was smarter than that now.

The truth was that Liv Peary was better suited for the task. She moved more quietly, and her eyesight was a little sharper than his. Not much, but possibly enough to make a difference.

Webb swallowed his personal pride and gave Liv the signal to close in.

She covered the fifty yards at a snail's pace. If she made a sound, it never reached Webb's ears.

Slowly she reduced the distance by half, and then reduced it by half again.

From a vantage behind a tree, she peered into the undergrowth for half a minute. And then she began a slow creep back to Webb's position.

When she was an arm's length away, she came in closer and put her lips next to Webb's ear. Her voice was barely audible. "False alarm. Old abandoned truck. No wheels. Looks like it used to be a campsite."

Webb nodded, but didn't speak. The presence of an old truck didn't necessarily prove the absence of missile launchers.

They crept forward together, until he was at an angle and distance to see for himself. Sure enough, it was an ancient deuce and a half truck. Nineteen fifties, or maybe even forties. True to Cuban tradition and mechanical ingenuity, it had long ago been stripped of all useful parts.

There were also some old corrugated tin sheets tossed around at random, like playing cards dropped on the floor. Lying half-buried in the dank leaf mulch. Rusted through, black with mold and the final stages of oxidation.

This was what the surveillance drones had cued on. Heat trapping from the old truck and the vaguely rectangular silhouettes of the discarded tin sheeting. Thermal images of obviously manmade shapes bleeding through the tree canopy.

Still, there was no reason to let down his guard now.

He motioned for Liv to continue her creeping search. He followed her, and they both combed the area, moving cautiously and quietly.

At last, Liv shot him an inquiring look and he nodded. "It's a bust," he said, speaking aloud for the first time since entering the woods.

"Shit," said Liv. "I really thought we were on to something."

"So did I," said Webb. "But there's no reason to stick around here. Let's head back."

The trip out of the forest was much faster, now that they no longer had to move in silence.

When they got to the road, Webb reached out to hold Liv's hand. He put on a smile that he definitely wasn't feeling. "Happy faces," he said. "We are happy tourists, doing happy tourist things."

Liv squeezed his hand and put on her own fake smile. "Happy faces," she repeated.

They walked down the road toward the town of Playa La Playita, laughing, holding hands, and looking very much like a carefree little couple.

Webb was already mentally composing the report he would make over the satellite phone when they got back to the *Foxy Roxy*.

Point Yellow was a false alarm. Wherever the North Korean missiles were, they sure as hell weren't here."

CHAPTER 55

SWIFT, SILENT, AND LETHAL:
A DEVELOPMENTAL HISTORY OF THE ATTACK SUBMARINE

(Excerpted from working notes presented to the National Institute for Strategic Analysis. Reprinted by permission of the author, David M. Hardy, Ph.D.)

While Horace Hunley and his associates were learning from their early failures in the American South, on the far side of the Atlantic, a Bavarian inventor and engineer named Wilhelm Bauer was adding to the composite knowledge of submarine technology with his own string of failures.

Bauer was an artillery engineer in the Bavarian Army. After witnessing his country's troops surrender the German state of Schleswig-Holstein to Denmark following a prolonged siege, he was impressed by the Danish Navy's effective blockade of the Prussian coastline.

He left the Bavarian Army to build a submarine, which he called the *Brandtaucher* (Fire Diver). His low military rank and lack of social standing made it hard to attract investors to finance his design. Eventually he developed a working miniature of the submarine and a series of successful demonstrations convinced government sponsors to fund construction at full scale.

Although the hull form of the *Brandtaucher* was unusual, the mechanics of the submarine were similar to other designs of the period. The only significant departure was a hand-spun flywheel propulsion mechanism in place of the more common hand-cranked shaft. This difference was not enough to make the craft seaworthy.

The *Brandtaucher* sank during a test dive near the port city of Kiel. Trapped on the bottom of the harbor for six hours, Bauer and his crew were finally able to escape when enough water had leaked into the crippled submarine to equalize surrounding water pressure. At that point it became possible for Bauer and his men to open the hatch and swim to the surface.

Bauer's next submarine, the *Seeteufel* (Sea Devil), was financed by the grand prince of St. Petersburg, Russia. The design was vastly superior to the *Brandtaucher*, and the *Seeteufel* is known to have made more than 130 successful dives before it also sank.

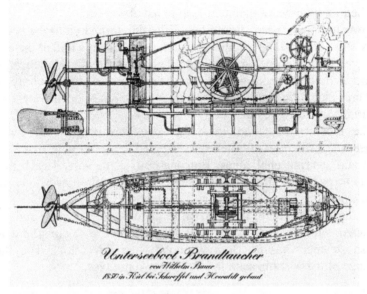

Brandtaucher design — 1850

Once again, Bauer and his crew were able to escape. It was after this second major failure that he began advocating for a propulsion mechanism to replace human power. He became fixated on building a submarine powered by an internal combustion engine.

At roughly the same time, the French Navy fielded the first submarine that was not reliant on human power. The *Plongeur* was equipped with a reciprocating engine which drew compressed air from 23 tanks at a pressure of approximately 180psi. The *Plongeur's* promise on the drawing boards did not translate into practicality. The French submarine was nearly unmanageable when submerged, with a top speed that disappointing.

Undeterred by the lackluster performance of his French competitors, Bauer continued to advocate for internal combustion engines in submarine propulsion. He spent more than a decade trying (and failing) to find a government sponsor for the idea.

In 1866, two years after Bauer began his fruitless quest for a new kind of submarine—and also two years after the *Hunley's* successful attack against USS *Housatonic*—a British-born naval engineer named Robert Whitehead built the first self-propelled torpedo.

Whitehead called his invention the automotive torpedo or locomotive torpedo. Supporters and critics tended to ignore his chosen titles and insisted on calling it the Whitehead torpedo. By any name, the self-propelled weapon was a quantum leap in naval warfare.

It was no longer necessary to tow a floating torpedo into the keel of an enemy ship, or ram the weapon against the target ship's hull at the end of a long spar. With a propeller powered by compressed air, Whitehead's new torpedo could be aimed toward the target and released to run on its own. It could cross hundreds (and later thousands) of yards of open water to reach and kill the intended vessel.

Like most new technologies, this one was plagued by numerous engineering difficulties. Whitehead struggled for years with depth control issues and steering challenges. But one-by-one, he solved each problem and his torpedoes continued to increase in range, firepower, and tactical effectiveness.

On January 25, 1878, the Russian torpedo boats, *Tchesma* and *Sinope*, conducted simultaneous Whitehead torpedo attacks against the armed Turkish steamer *Intibah*. Both weapons were direct hits. The flaming wreckage of the warship sank in less than two minutes.

A Whitehead Torpedo — 1888

After the sinking of the *Intibah*—and several other unlucky vessels that followed over the next few years—the words *automotive*, *locomotive*, and *Whitehead* were dropped from use. The weapon became known as the *torpedo*, with no qualifiers necessary.

It's clear from Whitehead's own writings that he considered his torpedo to be a surface warfare weapon: to be launched by surface vessels against other surface vessels. He had no way of knowing that his invention would rapidly transform submarines from mechanical curiosities into viable engines of destruction.

In 1875, three years before Whitehead's torpedoes sank the Turkish warship *Intibah*, an Irish engineer named John Philip Holland, Jr. submitted plans to the U.S. Navy for a submarine to be powered by an internal combustion engine. The Navy rejected the design as "unworkable" and Holland was forced to look elsewhere for backing.

A recent immigrant to the United States, he had contacts within the Fenian Brotherhood, an organization dedicated to establishing a free Irish Republic. The brotherhood agreed to fund construction of the *Holland I*, in hopes of using the submarine against the British Navy in a battle for Ireland's independence.

The vessel was launched on May 22, 1878, in Paterson, New Jersey. It was 14 feet long and was powered by a 4 horsepower Brayton engine connected to a single screw.

The operator was Holland himself. After several partial tests, he took the *Holland I* out for a full trial on June 6, 1878. The submarine ran on the surface at approximately 3.5 knots before submerging to a depth of twelve feet for an extended dive.

Overall, Holland was pleased with the submarine's performance, but persistent engine problems ultimately caused him to abandon the design. He stripped the craft of all usable equipment and scuttled the hull in the Passaic River.

Holland's next submarine, a three-man model called the *Holland II*, was also financed by the Fenian Brotherhood.

Unlike the boxy *Holland I*, the new submarine had a cigar shaped hull, tapered at both ends, with cruciform control fins at the stern—all features prominent in Whitehead's torpedoes.

A 15 horsepower Brayton engine overcame many of the propulsion shortfalls of the earlier prototype and the *Holland II* had one additional feature of note: a nine-inch pneumatic gun mounted along the centerline.

Engine power and reliability were satisfactory and the pneumatic gun was test-fired successfully a number of times, but Holland wasn't content with the sub's handling characteristics. Steering and depth control were not responsive enough to meet his self-imposed standards, so he built a scaled-down model, the *Holland III*, to experiment with alternative control mechanisms.

Work on the *Holland II* and *Holland III* came to a halt in November of

1883, when both submarines were stolen from their mooring place by the Fenian Brotherhood, following a dispute with John Holland over financial matters.

While both submarines were being towed up the East River, the *Holland III* began taking on water, possibly through an open hatch. The tow lines gave way and the sub quickly sank.

The *Holland II* was towed to New Haven, Connecticut, where the Fenian Brotherhood discovered that no one but John Holland knew how to operate the craft. The brotherhood approached him for help, presumably offering him a chance to continue working with his invention. Holland refused. After trying unsuccessfully to sell the submarine, the Fenian Brotherhood had the *Holland II* hauled out of the water and stored in a shed on the Mill River.

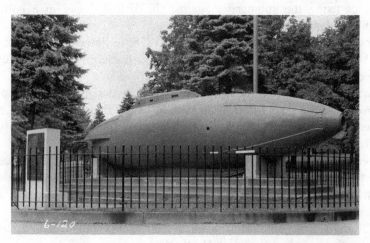

Holland II with pneumatic bow gun visible
(Photo by Nathaniel Ewan, Library of Congress — 1936)

Over the next few years, Holland continued honing his designs, developing two more experimental submarines in the process, predictably named the *Holland IV* and the *Holland V*.

His major breakthrough occurred on May 17, 1897, with the launch of the *Holland VI*, a privately funded submarine which incorporated all of his accumulated engineering knowledge. A 45 horsepower gasoline engine gave the submarine a top speed of 6 knots when running on the surface. For submerged operations, it was propelled at 5.5 knots by an electric motor connected to a battery.

The *Holland VI* had an operating range of 200 nautical miles when surfaced and 30 nautical miles submerged at depths of up to 75 feet. It was the first submarine capable of traveling extended distances under water, as well as the first to combine electric motors for submerged travel with internal combustion engines for use on the surface.

In addition to ballast and trim tanks for precision depth control, the sub was equipped with a conning tower, control planes, and many other features that would become regular components of submarine engineering for more than a century.

Armament consisted of a reloadable 18-inch torpedo tube and a pneumatic gun mounted in the bow. A second pneumatic gun in the stern was removed to make room for an improved engine exhaust system.

After naval observers witnessed a series of successful dives, the U.S. Navy purchased the *Holland VI* on April 11, 1900. Following six months of rigorous testing, the submarine was formally commissioned as the USS *Holland* on October 12th of that year. Her hull designation was *SS-1*, a numbering convention that the Navy maintains to this day.

Impressed with their first functional attack submarine, the Navy ordered six more subs of the same type. John Holland's newly-founded Electric Boat Company geared up to meet the demand.

USS Holland and crew at the U.S. Naval Academy (c. 1901)

Holland's design was quickly adapted by the British Royal Navy and the Japanese Imperial Navy, and they were not the only nations entering the race for undersea warfare.

In 1903 the *Friedrich Krupp Germaniawerft* dockyard in Kiel, Germany launched the *Forelle*, which is widely regarded as that country's first fully functional submarine. Powered by a kerosene engine and armed with a single torpedo tube, the *Forelle* was intended for the German Imperial Navy. When the German Navy failed to show interest, Krupp sold the submarine to Russia for use in the Russo-Japanese War.

Krupp's next submarine, was designated as the *SM U-1*, where the 'U' stood for *unterseeboot* (undersea boat). As Germany surged forward in the manufacture and deployment of attack submarines, the term unterseeboot was quickly shortened and Anglicized to *U-boat*.

The German Imperial Navy purchased the *SM U-1* and formally commissioned it as a warship on December 14, 1906. A larger follow-on model, the *SM U-2*, was armed with two torpedo tubes instead of one. This new more powerful U-boat was commissioned in 1908, and it triggered an avalanche of German attack submarine construction.

Four years later, the German Imperial Navy had 48 submarines of 13 different classes either in service or under construction.

Then came the event that spurred these machines into action. On June 28, 1914, Austrian Archduke Francis Ferdinand and his wife, Sophie Maria, were gunned down in the Bosnian capital of Sarajevo.

A month after his assassination, Austria-Hungary declared war on Serbia. Russia mobilized in support of Serbia, after which Germany invaded Belgium and Luxembourg and began moving towards France. World War I had begun, and the hour of the submarine had come at last.

Within weeks, Germany's U-boats achieved dominance of the seas surrounding Europe, stalking Allied warships and cargo ships, and sinking them at will.

The submarine became an instrument of terror. The U-boat captains of the Imperial German Navy raked their enemies with salvos of deadly torpedoes, spreading fire and destruction wherever they went. The bottoms of the North Sea and East Atlantic Ocean were transformed into graveyards for broken ships and the bodies of uncounted sailors.

From its position on the far side of the Atlantic, the United States, adopted a policy of strict isolationism. That changed on May 7, 1915, when a German U-boat torpedoed the British ocean liner *Lusitania*. Among the passengers killed in the attack were 123 American citizens.

Fueled by a rising demand for revenge, the United States entered the fight and the scope of the conflict became global. Before the First World War ended, the death toll would top 20 million, with the number of wounded reaching almost as high. But even this—the bloodiest conflict in the history of the planet—was only the beginning.

The interval between the end of that war and the start of the next was not a time of healing and peace. It was a respite in which the battered militaries of the world armed themselves for an even greater battle.

By the start of the Second World War, attack submarines were faster, deeper diving, longer ranged, more powerful, and many times more lethal. They would become still more deadly throughout the war, and in all the decades to follow.

The ship-devouring man-killing sea monsters of ancient myth had become real, and we had built them ourselves.

CHAPTER 56

Chaz Bradley signed the bottom of the document, ending the signature with his customary flourish. "That wraps up the Counterterrorism Summit, at least for the moment."

He closed the document folder and handed it back to White House Chief of Staff Jacqueline Mayfield. "What else have you got for me, Jackie?"

The chief of staff shuffled the folder to the bottom of a short stack and opened the one on top. "Looks like... the first draft of your press remarks for the oil spill in Prince William Sound."

Chaz waved the folder away. "I don't want to look at that yet. What's next?"

The rejected folder went to the bottom of the stack and another one was opened. "Let's see," said Jackie. "We've got... the State Department's latest markup of the Malaysia Free Trade Agreement."

Chaz accepted the new folder and rocked back in his chair. "How many times are we going to have to do this one?"

Jackie gave him a wan smile. "As many times as it takes, Mr. President. We've got to get this thing figured out; Malaysia is our nineteenth largest trading partner."

"You think that by itself would be enough to get their attention," Chaz said. "Before Muhyiddin Yassin put the brakes on negotiations in 2009, Malaysia was our *tenth* largest trading partner. Now they're down to number nineteen and still falling. While they've been busy playing the protectionism game, they've lost trade share to Brazil, India, the Netherlands, Italy.... Even Belgium is kicking their butts."

"I'm sure they're trying to do the right thing for their people, sir."

"Well they're going about it a funny way," said Chaz. "Because we're still their number *one* trading partner. Which means that the people who are mostly getting hurt by this are the Malaysians themselves."

"That's not something we can fix," Jackie said.

"I suppose not," said Chaz, and turned his eyes to the red-lined document.

His reading was interrupted by the opening of the door.

There were only a handful of people who could walk into the President's study unannounced. National Security Advisor Frank Cerney was one of them.

He closed the door behind himself and nodded in greeting. "Afternoon, Mr. President. Jackie. Can I have a moment of your time, sir?"

"That depends," said Chaz. "Is it gonna be something more interesting than the Malaysia Free Trade Agreement?"

Cerney smiled. "That's not my place to say, sir." He held out a folder. Not the blue embossed leatherette of a presidential briefing binder, but white cardboard edged with diagonal red stripes.

Chaz laid the trade notes on his desk and accepted the offered folder. "An update on the Cuba situation, Frank?"

"Two updates," said the national security advisor. "First, a P-8 Poseidon ASW aircraft out of Jacksonville detected and attacked the North Korean submarine about an hour ago. The engagement occurred northeast of the Cayman Islands, not quite two hundred nautical miles from the previous last known encounter with the sub."

"That thing gets around," said Chaz.

"Yes it does, sir. Literally like nothing anyone has ever seen before."

Chaz flipped up the cover sheet and looked at the after-action summary. "Holy cow! They dropped six torpedoes on this thing?"

"That's right, Mr. President. Six Mark-54s, all with fair-to-good placement. Against a normal target, any one of those weapons would have gotten a kill."

"Meaning that we didn't get any hits?"

"No hits, sir. Just like all previous engagements, our torpedoes were able to acquire the target, but they couldn't catch the submarine at supercav speed."

"Well, we're consistent," said Chaz. "We've got that much going for us."

He thumbed to the next tab in the folder. "Tell me that your second item is good news."

"Maybe *partial* good news, sir," said the national security advisor. "The Marine Corps Security Force Company out of Guantanamo has successfully inserted their scouting team into Cuba. They're checking out some of the five potential missile sites identified by satellite imagery and drone surveillance."

"That sounds promising to me," said the chief of staff. "What's the not-so-good part?"

"The report just came in from the first potential site, designated as Point Yellow. It's negative. Our Marines crawled all over the area. No missile launchers."

"Not the news I was hoping for," said Chaz.

He closed the folder and tossed it onto his desk. "We can't kill this damned submarine, and we don't have confirmed locations for *any* of the missile sites. Congratulations, Frank. You've somehow managed to turn the Malaysian trade mess into the high point of my day."

"Mr. President, it's not as bad as it sounds," said Cerney. "Point Yellow had the lowest confidence rating of any of the potential sites by a wide margin. Also, it was the only one that didn't correspond to the rough coordinates provided by Major Ri."

"Give us some calibration," said Chaz. "What was the confidence level for the site that turned out to be a false alarm?"

"The National Reconnaissance Office rated Point Yellow at sixty-two percent."

"And the other four locations?"

As usual, Cerney had come prepared. "Point Red and Point Blue are both rated at ninety-six percent plus. The Joint Chiefs believe that's high enough to justify suppressive bombing or missile strikes, and I concur. So does the Secretary of Defense."

"We'll talk about that," said Chaz. "What about the other two sites?"

Again, the national security advisor had the numbers ready. "The NRO rates Point Green at seventy-three percent confidence, and Point Orange at seventy-one."

"That's better than a one-in-four chance of being wrong," said Chaz. "Not good enough, Frank. I'm not prepared to authorize a strike on foreign soil with odds that shaky."

"I understand, sir," said Cerney. "Our Marine scouts are transiting to the next site now. With luck, we'll have confirmation on Point Green by about this time tomorrow, and Point Orange the day after."

"Why so long?"

"The scouts are travelling by sailboat," Cerney said. "Posing as vacationers. We ordered the Marines to keep the infiltration covert. This is how they chose to carry out the mission."

"If they get caught," Jackie said, "we could end up with a major diplomatic crisis."

"I'm not too concerned about the Cubans themselves," said the national security advisor. "We've got a gun pointed at our head, and—short of armed invasion—they'll understand if we take precautions to protect ourselves against nuclear attack. Especially since we've been careful not to lump them in with the bad guys on this one."

He picked up the red striped folder from the president's desk. "What worries me is that word could get back to Kim Yong-nam. If that happens, we'll be too busy dodging radioactive fallout to worry about diplomatic problems."

CHAPTER 57

Melly was writing on the whiteboard again, jotting rapidly with the nearly calligraphic penmanship that amazed Nathan and made him ever so slightly envious. Her lettering looked like one of the so-called 'hand printed' fonts: the kind that were supposed to resemble idealized human handwriting.

When Nathan made a deliberate effort to be legible, his own writing was somewhere between chicken scratch and minimalist hieroglyphics. If he was in any sort of hurry, things only went downhill from there.

The quality of Melly's penmanship did not seem to alter with speed. Her furious scribbles were every bit as neat as her more methodical notes. Nathan didn't see how that could be possible, but clearly it was. Yet another item on his growing list of reasons to be fascinated by this woman.

Her full name was Melanie Imogene Kimball; Nathan had been quite careful to listen during that part of the introductions. As far as he could tell she was exactly his height, and her voice had a tendency to squeak when she was excited.

Although she was possibly a bit plain by ordinary standards of physical attractiveness, Nathan found her long straight nose, wide hazel eyes, and pointed chin to be absolutely charming. But the most fascinating things about her were not physical at all.

Melly was a civilian software engineer from the Naval Undersea Warfare Center, and—even after Nathan had showered, slept, and rebooted his gray matter—she was proving to be at least his equal in terms of skill and intelligence, and probably his better. For some men, that would have been a turnoff. For Nathan Nguyen, it was the best of all possible worlds.

Not that he would have the courage to do anything about it. In his imagination it would all play out perfectly. Rum cocktails in some open air bar with a thatched roof.... A long walk on the beach.... A beautiful Key

West sunset.... Their hands drifting toward each other until fingers entwined of their own accord....

She cleared her throat. "You're not listening, are you?"

"No," he said. "I'm sorry. I wasn't."

"Where was your mind just now?"

"Uh.... Situational response algorithms," he said. "We're going to need to add another one."

Melly turned back to the whiteboard. "I don't think it's necessary. That's what I've been trying to say."

She pointed to a section of her notations. "Your existing code already cues on acoustic frequencies commonly emitted by the marine mammals that NOAA is interested in."

Her finger moved to indicate another section of notations. "You've even got a subroutine to maneuver the Sea Bat toward the axis of greatest signal strength, so that it swims in the general direction of the acoustic source, remaining within detection range of the dolphins, or whales, or whatever."

She capped her dry erase marker. "All we need to do is give the algorithm a different set of target frequencies to home in on."

Nathan shook his head. "It's a good idea, but you're forgetting two things. First, the maneuvering algorithm is slaved to signal strength. If the acoustic signal gets too strong, the Sea Bat turns aside and swims away for a hundred yards. The software was specifically designed to keep the units from getting in too close, and interfering with the normal movements and habits of the mammals under observation. And it's pretty difficult to attack something when you can't get within a hundred yards of the target."

Melly nodded. "And your second thing?"

"Second," Nathan said, "we don't have hardware or software for arming and detonating the explosive package."

"The second problem belongs to *them*," Melly said. She gestured toward the far table where Chief Goss and Eddie Sinclair were busy shoehorning something into the narrow interior cavity of the partially disassembled Sea Bat. "And I've got some ideas for solving the first problem."

"The situational response algorithms are written in ARIX-B," Nathan said. "It's a—"

Melly picked up the thread. "It's a proprietary language owned and controlled by Norton. I know all that."

Nathan smiled. "I was going to say it's a nightmare to work in. Once you get the wrinkles ironed out, ARIX-B does a nice job. But getting your code to that point isn't easy. A single wrong keystroke can have you chasing your tail for weeks. It's not anywhere near as forgiving as the first generation of ARIX."

"I know that too," Melly said. "Which is why we're not going to crack open the algorithms. We don't have the time to do it right, and we can't spend weeks—or even days—chasing our tails as you so eloquently put it."

"Then what are we going to do?" asked Nathan.

Melly put down her black dry erase marker, and picked up a red one. "Something like this...." She began to jot text and symbols in her neat calligraphic style.

After a moment, Nathan saw what she was getting at. "You want to modify the emergency recovery subprogram!"

Melly nodded. "Yep. It takes priority over all normal program functions. It can override the turn-away imperative in your situational response algorithms. And best of all—"

"It's written in URScript," Nathan finished.

"Exactly," said Melly. "Much *much* easier to work in than ARIX-B."

Nathan stood up and walked around the table to the whiteboard. "You're not rewriting my control code, you're *hacking* it."

"That's all we have time for," Melly said. "Don't take it personally. This is not a comment on your coding skills."

"Take it personally?" he said. "Are you kidding? You're a genius!"

They both blushed at this unexpected outburst.

Nathan picked up his own dry erase marker and began making frantic hen scratches. Melly went to work beside him, writing with equal speed.

And sometimes, when neither one of them were paying attention, their hands nearly touched.

CHAPTER 58

CUBAN REVOLUTIONARY ARMED FORCES HEADQUARTERS
HAVANA, CUBA
THURSDAY; 05 MARCH
0922 hours (9:22 AM)
TIME ZONE -5 'ROMEO'

General Rafael Garriga looked up as Allita showed Major Cardenas into the office. When the visitor was safely ensconced in a comfortable chair, the secretary gave Garriga a polite bob of her head, then made her exit from the room.

The major's head swung around like it was mounted on a swivel, his eyes never leaving the lush curves of the woman's retreating backside.

By the time the idiot managed to get his head turned back around in the proper direction, Garriga was ready with a conspiratorial leer—as if to say, *'yes, she's every bit as exciting in bed as you think she is.'*

In point of fact, Garriga didn't know what Allita was like in bed, and he didn't care. He cultivated rumors that she was his mistress, because such indulgences were expected of men with his position and power. He had no intentions of subjecting the woman to his unwanted advances, but he did draw a measure of satisfaction from the knowledge that his supposed interest kept Allita shielded from the grasping slobbering attentions of men who thought with their genitalia.

The lower left drawer of his desk was already unlocked. He lifted the lid of the mahogany humidor and drew out two *Hoyo de Monterrey* double coronas, keeping one for himself and holding out the other to Cardenas. "Welcome, Major. Please make yourself at ease."

The major accepted, and the next few minutes were devoted to the rituals of lighting a fine cigar.

When Garriga's was properly lit, he slid the desk drawer shut without reaching for the bottle of rum behind the humidor. Cardenas was just barely important enough to rate the cigars, and it was only his position as an officer of *Dirección de Inteligencia Militar* that made him worthy of a direct conference with the General of the Army.

Garriga blew a long plume of smoke and smiled toward the halfwit seated on the other side of the desk. "Tell me Major, what can the Army do for our compañeros in Military Intelligence this morning?"

"Today," said Cardenas with an overly solicitous expression, "it is about what *we* can do for the Army."

Garriga thumped a length of ash into a small porcelain bowl on his desk. "Very well, Major. Then what can *Inteligencia Militar* do for the Army this morning?"

The major's eyes darted sideways toward the door to the outer office, and lingered there for several seconds. When he looked back around, one of his eyebrows was raised in a suggestive manner. Could the imbecile be hinting at some kind of barter? Perhaps an hour with the general's secretary in exchange for whatever scrap of sordid information that the half-wit was carrying?

Garriga entertained a brief image of reaching across the desk to pound the life out of this little pulga. But the pleasure of snapping the man's neck would be fleeting, and there would be complications afterwards.

Cardenas repeated the eye motion, just in case the general hadn't caught the meaning the first time around.

"You seem to be reluctant to continue," said Garriga. "I'll be happy to speak to General Piñeiro if you're not comfortable talking directly to me."

"Oh, not at all!" Cardenas blurted. "I'm just concerned that someone could overhear through the door."

The lie was transparent. "If your information is as sensitive as that," Garriga said, "perhaps I should hear it from General Piñeiro. I'll have my secretary make the appointment."

"That won't be necessary," Cardenas said a little too loudly.

He lowered his voice. "It's the Yumas. They've infiltrated the north coastal region with military scouts. Marines, from the base at Guantanamo. They have orders to locate North Korean missile sites on our soil. Possibly for bombing strikes."

Garriga tried not to show his surprise. If this was true....

"How do you know this?" he snapped. "Where does your information come from?"

"I am not at liberty to say," said the idiot.

"In other words," Garriga said, "you don't *know* where the information comes from. Which tells me that it might be nothing more than rumor. Someone with an overactive imagination."

Major Cardenas shook his head. "No, General. The information is reliable. It comes from a trusted source."

"Pendejadas!" said Garriga. (Bullshit!) "If I act on this intelligence and it turns out to be false, I will nail your cojones to my door! And just so you understand, I do *not* mean that as a metaphor. I will personally nail them to my door, just before I have you shot!"

"The information is reliable," Cardenas said again. "DIM has a source inside the American base!"

Garriga snorted. "If your sources are so good, why are they spying on the Yumas? The Americans are not the ones hiding nuclear missiles in our country!"

Major Cardenas started to respond, but Garriga waved him to silence. "Is that it? Do you have more information for me, or is that all?"

Garriga stubbed out his cigar in the porcelain bowl. "Then you are dismissed!"

Cardenas left the room at a pace just below a run.

Sitting among the swirling cigar smoke, Garriga thought about this latest revelation. If it was true—if it didn't turn out to be a pile of sheer pendejadas—then the Yumas might try to destroy the launch sites before the North Koreans could fire their missiles.

He looked at the wall clock. His next prearranged call with the Korean was still more than three hours away.

Unscheduled calls always made the Asian angry. That couldn't be helped.

Garriga stood up, went to the old phonograph, and flipped the power switch. When the hissing crackle of bolero music filled the air of his office, he walked quietly to the door and slid the locking bolt into place.

CHAPTER 59

//TTTTTTTTTT//
//TOP SECRET//
//FLASH//FLASH//FLASH//
//051459Z MAR//

FM   COMSUBLANT//
TO COMSUBRON SIX//
USS ALBANY//
INFO COMFOURTHFLEET//
USS BOWIE//

SUBJ/CHANGE IN TASKING/IMMEDIATE EXECUTE//

REF/A/RMG/COMSUBLANT/260653Z FEB//

NARR/REF A IS ASW TASKING ISSUED BY COMSUBLANT
FOLLOWING 250408Z FEB ATTACK ON USS MAHAN IN
CARIBBEAN SEA.//

1. (SECR) REF A IS CANCELLED AND RESCINDED.

2. (TS) SUPERCAVITATING SUBMARINE OPERATING IN
YOUR AREA CONTINUES TO DEMONSTRATE SUSTAINED
SPEEDS EXCEEDING THREE-HUNDRED (300) KNOTS.

3. (TS) BASED ON USS ALBANY'S AFTER-ACTION REPORT
OF 02 MAR AND SIMILAR ATTEMPTS BY AIR AND SURFACE
PLATFORMS, SUCCESSFUL ENGAGEMENT OF THIS CONTACT
USING CURRENT INVENTORY ASW WEAPONS IS CONSIDERED
HIGHLY UNLIKELY.

4. (TS) USS ALBANY IS DIRECTED TO AVOID DIRECT
ENGAGEMENT OF SUPERCAVITATING SUBMARINE CONTACT.
IF THE CONTACT IS DETECTED, USS ALBANY WILL
MAINTAIN STANDOFF RANGE AND PROVIDE ACOUSTIC
TARGET CUEING TO USS BOWIE OVER TACNET VIA UHF
SATCOM.

5. (TS) IF ENGAGEMENT BY SUPERCAVITATING SUBMARINE
APPEARS TO BE LIKELY OR IMMINENT, USS ALBANY IS
ORDERED TO BREAK OFF CONTACT AND WITHDRAW TO A
SAFE AREA AS DETERMINED BY THE TACTICAL SITUATION.

6. (TS) ALL DIRECT ENGAGEMENTS WILL BE CONDUCTED
BY USS BOWIE USING NON-STANDARD WEAPONS AND
TACTICS.

7. (SECR) SUBOPAUTH WILL ISSUE ADDITIONAL ORDERS
AND AMPLIFYING INTELLIGENCE.

8. (SECR) SUBJECT CHANGE IN TASKING DOES NOT
REFLECT LACK OF CONFIDENCE IN USS ALBANY'S
READINESS, SKILL, OR CAPABILITY. THIS A NEW KIND
OF THREAT AND NEW METHODS MUST BE EMPLOYED TO
COMBAT IT.

9. (SECR) IMMEDIATE ACKNOWLEDGEMENT OF THIS ORDER
IS REQUIRED.

10. (UNCL) ADMIRAL POTTER SENDS.

//051459Z MAR//
//FLASH//FLASH//FLASH//
//TOP SECRET//
//TTTTTTTTTT//

USS ALBANY (SSN-753)
CARIBBEAN SEA, NORTH OF CAYMAN BRAC ISLAND
THURSDAY; 05 MARCH
1043 hours (10:43 AM)
TIME ZONE -5 'ROMEO'

Master Chief Ernie Pooler jabbed the message hardcopy with an angry finger. "Are you shitting me, sir? Are you *shitting* me? We play bird dog for a bunch of skimmers and *they* get to take the shot? Whose brilliant idea was *this*?"

Captain Townsend reached for the clipboard. "Don't scram your reactor, COB. I'm not any happier about it than you are."

"But, Skipper, they can't do this to us!"

"Yes they can, COB. They can, and they have."

The calm and rational quality of the captain's voice made Ernie conscious of his own tone and volume. When he spoke again, his delivery was closer to normal. "This order can't possibly have originated with SUBLANT. No way Admiral Potter would take the fight away from a 688 and hand it to a destroyer. This has to come from somewhere over his head. Some bright boy with too many stars on his collar, who doesn't understand what happens when a tin can gets in a scrap with an attack sub."

"You're probably right," said the Skipper, "about the first part, anyway. This isn't something Admiral Potter would do unless the order came from the top of the chain. Which means he's likely just as bent out of shape over this as we are."

"If that's true," Ernie said, "it doesn't come through in this message, sir. It sounds like he's singing along with the rest of the band here."

The Skipper flipped the cover page to the front of the clipboard, concealing the message hardcopy from view. "That's because the admiral is a good officer. He follows lawful orders—even the ones he doesn't like—and he treats them like they're his own ideas. Doesn't try to blame the bad ones on someone else."

"Well, this is definitely one of the bad ones," said Ernie.

"It looks bad to us," said the Skipper. "But we don't know what's behind this. We don't know what these non-standard weapons and tactics are supposed to be. Maybe it's something that can't be done by a 688 boat. Could be some piece of new hardware that won't fit into our tubes, or our signal ejectors."

"Maybe...." said Ernie grudgingly.

"Look at the bright side, COB. If this plan works, we may be able to provide an assist on the kill, and that's better than nothing. If it *doesn't* work, USS *Bowie* joins the *Mahan* and the *Winterburn* on the bottom of the Caribbean, and then we're back in the fight."

"To be honest, sir," said Ernie, "I don't like either option very much."

"Neither do I," said the Skipper. "Neither do I."

CHAPTER 60

FOXY ROXY
AT ANCHOR OFF LA BOCA, CUBA
THURSDAY; 05 MARCH
1324 hours (1:24 PM)
TIME ZONE -5 'ROMEO'

"Something's wrong," said Jon. "I can feel it."

Cassy shifted in her lounge chair. "Is your spider-sense tingling, or is this a full-on psychic premonition?"

Jon reached over with his left hand and took a lazy swat at his wife's knee. "It's my Jarhead-sense, and it's tingling like a son of a bitch."

"Then you're definitely imagining it," Cassy said. "Jarheads don't *have* any sense. I should know; I married one."

"I'm not joking," Jon said. "They should have been back by now. They're in trouble."

This elicited a sigh from Cassy. "Jonnie, they're U.S. Marines. They can handle their share of trouble."

"What if it's more than their share?"

"You're like a mother hen," Cassy said. "I love the fact that you care so much. But you need to remember.... They're not your Marines, and this is not your mission. Our job is to provide transportation and a believable cover story. We're doing that. Everything else is out of our hands."

"I don't like it," said Jon.

"Of *course* you don't like it. There are Marines out there somewhere, doing that Jarhead thing, while you're lounging in the shade sipping on a cool drink. You want to be out there too, covering their six, or their flank, or whatever it is that Jugheads cover. I know you won't admit it, but *that's* what's bothering you."

"Maybe," Jon said.

"No maybe about it," said Cassy. "Listen to Old Doc Clark. She knows about stuff like this. Just lay back, enjoy the shade, and let the Marines take care of themselves."

It was good advice. Jon knew that. Whether or not he could actually

251

follow it was a different matter.

Scout Detachment Bravo:

"Holy fuck...." said Fris in a whisper.

His words were barely audible to Elf, who lay under a bush not more than a yard away from his hiding place. Even so, the female Marine raised a finger to her lips, signaling for complete silence.

Although they were both corporals, Elf was marginally senior, and Sergeant Webb had placed her firmly in command of this scouting foray. Despite their equal ranks and nearly equal seniority, Fris didn't chafe under Elf's leadership. He accepted her orders readily, carried them out with few complaints, and rarely questioned her decisions. Beneath his sometimes mouthy persona was a solid Marine, who didn't let a wonky sense of humor get in the way of accomplishing the mission.

There was a time for joking around and acting the fool, and a time for shutting the fuck up and being a serious grunt. This instance fell into the second category. Maybe seventy yards away—partially hidden by trees and foliage—was an enormous ten-wheeled truck, painted in the low-contrast greens, tans, and browns of a forest camouflage scheme. In a cradle on the vehicle's back lay the unmistakable shape of a missile.

Fris could see parts of three other launcher vehicles in the distance. If the intel briefs were correct, there would be a total of six, but it wasn't necessary to see all of them. Even one would have been enough. Point Green was a missile site, no doubt about it.

Elf had her cell phone out, shooting video for later upload via the sat phone. Smart girl. That hadn't been part of the orders, but it was a damned good idea.

Fris was about to give her a silent thumbs-up when something moved in the bushes, much closer than the nearest truck.

He and Elf both froze, moving only their eyes as they scanned the greenery for the source of the movement.

It was a man, crawling out of a low camouflage tent that neither Marine had spotted earlier. The newcomer got to his feet and stretched, slinging the strap of a compact submachine gun over his shoulder as he did so.

Fris caught only a fleeting glimpse of the man's face. Dark hair, Asian features, and the lean and hard look of one accustomed to difficult living.

The North Korean soldier gave his surroundings a slow and careful sweep, and Fris suddenly felt that his decidedly non-camo civvies must be glowing like a highway flare in the green-dappled undergrowth. His kabar and M9 Beretta were both in the ridiculous tourist backpack. He wondered if he could get to them without making any noise.

He looked sideways and met the gaze of Elf, who seemed to be reading his mind. Her head turned a half-degree to the right, and then a half-degree to the left, the most minimal headshake Fris had ever seen. Her expression told him to be patient, but to also be ready.

The North Korean coughed, adjusted the crotch of his uniform trousers, and began walking toward the nearest launcher vehicle—evidently unaware of the two Marine scouts just a few feet away from him.

When the Korean had gone about thirty yards, Elf tapped Fris on the arm and motioned for him to back away.

The next forty minutes were spent meticulously picking their way through the undergrowth, putting distance between themselves and the missile site, gradually working back toward the road.

After they'd covered a half mile or so, Elf signaled that it was okay to risk a little noise and pick up the pace. They moved quickly now, relieved to be away from the enemy emplacement, and flushed with the excitement of a mission well performed.

They were just outside the fringes of the woods and breathing a collective sigh of relief when they heard the engine. One look at the approaching vehicle was enough. It was a truck painted in the lifeless green shade favored by militaries of many nationalities.

With no apparent hesitation, Elf dropped her backpack. "Take off your pants!"

That was literally the last thing Fris was expecting to hear.

"What?"

Elf peeled her shirt over her head, revealing a half-cup bra underneath, along with considerably more cleavage than her clothed form would have suggested. "Get your pants off, Marine! Do it now!"

Fris tossed his backpack on the ground and did as ordered. He wasn't wearing skivvies, so dropping the cargo shorts left him naked down to his socks.

That didn't stop Elf. She was in his arms a split second later, carrying him to the grass in a tangle of half-naked limbs, her mouth locked on his in a passionate kiss.

The sound of the truck was still approaching, but Fris tried to give as good as he received, returning Elf's kiss with equal vigor. She was really putting on a show too, moaning and squirming against his body like he was the sexiest hunk of man she'd ever seen.

The shriek of badly maintained brakes announced that the truck was stopping. Fris wanted to sneak a peek at the tactical situation, but Elf was demanding his full concentration.

She didn't break the kiss until they could hear male voices and the sounds of people jumping down from the bed of the truck.

Then she released her hold on Fris, glanced up, and squealed as though she was just now noticing the presence of strangers.

She squealed again, covered her brassier clad chest with one arm, and bolted for the nearest bushes—grabbing her backpack on-the-fly.

Fris, with his pants down around his ankles, got his first view of the interlopers. Six Cuban soldiers, dressed in the hunter green uniforms of their country's army. They laughed and traded remarks in Spanish as Fris scrambled to his feet and pulled up his shorts.

Elf could be heard making hurried fumblings behind the bushes. Although (if Fris knew her at all), she wouldn't be bothering with her shirt. She'd be rummaging in the backpack and recovering her 9mm.

There were six of them, not counting the driver in the truck's cab.

The M9 Beretta had a fifteen round magazine, and Elf was a hell of a good shot. With the element of surprise on her side, there was a decent chance that she could drop three or four of the Cuban soldiers before any of them could react.

Buttoning his waistband, Fris turned enough to spy his backpack. If Elf started shooting, he'd dive for the pack and try to get to his own 9mm.

This was a major downside of the tourist masquerade. It was impossible to keep your weapons close at-hand.

One of the soldiers stepped closer and rattled off something in Spanish.

Fris thought he caught the words *singar*, *casa*, and *Yuma*. He could only think of one sentence construction containing all three of those words. *Hey, you dumbass American, why don't you go home to fuck?*

He gave them a fake grin and raised his hands in a '*hey, you got me*' gesture, trying to radiate harmless stupidity even as he was considering the best way to break the man's neck.

The Cuban looked downward, frowned, and said something else.

Following the man's gaze, Fris looked down as well. The fly of his cargo shorts was still open. He grasped the metal tab of the zipper and rectified the problem.

The Cuban ruffled the Marine's hair in the kind of condescending gesture of affection that adult men bestow on small boys. Then the man laughed again, and tromped back toward the truck, followed by his five compañeros.

A minute later, they were gone, the truck leaving dark trails of diesel smoke as it receded from view.

Elf came out of the bushes, still shirtless, her M9 pointed skyward in a two-handed ready grip.

Fris took one look at her and grinned again, a real one this time. "Hey, Corporal.... Nice—"

Elf cut him off. "Stow it, shithead! If you even *think* about saying what I think you're gonna say, I'll put two rounds in your head and blame it on the North Koreans."

Fris held up his palms and tried to look innocent. "Come on, Elf. I was just going to say 'nice work'. That was quick thinking. You got us out of a tight spot there."

Elf snorted. "I'll bet that's what you were going to say."

"I *was*," protested Fris, putting all the sincerity he could muster into the fib.

"Fine," Elf said. "Watch the road."

Fris did as instructed, stealing glances out of the corner of his eye as the female corporal put her shirt back on.

When her clothing was restored and the M9 tucked out of sight in the backpack, both Marines started back toward the village, doing their best to simulate airheaded tourists returning from a long stroll.

"You *know*...." Fris said after a long stretch of silence.

"Don't say it!" Elf snapped.

So he didn't, and they walked another mile without talking.

Finally, Elf sighed. "Okay, go ahead. Just get it out of your system."

"I don't know what you're talking about," said Fris.

"Oh yes you do. You're dying to say it. So spit it out, and we'll be done with it."

"You're a good Marine," Fris said. "And it's a pleasure to work with you."

"That's not what you were going to say."

"Yes it is."

"No it isn't!" Elf said in a near shout. "Just go ahead and finish it. Nice... *what*?"

"Let's forget the whole thing," said Fris. "I almost said something unprofessional. Something that one corporal should never say to another."

"Tell me," Elf said. "Nice *what*?"

Fris shook his head. "No."

Elf gave him an elbow in the ribs. Not full contact, but hard enough to get his attention. "I mean it! *Tell* me! Nice *what*?"

Fris massaged the spot of the elbow strike. "Nice tits," he said.

She elbowed him again, harder this time. "Goddamn it, Marine!"

"I *told* you it was better kept to myself," he said. "I decided to be a good boy, and keep my mouth shut. You wouldn't let me."

"I should have shot you back there," she grumbled, "and left your body in the woods."

"You can shoot me next time," Fris said.

"Don't tempt me!" growled Elf.

But she was smiling. Fris could see it out of the corner of his eye.

CHAPTER 61

USS BOWIE (DDG-141)
CARIBBEAN SEA, SOUTHEAST OF CAYO ANCLITAS, CUBA
FRIDAY; 06 MARCH
1053 hours (10:53 AM)
TIME ZONE -5 'ROMEO'

Ensign Moore stood forward of the boat deck, watching the helo make its approach to the ship. The Sikorsky MH-60S was a dark insectile shape against the sky, its ovoid fuselage and tapered tail boom giving the aircraft a silhouette like a dragonfly.

Dangling on a cable beneath the dragonfly's belly were two expanded frame steel pallets wrapped in cargo nets, with nine rectangular fiberglass shipping crates strapped to each pallet. This was the third and final delivery, and it brought the total number of crates to fifty-four.

The helo grew larger as it came nearer, until the insect illusion was dispelled by the sheer size of the hovering machine and the mechanical tumult of its rotor wash.

The ensign's duties did not include observing vertical replenishment operations, and he didn't feel any personal desire to watch this one. But he couldn't make himself turn away.

This was all happening because of him. The VERTREPs; the changes in mission orders; *everything*. He was responsible for all of this.

He thought back to the strategy session in the wardroom. His idea had seemed like an intellectual exercise at the time. An out-of-the-box solution to a difficult problem.

But the captain and the XO had taken it seriously. They'd fired off a flash message to Fourth Fleet, and then the whole thing had taken on a life of its own.

Diverting assets from NOAA. Modifying hardware and software. Changing the operational tasking of ships and submarines. Who knew how many millions of dollars had already been spent because one naive ensign didn't know how to keep his mouth shut when smarter people were talking?

And the worst part was: his idea seemed less brilliant with every passing second. Now that the plan was being put into action, he had serious doubts about its viability.

"Is that the last of them?"

The voice startled him. He turned to see Captain Heller standing a few feet away. "Sorry, sir. I didn't hear you walk up."

The captain nodded toward the pallets being lowered to the flight deck. "Is that the last of the Sea Bats?"

"Yes, sir. This is all of them. Fifty-four total, as promised."

"I wish it was a hundred and fifty-four," said the captain, "but we were lucky to get this many on such short notice."

"I suppose so, sir."

"You don't sound very excited," said Captain Heller. "Your idea may open up an entirely new branch of ASW tactical doctrine. I thought you'd be turning cartwheels."

"I guess I'm just concerned, Captain."

"Concerned? Of course you are. You'd be an idiot if you weren't concerned."

"But what if I'm wrong, sir? What if I've wasted millions of dollars on a strategy that will never work? What if my big mouth gets people killed?"

The captain smiled. "Is that all you're worried about?"

"Isn't that enough, sir?"

The captain scuffed at the nonskid deck with the toe of his boot. "Todd, do you know what this high-tech bucket of bolts costs?"

"About two billion dollars?"

"More like two and a half billion," said Captain Heller. "And between officers and crew, there are one hundred and ninety-seven personnel aboard. Add in the civilian techrep we took on with the first helo, and it's a hundred and ninety-eight."

Ensign Moore nodded.

"So," said the captain, "every time I issue an order under combat conditions, there are two and a half billion dollars and nearly two-hundred human lives on the line. If I make a bad call, this ship—and everyone aboard—could end up like the *Mahan* or the *Walter W. Winterburn*. If I turn to starboard when I should have turned to port, we may not survive my mistake. If I hold fire a minute too long, or launch weapons thirty-seconds too soon, it can cost us everything."

"That's the nature of military command. That's what you're training for now. And that's also what you signed up for when you accepted your commission as an officer."

"I understand that sir," said Ensign Moore. "It's just—"

"It's just that you didn't expect to inherit this kind of responsibility quite so soon?"

"I suppose so, sir."

"Well, relax," said Captain Heller. "You came up with the idea, but *I* made the recommendation to DESRON, and it went up the chain from there. Admiral Turner at Fourth Fleet approved, and so did Admiral Cook at SOUTHCOM. Along the way, a whole lot of senior staff officers and tactical brains were in on the discussion. The final decision was made well above your pay grade and mine. Keep that in mind, and don't go weighing yourself down with all of the responsibility."

"But none of this would have happened if I'd kept the idea to myself," said Ensign Moore. "If things go wrong—"

"If things go wrong, they go wrong," said the captain. "We don't have the luxury of perfect foresight. If we did, we could tell in advance which tactics will lead to success, and which ones will lead to failure. That's not something we're privileged to know ahead of time. We take the best ideas we can think of, execute them to the best of our ability, and cross our fingers."

"Meaning that my brilliant idea could get us all killed."

"It might," said the captain. "The good news is: if your idea turns out to be a loser, you probably won't be around to regret it."

Ensign Moore responded with a weak smile. "That *is* good news, sir."

"Let's get up to the wardroom," said Captain Heller. "I want to round up our tactical thinkers and have a conversation with this civilian techrep. No more second-guessing yourself, Todd. We're committed now, and it's time to get back in the fight."

The ensign nodded. "Yes, sir."

He looked back toward the flight deck. The cargo had been delivered and the dragonfly shape of the MH-60 was disappearing into the sky.

CHAPTER 62

There was no beer this time. Maybe that was an omen. No teenage boys in homemade boats coming out to hock icy beverages to the Yumas at inflated prices. Not even fishing boats plying the bay between the coast and the outer cays.

Except for the sputtering runabout of the town's Guarda Frontera officer—which had come and gone an hour ago—there hadn't been another boat moving on the harbor since the *Foxy Roxy* dropped anchor.

All three of the visible piers had long ago collapsed into the bay, but there were a number of boats hauled up onto the beach, so some of the locals probably made their livings on the water. If that was true, what were the odds that every boat would be high and dry at the same time?

Was this an ordinary lull in the town's activity? Or had people been warned to stay away from the sailboat with the gringos?

Jon took a swig of lukewarm bottled water—a poor substitute for cold Cuban beer—and let his eyes drift down the shoreline. The water was a brilliant azure and the sand was the color of sugar.

He remembered the grubby strip of shingle in Playa La Playita. What could the people of that happy little village have done with a magnificent beach like this? But the inhabitants of Playa De Suerte appeared to have forgotten that they were living in a paradise.

The town had an aura of melancholy and decay. Many of the concrete buildings were crumbling into the streets, and Jon could see two hotels that had gone to ruin. There was none of the lazily festive atmosphere of Playa La Playita or La Boca. The natural beauty of the sea and coast did nothing to lighten the somber mood of this place.

But the Marines had taken the dinghy ashore anyway, continuing to play their given role as clueless tourists. It was the only cover they had,

STEEL WIND   261

even if it didn't fit the current situation very well.

Cassy yawned and shifted her legs in the lounge chair. "How's your Jarhead-sense doing?"

Jon didn't answer immediately. He'd more or less been asking himself the same question.

The town was certainly giving him a weird vibe, but that seemed to be a matter of long-standing economic issues, as if Playa De Suerte had fallen on hard times and never recovered. Now that he thought about it, this might have been one of the resort towns that catered to Soviet tourism during the Cold War, before the USSR went belly up. As far as he could see, there was nothing overtly hostile or dangerous here.

And last time, he'd gotten himself all keyed up for nothing. His sense of foreboding had been completely out of alignment with reality. The Marines had returned without a scratch, their mission successfully accomplished.

He shrugged. "My Jarhead-sense is quiet. I suppose that means everything is going fine."

His instinct had been wrong the first time. Jon didn't know it yet, but he was wrong this time too.

⚓ ⚓ ⚓

Scout Detachment Alpha:

"We are well and truly fucked," Webb muttered.

Liv plucked a long weed in passing and toyed with it as she walked. "Maybe not. We won't really know that until we get a decent look at the place."

The two Marines were acting out the happy couple routine again, strolling hand-in-hand one street north of their area of interest. Point Orange was an abandoned sugar mill just beyond the southern outskirts of town: a jumble of dilapidated metal buildings behind a wire fence that was more rust than barrier.

"That's the problem," said Webb, "we *can't* get a decent look. There's no way to get close without giving ourselves away."

His assessment seemed to be accurate. From their current vantage, the site was only visible through occasional gaps between intervening houses. Even then, the Marines had to satisfy themselves with sideways looks at the derelict facility. It wouldn't be smart to show anything more than a passing interest. But—limited as it was—their casual reconnoiter revealed the difficulty of the situation.

The sugar mill was set back from the road, and the surrounding terrain offered very little in the way of cover. Knee-high weeds dotted with a smattering of scrub plants, none of which were large enough to hide a person.

If this had been a movie, some Navy SEAL in uber-effective Hollywood camouflage would have belly-crawled through the weeds like a Ninja, silently dispatching six or eight guards along the way.

But this was real life, and the flat open ground surrounding the enclosure would support no such theatrics. It was a natural killing field for anyone foolhardy enough to cross it. One North Korean with an elevated observation post could keep every possible angle of approach under visual surveillance. And that wasn't counting video cameras, infrared cameras, or other warning devices, any of which could be hidden around the sugar mill's perimeter.

Inside the fence, the opportunities for concealment were greatly increased. The ground was littered with discarded machinery, rusted out sluice tanks, the ruins of collapsed outbuildings, and mounds of desiccated cane husks.

If the Marines could make it into the enclosure, they'd have a fairly good chance of remaining undetected, at least by eyeball. The problem was getting there.

"What if we circle around back?" Liv asked.

"I was thinking about that," said Webb. "But the terrain behind the mill looks like more of the same. Weeds and scrub. Nothing to hide behind."

He studied the house they were passing. Like most of the others on this street, it was deserted—the window frames bare of glass, the door sagging off its hinges.

"If we can't move in," he said, "we'll have to try going *up* instead. Get some elevation. Maybe we can find a line of sight through the windows in the main building."

"Those windows are pretty high," said Liv. "I'd say ten or fifteen feet off the ground."

"I'm thinking closer to ten or twelve feet," Webb said. "And some of these roofs are eighteen or twenty. If we can get up there..."

Liv shook her head. "They all look like they'd fall over in a stiff breeze. I wouldn't risk my neck on any of them."

"You won't have to," said Webb. "I've got this."

Liv stopped walking. "Are you serious?"

Webb stopped as well, looking upward toward the overhang of the nearest roof. "If you've got a better plan, now's the time to share it."

"No," Liv admitted. "I don't have a better plan. But that doesn't make this a good one."

"I agree," said Webb. "I just can't think of any better options."

"Neither can I," Liv said finally.

"That settles it," said Webb. "We try to pick the sturdiest roof we can find, and hope for the best."

Liv started walking again. "Not this one. It's got 'deathtrap' written all over it."

None of the next four houses seemed any more promising. The fifth one had no roof at all. The sixth and seventh houses were both vetoed by Webb, for reasons that seemed to be mostly instinctual.

The Marines stopped at the eighth house and gave the roof a hard look. It had the kind of barrel tiles commonly found in places with old world Spanish architectural influences. The half-curved terracotta slabs had kept a lot of their original orange-brown coloring, which might be a sign that the clay still maintained some of its structural strength.

Webb dug a pair of compact binoculars out of his backpack before laying the pack on the ground. "I think this is our best bet, and I want to be out of here before we run out of daylight."

He looped the binocular strap over his head and began limbering up his arms and legs.

"What am I supposed to do if you break your fool neck?"

"That depends."

"On *what*?"

"On when it happens," said Webb. As he spoke, he was sizing up the tumbledown house for possible handholds and footholds.

"If I find out what we need to know and *then* break my neck, you hide my body under the rubble and haul ass back to the boat to make your report. If I break my neck *before* I get a look into the site, then you're back to figuring out how to get inside the fence. You should still hide my body, so the local cops don't get bent out of shape about the dead gringo while you're trying to carry out the mission."

"That's not funny," Liv said.

Webb tested a handhold in the crumbling wall. "Wasn't meant to be."

He threw a wink at his fellow Marine. "I'd rather be back in the barracks drinking Bud Light and playing *Call of Duty*, but that's not on the schedule for today."

"You're really gonna do this?"

"Unless you'd rather do it for me."

"I'll pass," Liv said.

"Well then," said Webb, "stand back and watch the human fly at work. Remember, don't try this at home, folks."

He dug the toe of his left running shoe into a crack, put some weight on his first handhold, and began the climb. His ascent was slow and cautious, with none of the mini-emergencies or false slips so beloved by writers of adventure fiction.

Getting past the overhang of the roof presented the expected challenge, but—with some experimentation—he managed to swing one leg up over the eave. After that, it was just a matter of keeping his weight distributed across as many tiles as possible.

When he was turned in the proper direction and in what felt like a stable situation, he called out softly, "Hey Liv, can you do me a favor?"

"What do you need?"

"Take a look at where the rafters come out of the wall. Try to keep me lined up over two of them at all times, if you can."

"Roger."

She backed up a few yards and gauged his alignment. "You're okay on the left side, but a little wide on the right. Bring your foot in about six inches."

Webb adjusted.

"Yeah. Now bring your right hand in about the same amount."

He made another adjustment.

"Looking good. You think that's gonna help?"

"It'll help me feel better if nothing else," said Webb.

He started a steady crawl toward the peak of the roof, responding to periodic calls for adjustment from Liv.

About half way to his goal, the Marine began singing softly to the tune of an old Willie Nelson song. *"Mamas don't let your babies grow up to be Jarheads.... Don't let 'em wear camos and drive in Humvees...."*

"Getting too far left," Liv said.

Webb edged his body a few inches to the right. *"Make 'em be plumbers or Walmart trainees...."*

His next move brought a crackling sound, like the crunching of dry twigs. A tile under his right knee fell to pieces, fragments of clay falling through the new opening into the interior of the house.

Webb went motionless, listening and feeling for any signs of imminent structural collapse.

When nothing else happened for a minute or so, he resumed his creep toward the roof ridge, avoiding the gap where the missing tile had been.

"Mamas don't let your babies grow up to be Jarheads.... 'Cause they don't fold their napkins or use the right fork...."

The next line was hummed instead of sung. Webb hadn't come up with a good rhyme for 'fork' yet. None of the easy ones—*stork, pork, cork*, and *New York*—seemed to fit with the rest of the lyrics.

He made the last few feet of the crawl without singing, humming, or speaking. The only sounds were his breathing and the low scuff of running shoes on old clay.

At last, he was there, at the roof peak. He could raise his head a few inches and see over the tops of the uppermost tiles.

Still careful to move slowly, he found the binoculars and lifted them to his eyes. A three-quarter turn of the focus wheel brought the largest building of the sugar mill into sharp relief.

Webb started with the left side of the building. This elevation wasn't bad. Another few feet would have been nice, but he figured that he had sufficient down-angle for a workable line-of-sight.

The first few window frames had glass in them, the panes opaque with years (or decades) of accumulated dirt. Then came several that were boarded over with dry-rotted plywood. The next couple were glassless, but he could see nothing in the shadows within.

Then several more covered in plywood, followed by a long row with most of the panes missing. This was the opening he needed.

He began a methodical sweep of the exposed section of the building's interior, giving his eyes plenty of time to adjust to the shadows within.

There.... A rectilinear profile, marbled with the low-contrast greens, browns, and tans of forest camo. And a second shape; he could see the nearly man-high tires on this one, and the huge cylindrical form of the missile on its back. Fifteen degrees to the right was still another one.

"Pssssttt... Liv!"

"Yeah? What have you got?"

"Jackpot! I count three transporter erector launchers, and a possible fourth. There's also—"

Liv never found out was the '*also*' was.

She heard the impact of the bullet an instant before the muzzle report of the rifle. The top of Webb's head came apart in a cloud of red mist. Then he was tumbling back down the incline roof, his body already gone limp with the loss of muscle tension.

There was a half-second of freefall when he rolled past the overhang and plummeted to the ground.

Liv took one look at the ruin of her friend's face and confirmed what she already knew. Alan Webb was dead. There was no point in checking for vitals. All the CPR in the world would not bring him back from where he had gone.

Her immediate and instinctive reaction was a dizzying wave of sorrow, mixed with nausea, fear, and confusion. It crashed over her like a tsunami, and it could have easily carried her down into some dark internal place of quivering whimpering indecision.

But something clicked in her brain, like the tripping of an electrical relay. A shunting of mental circuit paths, routing her thoughts away from doubt, or sadness, or frailty. Energizing the part of her persona that was fearless Marine instead of ordinary civilian.

And just like that, her inner Jarhead reasserted itself.

She unzipped her backpack and groped for the M9 Beretta—her mind already buzzing with half-formed plans. There had to be a way to sneak in close to the fence. There just *had* to be. Some angle of approach; some line of sight, or feature of terrain. Some tricky little tactic that would give her a clear shot at the fucker who had killed Webb.

That's all she needed. One clear shot. One chance to send the asshole straight to hell.

She got a grip on the 9mm, pulled it out, and jacked a round into the pipe. The weight of the weapon felt good in her hand.

No. One bullet wouldn't be enough. She'd put the whole magazine into the bastard's head. Fifteen rounds of 9mm jacketed hollow-point, right in the face.

The sun was sinking now, the shadows growing longer. Lights were starting to come on in the windows of the few houses that were occupied.

She could wait for full dark, circle around to the left and move in from an oblique angle. Hug the dirt and creep toward that fence an inch at a time. Maybe....

That was the word that stopped her. *Maybe.*

Not a good word to use when you were planning an op. Not even an off-the-cuff job like this.

Maybe was another way of saying *maybe not.* Liv could deal with *maybe not* if her life was the only one on the line here. But it wasn't.

Except for the North Koreans (and maybe a handful of bad actors in the Cuban government) she was the only person on the planet who knew that Point Orange was hot. If the site followed the expected pattern, there were six nuclear missiles hidden in the old sugar mill.

Webb had seen three for sure, and a possible fourth. And somebody had put a rifle slug through his brain to keep that information quiet.

If Liv went for the shooter and got herself killed, the location of the missile site would remain unconfirmed. Which meant a half-dozen nukes pointed at American cities.

How many lives were at risk from those missiles right now? Hundreds of thousands? Millions? Maybe *tens* of millions?

She wasn't sure, but she was certain about one thing. Her mission was no longer inside the fence of the sugar mill. She had the information that she and Webb had come for.

Now she just had to deliver it to her people.

Her teeth ground together so hard that her jaws hurt, but she forced herself to eject the magazine from the grip reservoir of the M9. She shucked the round out of the chamber, popped it back into the top of the magazine, and reseated the mag in the grip of the weapon.

The 9mm went back into the backpack, and she began walking straight north, trying to keep the deserted house between herself and the sugar mill.

Her eyes blurred with tears, but they were more from suppressed anger than from grief. The back of her throat burned with unused adrenaline.

When she reached the other side of the street, something flicked past her left ear. An insect? A rifle bullet? Liv honestly didn't know. If it was a slug, she hadn't heard the muzzle report.

She ducked between two houses and zigged left, using the additional cover to (hopefully) stay out of the shooter's field of vision.

A block later, she felt like she had enough distance and enough intervening concealment to pick up the pace. Her walk became a trot, and then a jog, and then an all-out run.

The few locals stirring in the streets stared at this crazy Yuma, sprinting blindly through their town, tears streaming down her cheeks.

She didn't slow as twilight continued to fall, her heart pounding like a jackhammer, hoping that she hadn't gotten turned around somewhere. No longer completely certain that she could find her way back to the boat.

And inside her head, a single line kept repeating itself over and over again. *"Mamas don't let your babies grow up to be Jarheads...."*

⚓ ⚓ ⚓

Foxy Roxy:

Cassy stuck her face into the cabin. "Jonnie? Better get up here. A boat's coming, and it's not the dinghy."

Jon turned down the burner under the pot of simmering soup. He was on deck in a few seconds, Roxy at his heels.

Evening was giving way to night, and the stars were really starting to show themselves. The incoming boat was not easy to spot in the gathering gloom. It was dark in color and running without lights. Somehow he knew that neither was an accident.

From what he could see, the boat was a rigid-hulled inflatable. Something like a Zodiac Hurricane, but with the helm console near the stern. Decades newer than anything likely to be found in a jerkwater coastal town, and the outboard—now that Jon could hear it—was putting out a steady and healthy drone.

This was high-end equipment: the kind of stuff that Guarda Frontera and the local harbor cops only dreamed of.

Military? Could be. If so, it wouldn't be the local boys. The regular Cuban grunts would be making do with clapped-out Russian or Chinese handoffs, not the real tactical stuff.

Heavy customers, then. Bad news.

This evening was shaping up to be a real winner. First, the Marines hadn't come back on schedule, and now these guys.

Without realizing that he was doing so, Jon did a neck roll and began loosening up his shoulders. "Cass, grab Roxy and get below."

"But I—"

"Now!" Jon said. "No questions. Just do it."

Cassy grabbed Roxy's collar and led the dog down the companionway and into the cabin. A second later, the interior lights went out.

Jon smiled to himself. Good girl.

The boat was getting close now. He could see two forms crouched in the bow, and a third seated in the stern.

Three men, then. All dressed in black utility uniforms and assault helmets.

Bad news, alright. *Major* bad news.

CHAPTER 63

USS ALBANY (SSN-753)
CARIBBEAN SEA, WEST OF NIQUERO, CUBA
FRIDAY; 06 MARCH
1820 hours (6:20 PM)
TIME ZONE -5 'ROMEO'

The Sonar Supervisor motioned for Master Chief Pooler's attention. "Hey, COB. Looks like our North Korean buddy is back."

Ernie lowered his coffee cup and turned to examine the lower screen of the BQQ-10. The new sonar contact, designated as *Sierra One-Four*, was faint but it showed several of the acoustic tonals associated with *Han* class boats.

He nodded. "That's our boy, alright. Call it away."

The Sonar Supe keyed his microphone to make the report. When he was finished, he grinned and rubbed his palms together. "Your ass is *mine* now, Mr. Supercav. You've gone and fucked with the wrong people."

"Easy there, Shipmate," said Ernie. "We're not allowed to shoot this guy, remember? We're just going to tag him for the skimmers."

"You're serious? I thought you guys were joking about that."

"No joke," said Ernie. "We keep our distance and forward our contact data to USS *Bowie*."

"A surface puke against an attack sub? What mega-genius came up with that idea?"

"The order came from the top of the food chain," Ernie said. "We don't have to agree with it. We just have to follow it."

"COB, this is bullshit! The best way to kill a submarine is with another submarine. Even my brain-dead cousin knows that, and he could lose a battle of wits with a bowl of oatmeal."

"Your cousin doesn't make the Rules of Engagement," said Ernie. "So enough with your bitching and moaning. If we have to be a bird dog, we're gonna be the best goddamned bird dog in the history of the Atlantic Fleet."

"If you say so, COB."

"I *do* say so," growled Ernie. "Now, suck it up and do your job!"

269

⚓ ⚓ ⚓

USS *Bowie*:

"Sonar—USWE. Anything to report?" It was the third time in as many minutes that he'd asked the same question.

STG1 Wyatt keyed his headset. "USWE—Sonar. Negative, sir. Still no contact."

He released the mike button. "Jesus, does he think we're gonna keep it a secret?"

STG2 Denisha Jenkins was back in her favorite spot: the operator station for the aft towed array. "Cut the man some slack," she said. "He's an ensign. It always takes them a little while to get their heads out of their asses."

Wyatt said something in reply, but Denisha ignored it. Her mind was on the A-BAB display.

The colored dots were churning and mutating in their usual Brownian swarm. Never following a recognizable pattern, but never quite random either. Sending cryptic messages to the processing centers of Denisha's subconscious on a carrier wave that might have made sense to Jackson Pollock.

It wasn't there yet. The subtle and indefinable whatever it was that sometimes caught Denisha's notice. With A-BAB, she never really knew what her mind was reacting to. For the moment though, that unknowable something was absent.

She shifted to her lower screen and began paging through the aft beams of the array. There were plenty of contacts out there—fishing boats, small craft, merchant shipping, the oil rig off to the northeast—and all of their acoustic signatures showed up in the narrowband display. The frequency pattern of the North Korean submarine was not among them.

The hostile sub was definitely somewhere to the south. That much they knew, because the *Bowie* was receiving lines of bearing from USS *Albany*. But so far, the thing had stubbornly refused to make an appearance on any of the *Bowie*'s sonar screens.

Denisha reached the broadside beam and turned her focus back to the upper display. A-BAB was still doing its nonsensical pixel dance. The rhythmless shuffle of colored dots continued unabated. Still nothing. The *something* wasn't there.

She resumed paging through the beams, working from aft to forward as required by doctrine and training. Below her breath, she chanted in a singsong voice, "*Here, kitty, kitty, kitty, kitty....*"

Nothing again. Just the usual surface contacts. No sign of the acoustic fingerprint that so closely mimicked the old *Han* class boats.

She shifted back to A-BAB and found more of the same. Abstract pseudo-randomness, with nothing worth....

Wait a second....

Maybe there was something after all. Some faint and transitory kernel of pattern buried in the chaos. Denisha rolled her cursor over to the area that had piqued her interest, and examined the alphanumeric readout in the upper right corner of the display.

On her lower screen, she called up five adjacent beams, centered on the bearing of the A-BAB flicker. And there it was: the familiar not-quite-*Han*-class acoustic signature. The signal was weak—just starting to fade in above the ambient noise threshold—but it was definitely there.

Gotcha!

Denisha did a quick screen capture (just in case) and began tagging the target frequencies. "Sonar Supe, I've got him!"

Wyatt was at her elbow almost before the words were out of her mouth. "That's our North Korean alright!" He reached for the 29MC microphone. "All Stations—Sonar has passive narrowband contact off the port beam! Bearing one-three-three! Initial classification: POSS-SUB, confidence level high!"

He released the mike button. "Good job, Denisha! Tag it, bag it, and send it to fire control."

"Already on it," Denisha said.

⚓ ⚓ ⚓

In Combat Information Center, Ensign Moore watched a line of bearing appear on the screen of his Computerized Dead-Reckoning Tracer. The red line extended from the symbol for USS *Bowie* at an angle of 131 degrees. It intersected with a second red line extending from the original cueing platform, USS *Albany* at 199 degrees. The cross-fix provided an instant target range of just over 12,000 yards.

The ensign tapped a soft-key on the CDRT to send the range data to the Underwater Battery Fire Control System.

Then he keyed into the net. "TAO—USWE. POSS-SUB contact bears one-three-one at twelve-thousand."

Lieutenant Faulk was Tactical Action Officer for this engagement. She responded immediately. "TAO, aye. Your contact is now designated as *Gremlin Zero-One*. You are authorized to prepare weapons, but hold fire until you receive batteries released."

"USWE, aye. Understand hold fire on target *Gremlin Zero-One*. Break.

UB—USWE. I've got good bearing cross-fixes from *Albany*. Stand by for range updates directly from the CDRT. Target *Gremlin Zero-One* with Anvil, and inform me as soon as you've got a firing solution."

"UB, aye."

Two new bearing lines appeared on the CDRT as the sonars of *Albany* and *Bowie* both provided updated tracking information on the enemy submarine. This resulted in a new cross-fix.

With two known locations and an established interval of time between them, the fire control computer took about a millisecond to calculate the target's course and speed. The answer, 282 degrees at six knots, appeared in a small data window attached to the red hostile submarine symbol that represented the target.

Based on a single bearing and range update, this initial calculation would be approximate rather than exact, but it was good enough for the CDRT to project a line of advance for the submarine.

And there it was on the screen: the information they needed to move forward with the plan.

Captain Heller detached himself from a conversation with the TAO and strode over to the CDRT. "Got what we're after, Todd?"

Ensign Moore nodded. "Yes, sir."

The captain pointed toward a spot on the display. "What do you think? Come left to one-nine-five, and cross his track right about here?"

The ensign did an eyeball calculation. That puts us within six-thousand yards, sir. You really want to get that close?"

"I'd prefer not to get within a hundred miles of that thing," said the captain. "But we don't have all that many Sea Bats, and we can't afford to make our insertion points too far away from the target."

"I guess not, sir."

Heller caught the tone of the junior officer's voice. "Having second thoughts?"

"About accepting a commission in the Navy? Now that you mention it, I am. Should have listened to my mom and become a dentist."

As jokes went it was not exactly a knee-slapper, but the captain responded with a smile.

"If your brilliant plan doesn't kill us all, you can always apply for dental school. Probably get free dental floss for life."

The ensign returned the captain's smile. "Who could pass up an opportunity like that?"

⚓ ⚓ ⚓

Foxy Roxy:

Jon kept his voice low enough to barely carry over the sound of the approaching outboard. "Here they come."

There was a sound from inside the cabin, but he didn't know what Cassy was doing in there.

Even as he watched the boarding team approach, he was mentally deconstructing their methods. If they wanted the element of surprise, they should be coming in from the seaward side, so their silhouettes wouldn't be visible against the lights of the town. Also, the noise of the outboard was broadcasting their presence. They could have prevented that by running on an electric trolling motor. Slower, but much quieter. And how hard would it be to catch a sailboat at anchor, even if your top speed was limited to three or four knots? With a little more forethought, these guys might have slipped aboard without being detected.

Maybe their failure to take the extra steps was a sign that they didn't care about surprise. It could also be a case of cultural machismo at odds with tactical thinking. They paid lip service to the need for stealth by dressing in black and running at night with no lights on. But they couldn't resist the sense of masculine dominance that came from the throaty roar of a powerful motor, and their pride wouldn't allow them to sneak in from an unexpected angle when *real* men charged straight in the front door.

Or maybe all of that was wrong. Jon was hardly an expert on the social customs of Cuban roughnecks.

The boat's coxswain throttled back his motor about ten yards out, and guided his craft alongside the port stern of the *Roxy*.

Jon kept his hands in sight and tried to look nonthreatening as the two men in the bow looped lines over a pair of cleats, and swarmed over the gunwale into the cockpit of the sailboat.

The soldiers (or whatever they were) had worked out their tactics ahead of time. Either that or they'd been in similar situations before. One maintained as much distance as he could manage in the small cockpit, keeping a hand on the butt of a holstered sidearm. The other moved in closer.

Clearly the plan was for Thug Two to keep Thug One—and the threat—covered from a safe distance. The technique might have been effective in a place with more elbowroom, but the cockpit of the *Foxy Roxy* didn't have much open deck space. With one good step, Jon could be within grabbing distance of Thug Two.

Which he wouldn't do unless he had to. Much better to submit to some questions, produce the cruising permit and license of exception—with all the stamps and seals attached—then play the dumb (but officially sanctioned) tourist.

It wouldn't work, of course. These guys weren't Guarda Frontera or *Policía Nacional*, and they hadn't come to inspect travel papers. This had the look of a rapid action team; the kind of jackbooted toughs who did the dirty work that few governments would admit to.

"Welcome aboard," Jon said. "What can I do for you gentlemen?"

Thug Two said something in rapid Spanish.

"Put your hands on your head," said Thug One.

It was now too dark to make out the man's features, but he was undoubtedly wearing his best badass look.

Jon did his best to sound surprised. "Am I under arrest? What are the charges?"

"Hands on your head!" said Thug One again, and this time it was a shout.

"I'm an American citizen with legal travel papers," Jon said. "And I've broken no laws."

Thug One shot out a gloved hand and shoved Jon backward against the aft bulkhead of the cabin. Then the man reached for his weapon.

That's when Cassy's voice came from the open companionway. "Jonnie! Soup's on!"

Back still against the bulkhead, Jon slid a half-step away from the darkened opening.

Thug One glanced instinctively toward the sound of the voice just in time to catch the contents of the soup pot right in the face. The liquid was boiling hot. The man screamed, and threw his hands up to cover his scalded flesh.

Jon launched himself off the bulkhead, slamming his left shoulder into the blinded man's chest, driving him back into Thug Two.

The three of them went down, with Jon on top. He grabbed Thug One's helmet, pulled it upward a few inches, and then slammed it downward with all of his might—trying like hell to jam the hard surface into the unprotected face of Thug Two.

He did it again, and again, with Thug One screaming and thrashing the entire time.

There was a flash and sound like an explosion close to Jon's ear as Thug Two squeezed off a round from his sidearm. The man's arm was flailing, struggling to reach around his convulsing partner and draw a bead on this crazy Yuma.

Half-deafened by the gunshot, Jon gave the helmet in his hands an abrupt and vicious twist, trying his best to snap Thug One's neck. It looked easy when Jet Li did it in the movies. In real life it turned out to be not quite as simple.

Thug One was in pain, but he had not lost his physical strength. He managed to slam a fist into the side of Jon's head, and Jon went rolling off of him.

Suddenly Roxy was in the middle of things, snapping, biting, growling with a ferocity that Jon had never heard from his sweetheart of a dog. Leaping into the tangle of convulsing limbs, the Staffordshire Terrier latched on to the inner thigh of Thug One and began trying to rip the man's leg off.

Down in the inflatable boat, the coxswain (Thug Three) was yelling in Spanish.

Scrambling to his knees, Jon spotted the empty soup pot and grabbed it. A half-second later, he was hammering the hell out of Thug Two's gun hand, trying to knock the weapon out of his grasp, or at least keep the man from putting it to effective use.

The pistol went off again, blasting a crater in the fiberglass near Jon's left knee. Thug Three's weapon was out now too. Jon caught sight of his form in the dark, standing unsteadily in the stern of the inflatable boat, trying to line up a shot that wouldn't endanger his own people.

Jon hurled the soup pot toward the man's head, and then seized Thug Two's weapon hand, bending the wrist and rotating it inward.

If he had thought about it, Jon would have recognized the move as a pronating wristlock: one of the techniques he had learned in Marine Corps unarmed combat training. But he wasn't thinking. He was reacting instinctively, and the split-second maneuver took his opponent by surprise.

A pronating rotational attack can be difficult to counter, because it forces motion in a direction that human musculature is not designed to oppose. Thug Two—still being crushed by his floundering partner, and all too aware of the furious beast snarling and tearing flesh just centimeters from his groin—did not instantly apply the counterforce necessary to prevent the rotation before it passed the point of no return.

The gun hand turned inward, and Jon increased the pressure, bringing the pistol back around toward its owner. With both hands, he squeezed the man's fingers with all his might, forcing the finger inside the trigger guard to contract.

The weapon bucked in its three-handed grip as another gunshot rang out. Jon repeated the bone-crushing squeeze and the weapon fired again.

Thug Two stopped struggling. Like his black-clad partner, he was wearing a flak vest. If the shot had been from a few feet farther away, that might have saved him. But very few pieces of wearable ballistic protection can stop a large caliber slug at point blank range. This was not one of those rare exceptions.

Snatching the weapon from the limp hand, Jon popped off two shots in the general direction of Thug Three. The man dived for cover in the bottom of his boat.

Jon leapt to his feet, stepping up onto the transom bench to get a good angle down into the inflatable boat.

Before Thug Three could recover, Jon peppered him with five quick rounds. Unlike the two boarders, the coxswain wasn't wearing a flak vest, and at least two of the shots caught him high in the back.

Then Jon turned his attention back to Thug One, who was trying to keep the slavering dog from eating his crotch.

For an instant Jon thought about putting a couple of bullets in the bastard's chest, to take him out of the game permanently. But the fight was over now, and that no longer seemed necessary.

He brought the barrel of the automatic down hard on Thug One's face. The man stopped struggling, despite the fact that Roxy had not paused in her attempt to tear his leg off.

Jon pulled the sidearm out of Thug One's holster, and then checked to be sure that Thug Two and Thug Three were not moving. Only then did he start trying to calm Roxy down, and disengage her jaws from the unconscious man's leg.

There was a moment when he didn't think she was going to let go, and he wondered if the first taste of violence might have pushed her over some edge from which there was no coming back. But after a few seconds, the sound of his voice seemed to filter into her brain. She released her jaws, and backed away, almost tripping over her own paws as if she was completely disoriented.

Jon knelt and caught her, stroking the dog's head and crooning to her in soothing tones. She was trembling, and she wasn't the only one.

He turned to face the open companionway. "All clear, Cass. Bad guys are down."

Cassy came out on deck, the boat's flare gun in her right hand, and a boning knife in her left. Both improvised weapons clattered to the deck as she threw her arms around Jon's neck and began to sob.

"I was going to help..." she sniffed. "I was ready to help.... But—"

"You *did* help," Jon said. "You were right on the ball when it counted. I'm pretty sure your soup trick saved my life."

Cassy pulled back abruptly as she realized that her hands were wet and sticky. "You've got blood all over you! How bad are you hurt?"

"Steady there, Doc," said Jon. "That's not my blood. Or I don't think so anyway."

He gave Cassy a final hug and got painfully to his feet. "I'm gonna toss these two Bozos into the boat with their buddy, and set them adrift. Then we're going to do some fast clean up, in case somebody else comes nosing around."

Cassy sniffed. "And *then* what?"

"Then, I'm going to leave you with one of these weapons and Fearless Roxy while I go ashore to hunt for our lost Marines."

"Jonnie, you can't!"

"Those guys are in trouble," he said. "They should have been back hours ago."

"They're Marines," Cassy said, "and you're not the U.S. Cavalry. It's not your job to go charging to the rescue if their mission goes sour."

Jon looked toward the beach. "Okay, you convinced me. I'll wait here."

"Wait.... *What?* You can't change your mind that fast. I think you just gave me whiplash!"

Jon pointed. "I don't have to go after them. They're coming back."

Cassy got to her feet and looked for herself. Sure enough, the dinghy was inbound.

"Hang on," she said. "There are only three of them. They're missing somebody."

"I can see that," said Jon. "Get below and start the diesel."

⚓ ⚓ ⚓

Sea Bat 035:

Officially, Sea Bat was an acronym, short for <u>S</u>ubmerged <u>E</u>xtended <u>A</u>utonomy <u>B</u>iological <u>A</u>coustic <u>T</u>racker. Unofficially, the term was a *backronym* rather than a true acronym, meaning that the project team at Norton Deepwater Systems had decided upon the name first, and then cherry picked supporting terminology to fit the resulting letters.

Unless ordered to testify under oath, the Norton personnel in question would probably have denied the name's origin as a backronym, such linguistic manipulation having connotations of unprofessionalism in the industry.

Sea Bat 035 knew nothing of these things, and it cared not a bit what title it was called by. Like the other Unmanned Underwater Vehicles of its design series, the Sea Bat had no awareness of humans or their affairs. It was interested in only three things: the acoustic emanations of specific aquatic mammals, the movements and migratory patterns of those creatures through the ocean environment, and compliance with certain operational and maintenance related programming imperatives.

In configuration the UUV was a glider, cruising slowly through the sea on tapered wing-like foils that blended smoothly into the body of the hull form. It was dolphin-like in shape, partly to appear less threatening to the marine life it was built to study, and partly because the length-to-diameter ratio of 4.5:1 created minimal hydrodynamic drag (a lesson learned from the dolphins themselves).

Under the original production contract with NOAA, this particular series of Sea Bats had been configured to detect, approach, and follow acoustic emanations from members of the genus and species *Balaenoptera musculus*, more commonly known as blue whales. Each of the UUVs had carried a library of signatures containing frequency sets in the 10-40Hz range most often used for blue whale vocalizations.

For Sea Bat 035 and its brother units now swimming in the vicinity, the signature library had been overwritten with frequency patterns associated with a North Korean supercavitating submarine. The Sea Bats were not aware of this change, of course. They detected acoustic signals, compared them to target frequencies from the signature library, and acted as the situational response algorithms in their software dictated.

As far as the Sea Bats were concerned, anything emanating the proper target frequencies *must* be a blue whale. Their programming imperative was to move in close enough for easy observation.

So it was with Sea Bat 035. The UUV's acoustic sensor package had detected two of the target frequencies. It made a gentle turn toward the axis of highest signal strength, and began its unhurried glide toward the source of the noise—wings pinioning in a slow-motion flap not unlike that of a penguin.

After fifteen minutes, the two target frequencies were joined by a third. Another few minutes of swimming brought a fourth frequency, and then a fifth. Sea Bat 035 glided on.

Eventually, the signal strength passed a critical threshold. The Sea Bat's operational program instructed the UUV to turn aside, but that order was immediately countermanded by a higher priority command from the emergency recovery subroutine.

The turn-away command was ignored. Sea Bat 035 continued to close in silently and serenely on its "whale."

The Sea Bat series gliders were designed for an operational lifespan of five years, and a maximum mission duration of six months.

Sea Bat 035's lifespan was somewhat briefer than that. One hour, four minutes, and eleven seconds into its very first mission—at a distance of less than two feet from the "whale" it was tracking—the UUV satisfied the final arming conditions for the small (but significant) explosive charge carried in its belly.

Seven and a half pounds of plasticized pentaerythritol tetranitrate detonated with a force equivalent to ten M67 fragmentation grenades.

Sea Bat 035, which had not been designed with such capabilities in mind, was not expecting this abrupt and terminal change in its fortunes.

Neither was the "whale."

CHAPTER 64

STEEL WIND (KANG CHUL POONG)
CARIBBEAN SEA, SOUTHWEST OF NIQUERO, CUBA
FRIDAY; 06 MARCH
2007 hours (8:07 PM)
TIME ZONE -5 'ROMEO'

The explosion jolted Hwa Yong-mu awake. He lay in his hammock for a second, trying to figure out whether he had dreamed the earsplitting noise. Then the sound of shouting voices told him that the detonation had been real.

He rolled out of the cramped sleeping area, jammed his feet into his shoes, and hurried toward the control room. He pretended not to notice the clumps of hair left behind in the hammock.

When he reached the control room, his first officer, Lieutenant Po Hyun-su, was half out of the command chair, gesticulating toward an electrical junction box. "Cut the power!"

Two crewmen were struggling to stuff rags into the narrow space behind the electrical box, where rivulets of water could be seen coursing down the bulkhead.

It wasn't much more than a trickle, but there shouldn't have been any water at all. There was no piping in the control room, for this very reason. The only possible source was the sea itself: a penetration of the pressure hull. And that was not good.

"Shut off the circuit!" Po shouted. "Before you *chon-noms* electrocute yourselves!"

One of the crewman rushed to a breaker panel and did as ordered, locating the proper circuit and flipping the power switch to the off position. Part of the control room lighting went dark, along with two of the display screens.

Hwa Yong-mu caught Po's eye. "Comrade Lieutenant! Make your report! What happened?"

"We don't know, Comrade Captain. There was an explosion; I believe outside the hull. Perhaps we struck a mine."

"A mine?"

"Just a thought, sir."

Hwa Yong-mu gave the logical order. "All engines stop!"

If there was any chance that the explosion had been caused by a mine, he wasn't going to risk hitting another one. Better to stay put and assess damage.

"Sir! All engines are stopped!"

Hwa turned toward the sonar station. "Report all contacts!"

"Comrade Captain, we are tracking two fishing boats at medium to long range, bearing three-zero-four and three-three-seven degrees. Also, we have an oil platform at long range, bearing zero six zero, and a long-range merchant ship bearing one-five-two."

"Close aboard contacts?"

"None, sir."

By now, another pair of crewman had arrived with tools and a patching kit. They began unbolting the electrical box from the bulkhead.

Hwa motioned for Po to vacate the command chair. "Form an inspection team, Comrade Lieutenant. We need to be certain that we're not taking on water anywhere else."

Po acknowledged the order and headed aft.

Hwa settled into the chair. Wouldn't a mine have done more damage? Maybe this hadn't been a mine. Perhaps it was a stress crack in a weld, brought on by water pressure.

That couldn't be right; the *Steel Wind* was only sixty meters down. He did a quick mental calculation. The water pressure at this depth shouldn't be much more than 600 kilopascals. Not enough to cause hull failure. Unless this was an aftereffect of damage done by an earlier dive, or possibly the structural strain of operating in supercavitation mode.

Besides, he had distinctly heard an explosion. Not the crack of a failing weld or a buckling hull plate. Quite definitely an explosion.

And the source did not appear to be inside of the hull. The only other possible source was *outside* of the hull, which would seem to indicate either a mine or a torpedo. But sonar had detected no hydrophone effects from the high speed propellers of a torpedo, and the blast yield would have been much larger for any torpedo warhead or mine.

Which brought him back around the circle again. Not a mine, or a torpedo, or a mechanical hull defect. What did that leave?

He was pondering this question when the second blast went off.

The shock wasn't powerful enough to jar Hwa from his seat, but it rang the hull like a gong. The remaining control room lights flickered, and red warning lamps began flashing on the Weapons Console.

Hwa jerked his head around toward the bow, the apparent direction of the detonation. "*Si-bal!* (Fuck!) Are we making way?"

"No, Comrade Captain!" said the helmsman. "We're at dead stop, as you ordered."

"Then we couldn't have hit another mine," Hwa said. "So what *was* that?"

No one had an answer.

The Weapons Officer looked around from his station. "Sir, torpedo tube number one is showing a critical fault. The torpedomen are investigating."

"Si-bal!" said Hwa again. The *Steel Wind* only had two torpedo tubes. The loss of one tube represented a fifty percent reduction in the submarine's firepower.

That was bad enough, but not knowing the cause of the explosions was worse.

"Ahead one-third," Hwa said. "Take us to periscope depth."

The order was sufficiently rare to catch the Diving Officer by surprise. The *Steel Wind* hunted and navigated almost exclusively by sonar. The submarine's most reliable defense was the ability to transition to supercavitation mode in seconds, outrunning all enemy weapons. That transition wasn't possible with ten meters of periscope extending beyond the supercav envelope. The resulting hydrodynamic drag would slow the submarine (possibly below supercavitation speed), and (potentially) rip the periscope out of its mountings—allowing seawater to rush in through the broken fittings.

The extra minute or so required to fully retract the periscope and avoid such a disaster might turn out to be more time than the submarine could afford.

"Do I have to repeat myself?" Hwa snapped.

The Diving Officer shook his head. "No, Comrade Captain!" He turned and began relaying orders.

Fifteen minutes later, after the usual pause at the forty meter mark to check for shapes and shadows, the *Steel Wind* reached periscope depth.

Hwa stepped to the scope stand, reached up and gripped the hydraulic control ring encircling the upper hull penetration for the periscope. He turned the control ring ten degrees to the right.

With a muted bump and a low hydraulic whine, the periscope emerged from its form-fitting recess below the deck plate. As the optics module rose into view, Hwa flipped the periscope handles into position. When the scope had risen about a meter, he crouched and pressed his face into the light shroud surrounding the eye piece.

He followed the optics module as it continued to rise, starting from a crouch and gradually straightening to his full standing height as he turned the scope through a 360 degree revolution.

Halfway through the circle, his concentration was disrupted by the third explosion. Somewhere aft by the sound of it, a suspicion that was quickly confirmed by muffled shouts from the direction of the engineering plant.

His eyes missed the shape on the first rapid sweep, but he spotted it on the second time around. Off the starboard bow, bearing two-seven-eight: a dark silhouette, running without lights.

A flick of a thumb tab engaged the scope's light amplification mode. The image became grainier, but the shape took on sharper visual contrast. A destroyer, moving from starboard to port, crossing the *Steel Wind's* line of advance.

The click of another tab called up the stereoscopic range finder. This created two ghostly images of the ship, and Hwa spent a few seconds turning the handgrip that adjusted the range finder's prisms, until the images overlapped and merged.

He checked the estimated range from the readout at the top of the image. Six-thousand four-hundred meters. *Jen-jang!* How had the enemy ship gotten in so close without being detected by sonar?

Hwa could ask such questions at another time. For now, he had to move quickly. "Ready tube two! Prepare for a snap shot!"

"Comrade Captain!" said the Weapons Officer. "Tube two is now reporting a fault in the firing circuits."

"Is the local firing mechanism operational?"

"Yes, sir! It seems to be, sir!"

"Then we'll fire locally," Hwa said. "Inform me when the torpedo is ready."

He felt a tickle of something on his upper lip. His fingers swiped at it automatically and came away wet. His nose was bleeding again.

No time for that now.

"Sir, tube two is ready!"

Hwa adjusted the angle of the periscope to keep the destroyer in his crosshairs. His grip tightened on the handles.

⚓ ⚓ ⚓

USS *Bowie*:

"All Stations—Sonar has hydrophone effects off the port quarter! Bearing zero-nine-six, correlated to current position of *Gremlin Zero-One*. Initial classification: supercavitating torpedo!"

Ensign Moore jabbed his mike button. "Bridge—USWE. Crack the whip! We have an in-bound hostile torpedo. I say again—crack the whip! Break! UB—USWE. Kill *Gremlin Zero-One* with Anvil!"

The deck began to tilt as USS *Bowie* heeled into the first turn of the crack-the-whip evasion maneuver.

"UB, aye! Going to launch standby. Launch ordered. Weapon away— now, now, NOW!"

The entire ship vibrated as an ASROC missile blasted out of the forward vertical launch module and shot toward the sky. "Anvil away, no apparent casualties!"

On the screen of the CDRT, the red hostile-torpedo symbol had already covered half of the distance that separated the *Bowie* from the North Korean submarine.

It was the speed differential again, and USS *Bowie* was on the wrong end of the curve. Although it could not have emerged from the tube at its top speed, the supercav torpedo was probably moving at two-hundred knots by now. There was just no hope of outrunning the thing.

The commanding officer's voice came over the net. "Bridge, this is Captain Heller. I have the conn. Hard right rudder! Steady on new course three-two-five!"

The Officer of the Deck acknowledged the order, and the ship rolled heavily as she came about.

Ensign Moore watched the screen, trying to figure out what the CO was thinking. This was nothing like the evasion maneuvers taught in the USWE course, and he couldn't remember anything similar from the tactical manuals.

The OOD's voice came over the net. "Steady on three-two-five, sir!"

"Very well," said Captain Heller. "All stop."

"All stop, aye, sir!"

This new order was just as confusing to Ensign Moore as the captain's earlier commands had been. All stop? When they were running away from a torpedo? Wasn't that the exact opposite of what you wanted to do in this situation?

The CO patched his headset into the 1MC general announcing circuit. When he spoke, his voice was heard from every speaker on the ship. "All hands, this is the Captain. Brace for shock!"

Ensign Moore gripped an overhead grab rail with one hand, and the edge of the CDRT console with the other. Just as he'd been trained to do, he bent his knees to absorb at least some of the shock that would be transmitted through the deck plating, and opened his mouth to keep the overpressure of the coming explosion from blowing out his eardrums.

He wondered if these precautions would offer any real benefit at all. And then he wondered if he was living out the last few seconds of his life.

⚓ ⚓ ⚓

Supercav Torpedo:

Contrary to the speculations of the U.S. Navy's acoustic analysts, the incoming weapon was not a Russian-built Shkval, or even the similar (but less capable) Iranian counterfeit model known as the *Hoot*. It was a *Superkavitierender Unterwasserlaufkörper* (Supercavitating Underwater Running Body) built in Kiel, Germany by the international arms firm *Ozeankriegsfuhrungtechnologien* (Ocean Warfare Technologies).

The *Steel Wind's* torpedoes had been procured through an astonishingly complex chain of false fronts, weaving through six countries on three continents. The CIA and Office of Naval Intelligence would ultimately devote more than two years to unraveling the twisted trail of evidence. Even then, the investigators would never uncover proof that the German company had knowingly sold advanced armaments to North Korea in violation of UN Security Council Resolution 1718.

None of these details mattered to the torpedo closing in on USS *Bowie*. And no one aboard the destroyer had the slightest interest in the provenance of the weapon that was coming to kill them.

The supercav was still accelerating when the arming section of the warhead detected the magnetic signature of the target vessel. Approximately two seconds later, the signal strength crossed the minimum threshold required to trigger the detonation sequence.

A relay in the arming section should have tripped, providing electrical power to the detonator circuits. Damaged by concussion from the second Sea Bat attack, the relay armature was jammed in the open position. The intended explosion did not occur, but the result was nearly as bad.

Even without its warhead, the supercavitating weapon was three tons of underwater missile moving at 192 knots.

USS *Bowie*:

The torpedo impacted the stern ten feet left of centerline and just above the keel. The weapon's conical nose acted as a force localizer, providing a degree of penetration that the German designers had never intended.

It tore through the reinforced steel hull like a rocket-powered wrecking ball, shattering welds, mangling I-beams, cracking support structures, and buckling deck plates as it went. Behind this moving locus of chaos came the sea, rushing in through the ruptured hull in an unstoppable torrent.

The engineering compartment known as Aft Steering took the brunt of the initial destruction. Housing the immense hydraulic motors that turned the ship's twin rudders, the compartment was crewed during battle stations. Two enlisted engineers were standing by to take local control of the rudders in the event of a steering failure.

The first engineer was torn apart by shrapnel when the hostile torpedo came bursting through the hull. The second engineer died an instant later, as the inrushing wall of water slammed her into the forward bulkhead with enough force to cave in the side of her head.

Inertia not yet expended, the enemy weapon lanced through into the next compartment, Shaft Alley, trailing more devastation and flooding in its wake.

If the screws had still been turning, the mechanical stresses imparted by 105,000 horsepower per shaft would have magnified the damage several times over. With both propeller shafts stopped, the metallic juggernaut severed electrical cables, shattered piping, and damaged everything in its path, but it did not tear the aft end of the ship apart.

Forward of Shaft Alley was Main Engine Room Number Two, containing a pair of the ship's gas turbine generators and the electric motor for the port shaft.

Reduced now to a mangled core of burning scrap, the remains of the supercav weapon plowed into the engine room where it struck the isolation enclosure for a Rolls Royce RR4500 turbine. Fragments penetrated the walls of the enclosure, pulverizing the generator and setting fire to fuel that spewed from cracked pipes.

An engineer on the lower level was caught in the expanding fireball. Three others ran for the nearest ladders and began trying to climb faster than the floodwaters.

The broken piping continued to gush fuel, and the flaming oil slick spread itself across the surface of the rising water.

Electrical junction boxes shorted out and power to the engine room failed. The cavernous compartment was plunged into darkness. Battery-powered emergency lanterns tripped on, throwing circles of illumination in the smoke-filled gloom.

When they reached the upper level, the evacuating sailors dogged the watertight door behind themselves. The senior engineer on watch, Gas Turbine System Technician–Mechanical First Class Craig Wagner, broke the plastic seals on the activation handles for both of the main space fire suppression systems.

"Get to a phone and call CCS!" he said to the nearest sailor. "Report a class bravo fire and major flooding in MER 2. Tell 'em that I'm dumping foam and PEAT!"

The junior engineer ran for a telephone, and Wagner twisted the activation handles.

The first system sprayed hundreds of gallons of high-expansion foam from sprinkler nozzles all over the engine room, blanketing the fuel slick under a layer of suppressant chemical bubbles.

The second handle triggered the new PEAT system (Propelled Extinguishing Agent Technologies), lighting off powdered aerosol dispensers in the overhead of the compartment—pumping out clouds of micron-sized fire retardant particles.

When the status lamps for both systems showed that they had been properly actuated, Wagner nodded toward the remaining engineer. "Let's get to Repair 2 and report in."

Both sailors took off up the passageway at a trot.

⚓ ⚓ ⚓

A blue circular icon appeared on the CDRT screen near the current cross-fix for *Gremlin Zero-One*. It was the water entry point symbol for the *Bowie's* Anvil.

The Sonar Supervisor's voice came over the net. "USWE—Sonar, we have weapon startup."

Ensign Moore thumbed his mike button. "USWE, aye. Let me know if it acquires."

The deck was listing aft and to port, the angle becoming increasingly noticeable as tons of seawater poured in through the gaping holes in the hull.

It was all going wrong. The propulsion plant was out; the ship might be sinking; and some of the crew—he didn't even know how many—were dead. All because of his stupid idea.

The Sea Bat plan had seemed so ingenious. Such an innovative way to go after the North Korean sub.

Now they were seeing the result of his cleverness.

He watched the blue friendly torpedo symbol close in on *Gremlin Zero-One*. Any second now, the sub would shift into hyper drive and leave his too-slow weapon behind.

The Sonar Supervisor's voice came over the tactical net again. "USWE—Sonar. Weapon has...."

His report chopped off in mid sentence as the power tripped off line in CIC.

The CDRT screen went dark, along with the displays of every radar console and operator station.

USS *Bowie* was now blind, as well as crippled.

⚓ ⚓ ⚓

Steel Wind:

"Sonar has torpedo hydrophone effects off the port bow!"

Hwa didn't hesitate. He stabbed at the transmit button on his communications panel. "Emergency Mode Alpha! Execute!" Then, he jerked the hydraulic control ring to the left, and the periscope began to retract.

Emergency Mode Alpha was the order for immediate transition to supercavitation mode. There was no time to wait for full retraction of the periscope. He would have to risk the consequences of potentially losing it.

There were the two usual heavy thumps as the Chief Engineer hit the solenoid switches for the huge electrically powered dump valves. Next would come the rumble of seawater being rammed into the reactor vessel, where it would flash to steam for the rocket thruster and the capillary bow vents.

But the familiar sound didn't come. Instead, the heavy thumps were repeated as the Chief Engineer cycled the solenoid switches a second time. And then a third.

The report that came next was no surprise. "Comrade Captain! The solenoids are operating, but the dump valves will not open!"

"Find a way to open them!" Hwa shouted. "Do it *now*, or we are all dead!"

He wiped his bleeding nose against his sleeve: a crudity he had not allowed himself since childhood. That thought brought back something else from his youth: the memory of a puzzling phrase once spoken by his father's father. *A tiger brought down by crickets.*

As a boy, Hwa Yong-mu had never understood the reference. How could a fearsome beast like the tiger be brought down by insects?

The phrase was no longer a mystery to him. The *Steel Wind*, built to outrun every antisubmarine weapon in the arsenals of the fatherland's enemies, was being killed—one tiny insect bite at a time.

He grasped the periscope's control ring, cancelled the retract signal, and reversed it to re-extend the scope. If he couldn't accelerate to supercavitation speed, at least he could continue the fight.

He returned his face to the light shroud and peered through the scope. The American destroyer was down by the stern and listing to port, but stubbornly afloat. He would change that. It might be too late to save his own vessel, but he would take his enemy to the grave with him.

"Weapons Officer, ready tube two! Prepare for a snap shot!"

"Comrade Captain, the outer door of tube two will not close! We cannot open the inner door to load the tube!"

"Of course you can't," Hwa said to himself. "I should have expected as much."

The American torpedo was now close enough to be heard through the hull. The high-pitched howl of its screws grew louder and more shrill, like the buzzing of an angry insect.

And that was fitting, Hwa supposed. One last cricket, come to bring the final sting of defeat.

⚓ ⚓ ⚓

USS *Albany*:

"Conn—Sonar. Loud underwater explosion off the starboard bow, bearing two-two-nine! Correlates to bearing of contact *Sierra One-Four*."

Ernie Pooler was through the door of the sonar room before the report was complete. "Any secondaries?"

The sonar operator held up a hand in a wait gesture. "Standby, COB. Standby.... Affirmative! We have definite secondary explosions! Target is breaking up! Score one for the skimmers. Looks like those boys have killed themselves a submarine!"

Ernie chuckled and patted the operator on the back. "Bound to happen sooner or later, Shipmate. Even a blind squirrel finds a nut once in a while."

CHAPTER 65

FOXY ROXY
NORTHWEST OF PLAYA DE SUERTE, CUBA
FRIDAY; 06 MARCH
2118 hours (9:18 PM)
TIME ZONE -5 'ROMEO'

Cassy came up through the companionway with a mug of coffee in her hand.

Jon reached for it. "Thanks! I can use that."

Cassy held the cup out of reach and took a sip. "What makes you think this is for you?"

"It's only fair," said Jon. "You gave my soup to some Cuban guy. The least you can do is bring me some coffee."

After a second (and much longer) sip, Cassy surrendered the mug. "You're not nearly as funny as you think you are."

Jon took a swallow. "So you keep telling me."

"How's Eagle Eye doing?" She nodded toward the spot on the upper deck where Fris sat cross-legged with his back toward the mast, scanning the horizon behind the boat with a pair of binoculars.

Jon shrugged. "I told him we're outside the twelve mile limit and that nobody's going to come after us now. But I don't think he's gonna come down from there until we're within sight of Key West."

"Maybe I should bring him some coffee," said Cassy.

"Probably a good idea," said Jon. "He didn't get any soup either."

Then he dropped the levity from his voice. "How's Liv holding up?"

"She's still just sitting there," said Cassy. "I don't think she's said a word since she called in her report. She needs a good cry to let some of it out."

"Maybe she *can't*," said Jon. "Sometimes, you get so wrapped up in being a good Marine that you forget how to be human."

Cassy sighed. "You think she's going to be okay?"

This brought a snort from Jon. "What are you asking me for? You're the doc."

290

"Yeah," said Cassy, "but not *that* kind of doc."

Jon downed another swallow of coffee. "We'll be in Key West in a couple of days. The Corps can either fly her back to GITMO for treatment, or get her into counseling right there at the Naval Clinic."

"I guess the real doctors can figure it out," Cassy said.

Jon held up the coffee mug in a toasting gesture. "Chesty Puller always claimed that Navy Corpsmen were the best doctors in the business. I'm betting you can cure her by the time we get to Florida."

Cassy shook her head. "I'm not sure this is something that can be cured."

"Then it can be treated," said Jon. "If I was a shrink, I'd prescribe an extended vacation on a beat-up old sailboat, with a beautiful woman and a faithful Staffordshire Terrier. Maybe that's not the cure for PTSD, but it's a damned effective treatment regimen."

"I don't know if Liv leans that way."

"What? She doesn't like dogs?"

Cassy elbowed him gently in the ribs.

"Although," said Jon thoughtfully, "if she's going to do the sailing vacation thing, she can probably skip the nuclear explosion part."

"And the gunfight on the boat," said Cassy.

"Right," said Jon. "She can skip that part too."

CHAPTER 66

The Chief Engineer plodded into the wardroom, ambled to the coffee urn, and slouched into a chair with the weariness of a man near to collapse. His coveralls were wet, smeared with grease, and torn in several places.

Captain Heller came in a few seconds after, somewhat less bedraggled, but showing his own signs of exhaustion. He also went straight for the coffee urn. "So, Cheng, what's the verdict? Are we going to sink, or not?"

"That depends," said the Cheng. "Are you planning to recommend me for commander?"

"Not if we sink," said the captain.

The engineer yawned. "Then I reckon I can keep us afloat. Well, maybe not me personally. But my people can do it."

Heller responded with a yawn of his own. "That's the spirit! Seriously though, how are we looking?"

"We've got power restored to critical systems and most of the crew areas. Between pumps, eductors, and liberal use of fairy dust, we've got the water level in MER 2 down to about fifty percent. That's as good as we're gonna get, I think. Not much we can do about Shaft Alley or Aft Steering. We can't get a patching team into either compartment without opening a watertight door. If we do that, we end up flooding the adjoining passageways. And we can't afford to take on much more water, or we really *will* sink."

There was another (unspoken) reason for wanting to access Aft Steering. The bodies of MRFN Jessica Marsh and MR3 Dale Hanning were still in there.

For the first several hours following the attack, everyone's hands had been full just trying to save the ship. Now that the flooding was under control and things seemed to be stabilizing, there would be time to recover

292

the remains of their casualties.

The body of GSM3 Vincente Petrillo should be the easiest to get to. Main Engine Room Number Two was accessible, and they had a fairly good idea of where the sailor's remains should be.

Aft Steering would be a lot more challenging. Getting in there would take some work, and a lot of thought. Neither officer was ready to tackle that problem yet.

Captain Heller moved on to the next question on his mental list. "Do we have enough power for radars and weapon systems?"

"Should be okay. We've got two of the main generators on line, plus one of the auxiliaries. Enough capacity to handle the load."

"How about propulsion?"

The Cheng stared into his coffee cup. "I'd just as soon not mess around with that, sir."

"Why not?"

"The port engine shorted out when MER 2 flooded," said the Cheng. "Starboard engine stayed dry and looks to be okay, but I wouldn't want to put torque on the starboard shaft until I see how badly things got beat up in Shaft Alley. A few million foot pounds of rotational force can cause a lot of bad mojo if we've got a locked line shaft bearing or something. By the way, Captain, that was a good idea: stopping the shafts when that torpedo was after us."

"Thanks," said Heller. "I figured there was no chance of outrunning that monster, so the best I could do was limit the damage."

"Well, it worked," said the Chief Engineer. "We may have to drift around and wait for a tow, but at least we go home in one piece. Mostly."

The captain stood up and stretched his muscles. "I'll settle for *mostly*, Cheng. It beats the hell out of the alternative."

"Yes, it does, sir," said the engineering officer. "It most certainly does."

⚓ ⚓ ⚓

USS *Albany*:

At 0940 Zulu (0440 hours local time), a hatch opened in the curved upper hull of the *Albany's* bow, exposing the dome shaped waterproof cap of a vertical launch missile cell. Three seconds later, the cap shattered along a series of pre-stressed structural points as a Block IV UGM-109E Tomahawk Land Attack Missile blasted out of its cell and roared toward the surface of the water in a turbulent shroud of smoke-filled bubbles.

When it broke through the wave tops, the weapon climbed into the night sky on a column of gray-white exhaust gasses. At a predetermined altitude, the solid fuel booster broke free and tumbled back into the sea.

The missile transitioned to cruise mode, stubby wings extending from the fuselage and a Williams International F107-WR-402 turbofan taking over the job of propulsion.

The guidance section locked onto down feeds from four GPS satellites, and used three of the signals to perform a Cartesian position calculation using a branch of circular geometry known as trilateration. By comparing the resulting "fix" with the signal from the fourth satellite, the guidance computer was able to determine the missile's attitude with an error factor of less than one inch.

It was right on course, cruising at 550 miles per hour toward the North Korean missile site designated as Point Orange. It would reach its target in twenty minutes and seventeen seconds.

The second missile in the Point Orange fire mission broke the surface of the water twenty seconds after the first. The third missile broached twenty seconds after that, and the firing pattern continued until six Tomahawks were inbound to Point Orange.

The second fire mission, targeted on Point Green, began eight minutes later. It also consisted of six Tomahawks launched at intervals of twenty seconds. Between them, the twelve missiles comprised the entire land attack cruise missile inventory of USS *Albany*.

Each weapon followed a slightly different flight path, and they were all timed to arrive on target simultaneously.

There were identical fire missions launched from USS *Philippine Sea* and USS *Lassen*, timed to strike Point Blue and Point Red at the same instant as the *Albany's* Tomahawks.

Standing ready for follow-up attacks were USS *Hué City*, USS *Farragut*, and USS *Gettysburg*—ready to deliver a second volley of cruise missiles if any of the North Korean launch sites survived the first strike.

The mop-up attacks were not necessary. Twenty-one minutes after USS *Albany* fired the first Tomahawk, the last of the nuclear missile sites had been eradicated from Cuban soil.

It wasn't the sort of victory that Master Chief Ernie Pooler and his fellow submariners had hoped for, but it would have to do.

CHAPTER 67

The three B-2 *Spirit* bombers came in at 50,000 feet, slipping through North Korean air search radar coverage like electronic wraiths. Although not completely invisible to microwaves, their reflective cross-sections were low enough to keep any return signals below the threshold of atmospheric clutter. Coupled with infrared signature suppression, and the fact that the slate gray batwing shapes were extremely difficult to spot visually in the night sky, this made the B-2s as close to undetectable as current technologies permitted.

Based out of Whiteman Air Force Base, Missouri, the stealth aircraft were half way into a thirty-two hour mission. As long as the flight had been so far, and as much of it as still remained, the mission was twelve hours shy of the standing record.

On such long duration flights, the pilot and the mission commander (also a pilot) took turns sleeping in a folding cot aft of the cockpit. But no one was napping aboard the three bombers now as they made their final approaches to the target.

Coming up nine and a half miles below them was the Ryongsong Residence, the official presidential palace of Kim Yong-nam. Built for Kim Il-sung in the early 1980s by a construction brigade of the Korean People's Army, the 4.6 square mile compound enclosed a seven story mansion, several lesser mansions, lush gardens, lakefront banquet halls, swimming pools, waterslides, athletic fields, horse stables and riding trails, a shooting range, and a race track for sports cars.

The complex also contained an underground command center intended to serve as wartime headquarters for the North Korean military, as well as subterranean railway tunnels connecting the facility to at least eight other residences of the Supreme Leader.

Kim Yong-nam was known to spend the night here frequently, although defectors from his regime reported that the man often awoke at random hours and rode his private subway to another of his highly-guarded palaces. This ever-shifting game of sleeping places was assumed to be a hedge against assassination attempts and military strikes.

Kim could be snoring peacefully down there, in some palatial bed chamber at this very moment. Or he might be someplace else entirely. The B-2 crews had no way of knowing, and it wasn't their responsibility to find out. Whether they got lucky with Kim or not, their payloads were about to put a major dent in the military command and control structure of North Korea, as well as sending an unmistakable message to the Supreme Leader, his cronies, and potential enemies of the U.S. all over the world. *This is what happens when you fuck with the United States of America.*

At a precisely calculated instant, the lead B-2 dropped a GBU-57 Massive Ordnance Penetrator, more popularly known as the 'bunker buster.' The ungainly looking 30,000 pound bomb fell clear of the ordnance bay, pitched over into a nose-down attitude, and used variable angle tail vanes to zero in on the GPS coordinates programmed into its guidance package.

The most powerful non-nuclear weapon of its kind, the GBU-57 was designed to penetrate and destroy hardened bunkers, armored missile silos, and other deep-buried fortified targets that were generally considered to be impenetrable.

It slammed into an ornate water fountain that happened to sit astride the specified coordinates, blew through the shallow pool of water and its stone containment basin, blasted through forty feet of hard-packed earth, and then lanced through twenty feet of steel reinforced concrete, before detonating in the open area beneath the armored roof. The 5,300 pound warhead shredded, pulverized, and incinerated nearly everything within the buried command and control center, including more than 100 military personnel standing the late night watch in the facility.

The tunnel leading back to the surface became a chimney, drawing in air to feed the flames below, and venting gouts of smoke into the night.

About 600 yards away, a second GBU-57 drilled through a parking lot, bored down to the railway station beneath, and brought down the roof of the subway for 150 feet in all directions.

Only the lead B-2 was armed with bunker busters. The remaining two aircraft each carried three GBU-43/B Massive Ordnance Air Blast bombs, to continue the pattern of destruction in the above ground sections of the complex.

Carefully spaced to spread their yields over the largest possible area, the six enormous weapons leveled every building, vehicle, or tree within their footprints of desolation. And when their shockwaves and fireballs had subsided, nearly everything in the compound was broken and burning.

Nine and a half miles over head, the trio of stealth bombers turned east and began their exit from North Korean airspace.

Even as Ryongsong Residence was being hammered into oblivion, Kim Yong-nam's alternate palaces at Changgyong, Kangdong, Sinuiju, Ryokpo, Samsok, Pyongsong, Wonsan, Changsuwon, Nampo, Paektusan, Hyangsan, Ragwon, Changsong, and Anju were all on the receiving end of coordinated Tomahawk strikes, launched from ships and submarines in the Sea of Japan. The devastation at the additional residences was not as extreme or as thorough, but very few of the structures left standing could be considered worthy of habitation by the lowliest street urchin, much less by the exalted Supreme Leader of the fatherland.

It was a night of fire, and blood, and death. It was also a night of communication without ambiguity. The President of the United States had delivered his answer to the North Korean ultimatum ten hours before the deadline, in a language that could not possibly be misunderstood.

If Kim Yong-nam had been around to receive it, he would have gotten the message immediately. But Kim was lying crushed beneath six tons of rubble in a collapsed mansion outside of Wonsan.

The headaches would never trouble him again, and he would definitely not be dying from the tumor in his head.

CHAPTER 68

Ri Su-mi lay in the bed of her tiny one room apartment, listening to distant shouts and sirens, trying to decide what to do. She'd heard at least five or six explosions since the one that had awakened her. Possibly more. It was hard to tell, because they sounded far away, and sometimes it seemed like multiple blasts might be overlapping one another.

There was clearly some kind of emergency going on. Her instincts as a nurse made her want to get out there and help people. Perhaps she should walk the eight blocks to Bonghwa Clinic and see if she was needed.

But she had not been called for, and her culture did not look kindly on unprompted acts of initiative. Overly eager people could be unpredictable and they were often ambitious, both of which were considered dangerous traits. A loyal Korean followed orders, believed what she was told, did not complain, and did not ask questions.

Su-mi no longer counted herself as a loyal Korean, although she pretended quite carefully to be one. She could follow orders; she never complained; and she kept her questions to herself. It was the *believing* part that she found difficult.

She had worked at the clinic too long. Her experiences there had become a slow corrosion, eating away at her conviction in the teachings of Juche, and the moral integrity of the party elite.

It was a beautiful facility: sterile, well lighted, professionally staffed, and outfitted with the finest medicines and medical equipment available in Europe and the United States. (That by itself raised a question which Ri Su-mi had never dared to ask. If the People's State was truly a paradise of technological self-reliance, why did all of the best instruments and supplies come from decadent western imperialist countries?)

She also had never dared to ask the other question that was never far from her mind. Why was a superb medical facility like the Bonghwa Clinic reserved for fewer than ten senior members of the party? It could support twenty times as many patients. With careful scheduling, perhaps fifty times as many.

But the clinic sat empty on most days, except for the doctors and nurses in their starched white uniforms, the gleaming racks of instruments, the barely used equipment, and the stone faced guards who kept ordinary citizens from even approaching the gates.

Su-mi knew what the clinics and hospitals for the workers were like. Squalid, ill equipped, and crowded, with acupuncture and herbal home remedies taking the place of real medicines and decent instruments. Antibiotics—when they could be had—were frequently expired or counterfeit. There was often no electrical power, and no running water. This, in the Democratic People's Republic, where all men and women were supposed to be brothers and sisters.

Where was the equality of socialism? The sharing of hardships and good fortune alike?

Those things *were* shared, she knew, only not in the way promised by the ideal of Juche. Fear and privation were shared among the masses, while privileges and luxury were shared among the party elite.

A siren went past her window, and she wondered again if she should go outside to help anyone injured by the explosions. Was it safe to display so small a sign of personal initiative? Just enough to render aid and comfort in an emergency?

The knock on her door was so soft that she barely recognized it. Not much more than the repeated pressure of fingers touching wood.

She threw back the covers and got to her feet. It was the clinic, calling her to work.

But she knew before she reached the door that it was not anyone from the clinic. That would have been a summons. A decisive rapping of knuckles, which allowed for no argument or delay.

She was at the door when the nearly inaudible sound repeated. It was cautious. Furtive. Meant to be heard by her, and her only.

The realization set off feelings of alarm quite apart from the uncertainties of explosions and sirens. In the People's State, the party was allowed to have secrets. The citizens were not. Any attempts at secrecy were automatically dangerous.

But the knock came again, not quite as softly this time.

She knew instinctively that her clandestine visitor would not go away until she opened the door. The knocking would get gradually louder until one of the neighbors investigated.

A shiver of raw fear ran down her spine, but she quietly slid back the latch and opened the door two or three centimeters, putting her eye to the crack.

She had never seen the man before. He looked like any of a hundred other men in her neighborhood. About forty. Thin. Dressed in clean (but worn) work shirt and pants.

He stood with one hand over his own mouth, as though signaling for her not to speak. His other hand held out something for her inspection. A photograph.

The instant Ri Su-mi identified the subject of the photo, she opened the door wider and took the picture from the man's hand. It was her brother, Ri Kyong-su, standing in his camouflage Army uniform—a broad grin on his face. Su-mi felt herself begin to smile automatically in return, before the general anxiety of her situation reasserted itself.

Even more puzzled now, she looked back to the man in the hall. He still had one hand over his mouth, but his free hand was motioning toward the photo in a twisting gesture.

Ri Su-mi turned the photograph over. On the back, in her brother's confident pen strokes, was a message. '*Trust this man, Happy Little Pig. He will bring you to join me in freedom.*'

The nickname, Happy Little Pig, brought Su-mi another tremulous smile. It had been Kyong-su's favorite name for her in their childhood. A reference to the plump cheeks of her ever-smiling face.

But join Kyong-su in freedom? What did that mean?

The stranger in the hall gestured for Su-mi to open the door and let him in.

She hesitated only a second, then motioned him inside.

When he was in with the door closed behind him, the stranger lowered the hand from his mouth and brought his lips close to Su-mi's ear. His voice was scarcely louder than a breath. "Your brother is in America. He wants you to join him there."

Su-mi brought her own lips close to the stranger's ear. "What about his wife and daughter?"

"Someone else is taking care of them," breathed the stranger.

"But they are going?"

"Yes," whispered the man. "They are going. Will you come?"

Ri Su-mi didn't know this man. She had never seen his face, and knew nothing about his history, his personality, or his trustworthiness.

"Is it dangerous?"

"Very dangerous. *Gravely* dangerous. If we're caught, we'll be lucky if they shoot us."

"Can you do it?" Su-mi asked. "Can you get us to America?"

"We will try," said the man. "If everything goes to plan, we will get out. Otherwise...."

He didn't have to explain what would happen otherwise.

Ri Su-mi looked again at the photo of her brother's smiling face. If this stranger was an agent of the party, it would be suicide to go with him. Even if this man was honestly here to help, there might be no escape from the Democratic People's Republic. She might be going to her death, or something worse.

She handed the photo to the stranger. "Hold this for me. I need to get dressed."

EPILOGUE

In unison, the warning light on every camera toggled to green, and the president began his address to the nation. His tone was somber, but a little of the old Chaz Bradley twinkle had returned to his eyes.

"Good evening. Tonight, I can report to the American people and to the world, that the threat of North Korean nuclear attacks against the United States has been eliminated.

"In the pre-dawn hours of this morning, acting under my orders, ships and submarines of the U.S. Navy conducted precision cruise missile strikes against the North Korean nuclear launch sites on the island nation of Cuba. Post mission battle damage assessment confirms that all twenty-four nuclear missiles were destroyed, along with the launch crews assigned to guard and operate the weapons.

"The second Cuban Missile Crisis is ended. A lot of people—in and out of government—worked diligently to bring this emergency to a successful conclusion, but the real credit must go to the men and women of our armed forces. As they have done throughout the history of this great country, they have once again placed themselves in the path of danger to protect their fellow Americans from harm. Too many of them, I'm sorry to say, have paid the ultimate price to end this threat to our nation.

"No words that I can speak will bring back even one of the heroes who perished at the hands of our North Korean attackers. Just as no power on Earth can restore the lives lost during the unprovoked attack on the city of Franklin, Tennessee. We cannot soothe the grief suffered by the families who have lost loved ones during the crisis, nor can we fully heal the wounds of those injured in this ignoble assault upon our nation and our very way of life.

"But we can remind the enemies of freedom and democracy that acts of aggression against the United States do not come without consequences. We can punish those responsible, and we have done so.

"Our naval forces have engaged and destroyed the North Korean submarine operating in the Caribbean Sea. It can no longer threaten our warships or disrupt peaceful commercial shipping in the area.

"Also on my orders, at noon Eastern Standard Time today, U.S. ships, submarines, and aircraft launched coordinated missile strikes and bombing attacks against fourteen separate facilities in North Korea. The targets included military command and control installations, as well as all residences known to belong to the Supreme Leader of that country.

"Let there be no mistake. My intent was to kill Kim Yong-nam, and I believe there's an excellent chance that we succeeded in the goal. If it turns out that Mr. Kim somehow survived our initial attempts, we will redouble our efforts until I am satisfied that the job is complete.

"The United States does not have diplomatic relations with the Democratic People's Republic of Korea, so Kim Yong-nam has no entitlement to the protections of diplomatic immunity. Moreover, this man is responsible for the slaughter of thousands of innocent Americans. He has threatened our cities and our citizens with weapons of mass destruction. And he has issued an ultimatum which can only be described as nuclear blackmail.

"His actions can be construed as terrorism, or as an act of war. There is no third interpretation. In either case, he is a legitimate military target, and we *will* take him down—if we haven't done so already.

"The world now bears witness to America's response to Kim Yong-nam's failed attempt at international extortion. In the unlikely and unhappy event that this barbaric tyrant remains alive, I give you my personal assurance that his reprieve is only temporary.

"To the people of North Korea, I say this.... Your so-called Supreme Leader has led you into the greatest peril that your country has ever faced. If you turn away from his foolish and criminal path, you will find that the United States can be merciful and forgiving even to our past enemies. But if you persist in attempting to harm our citizens, our country, or our national assets, you will find out what it truly means to be the enemy of the United States.

"Do not mistake our benevolence for weakness. Do not mistake our tolerance for indecisiveness. Do not mistake our love of peace for an inability to make war.

"What you have seen today is barely the tip of the sword. If you give us any further provocation, we will bring down the blade of that sword with a power and a fury that you have not imagined in your darkest nightmares.

"You have been warned. I urge you to choose carefully.

"To my fellow Americans, I say that we will rebuild that which has been broken. We will tighten our defenses, strengthen our alliances with friendly nations, and keep a closer watch on our potential adversaries. We will examine our mistakes, and learn the painful lessons they have to teach. And in so doing, we will emerge from this ordeal stronger, wiser, and more resolute than ever.

"Goodnight. God bless you all. And may God bless these United States of America."

⚓ ⚓ ⚓

Cuban Revolutionary Armed Forces Headquarters:

General Garriga jammed the power button of the remote control, and the television went dark.

He fought down the urge to hurl the remote through the screen, where the ghost of the American president's face was still faintly visible. Instead, he forced himself to set the plastic device down on the top of his desk.

Damaging the television would accomplish nothing. America would still be there, looming like a poisonous cloud less than 150 kilometers to the north.

Unpunished. Undestroyed. Barely affected by what should have been their apocalyptic demise.

Where was the fiery death that had been promised? Where were the heaped piles of smoldering corpses? What had happened to the glorious radioactive pyres that were supposed to level and devour the cities of Cuba's greatest enemy?

He thought about reaching for the satellite phone and trying the call yet again. But he had already called eight times, and the Korean had stopped answering the phone. Perhaps he was no longer capable of answering.

Assuming that the American president's speech was more than empty braggadocio, Garriga's Asian contact could be lying dead under a pile of burning rubble right now.

There was no point in calling the man anyway. The North Korean plan, for all of its original promise, had failed. If there was going to be revenge, it would have to come from somewhere else.

Garriga leaned back and closed his eyes, rocking slowly in his fine oak swivel chair. There *would* be vengeance. There *had* to be.

His eyes snapped open. What if....

It was only the beginnings of an idea. He could already think of ten or twelve obvious problems, and he'd barely begun to consider it.

But problems could be solved. It would take time to put his new plan into action.

Time was something he had in abundance. He'd been waiting for revenge since before his seventh birthday.

He could stand to wait a little longer.

AUTHOR'S NOTE

If you've every served in a Harbor Patrol Unit, you know that I've taken some liberties with the port security procedures at Naval Station Guantanamo Bay. The methods I've described are straight out of my imagination, with no attempt to reflect any of the techniques in use. For the record, I have only the vaguest idea of the current force protection measures used to defend Navy ports against intrusion by small craft. That's not my area of expertise and it never was.

My original plan was to fill this gap in my knowledge with research, but even casual forays into the topic reminded me that there are human lives at stake. Telling a good story is important to me, but maintaining operational security is important to the safety of real people, both in and out of uniform. That made it a no-brainer decision. Instead of trying to study and describe actual force protection methods, I just made stuff up. (That's kind of what I get paid for anyway.)

I've also used some artistic license with Executive Order #12968. The order itself is real. It was signed by President Clinton on August 2, 1995, and it's still in effect. As alluded to by Colonel Dawkins in the story, Section 3.3 of the order includes provisions for granting temporary access to classified information under "exceptional circumstances." However, the language of the order probably couldn't be stretched far enough to cover people in Jon and Cassy Clark's situation. So I ignored some of the restrictive conditions to move the narrative forward. Readers with a penchant for strict and literal interpretations of legalese are invited to send me disparaging comments by email. Extra points will be awarded if any nastygrams are written in iambic pentameter.

Any misstatements about the woodlands and terrain of Cuba were not artistic license. I studied forest overlays, vegetation density maps, and satellite images in selecting the hiding spots for each of the North Korean missile sites. I also Googled my fingers to the bone in my attempt to get it right, but the amount of available information about Cuba's undeveloped areas is spotty at best. My mistakes here are the product of ignorance, not of the blind and willful sort, but of the *I-honestly-can't-find-out* variety.

If (or when) you encounter errors not described in this note, it's a safe bet that they resulted from some similar decision or oversight on my part. As always, I throw myself on the mercy of the court.

— Jeff Edwards

A TAIL OF TWO PUPPIES

As some of my readers know, I occasionally name characters after real people—partly as a sort of inside joke, and partly as a way of recognizing and celebrating people whom I like and respect. There's a bit of that in *Steel Wind*, if you know where to look. In this book, I've also expanded the idea to include a few members of the animal kingdom.

The Secretary of Defense's Golden Retriever, Knut, is based on the beloved companion of the real-world Mary O'Neil-Broerman. Knut was a champion surfer, a tireless tennis ball chaser, and the friend of every person and dog lucky enough to meet him. He passed away in 2016, after a long battle with cancer, but he kept his good spirits and sense of playfulness right up until the last. He lives on in the hearts of all who knew him.

The American Staffordshire Terrier, Roxy, is the fur child of the real-life Jon and Cassy Clark. (Sorry to disappoint anyone who thought Jon might be a nod to Tom Clancy's character of similar name.) Roxy is ten years old now and still bounces around like a puppy. As far as she's concerned, any morning that doesn't include playing Frisbee with Jon is a complete waste of time. Her favorite things are scratches behind the ears and unguarded bacon. Let's hope she continues her career as a canine blanket far into the future, bestowing snuggly-drooly protection on her humans for many years to come.

Real heroes don't look like movie stars.

More often than not, military novels and movies portray heroes as larger-than-life characters endowed with stunning good looks, superb physical conditioning, amazing technical capabilities, and combat skills that border on the supernatural. In nearly two and a half decades of active duty, I never met anyone who resembled the kind of lone-wolf superheroes who populate many of the books in the military thriller genre. Real military heroes are ordinary men and women who work together to accomplish extraordinary things. Their only superpowers are training, hard work, dedication, and teamwork.

Those are the kinds of heroes that I write about. Soldiers, Sailors, Marines, and Airmen who know what it's like to accomplish the mission in an imperfect world; to struggle with faulty equipment, often while hampered by rules of engagement that make their jobs many times harder than they need to be. Men and women who step forward to risk their lives for a citizenry that all too rarely recognizes or appreciates their sacrifices.

The novel you're holding in your hand was written with those men and women in mind. I've tried to make it entertaining, but—of equal or greater importance—it's intended as a salute to the real heroes who keep this country strong.

Now that you've turned the last page, I'd like to ask you for a small favor. Please pass this book on to an American service member on active duty, or to someone who once wore the uniform, and remembers his or her service with pride.

In other words, *hand this to a hero*.

Respectfully,

STGC(SW), USN (Ret.)

YOU KNOW WHAT'S COMING NEXT...

This isn't the first time you've finished a book, so you already know what comes next: teasers for more books, right? Nothing unusual about that. It's pretty much standard practice in the publishing industry.

Let me tell you what's different here. The books and authors on the following pages are not part of some carefully-optimized marketing campaign. They weren't selected by an algorithm that monitors your purchasing preferences. They were hand-chosen by me. These are my personal recommendations.

When I first read John Monteith's *ROGUE AVENGER*, I paid the book my highest compliment by saying that I wished I had written it. (In the spirit of full disclosure, I *still* harbor that wish.) I had a similar thought when I read *A SWORD INTO DARKNESS*, by Thomas A. Mays. It is, quite simply, the best space combat novel I have <u>ever</u> seen. Kevin Miller's *RAVEN ONE* put me in the cockpit of a U.S. Navy fighter with a visceral human realism that I haven't felt since my first viewing of the movie TOP GUN. And *THE HITLER DECEPTION* by Alan Leverone has made me a lifelong fan of his Tracie Tanner series.

I also think rather highly of some of my own novels, so you might see a few mentions of my work. These are the kinds of books I recommend to my friends. I sincerely hope you enjoy them as much as I have.

CUTTING-EDGE NAVAL THRILLERS
BY
JEFF EDWARDS

ORIGINALLY PUBLISHED AS "TORPEDO"

JEFF EDWARDS
SEA OF SHADOWS

"A TIMELESS WARRIOR EPIC. JEFF EDWARDS S...
A STUNNING AND IRRESISTIBLY-BELIEVABLE TA...
OF SAVAGE MODERN NAVAL COMBAT."
—JOE BUFF, Bestselling author of "SEAS OF G..."
and "CRUSH DEPTH"

JEFF EDWARDS
THE SEVENTH ANGEL

"...A SUPERB THRILLER THAT GRIPS THE READ...
FROM BEGINNING TO END. A TRULY SPELLBIND...
TALE OF INTRIGUE... BRILLIANTLY EXECUTED..."
—CLIVE CUSSLER, International bestselling aut...
of "THE SPY" and "RAISE THE TITANIC"

JEFF EDWARDS
SWORD OF SHIVA

"A FANTASTIC AND CHILLING TAKE ON HOW CLOSE
TO THE EDGE OF DISASTER OUR WORLD ACTUALLY
MIGHT BE. THE ADRENALINE-FUELED WRITING
SENDS YOU HURTLING FORWARD LIKE A MISSILE."
—GRAHAM BROWN, International bestselling author
of "THE STORM" and "THE EDEN PROPHECY"

www.braveshipbooks.com

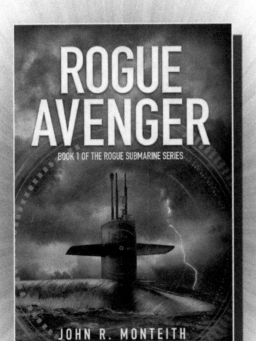

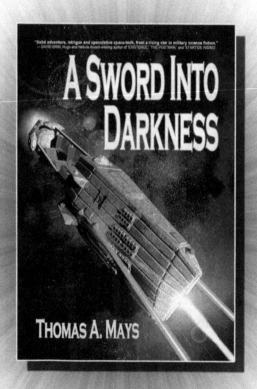

HIGH OCTANE AERIAL COMBAT

KEVIN MILLER

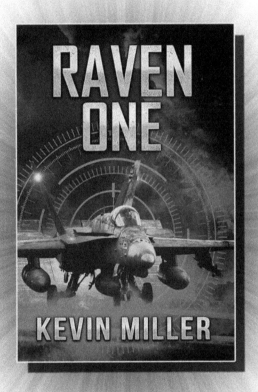

Unarmed over hostile territory...

www.braveshipbooks.com

**THE THOUSAND YEAR REICH MAY BE
ONLY BEGINNING...**

ALLAN LEVERONE

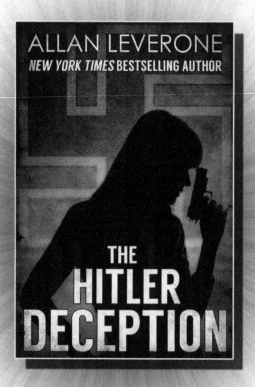

A Tracie Tanner Thriller

www.braveshipbooks.com